The Lava in My Bones

The Hand in the Dark

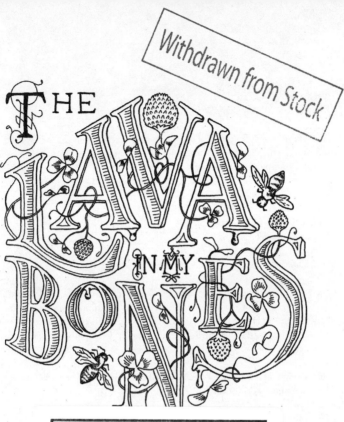

THE LAVA IN MY BONES

Arsenal Pulp Press   Vancouver

THE LAVA IN MY BONES
Copyright © 2012 by Barry Webster

ARSENAL PULP PRESS
Suite 101 – 211 East Georgia St.
Vancouver, BC V6A 1Z6
Canada
arsenalpulp.com

The publisher gratefully acknowledges the support of the Canada Council for the Arts and the British Columbia Arts Council for its publishing program, and the Government of Canada (through the Canada Book Fund) and the Government of British Columbia (through the Book Publishing Tax Credit Program) for its publishing activities.

This is a work of fiction. Any resemblance of characters to persons either living or deceased is purely coincidental.

Cover illustration by Carey Ann Schaefer
Book design by Gerilee McBride
Editing by Susan Safyan
Author photograph by Maxime Tremblay

Printed and bound in Canada

Library and Archives Canada Cataloguing in Publication

Webster, Barry, 1961-
     The lava in my bones / Barry Webster.

Issued also in electronic format.
ISBN 978-1-55152-478-8

     I. Title.

PS8595.E343L39 2012   C813'.6   C2012-904789-9

For Brian D. and Stephen N.

I am among those who think that science has great beauty. A scientist in his laboratory is not a mere technician: he is also a child placed before natural phenomena that impress him as though they were fairy tales.

—Marie Curie

I cannot understand why my arm is not a lilac tree.

—Leonard Cohen, *Beautiful Losers*

Contents

Sam rifled through his lover's drawer and discovered a dog-eared book called *Fairy Tales of Flesh*. He flipped the pages hoping to find evidence of himself.

He read long stories about witches with phalluses for teeth, men with breasts for testicles, huge walking elbows, chins, and disjointed body parts who performed elaborate Maypole dances together yet couldn't synchronize themselves enough to form a functioning human body. One tale described two ghosts who had sex; their ephemeral skins flowed into each other, and the erect penis became so foggy you could run a hand through it. Sam read of rock people who made love with such violence that their bodies fractured, crumbled, and were blown away in the breeze. There were tales about women whose body fluids drowned entire civilizations, lovers who bit off each other's organs and when they opened their mouths, birds flew out.

The final story described a free-floating world where Mr. Potato Head-like people could remove and try on each other's body parts as if they were brooches or clip-on bowties; of course, sexual organs were most in demand and people started hoarding. National outrage ensued when police discovered a woman with fourteen breasts and sixteen penises pointing in all directions like the quills on a durian fruit.

Although Sam couldn't put his finger on exactly how, he knew these tales were telling the very story of his life.

PART ONE

🌿 *Rock*

Sam stares through his barred window at a spot of earth that looks no bigger than a postage stamp. Soon the guard will unlock the door and offer him dinner.

Sam's not sure if he's in prison, a hospital, purgatory, or hell. If this is heaven, he thinks, how disappointed his mother will be.

From the hall he hears boots stamping, the squeak of trolley wheels, voices over the loudspeakers, "Ted Murphy wanted in the L-wing."

Sam puts his head against the crisscrossing bars. The metal is cold against his forehead.

Has the scientific community reacted to his collapse with horror or delight? Surely not indifference. If Franz knew, he'd be mortified. "I had no idea Sam was like that. *Scheiss.* I should be careful who I hang out with." Sam's mother and sister haven't come banging on the door, which shows he's made progress in life.

Is Sam ashamed of what he did in full view of the whole world? Studying the snow-covered lawn outside, he realizes he feels no shame, and this self-assurance amazes him.

He remembers the rise of Franz's stone-solid chest, with scattered hairs bending like windblown grasses.

A few months prior, Sam had lived in a Toronto basement apartment that was empty but for a desk, bed, computer, and stacked plastic cubes containing rock samples. The microscope was never put away but stood defiantly on the desk. While he slept, his hand would twitch in empty space on the bedspread as, with his ear pressed to a pillow pressed to a futon pressed to the earth, he'd hear the fire burning at the Earth's centre. There, lava coagulated into gigantic globules that collapsed downward into a sea of fire that broke apart and rose up to join other steaming, shifting masses in a subterranean landscape that perpetually devoured and recreated itself. In the morning when Sam woke, his friend was everywhere. Franz's shoulder was the rock sheath jutting from the dirt beside the apartment parking lot. Protruding stone spheres behind the corner store were nodules in Franz's spine. The lakeside cliffs were the edges of his forehead and nose. With his hands on his ears, Sam would run down Toronto's cement-walled streets, through car-flurried intersections, across deserted squares, over empty, wind-whipped fields, but no matter how fast he raced, no matter how many buildings he circled, there was always the sudden, scuffled scrape of stone beneath his feet and the fire roaring at the Earth's centre.

Franz was everywhere.

But then again, he was nowhere.

Sam stood on the edges of oceans, straining to see his friend's face in the horizon. He shouted his name into windstorms, waved huge placards from atop mountain cliffs, but the world was too vast, distances were too great, and the Atlantic Ocean was like a wall.

Now Sam touches the gridwork of metal bars with the open palm of one hand. He does not know why desire destroyed him, why his own frail frame couldn't bear the force of what is a part of human nature.

❦

One year earlier, Sam sat nervously on a plane bound for Europe. He fingered the steel seatbelt-buckle that flickered like a winking eye. Tomorrow, at a climate-change conference, he'd give his first lecture ever. At university Sam had avoided public speaking. Now this "genius" who'd gotten a BA, MSc, and PhD in eight years would visit another continent. "Talking," he muttered as the plane shot like a bullet from the runway, "is necessary. Nothing else works." Despite all his journal articles and studies for the Science Council of Canada, ice caps were still melting and temperatures were rising. Canadians only half-listened to him, but Europeans were more environmentally aware; at last, he could have an impact.

When Sam passed through Swiss customs on the morning of June 5, he felt he'd burst through a membrane he hadn't known existed until then. Before him lay thirty long, juicy days in Switzerland. A clock began ticking the countdown to his tragedy.

His first days in Zurich, he wandered as in a dream; the snow-capped mountains loomed in the distance and everything confused him: the slope-roofed Tinkertoy buildings, breezes smelling of baked bread and *parfum Givenchy*, cobblestone streets that forked or headed in all directions at once. Sam snaked his fingers into his pocket, touched the card with his hotel's phone number. In unfamiliar cities he got lost easily. Was that so bad? Sam had no friends to telephone, no one to send postcards to; he hadn't seen his parents in years. He tried not to think about this.

The streets of Zurich were perilously empty; agitated, Sam searched their polished surfaces for something to occupy his mind. There, a window display of baguettes lined up like artillery. Notice it's interesting. A tour guide talking about cheese and watches because she doesn't know what else to say. Remember her.

In the late afternoon, Sam collapsed exhausted onto a chair at a café. The table-top was a perfect circle—the beige marble cool against his palm. The waitress smiled, her lips a pert crescent moon; pigtails hung down the front of her blouse. Sam chuckled. Heidi of the High Alps. Yes, he will think of this waitress if, before his lecture tomorrow, his mind goes blank and he panics. Skirt pleats curved round her large hips and comma-shaped dimples bracketed her lips. Like most women she'd seem attractive until she spoke.

"Ready to order?" she asked in English. The linguistic skills of the Swiss humbled Sam. He admired the gentle swell of the woman's bosom. Her face curved like a Valentine heart. Yet she lacked mystery. Five minutes alone with her and you'd know everything.

"Just some tea." Sam rarely had an appetite. A line he'd once heard: "If you love something, you put it in your mouth." He never understood people who were always hungry.

Behind him, two women were speaking English with

American accents. They were from far away, like him, and Sam felt reassured.

"We'll take the Lake Zurich cruise earlier or we'll miss the symphony."

"I so want to see Bamberger conduct."

"His daughter once dated Tom Cruise."

Sam often wondered why people had conversations. Nothing new was ever said. Should he start listening? If he changed his behaviour, would the Earth change too? Everything was connected, after all.

Sunlight gleaming on the tabletop hurt his eyes. He was jet-lagged. Yet he sensed something significant was going to happen. He'd dragged himself across the ocean and was farther from home than ever before. If you changed the position of one compound, the elements surrounding it changed too.

Heidi returned with tea. "Here's your drink," she sang. Her eyes were lit. She was becoming friendlier. Sam looked away. The *click-click* of her receding footsteps was like a metronome ticking.

Lately, he'd had nightmares in which he looked into a funhouse mirror, his teeth grew as long as a rabbit's, his eyes expanded to cover his cheeks, and his ears protruded like parking meters. His face became a baby's, a gerbil's, a cow's.

Sam sipped the tea; it scalded his tongue—he spit it out. *What's with Heidi, bringing him this?* Through the window, distant mountains rose and fell like the curves on a woman's body. The few patches of glaciers were blindingly bright. These mountains looked different from the ones on the placemat. The photos must have been taken around 1983, as every summit was topped by a crown of ice; now, only ten years later, half of Switzerland's glaciers had melted and landslides occurred regularly.

Women passed on the street like figures on a television screen, yet they were real, and he could touch their skin if he wanted. At night he'd wake with an erection pointing skyward like a finger testing the wind. What happens to energy that isn't expended?

There was a stack of *petit pains* on the neighbouring table; he could smell their sweet butter scent, and his stomach growled. *If you love something, you put it in your mouth.* He reached, snatched one, two, three rolls, swallowed them whole.

Back at the hotel, he strutted through the lobby, and the desk clerk chirped, "The guests are looking forward to your speech tomorrow."

Sam hoped that when he stepped up to the podium, his voice, normally a mumbled rasp, and his arms, which hung down like pendulums, would transform—his arms dramatically jousting at unseen opponents, his voice resonating. "See my emaciated body," he'd be saying silently, "these stick-thin forearms, my wrinkled jacket? I'm nothing, for I've sacrificed all to save the world. Adore me. I only ever had one girlfriend and I didn't love her. Take me on your shoulders and parade me through the streets." At unguarded moments he admitted he was grateful for global warming because it distracted him from his own life and made strangers respect him.

That night Sam dreamed he was seated before crowds of men

with electric sockets for eyes. Someone kept calling "Where's the plug?" He noticed a two-pronged plug lay on his knee. Nearby, tips of volcanoes puffed like lips exhaling smoke.

In the morning Sam arranged his papers and practised his first sentence, "Good morning, ladies and gentlemen. Good morning. Good."

At last he was sitting at a table before a room full of scientists. In his bag were gleaming cobalt, pyroxene-filled trachyte, sharp-edged obsidian, pock-cratered basalt. To one side, the podium where the German doctor was speaking. Sam's knees trembled; goosebumps prickled on his forearms. Was he tense because he'd crossed the ocean, something he'd once felt forbidden to do? Or was this the same edginess he'd experienced in his Toronto apartment, now magnified in the absence of his university degrees on the wall? He recalled the mall at the end of his street, its fake palm trees beneath the glass pyramid skylight, people eating chop suey with styrene forks at Gourmet Fair. A world made of plastic.

Applause. The German scuffled to his seat.

Sam clutched the bag full of stones, stood up, took two steps to the podium, and pulled the mic to his lips. "Ladies and—." Germs. Yes, he almost said, germs. "Gentlemen." His voice boomed so loudly that it startled him. "We have been paying attention to the poisons that kill the world, such as carbon dioxide, which heats up the atmosphere and is melting our ice caps." Before him the dark mass of people throbbed like a giant restless amoeba. He forced out the words: "The polar regions are warming up and the tropics are overheated. The two extremes—heat and cold—must be maintained for life to exist." Spectators shifted in their chairs; they'd heard all this before. "Until now climatologists have given warnings, but have politicians listened to these scientists of the air? The recent Rio Summit achieved little. Geology—" he said challengingly, "holds the answer."

He plucked a stone from his bag, held it up; his trembling fingertips pressed its contours, the jagged crevices, twinkling crystals. Get personal, he thought. Tell them about your life. His speech coach said that spectators love personal anecdotes. "Rock is why I became a geologist." His cheeks felt warm. God, was he blushing? "Rocks are intimately connected to us. No matter what we do, we are standing on stone." He repeated his memorized lines. "Rocks bear the imprint of the weight of our bodies and, like snowflakes, no two are alike. They *are* us. I am in love with rock"—his voice became husky—"more than I love myself. This rock from Labrador *is* me. Labrador is where I spent my childhood. Look into a rock from your home; you're looking into something essential to you." Now his main point. He deliberately banged one fist on the podium, which wobbled drunkenly. A sound in the dark. Giggling? "Instead of focussing on the poisons destroying the Earth, we must study rocks and the forces protecting our planet. Rocks are the immune system fighting toxins in our atmosphere. Rocks are less affected by global warming than water or air. They are part of that larger force that isn't conquered ... Yet what exactly is this force that spins the world?" Perspiration ran through the hair on the back of his scalp. "If some scientists question God's existence, where then do they think rock's energy comes from?" A complete hush. Were spectators bored or captivated? "If rocks embody the power that moves the world, we must find that force and strengthen it. Only then can we halt the Greenhouse Effect."

The empty silence lasted.

When the lights were turned on, three arms flew up. The shadowed, outer edges of the crowd pressed against walls that seemed to push inwards. Had he spoken well? Would the world change? He was struck by his egotism.

Answering the few questions, Sam noticed a man sitting in the front and centre of the room, as still as a boulder.

At last, coffee break. Relief flooded him. Sam fingered a Styrofoam cup. "Very bad for the ozone," he murmured.

Then the man approached him. Cautiously. The man from the centre. Later Sam would find out that he rarely approached people; people approached him. Uncharacteristically, he shuffled his feet. His head hung shyly. Also, atypical. On the day he met Sam, Franz was a man he had never been before and never would be again.

With one glance, Sam labelled him a frivolous peacock. The man wore a feminine mauve blouse that glimmered in the light, shiny canoe-shaped shoes with steel tips, and tight, herringbone-patterned jeans. He was the only man not wearing a suit, and Sam wondered why they had let him in.

Sam turned away and sauntered to the snack table, unaware that walking ten metres to speak to Sam was the hardest thing Franz had ever done, and it was followed by rejection, something he'd never experienced, especially in public.

Sam chatted with the Finnish biologist: "...and I'll be studying felsite deposits on rocks below the Matterhorn next week…"

When the biologist excused himself—"I forgot to pick up a nametag"—Franz stepped into the space he'd vacated. He scrutinized the rock Sam was still clutching, then examined the space above his head. Was this man timid or mentally ill? Sam wondered. Months later he would learn the meaning of all this.

"Mr Masonty," he said. "My name is Franz Niederberger. I notice that your rock belongs to a stone mass bigger than all of Switzerland." He stared directly into Sam's eyes, then again at the space beside his cheek.

Sam answered as if reading from a textbook. "Yes. The Canadian Shield stretches 3,000 kilometres from the Arctic Circle to the forty-ninth parallel." This wasn't news to anyone.

Franz's eyes worried back and forth as if erasing the line separating Sam from the surrounding air. His lips quivered. His eyes fixated on Sam's rock; next, he studied Sam's chin.

Sam became conscious of his own appearance; his un-ironed pants and stained tie, the jacket he'd had since he was eighteen, the unwashed hair he couldn't remember combing today. This man had tight, tanned skin, gleaming blue eyes, and wet lips (his tongue kept gliding over them); he was someone women probably considered attractive. Sam thought: Do I deliberately make myself homely so no one shows interest?

Franz stated, "You said something wrong. Rocks around the world are different? *Das ist nicht richtig.*" He tilted his head cockily. "Rocks are the same everywhere. All rocks are hard."

Surprised by this silly challenge, Sam answered, "Our presence affects how rocks erode."

"But why study the surface of rock?" the man continued. "Even in Canada, what's below is more meaningful than what you see."

Why was Franz so poetic that day? Why did he become so ridiculous later?

Sam tightened his grip on the stone as Franz glared at it. For a second Sam felt violated.

"You should go to Canada," he muttered. "If it interests you." Sam studied the rising arc of the man's pompadour. He must have spent the whole morning arranging it.

"No, I'm…I get afraid of… of leaving Switzerland. You see, I've never been to another country. *Das ist scheusslich.* I don't know what would happen if I crossed a border and entered France or Italy. I'm afraid I'll dissolve or something." Sam had always had the same fear but only now realized it. "Because I am an artist but have been blocked for years. Nobody knows this. Everybody thinks I'm a great professional but, *Scheiss*"—why was he telling Sam this?—"nature should help, and there's so much of it in your country. I saw 'Canada' beside your name on the conference poster and so I knew I had to come here. Something might *begeistern*—inspire me. And seeing you talk about your enormous home while holding a real Canadian rock in your bare hands, *mein Gott!*" The man choked. "You're from so far away." Then he reached for the stone but instead touched Sam's forearm. His fingertips were warm on Sam's skin. The man's hair swirled luxuriously around two ears, curling, Sam thought, like the wave-rippled coves near his hometown in Labrador.

Sam stepped back and replied with forced sternness. "Sir." Franz flinched at the coldness of the word, but Sam repeated,

"Sir—what did you hope to gain from this conference?"

The man was breathing heavily. "It's funny, but when I see you, I don't really see you. I just sense something coming from inside you. And I put on these clothes—this shirt is 100 percent silk, and my jeans are the latest Diesel—as a …" he searched for the word "*Bollwerk*—bulwark?—against everything here, so I wouldn't get … consumed. Since I stopped painting, I design ads and go to bars and eat out with my friends, but it's only the *verdammt* surface—and I need risk. I need to be a risk-taker. 'Cause I'm a total coward. I don't tell friends this, and they can't imagine I'm frustrated. But your country is such a vast space and has so much nature. You can absorb anything."

Sam stood rigid. No one had ever talked to him about personal feelings. His colleagues only discussed stone formation.

Suddenly Franz grabbed the rock from Sam and cried "*Christus!*" He stared at the rock in his trembling hands, and his body wavered as if buffeted by winds.

Alarmed, Sam asked, "Are you all right?"

"This rock doesn't reflect light, *nicht wahr?*"

"No."

"Is it dangerous?"

"Dangerous?"

"Will this rock harm me?"

Sam was dumbfounded.

"Do you really think it's personal?" Franz asked.

"What?"

"What you said. That rocks record the details of someone's life. Do you believe that?"

Sam nodded.

"Then it will help me."

"With what?"

"*Mit was ich brauche*—with what I need!"

And then it happened. The moment that jumpstarted everything and determined the course of Sam's life.

If you love something, you put it in your mouth.

Franz brought the rock to his lips, shoved it into his mouth, and swallowed hard. His Adam's apple leapt forward as if a tiny man trapped in his oesophagus struck his fist once against the inside of Franz's throat.

Both men looked at each other. It was impossible to tell who was more surprised.

Around them, life went on. The woman at the beverage table stirred hot chocolate. Scientists quarrelled before the exhibition booths; the Finn put his finger on a graph-line. Outside, the traffic light was red, then green, then red. Pedestrians crossed streets. In the sky, CFCs gobbled the ozone layer. At the outer tips of the world, sunrays sliced the Earth like razors.

After a moment, both men came to.

"You just swallowed a rock," said Sam.

Franz began hyperventilating.

"That'll rupture your oesophagus—or shred your stomach muscles! *It could kill you!*"

Stunned, Franz could only gawk at the palms of his hands.

"Ambulance!" Sam shouted. "We need an ambulance!"

Sam sat beside the Swiss stranger on the way to the hospital. He said, "Why the hell did you do that? Who are you, anyway?"

He expected Franz to gasp in pain, but his voice emerged a resounding baritone. "*Ich weiss nicht.* I don't know—I'm horrified. I expected I'd do something here but not that. You awoke this in me. Thank you," and again he touched Sam's hand. "I get so tired of fighting myself." The ambulance went over a bump, and the stone rattled in his oesophagus. "I told myself not to risk a conference on nature, but I came. I got filled up with this intense craving yesterday at nine o'clock." Sam's plane had landed at nine o'clock.

At the hospital, X-rays showed that Franz's rock had miraculously dissolved and been absorbed into his bloodstream. Astonished, Sam gazed at the translucent sheet lit up like the iridescent forms of the aurora borealis. Sam immediately felt he was in a fairy tale that he had never read but would one day be written.

Ecstatic, Franz turned to Sam. "How long are you in town for?"

"One month."

"Just a month? Good. Let's experiment with this. Can I ask you on a date?"

"A date?" Then he understood. "I'm not…that way."

"Come now, are you serious?" Franz rolled his eyes.

"What's that supposed to mean?" Sam retorted angrily. How could this man know anything about him? Sam became confused. Interest in someone of his own sex seemed too violent a break with his placid past. Still, like the compounds of the Earth, we are not one thing but several. If someone thought he was gay, fine. Homosexuals are marginal, and Sam liked being marginal.

He examined Franz's muscled torso spread out on the stretcher. Impressive. Yet Sam knew there was more to it than this. He had to uncover Franz's secret. Here was a man who had struggled with stone and conquered it. Sam wanted to get closer to his power.

"Fine," answered Sam. "Let's meet."

"Tomorrow morning at nine. I want to hear about the country you live in."

The country he lived in? Sam came from a place people rarely visited and which, for some, hardly existed. He immediately saw himself alone in an empty field, crouched and staring at a rock in his hand, yet as winds blew all about him, he dared not lift his head to see where he lived because, if he did, the precious stone he clutched, its glittering crystals and asymmetrical ridges, would dissolve into dust and vanish in the wind.

※

Sam had experienced flings before. He'd spent the night with women who were like breezes that scuttle along the Earth's surface, disturbing not a leaf. He'd had discussions with scientists who'd forget him. He'd written articles few people read. He was a man who lived in a basement apartment and looked through a microscope lens and never asked for anything more.

Sam hadn't always been so placid. Years ago he'd been in love with a girl. Esther. She was in his grade five homeroom class. Her blonde hair rose in an elaborate, twisting labyrinth. On her shiny pencil case gleamed a picture of a mountain, and inside—this was the exciting part—she carried a jerky-limbed wooden man with hinged joints, bulging thigh muscles, and sequins for eyes. At night Sam dreamed the man leapt from her pencil case and dance-kicked his square feet, flapping his arms in the air. *Clatter-clatter*, he'd go. *Clatter-clatter*. From his desk Sam eyed Esther, hoping she'd zip open her case.

One day he gathered stones by the seashore, fastened them together with knotted dandelion stems, and tied a flower on top. At recess Esther moseyed through the empty hopscotch court when Sam shuffled over and shoved his gift into her hand. Her cheeks reddened, her eyes watered, but with pain or gladness Sam couldn't tell. Then she frowned and said, "I don't want any of your stupid presents," and smashed his rock-bundle against the school wall. Dandelion stems oozed juice onto the pavement.

"Can I at least see the man in your pencil case?"

Esther gasped, slapped him on the face, ran to a teacher, and complained that Sam had tried to put his hand between her legs.

His parents were notified. His father scoffed, "'Tain't no harm in what he did." Mortified, his mother demanded that Sam attend the Friday night Bible-study group. Sam was expelled from school for three weeks and later placed in a different class than Esther. He was distressed because now he'd never learn the secret to her wooden man. Who and what was he?

On Halloween, he discovered the truth. Everyone wore costumes to school, and Sam was able to crouch incognito in a robot outfit outside Esther's homeroom. His lips trembled as he watched her slip the man from the case; she stuck a pencil into a hole hidden in the top of his head and began to grind, grind,

grind until the man's brains were full of sawdust. He was only a pencil sharpener!

Sam soon realized he was over-imaginative and expected too much. Years before, his mother had coyly said the tooth fairy didn't exist and he stopped eating for five days. Learning that the Easter bunny was a fantasy, he raced into the kitchen, snatched the coloured eggs from the fridge, and smashed each one on his father's armchair. The Christmas his mother announced that Santa was make-believe—"The pastor says these lies are Satanic. Forgive me for not knowing sooner"—he refused to open any presents. "I'll have them all for myself then," Mother crowed, "for only God and Jesus exist." Sam knew this wasn't true. At their church everyone waved their hands in the air, wailing, screeching, straining so hard toward belief, Sam sensed the whole thing was fake.

At the age of eleven, he devoted himself to reading the science journals in the town library. From now on he would know the world exactly as it was and not be wounded by unwelcome surprises. Two years later, hormones shot through his bloodstream and body parts spun round his brain like clothes in a dryer. Still, he would never again allow himself to feel desire mixed with a belittling hope. The first time he masturbated, the drop of sperm on his thigh caught the light and winked up at him like an eye.

In high school, Esther re-entered Sam's life. She remembered her earlier cruelties and felt responsible for his becoming an anti-social outcast. Now she pitied him. Esther assumed Sam was still attracted to her, and any boy who desired her automatically became a friend. In the high-school hierarchy, a guy who liked you, no matter how peripheral, earned you a point, and she wanted more points than anyone.

Sam didn't want to date Esther, but enjoyed watching her. He'd discovered girls were most attractive when seen in the distance. He still loved the labyrinth of hair on Esther's head; he sensed unresolved mysteries there.

Life changed drastically in October 1984 when Sam won the school science-fair prize for his rotating wheel labelled with the planets of the solar system; the next month he was awarded the Labrador Science Trophy, and his picture was in the *Cartwright Gazette*. His mother believed the attention was making him arrogant and stuck the trophy in the garbage. But at school Sam was a hero. Briefly. Esther cornered him on the volleyball court and said, "If you want to go to the Dairy-Freeze with me, I'll buy my own ice cream." Sam knew that if he rejected her, she wouldn't let him watch her anymore. He answered, "Okay, let's do something."

He took her to the hamburger joint and she studied him while he ate. He was always hungry in those days. Esther said, "I'm not ordering because I gotta watch my figure. Besides, grease drips," and she pointed to her dress. "I don't want to look like those piggy girls that act like boys."

After a month of dating, Sam and Esther had sex in his father's car. Sam found it cumbersome; her body was as slippery as a fish's, making her hard to grip, and he kept getting her hair in his mouth. She'd mechanically roll her head back and forth murmuring "Kiss me, boy, kiss me," but each time he tried to kiss her, the timing was off and he'd end up pressing his lips against the side of her head. As he stared into the swath of hair whirling round one ear, he thought: I'm making love to a gorilla.

Afterwards she excused herself and said, "I gotta pee," stepped out of the car and squatted in the bushes; Sam reached into her bag and snatched the pencil case. As her urine splattered on leaves, he pulled down the zipper. Inside, he discovered some spindly pencils. The little man was gone. She'd long ago thrown him in the garbage.

His mother believed he shouldn't date until he was eighteen. Panicking, she phoned Esther's mother. "Years ago your daughter brought out something bad in Sam. I don't know what they do when they're out, but he's been doing things with her…in his mind. I find these new stains in his underwear from…his thinking. I worry what could happen. If you don't believe me, I'll show you the stains." Esther's mother told Esther who laughed and said, "Good for him."

Sam began to feel Esther had little to offer. In conversation she said the same things over and over: "Dairy-Freeze's snow-cones are sweeter than Mr. Softy's" or "Dresses that come to the knee are way cooler than the mid-thigh ones." Some days the *clackity-clack* of her voice was like a hockey card flapping in bike-wheel spokes; sex with her began to seem repetitious. It satiated a hunger, but nothing new ever happened. Esther said, "You're different for me because you got brains. I'm starting to think footballers are gross. Now I'm dating the guy who won the science fair! My parents can't believe it. You like to do experiments, Sam? Do one on me."

He mournfully studied her labyrinth of hair; beads of water

nestled in its curves and glittered in the sunlight. Observing her put her hair up each day had not diminished the mystery. But whatever was there remained beyond him. Just before Christmas, he broke up with her.

He confronted her in the cafeteria. "I don't think we should continue dating. I'm applying to some good universities and need to spend my time studying."

Esther was momentarily stunned. Then she screamed so loudly that everyone at the nearby tables heard her. "I'm the prettiest girl and I deigned to go out with *you!*" The labyrinth on her head trembled like a giant jelly salad. "I coulda gotten a guy a thousand fuckin' times better! I'll get back at you bunch of assholes." He assumed this meant his family. Finally Esther told the whole school the underwear stain story and Sam became known as the boy whose mom loved his undies. The next spring, after graduation, Sam left Labrador and never returned.

All of this happened in the early days of the world, before glaciers started melting and ocean levels rising, during a time when the tropics were hot and the North and South Poles frigid. The world's climate was in perfect balance.

His second morning in Zurich, Sam noticed the sun perched on the lower lip of the valley. He was curious about what would happen today. He'd refrain from lecturing Franz on global warming. In the mirror, the skin on Sam's face looked smooth, unblemished. He fingered the gentle bump of his barely visible cheekbone, the budgie-like beak of his nose. In his life, there was no largeness of gesture; when someone offered him pleasure, albeit peculiar and fleeting, he knew he should accept and be satisfied with it.

The tram made a high-pitched, humming sound as it slid along its steel rails, moving so smoothly through the cobbled streets that Sam felt he was floating on air. The metal-slat seat vibrated beneath him. The city was calm. Zurich always looked calm. Gleaming silver-trimmed cars glided soundlessly along streets, boys on shining bicycles seemed to drift in slow-motion up the city's small hills; an elderly woman wearing a hat decorated with a stuffed bird carefully sipped her coffee at an empty sidewalk café as a teenager with safety pins in his cheeks crouched down to comb his orange rooster-tuft before a shop window. At intersections everything came to a stop as groups of men in identical, square-shouldered suits and women carrying shopping bags draped with floating wisps of gauze walked in single file between parallel lines printed on uncracked pavement. One man's tie blew over his shoulder and he stopped walking to tuck it back in.

When the train passed Zurich's little lake, there was not a ripple on its surface, and all the small boats were docked. The whole city appeared to be waking up but, in truth, it was the height of day.

Little did Sam know that below the ground, continental plates were shifting, buckling their shoulders hard up against each other, and that steam was building up below the Earth's crust.

Finally, at the thirtieth tram stop, Franz stood leaning against an oak tree next to a cluster of squat pines. He stepped forward, held Sam's fingers with moist hands. "Come," he said marching between the trees. "Hope you're hungry."

In the clearing, Sam discovered a picnic table covered with paper plates and piles of sliced cheeses and meats and paper cups and thermoses of drinks. "Why are you doing this?" Sam felt embarrassed. He wasn't used to people giving him things.

"I bring you a typical Swiss breakfast because I'm a typical Swiss guy." For the first time, Sam saw Franz smile—so broadly, his eyes twinkled. He was wearing a checked T-shirt and suit jacket. A bit overdressed for a picnic? Noting Sam's gaze, he explained, "To prevent me from going wild in the forest."

"You do that?"

"I ate a rock yesterday. You make me go crazy. I could get weirder today if I don't watch out."

And then the men ate food. Sam swallowed things Franz's hands had recently touched: thick slices of salami that left grease dripping from their lips, acrid olives that singed tongues and palates, moisture-beaded grapes that exploded between teeth, and Franz's own concoction—"that I invented one day when it wouldn't stop raining and my fridge was too full"—yogurt mixed with cranberries, pomegranate seeds, muesli, and sliced apples.

Then Franz cocked one eyebrow. "That breakfast wasn't enough. I'm still hungry as a *Schwein*."

Sam feared what would happen next.

Franz bent over and scooped up a handful of rocks. Molasse pebbles. His forehead creased. "There's no choice." He looked at Sam, took a deep breath, shoved them into his mouth, and swallowed. He clenched his eyes shut, his brow knit. Then his whole face relaxed and he smiled a second time. He offered Sam three beige stones and said gently, "Your turn."

Sam studied the rocks like pulled teeth in his palm. He hesitated, placed them on his tongue, tasted earth, dust, gravel. Everything in him said not to. His Adam's apple popped forward once, twice; the stones plummeted down his gullet, and there was a warm detonative trembling in the centre of his stomach. He had the sudden impulse to gobble up all the pebbles scattered about his feet.

Franz looked him in the eye and said again, "Your country, Sam. Tell me about your country."

And again Sam was in an empty field staring down at a pock-marked rock, and although winds blew all around him he dared not lift his head.

"Who cares about my country?" He playfully picked a blade of grass and twirled it. "Tell me about yours."

Franz leaned back, chuckled. The sun shone right above his head. "*Mein Land?*" he said raising both hands. "This is it."

And so Sam followed him into the wooded park on the edge of the city and up along rock-strewn paths, over twisted tree roots that clutched the earth like gnarled fingers, past moss-mouthed caves where stalactites had been dripping for the past one thousand years, and when they reached the edge of a limestone pit, Franz took off his suit jacket.

The two men were sweating. Dark blotches marked the back of Franz's T-shirt, his armpits, the top of his chest. Overhead, leaves rustled; Sam watched light-flecks dance over Franz's narrow nose that jutted like a ski-jump, his low forehead with bangs that, from here, seemed unevenly cut, his thick thighs and wide kneecaps. A woman's body would be more different from my own, Sam thought, hence more separate. Again, he felt bewildered.

Franz spoke to Sam in a hushed voice. "Thanks for coming, stone-man."

Sam could only reply, "You're welcome."

A shadow flickered on Franz's cheek. "I live in a small house up ahead, on the edge of this park. My stepfather was the mayor, and he bought it for me. I'm a spoiled *Arschloch*; most people only dream about having my life." He ran one nail-bitten finger across his chin. "You see, I moved here seven years ago because I thought being near nature would help my art—and it did for a while. I painted every day! So many trees here, but *mein Gott*, your country has so many more. Eventually the trees began to bother me. I get afraid sometimes and will probably move back into the city soon, *glaube ich*. 'Cause I forget who I think I am when I'm out here." He looked at the sky. "I don't *verschmelze* with nature well, though I want to. *Das ist mein Problem.* So I was a daredevil to flirt with you and your country yesterday, your giant country of rock and trees. After meeting you, I actually painted a picture—the first time in years—of trees and light that shows how everything's connected."

Sam listened in silence. He'd never heard someone talk so candidly. The words flowed gently into his ears.

"I'm surprised I like you."

"You like me?"

"Yes. You're small like a *Vogel*. You're not my type, and I usually get who I want. I actually barely notice what you physically look like. Funny. Usually someone's body is all I see. You're sweet. *Du bist wirklich ein süsser Mann.*" A breeze moaned through the treetops. He moved toward Sam and quickly and unobtrusively kissed him on the lips—Franz's mouth was harder than a woman's, the lips thinner, dryer, and beneath, the solid bone-plate of jaw. Sam smelled sweat, aftershave, a cinnamon-soap scent. Franz stepped away and sat on a flat rock protruding from the ground.

Sam wondered if anyone saw the kiss, concluded this was irrelevant. He crouched on a stone outcropping.

Franz pulled out a knife and cut an apple. "Are you still hungry?" He handed Sam a slice. "We could've gotten to my place a lot faster, but the scenic route is better." He looked straight at Sam and said, "Or maybe I'm delaying 'cause I'm scared." He held Sam's gaze for a long time and Sam felt he was being offered something. "Sometimes I pretend I'm far from Zurich." He pointed his knife-tip south. "But in that direction another town begins. Head in any *Richtung*, and you'll hit a border, the German, Italian, or Austrian. I'm surrounded by borders. Unlike yours, my country is so small, some days it seems I know everyone in it." Franz fingered an apple slice. Again he stared directly at Sam. He said, "I feel trapped."

How strange to talk about sentiments. What should Sam say? He'd mirror Franz. "I've been feeling peculiar lately too. It's one reason I came to Europe. I thought if I corrected my own life, the world would fix itself as well. Funny, eh?"

Then the conversation shifted, rose like a wave, and the two

men started talking about a thousand things: hiking boots, airplane tickets, the difficulty of tying sailor's knots, ice cream that's
been refrozen, fire extinguishers, and the hard pit at the centre
of avocadoes they both always wanted to eat but couldn't. Franz
kept saying, "You're right," while Sam responded, "Yes. Yes, yes."

Winds swept softly through the underbrush. Light-flecks
scuttled over Sam's thighs. A cool breeze brushed his eyelashes.
He thought that everything was normal in his life and nothing
was changing. He didn't know that on the far side of the world,
earthquakes were happening in the country where he lived, granite mountains were imploding, and shale cliffs were falling into
the sea.

He lifted the piece of apple Franz gave him, put it into his
mouth.

Franz pointed at the dark cleft in the centre of the limestone
pit. "Fall in that, and you'll keep falling and never stop."

And for the first time Sam heard it, the sound that would
follow him for the rest of his life: the fire burning at the Earth's
centre. Molten lava separated to join swelling masses that broke
apart to meld with other shifting masses ...

Sam looked at Franz and Franz looked at Sam and their apples
cracked between their teeth. A bird flew overhead. Somewhere,
water trickled. The forest was dark and then light and then dark.
Franz took Sam's hand in his—a hairy, rough-skinned hand—
and led him the rest of the way down the twisting trail until they
stood in the clearing where, years ago, Franz had built his sculpture garden. Studded about the square yard was artwork that
would remain in Sam's mind for a lifetime: large stone circles

with lines through them and clay spheres penetrated by steel rods that went in one side and out the other; everything round was divided yet connected by lines that criss-crossed at multitudinous angles, and everything was chopped into segments that fit into a framework that was spherical. Plastic slatted wheels rotated on metal axles, wooden hoops adorned with streamers whirled round iron poles, as huge metallic disks spun in the wind, their styrene spokes clattering against out-thrusting metal prongs. Everything had an axis as well as an outer surface, and suddenly Sam realized that if you drew a line from Canada to the Earth's centre, it joined a similar line from Switzerland and the two countries were connected in an obvious, logical, not-even-mysterious way. All at once Sam saw himself in his own barren field studying the crystal-flecked surface of a rock, and as Franz's words pushed relentlessly against his eardrums, "Now tell me about your country, tell me," he finally let the rock drop to the ground, lifted his head, and saw where he lived.

He beheld a vast plain and a forest and beyond, another forest and lakes and cliffs and more forests and trees and plains and rocks, and suddenly a shrieking wind from the Arctic Circle hurtled down across a vast distance to blast every cell in the surface, subsurface, and deepest layers of his body.

He'd never seen himself so clearly.

Sam said, "Franz, my country is—" and as spiked disks clattered furiously at the back of his head, he told Franz everything: How the fierce, ravenous, northern winds roar down across seven billion forests full of 1,000 billion trees where they tear off pine branches, fracture birches, uproot junipers and wild crocuses, drag up rocks from the earth, and dash grey, gritty water against cliffs; the air is full of the piercing wail of starved coyotes and grizzly bears; snow falls in avalanches from the sky and becomes an army of ice-pebbles beating your cheeks as, gazing at empty horizons, you call out for a warm breeze that never comes—for your heart can pound all it wants, but your blood will never be enough to warm the extremities of your body, and your thigh muscles can strain all they can, but will never hold your torso straight against the wind, and you can barricade your doors and windows behind mountains of wool blankets, but the gales will smash every window of every building you've ever been in, hurl your wool coverings to the farthest corners of the Earth, and drive its steely, icy claws into every pore in your skin at once.

In the country he lives in, it is always minus 7,000 degrees Celsius, the wind has never stopped blowing, and winter is 1,000 months long.

Seeing Franz before him, Sam hurled himself onto the inexpressible warmth of his body and, as his mouth wandered wildly over the rock edge of Franz's chin, the hard, level expanse of his chest, the solid protuberance of his groin, an Arctic wind beat at his back and neck, drove snowflakes through his hair, striking faster, colder as Franz's flesh burned like fire beneath him.

That day, for the first time in history, there was a snowstorm in Switzerland in mid-summer. Shopkeepers goggled in disbelief as white flakes appeared in the formerly blue sky; the bankers stopped walking and checked to make sure the date dials on their watches were correct. Soon, the streets were clogged, tram cars couldn't run; the café owners took their tables inside and changed the day's special from pasta salad to fondue.

When Franz and Sam finished making love, they looked out at a world transformed into an endless series of ghost-like mounds of pure white snow.

❧

When Sam woke the next morning, he lurched upright in bed. Why had a man's body brought him pleasure? Was he himself a man? Two men together was pointless—they can't produce babies. What's happened to logic? Does science have anything to do with this? With a flash of panic, Sam thought: the world is still dying and I'm doing nothing about it.

That week Sam ate rocks every day; he couldn't resist their beckoning curvaceousness, their ribald density and earthy flavour. They swelled his libido, and Franz ate rocks with him. He became accustomed to Franz's maleness, the deep voice vibrating the chest cavity, the hardness of his eyebrow-ridge, wiry hair curling in unexpected places, and the raw apple scent of his groin.

❧

Sam steps away from the barred window and sits on the cot in his bare-walled room.

I'm imprisoned now, he thinks, *in Ontario*.

Light gleams on the floor tiles, and the air smells of antiseptic. He hears a staticky radio from the room next door. Someone coughs outside his door. The door does not open.

Sam puts his face in his hands. He knows that organisms are never completely at one with their environment. The world is 4.6 billion years old, and the subterranean plates of its continents have shifted and readjusted themselves many times. The Earth is so altered from what it once was and has become so multifarious that it's impossible to find an organism aligned with every element in its habitat. Yet that's the way Sam still remembers his first week in Zurich. He is sure Franz remembers too.

Although Switzerland has closed its borders to him, the café-awnings are folded up, and the bankers' briefcases locked tighter than ever, Sam is sure there are moments when Franz sees his friend's face in a flash of light reflected in a shop window or in the blurred flutter of wings as pigeons fly from the fountain beside the statue of Alfred Escher, and at times, in darkest night, when Zurich is engulfed in its tomb-like silence, Franz can hear the faint, barely perceptible sound of Sam weeping on the far side of the world.

If Sam could forget how they wandered arm-in-arm down the city streets as snow banks rose on all sides, growing higher and higher, glittering beneath a crystal sun in a subzero cold he could no longer feel. Sam forgot calendars existed. He was deaf to the sound of the Swiss time-pieces ticking in the windows of every shop, on the wall of every restaurant, on the wrists of people who glanced at the two men in the streets. The silent snow, the rise and fall of its knolls and dales, was everything to him, the laughing children throwing snowballs across the street, the water dripping down the steamy insides of café windows, the icicles hanging like metallic spears that everyone feared would drop. And that day Sam made a magnificent, life-sized snowman of Franz right there in the middle of the financial district, and it lasted two days before a plough came.

Sam could press handfuls of snow against his cheeks and feel no pain, and when he touched the nylon surface of Franz's winter coat, though it seemed as thick as the internal layers of the Earth, he could feel Franz's heart beating deep inside. How he came to know Franz's body in that short time, its stone ridges and hidden valleys. He knew it as he once knew the mall at the end of his street, the grey walls of his Toronto apartment, his trays full of rocks, and the night-black computer screen.

How glorious Franz looked feasting in that Italian restaurant, his hands stuffed with bread. He could chatter so in the cinema where they saw a terrible movie about bank robbers stranded in the Sahara desert; but Franz could be serious too. He told Sam about his father's death; he'd been young and it was unexpected. His dad had always wanted to be a deep-sea diver, but had ended up living his life here in Switzerland, the most land-locked country in the world. Franz would press his face into Sam's shoulder and let him stroke his hair as Sam described wind-swept glaciers, flowers that bloomed once a century in the sun-starved tundra, and the vast outer reaches of the Arctic Ocean covered with ice that he hoped would never melt.

❦

On his fifteenth day in Zurich, Sam was horrified to discover he didn't want to leave. Toronto now seemed a place of exile.

He'd only tolerated it because his Labrador childhood had been worse. Here the Alps undulated like roller-coaster hills, and Franz's body rose on the bed like a mountain range beside him. He no longer obsessed over global warming; there was snow in every street, and the weather was simply too cold.

At the conference, the shocked scientists had no choice but to defend themselves. "This uncharacteristic cool spell is exceptional and doesn't contradict the forward progression of global warming."

Everywhere Sam heard the sound of the fire roaring at the Earth's centre. It roared when he slept, and it roared when he woke. There it was, thundering beneath the blare of the kitchen radio, behind the shout of the newspaper delivery boy, under the chirping of birds in the park and the rumbling of street traffic. The sound drowned out babies crying, cars honking, organ music from Grossmünster cathedral, the thumping disco beat in fashion boutiques, Franz's snoring, and Sam's own heartbeat. The roar intensified the more rocks he swallowed. How could he have never noticed before and why did only he seem to hear it? There is fire at the Earth's centre and ice on its surface. These two extremes had never existed in Sam's monochrome life before, but now the world was in order.

Sam had twenty-five days left until his flight home, then twenty, then fifteen. He wouldn't stay in Zurich forever, but he couldn't leave yet. He had to discover why the world was breaking into pieces and holding together at the same time. Besides, he'd never been so happy.

Franz stepped out of a snowstorm and through the door. He

embraced Sam. "I'm confused too about what's happening with the weather in Zurich. I'll have withdrawal symptoms when you and the rocks leave. You have fifteen days left in my country. You are a scientist. Why not move out of the hotel and we'll finish our experiments here?"

Sam packed his bags in the Schweizer Inn and called the receptionist. "I'll be staying somewhere else. Don't worry about me." He didn't care if the other scientists knew he was "having an affair" with that odd Swiss painter. His name in the same sentence as "affair"! Giggling, he pushed through the hotel's revolving door.

Franz watched Sam hang his flannel pants and button-down shirts in the closet. For the first time, Franz realized he disliked Sam's clothes. With Sam present, the pinesap scent from the trees outside seemed more intense. Rocks were stacked in the corner and Franz's stomach growled.

Franz was always smiling and never mentioned an exact departure date, so Sam assumed he could stay as long as he wanted. He headed to the Swissair office to cancel his return flight.

"Mr Masonty, we can reschedule your return for another month, but that's the limit allowed for this ticket."

Sam would discover that life's greatest disappointments involved planes. He did not belong in the air but on the fire-centred Earth. He decided to miss his flight and go home when he was ready. He'd tell his university that he was doing research.

At night Sam and Franz lay across from each other naked and strangely shy. In his fingers Franz clutched a rock tightly as if dropping it would leave an irreparable dent in the Earth's surface.

He kissed Sam's chest, and Sam's body shivered. He offered him the stone, and Sam cradled it in his hands. Dolomite-stone coated with Franz's fingerprints, the dew-drops of his perspiration and pheromones, a Swiss rock bearing the weight of his twenty-seven years. Its surface had touched both Franz and the Earth. Trembling violently, Sam inserted the stone into his mouth, and it shimmied toward his Adam's apple, then paused on the line separating head from body. Each time he feared the rock would slide into him like a machete, lacerate his digestive tract and emerge from his anus blood-drenched and sticky with viscera. Yet he remembered that Franz's sweat had saturated it, and when the rock finally dissolved in his stomach acids and its fragments shot to the farthest reaches of his body, he felt united with Franz and the Earth. His body became rock.

"How funny," Sam commented. "All my life I've analyzed the natural forces of the world and now I've become one. These rocks are a natural Viagra."

Franz stared at the forest outside the bedroom window. He said, "I hope we don't disappear."

Sam studied the room—bottles of cologne on the dresser, beige and burgundy T-shirts in the closet. The carpet was thick, plush broadloom, and the end-table lamp curved like a woman's body. Inside the lamp, goldfish swam around her navel. The French curtains were drawn; the air smelled of spicy cologne and damp wool.

Franz began to chat. "People I know would be amazed to see me with you here. It'd wreck my image." He chuckled and held Sam tighter.

"Because I'm a scientist? You only know artists?"

"That's partly it. Everybody I know is actually in advertising. But my friends look and judge. They think I'm great—and I believe them. I love the attention. I can't live without it. It's my weakness. My friend Delial always compliments me on my clothing choices. He says I look good in Dolce & Gabbana, but I wear Diesel." Sam became aware of huge differences between himself and Franz and wanted to discover more; they made their relationship seem improbable, hence miraculous. Sam glanced at the party invitations on the night table, at hairbrushes lined up like *objets d'art*. This was the insipid surface of Franz that the world saw and that had nothing to do with the rock-eater at his centre. "Delial doesn't know the difference since he works in ladies' *Kleidung*. I guess the fabric is thinner for women. Men are stronger so the material's tougher or we'll tear it with our larger muscles." Was he serious? Such a silly comment. "Diesel probably has outlets beside Italian Customs on our border. It'd make sense because their brands arrive here before the others." Sam snickered. He remembered the first thing Franz said at the conference, "Rocks are hard." Franz could be hare-brained but was adorable. Sam kissed the crook of his arm.

"These people who admire you … are they men or women?"

Franz sat up. "I hardly know any women. I work alone here so I don't have colleagues. At the bar I frequent, everyone's male." So Franz's social world was crowded but miniscule. "Of course, I have a mother, this prissy over-elegant *Frau* living in Oberstrass. And I see women there—" Franz reached and flicked on the television remote. A woman in a red skirt was soundlessly running up and down supermarket aisles. "Someone ordinary like her is lucky. She can go where she wants and no one pays attention. Women don't have to be so tough all the time." Franz spoke sadly. "Some days I want to become someone like that, someone who's…peripheral. I get tired of getting looked at, but I look too, I assess. I'm picky—except with you, Sam"—he turned to him—"who I don't seem to see." His lips closed around Sam's. "I have a family, of course, my stepfather and brothers. I see them once a month for dinner. My parents are angry that I'll never give them grandchildren."

"Having babies is bad," Sam said reassuringly. "There are too many people on Earth already." He had started to confess his private thoughts. "The average person in the First World creates 726 kilograms of garbage a year. A person like me releases 450 litres of carbon dioxide daily. To be frank, I've never known why people exist. The Earth would be better off without people."

"Without people!" Franz cried. "Then we'd be in a…*Leere*—a void." Shivering, he got up and put on a silk shirt, wrapping it tightly around him. "What would be here then, Sam? Only trees and the ground? The world is full of people, *Gott sei Dank*. Sam, tell me something about you involving people, something that isn't abstract or about this 'force that moves the world' stuff."

"That 'stuff' is important. I'm glad you keep attending the conference, but did you notice the media stopped reporting?"

"So?"

"I'm more responsible for all of this than you are. I have knowledge and that makes me accountable."

"Sam, say something simple about yourself."

Sam pondered. "When I was a child, I was fascinated by trout swimming upstream."

"Good. How about *deine Familie*? Your father?"

"My father? Hmmm. I haven't seen him for years. He is kind of...bizarre. He works as a fisherman. He lives with my mother and sister but has always ignored everyone." He ran one finger along Franz's knee. "I think he still spends all his time on his boat. He'll sit there for hours, staring down into the ocean. Some have said he's looking for mermaids."

"Mermaids!"

"Yes, he wants to make love to one. Really. He believes a mermaid with golden hair will appear and he'll fall into the water and live with her forever."

"You're serious? Like in a fairy tale? Fairy tales are exciting but dangerous, Sam."

"You mean I'm not in one now?"

"You think I'm Prince Charming? I'm too neurotic to be Prince Charming."

Sam laughed. "I think my father looks for mermaids in the same way I always eyed women from a distance or in magazines, fixating to anaesthetize myself and forget my boring life. I'd watch movies to find out how normal people lived."

"How is *Mutter*?"

"My mother is... also special. She's religious and hated that I did well in science. It offended her values. I think she just didn't want me to become separate from her; without me and Dad, she had no men in her life. Once, I started dating this girl, Esther, and she tried to stop it. At one point she got so angry that she trashed my precious rock collection. It was a great collection. I'd been working on it since childhood … It's weird, but whenever I was alone and tried to jack off, that woman would walk right in. She had a sixth sense, and I guess she didn't want me up to any monkey business. It was like living beneath a giant searchlight. I couldn't hide. She never understood that forcing people doesn't work."

"Hearing you talk about yourself," Franz said unhappily, "makes me like you more." Clutching his elbows he hurried into the bathroom.

Sam listened to the gentle hiss of Franz's urine striking the rim of the toilet bowl and remembered Esther crouching in the leaves. He eyed the alabaster brightness of the skin on Franz's behind, the muscle that twitched in his dimpled bicep, the elegant curve in the small of his back. Astounding to think that just a few weeks ago Sam had not been sensate to such beauty. He remembered Esther's body and recalled his adolescent self masturbating to body parts swirling about his brain like blots in a kaleidoscope. Too often women reminded him of his mother, but he'd liked the labyrinth of Esther's hair, the way he sensed no one could get to the centre of it. If a woman had eaten rocks, would it have affected him as Franz had? Probably. So much in life was accidental. He'd liked Esther's freckled nose, her pointed chin, and now here he was with Franz's earlobes, flat pectorals, tangled armpit hairs, rough-skinned testicles, and thighs that sloped inward like celery stalks. What relationship did each part have to the body as a whole and how did they connect to the person inside? Penises, toe knuckles, bellybuttons, vaginas. Sam felt the expansiveness of his own desires as he sensed, stretching away on all sides of him, an endless forest of jutting elbows, erect penises, stiff nostril hairs, clitoral flaps, quivering eyelids, testicles round as ice cream scoops, and pert feisty nipples—a wonderful wilderness he could get lost in and explore for the rest of his life.

It was then that Sam told Franz about the wooden man in the pencil case. He asked him, "Are you that man?" Franz jump-spun in the air and, whooping, danced a can-can, kicking his feet and spinning his arms like windmills.

Sam laughed so much his abdominals throbbed, and he wondered if he'd ever truly laughed before. Franz could hold back no longer. He tumbled into bed on top of Sam, and as the two made love, snow piled up outside the window, on the carpet, and finally over their bodies. Franz shivered and his teeth clattered.

In the middle of the night Sam woke. All the snow was gone. The clock ticked loudly as if someone were striking two sticks together. He blinked once, twice, and realized that a woman was standing at the foot of the bed! It was his mother, one arm stretched out, fingers pointed. The edges of her body wavered as if under water. He tried to cover himself, but she'd seen everything. "Abomination! Sinner!" How odd that she'd show up when he was with a man; it was women she hated—"like prostitutes," she often said. He covered his eyes with his hands, slapped his face, but the apparition wouldn't vanish. Then he saw his father hunched over on the desk in the corner. A girl limped into the room; her long hair fell like taffy over her plaid shirt, and her mouth opened and closed like a fish's—Sam's sister, whom he'd left behind in Labrador. His mother turned and walked into the closet, slamming the door so loudly that Sam was surprised Franz didn't wake. Sam never had these nocturnal family visits in Toronto. Why were they happening in Switzerland?

The next day, snow fell while Franz huddled over his desk eagerly working on a new ad for Credit Suisse, and Sam sensed his family was everywhere. His sister's ghostly head peeked over the railings of snow-covered balconies; his mother's face appeared on statues or in museum paintings in which only the eyeballs moved. He saw his sister's scribbling on graffitied walls: "Please help me!" and "How could you desert me?" Sam and Franz attended a soccer game at the indoor stadium, but when the first goal was scored, the voice over the loudspeakers morphed into his mother's: "You think you're so smart, abandoning your nearest and dearest. Listen, hotshot, we've been following you a long time, but you were too frightened to see us."

Franz watched his Canadian lover bat at clouds of dust and stumble into snow-drifts.

When Franz agreed to paint Sam's picture, the ghosts vanished. Sam sat quietly as—*swishity-swash*—the brush swept back and forth across the canvas. The result: no face, arms, or hands, but violent slashes of ochre, throbbing purple globes, orange lightning-bolts. Never had Sam suspected such things existed inside him. Never had anyone noticed. Franz said, "Tell me about your country again, Sam, tell me…" and Sam felt possessed of real power.

If Sam stayed longer than three months, he'd need a visa. It was best to apply early so he headed to the Swiss Immigration Office.

He struggled through a form in four languages, none of them English. The French instructions helped him most.

When his number was called, he approached a man sitting at a wooden desk and stamping strips of paper. Behind him sat similar people at similar desks with similar paper strips. "Hello," Sam said.

"*Guten Tag.*" The man had pointed diagonal streaks of grey in his jet-black hair; he wore rectangular glasses whose thick lenses made his eyes look pinched.

Sam offered him the form. Some boxes weren't checked off and lines were left blank. "Sorry, but I couldn't understand these languages well."

The man's eyes flickered. With lips pursed, he looked over what little was written. He took Sam's passport and flipped through it peremptorily. He asked, "So what will be you doing in Switzerland? You have been offered a job?"

"No, not yet, but I'll get one."

"What is your field?"

Sam knew immigrants in nursing or medicine were in demand. "I'm a geologist."

The man glowered. "So what would you do here, then?"

Sam immediately felt bashful, the way he'd been in Toronto. He was regressing as if Franz had never happened. "I can look at a rock and, among other things, determine its chemical content."

One of the man's eyelids lowered slightly. "Mr—" he glanced

at the sheet, "Masonty. We do not give out residence or work permits for spontaneous demands unless there is an urgent reason involved. What is the reason?"

Sam gulped. He'd tell him everything. "I really like somebody. For the first time ever. And he's of the male sex so I can't legally marry him and stay here. But if I were here, I could help him with his art. I could oil his sundials and the spinning, plastic wheels on his lawn. I think it will be good for me ... for us, which will be good for the whole country."

The man burst out laughing. Then he removed his glasses, wiped his eyes, and put his glasses back on. "Switzerland has a great love of the homosexuals." Sam bristled at the sound of that word. "We would never put you in camps or force you to walk down the street wearing funny hats. But such unions have no legal status here. They have no effect on the speed of our tramways or the quality of nuts in our chocolate or the price of gold bullion. As for work opportunities, we have no need for rock examiners in Switzerland." He grinned ironically. "Our economy isn't built on rock but on money made of metal." With a dramatic flourish, he reached into his pocket and let fall a handful of coins that clattered on the desk. "If our banks were full of rocks, you could spend your time counting them. But we have no rocks in any banks here. We have many rocks in the Swiss countryside but prefer to leave them unexamined. So I'm sorry, Mr Masonty," and then he stamped—*bang!*—a black square in Sam's passport. "You must leave before the date stated." He handed him the blue booklet labelled with the name of Sam's country and said, "Sir, enjoy your visit."

Outside, it had stopped snowing. A cold wind pierced the fabric of Sam's thin coat. He peered into the frozen waters of Lake Zurich. He'd find a way to stay in Switzerland even if it meant breaking the law. Sam was amazed at himself; he'd never believed himself capable of courage. White powder blew across ice and a distant fire roared.

※

A week later, Sam announced to Franz that he'd called his university and they'd allowed him to stay longer. His department assigned to him two more lectures at the University of Zurich plus field research.

One half of Franz's mouth twisted upward, the other half curled down. Sam was supposed to be here temporarily. Franz walked into the bedroom and closed the door, but later spent the rest of that morning and the entire afternoon out shopping. He arrived home with three Armani suits and bags of glittering scarves and belts. Sam believed he'd bought these clothes to impress him. Then Franz spent the whole evening on the phone with his friends Darcy, Darlene, and Delicia—"all pet names because they're all my pets." Sam couldn't understand the conversations in German but assumed Franz was talking about him.

That night, while making love, Franz said, "Sam, you're not very good at this."

Sam gasped, but had suspected that, yes, he was lousy in bed. He had a penis but only recently realized his pelvis was attached. Sam had to remind himself that these limbs and this torso were his. He mentally desired his lover, but his fingers would brush inanely through the air around Franz's body while scientific formulas ($xy^{33}z^{2}(bo^{3)33}s^{12}o^{12}$) whirled unimpeded through his brain. How could he activate his body and make it his own?

Afterwards Franz looked out the window and said, "I worry now that I shouldn't have gone to that conference. Today I looked at a Versace shirt, but it didn't interest me any more. Then I saw this cute salesman, *sehr schön*, with a flat-top haircut—the kind I like—and I gawked at him for ten minutes but didn't get excited. I only want you, Sam. I still can't visualize you when I'm away. And when I'm with you I hardly see you. I hear things."

"Hear what?"

"Winds blowing. Animal sounds—moose? Sam, what if I'm … disintegrating?"

Sam threw himself onto Franz's body. Never had he wanted him as much as he did then.

Sam began to struggle. His boyfriend's masculinity attracted him, but sometimes when Franz softened and kissed him murmuring *"Mein Schatz,"* he seemed diminished and Sam's desire shrank. Yet when Franz turned away, Sam entered a zone of strange agony. Franz tumbled toward him in bed and Sam's body braced; he fled Franz's longing and returned in desperation when the ardour cooled; the two became hot, then cold, and then hot just as the Earth's surface heats and cools; they chased each other across the bedspread that seemed as vast as an Arctic plain. Sam wondered if sexual relationships between men were always so difficult. Through the window he observed numerous Esthers drifting past snow-topped hedges. If he could reach out and touch that blonde hair—but it'd dissolve like candy floss in his hand.

One afternoon, rummaging in Franz's drawers, he came across *Fairy Tales of Flesh*, a book written by an unspecified author from an unknown country. Sam spent all afternoon reading it.

"Franz, these tales are fantastic!" he cried, running into the study. "There's this neat story about a free-floating world where Mr. Potato Head people can exchange and try on each other's body parts. One lady loses her false teeth and instead wears matching toenails in her mouth; this other guy attaches two boobs to his head like Mickey Mouse ears and is overjoyed. The message is that the inside of people is the most important, and the outside of the body is just ornamental."

Franz felt as though Sam had brought a loaded gun into the room. "Get that *verdammt* thing out of here. I bought that when I first moved out here. I didn't think I still had it."

Some days Franz was thrilled when his boyfriend arrived home. He took Sam in his arms. "I thought about you all day. I couldn't work but kept drawing circles," and to prove it, he showed him reams of paper covered in spiralling ovals. Other days he said, "Back so soon? Thought you had work to do. Remember: If you stop researching global warming, you'll have one of your guilt trips." One afternoon Franz said, "*Christus*, can't you give me a moment to myself? IKEA wants their catalogue design tomorrow, and I can't work with you mooning around."

Sam found these puzzling changes cute; Franz was one of those temperamental artists he'd always heard about.

Snooping, Sam discovered a dozen new paintings stashed in the living room closet. Franz had been painting when Sam was out. Each showed trees interspersed with elongated squares of light. He began to regularly ogle these hidden images.

One night Franz panicked and grabbed Sam's forearm, pressed it against his own, and exclaimed, "You're you and I'm me, right? This damned line between us"—he pointed at the crack separating their skins—"can't be crossed—we won't become each other, *nicht wahr*? Even though I speak to you in your mother tongue there's no way I'll start being like you?"

"Of course not. And I won't become like you either." Yet Sam wasn't sure of this.

"Look at how you dress. I'd never wear clothes like yours."

"And your interest in advertising bores me. I could never care about that."

The men looked uneasily into each other's eyes yearning to hear a giant "Yes" from the universe. Sam knew it was essential they remain separate; just as snow and fire must exist for the Earth to survive, the two men must not neutralize each other's extreme qualities.

Sam became troubled about how the opposite sex fit into all this. With women he had a script to follow. He knew who should open the door, pay for dinner; sex seemed more straightforward, less negotiable.

One evening Sam guiltily snuck over to south Bahnhofstrasse, where female prostitutes paced, smoking and scratching their armpits. A woman in a micro-skirt and twisted halter top that pushed one boob up and the other down chewed gum in a darkened doorway. Sam was not dressed as elegantly as the Swiss men, so she said in English, "Hello. Want some *Spass?*"

He took a step toward her and grimaced. In one quick movement she grabbed him by the arm and manoeuvred him into a dark room with a mattress on the floor. She asked him to show his money, which he did. "Take off your clothes," she said.

Sam undid his belt, not quite knowing why he was here. He didn't want to abandon Franz, but hoped that making love to a woman would clarify his mind. When she was finally naked in his arms, he realized his desire for her was too lukewarm to act on.

"Nothing personal," he muttered. "But I could only be happy with you if you had Franz Niederberger's body and voice."

"I'm good at doing imitations."

"I want to eat rocks." He paid her and left.

On the tramway, wheels clattered and the air smelled of gasoline and wet socks. At station stops, people wearily shuffled on and off. Sam studied a dozing banker, a mother holding a sleeping baby, a bent elderly lady with watery eyes, an adolescent picking at his pimples with the end of a comb. The whole scene seemed pervaded with an indefinable grief. He felt sorry for every single person there, longed to take each rider's hands in his and comfort them, saying, "In the past, I was solitary and desperate, just like you. I never realized we were so alike."

Arriving home Sam caught Franz finishing up a painting. Franz blushed; he didn't put the canvas in the closet right way but turned from his easel and took Sam in his arms. As Sam felt Franz's hands warm against the small of his back, he looked at the painted tree trunks sloping upwards, branches like fingers clawing at the sky, and the lights like eyes flashing fire.

Days passed. This was the first time since he'd left Labrador that someone always greeted Sam when he arrived home, the first time someone said goodbye when he left, the first time he told someone the trivia of his day (and how much more meaningful that seemed than his scientific ideas), the first time someone laughed at his jokes, talked to him at midnight, looked out the window beside him, prepared his breakfast, lunch, and dinner.

Franz gave him a haircut. With each snip, the follicles in his skull tickled. "*Scheiss*, Sam, what bastard did this to you? It's good you met me so I can repair your 'do'." Sam enjoyed feeling Franz's fingers move about his head like delicately stepping spider's legs. Then Franz asked, "When are you going home, by the way?"

"I'm not sure. It's my university's decision." A lie. Sam knew that at any given moment Franz could simply tell him to go back to the hotel, but he didn't. If this were a fairy tale, that meant the dragon had been slain. Or hadn't arrived yet.

When Sam gave his next talk at the University of Zurich, he spoke before a near-empty auditorium. "If we can discover that force that jump-starts energy combustion, we can align our technologies to it, and our lifestyles will not kill our planet. But what could that initial force be? The energy created when electrons collide? The friction caused by water eroding rock? Somewhere in the relationship between rock, water, ice, and air is the secret of that robust energy that moves our Earth and fights its destruction." In the front row one man snored, his head bobbing. Two women in the back were reading magazines. "Do you know what I'm talking about? Do you have any idea what I'm saying at all, you bunch of brain-dead morons?"

The sleeper belched.

Meanwhile, Franz went to Excelsior's to seduce the salesman with the haircut. Later, on the man's pitching waterbed, Franz felt seasick and threw up in the night-table drawer. "I don't know what's wrong with me." He clutched himself, rocking on the rug. "Normally you're my type. I don't know what's happening to me." He went home and couldn't stop painting trees and beams of light.

The next day Franz told Sam, "I'm going to change the locks on the door. You won't be able to come in unless I'm here, but it's no big deal." But Franz didn't change the locks. Then he prepared a Spanish quiche but ate it all himself, saying, "Didn't think you'd be hungry." He washed his clothes but not Sam's. The grease-stained pillow lay beside Franz's clean one.

They went to a fancy party, and Franz "accidentally" spilled red wine on Sam's lapel, then later "inadvertently" pushed Sam's face into a bowl of trifle. Franz apologized profusely, and on the way home started crying.

"What's the matter with you?" said Sam. He'd never been in a same-sex relationship and wondered if this was standard.

"I thought you were here for a short time. And now I can't end it. I'm afraid. *Ich habe Angst.*"

"But I'm not going to do anything bad to you."

At home Franz took the latest painting off the easel. "Take this as a present. I don't want to look at it."

All the next day, Franz's face continued to twist into myriad patterns until he finally said, "We've got to get out of this room. Let's go to the city." He grabbed Sam's hand. "Tour! I'll give you a tour!"

Sam became more confused than ever. Together they visited the Zunfthaus zur Waag, "where hatmakers met regularly during the Renaissance," explained Franz. On the Quai Bridge, Sam saw Lake Zurich on one side and the medieval city centre on the other. At Zurich's original Roman customhouse, Franz pointed at the plaque commemorating the women who'd saved the city from disaster. "The Hapsburg armies were near; all the men had died, so the women put on soldier's uniforms and marched. When the Austrians saw the soldiers coming, they didn't wait to see what bodies were under the uniforms and fled."

Yet Sam felt he was not in Franz's home country but in his own. Was it the occasional flash of metal and steel amidst all the wood and cement? Or the still air, the lack of odour, the discreet way people walked down streets, speaking only when necessary? Or was it simply rock, the same rock beneath his feet and before his eyes? Sam wondered if narcissism was the cause of the world. After the Big Bang happened, did a billion gases come racing together because everything was in love with itself?

Franz asked again, "So, next Wednesday you fly off?" His repetition of this question was starting to really bother Sam.

"No, I don't have to leave yet. I still have to do my Matterhorn studies." This was true. Since meeting Franz, he'd abandoned his research, giving himself up to eating rocks rather than studying them.

Franz's head swung up and he stared into the distance. Sam studied the furrowed brow, twitching cheeks and lips. Sam had never before witnessed intense inner struggle on his account. His mother and father had simple, unimpeded desires, but inside Franz great forces were pressing together, creating—what exactly? The Earth's lithospheric plates move back and forth and are in constant tension; the internal pressure creates substances below the surface, hard, compact, scratch-resistant matter. Franz contained even more contradictions and tensions than the Earth. Something solid was growing below the surface. Sam remembered the elongated square lights in Franz's paintings. They reminded him of diamonds. Was Franz creating a diamond? Sam yearned to be present when what was forming inside Franz was pushed to the surface.

Then his lover's face softened. Something in him shifted, unlocked, and he gushed, "I'm so happy you'll stay longer," and Sam felt he was being given the universe.

Then Franz stepped back. He again clenched his lips, squinted, and barked, "Disco. Tonight we have to go to the disco. There's no other choice."

✻

The room was a sea of half-naked, gyrating bodies, thumping music, multi-coloured flashing lights, and clouds of dry ice. The bass beat was so loud that Sam's collar vibrated against his neck.

The room smelled of stale beer, marijuana, and dry dust.

Franz marched proudly into the disco. All the disparate parts of himself were rushing together like balls of mercury. He seemed solid, lacquered. He said to Sam, "Don't start talking to people about geology here. No one will be interested. And I have to confess: when you go on about your greenhouse effect, *Scheiss*, I listen, but I don't get a third of what you're saying."

In a quiet alcove, Sam met Franz's friends. Although their names were different, they seemed to be the same person repeated five times. Each wore a matching belt and trouser set and a tight black T-shirt cut off at the shoulders. Their hairstyles matched: short and wavy, curling around their ears—like Franz's; they each wore spicy orange cologne. Even their faces resembled each other's, square-jawed with pronounced cheek bones—had they had plastic surgery? Sam noticed that everyone in the bar, including Franz, had similar bodies—round biceps, thick forearms, and pectorals so developed they came perilously close to resembling women's breasts.

The friends' eyes glittered as they regarded Sam's narrow face, skinny arms, laced shoes. His white shirt hung on his bony shoulders like lopsided curtains, and his too-short pants revealed that his socks didn't match. For the first time Franz had refused to lend him some clothes. Franz eyed the creased shirt, trying to fixate on Sam's flaws.

Franz made the introductions. The clone-men pursed their lips and shook Sam's hand.

"You're the one who's stolen our Frankie away."

"I guess I'm the robber," Sam admitted.

"We hope you'll give him back in one piece."

"And Franz's piece is too good to be broken." The five men let out a uniform titter.

"You mean, you've all had sex with him?" Sam assumed that in this milieu, despite the threat of AIDS, everyone screwed everyone. That's what they said in the newspapers and movies.

The men choked on their drinks. "That'd be incest," one man cried. "Like having sex with Aunt Beatrice."

Franz said, "Sam is new to the community. He doesn't know a lot of things."

"So that explains it," replied Darcy. The tip of his thin tongue stuck briefly from his mouth like a pointing finger, then vanished between lips. A lizard's tongue, thought Sam.

"Hey, Franz!" the bartender yelled. "Where'd you get the shirt?"

Franz hurried over. "C&A. Lycra-cotton blend, for 240 francs."

The bartender pretended to applaud hysterically. Franz ordered drinks. A man on a stool patted him on the back and another ran up to say hello. Everyone here knew Franz. This is not the real Franz, thought Sam, but the one that dominated before I arrived and cracked his shell.

On the packed dance floor, shirtless men moved their arms like pistons and pumped their biceps to the disco beat.

Baby, we're shakin' it, groovin' it,
Makin' it, movin' it . . .

A man's sweaty ponytail whipped back and forth; thighs bulged from satin shorts; boys clad in white underwear wrestled in elevated dance-cages; men stamped their feet, dramatically banged their fists and arms against walls; heads pivoted on thick-muscled shoulders. Sam was amazed by the fetid intensity of this throbbing testosterone-filled space. We live in bodies that are worlds unto themselves, self-enclosed, skin-prisoned, he thought. He studied his own forearm, the subtle bump of a knuckle, his milky skin—this container he'd scarcely noticed before in which he lived.

After handing Sam a drink, Franz leaped onto the dance floor. He flung one arm in the air, spun round, shook his little butt. He made whooping sounds, blew air-kisses to spectators. Sam couldn't bear to watch him. At home Franz kept his voice low, as if in a cathedral, but here he shouted and strutted, chattered inanely to whoever and watched his own pelvis whirling as if it were a new toy he was mesmerized by.

When the song ended, Franz shouted to Delial, "I can't stand Tom, that silly queen!" A man tapped him on the shoulder; Franz turned, shrieked, "Tom!" and embraced him. For an instant Sam feared his obsession with Franz was a precious rock that could disintegrate.

At midnight Franz began chatting up a man in a tank top with tattoos of anchors on his huge biceps. Franz reached over and jerkily stroked the man's chest with uncharacteristically awkward gestures. Sam became so angry, he surprised himself. He pushed through the crowds. Sam knew he was ridiculous; he'd become a character in a soap opera doing the kind of thing he once scorned. Straight from a Harlequin romance, Sam defiantly positioned himself between the two men. Sam faced the tank-topped man, who said, "*Entschuldigung!*"

"Franz and I are together, so you'd best leave now." Sam was glad he'd seen those movies. The words felt fresh in his mouth.

"*Du bist mit ihm?*" the man blurted. He flicked his finger against Sam's collar and disappeared into the crowd.

"It's not what you think," Franz said. "I didn't really want him. I wished I did; I just wanted to prove... *Scheiss*. I don't know what to think anymore. *Ich weiss nicht.*"

"Has it occurred to you," Sam said at last, "that I don't understand the German you keep using?"

"Well, I understand it, and that's what counts. After all, they are my words."

Sam couldn't forget Franz's hand lingering beside the anchor tattoo. The next morning, Sam wasted no time. He found Delial's number in Franz's phone book and called him.

"I need help, Delial." How odd it felt to ask for aid. "I need to learn how to keep Franz with me and," he admitted angrily, "away from the others. His attachment to me is...weaker than I'd hoped. I felt so uncomfortable last night and he made no concessions to me at all."

If Franz wouldn't live in Sam's world, then Sam would learn to live in his.

Delial chirped, "That is a magnificent thing to say, and you are a magnificent man for saying it." He proceeded to make suggestions and Sam agreed with everything. First Delial recommended a gym, "Atlas Special. Franz never goes there. Way too hetero for him."

Over the next week, Sam secretly lifted weights. He marvelled at how his forearm veins bulged after his workouts. He ate a high-protein diet and studied muscle metabolism charts. Sam knew bodies weren't separate from minds, yet he worried that he was interfering with a natural process. In that disco, desire seemed twisted into such narrow shapes, it nearly choked to death. Sam considered plastic surgery to give him a chiselled jaw and pectoral implants. "That takes months!" exclaimed Delial. Why weren't things as instantaneous as society promised? "How long are you here for, anyway?"

"That's the million-dollar question."

Delial suggested an image consultant. "Madame Inga Binga from Hollywood. The advisor to the rich and famous. She'll make you a star." After just one meeting Sam could smile engagingly, wave his hand in the air just so, walk suavely without tripping; now he could shake hands with a solid grip and get through a short conversation without mentioning geology.

"But my problems are deeper than all this," Sam later confessed to Delial. "I hate to say it, but I'm a lousy lay. That's more important than I thought at first."

Delial shook his head. "Poor boy. That's something you must never admit out loud." Together they browsed the bookstore's self-help section. Sam bought and read *Give Him the Boner from Paradise*.

"This isn't going to work," he cried, exasperated. "The problem is more profound. The breach between the mind and body can't be healed by more knowledge."

"Then we'll go shopping. It's the only way to solve a crisis."

Darcy joined Delial and Sam, and they spent the entire weekend in designer clothing boutiques.

On Monday Sam arrived at the chalet with his hair cut and

gelled, cerise Ermenegildo Zegna jeans and a skin-tight Lycra vest that pushed his meagre pectorals up and forward. Franz's chin dropped, and Sam understood he'd made a huge mistake.

"That's not how you dress," Franz shouted. "It's how I dress."

At dinner when Franz commented on an art exhibition in Italy that he was too afraid to visit, Sam finally understood what had made him attractive to Franz in the first place: his country.

Next came the fight to the finish. Sam blanketed the walls of Franz's house with photographs of Canadian forests, Lake Louise, prairie grain fields, fjords on Baffin Island, caverns on the Bruce Peninsula, mountains in the Yukon; he covered the coffee table with rocks labelled with provinces' names. He installed a boom-box and played tapes of icebergs creaking, loons crying, the north wind wailing through juniper branches. Franz entered the living room to see a projector shooting a vermilion light across the ceiling. "The aurora borealis," Sam explained. To his delight, Arctic winds began pounding the windows, snow piled up in the bedroom, and icicles formed on the shower curtain rod. Franz covered his ears as he stumbled through snow-clogged rooms.

He retaliated by hooking up speakers that played Donna Summer tunes and hanging a spinning glitter ball that transformed the dining room into a discotheque. Overnight, piles of clothing appeared everywhere. Sam got stuck in swelling dunes of Italian T-shirts outside the washroom, squeezed past hedges of Ascot Chavez vest and jacket sets. Piles of sequined shirts glittered like coral; satin vests floated in dizzying eddies while faux goat-leather belts thrashed like snakes in fast-moving streams of silk socks and Tommy Hilfiger underpants. Franz maxed out his credit card and received a call from his stepfather: "Your bank account's empty. What the hell are you doing with our money?"

Sam and Franz no longer listened but shout-talked at each other. Sam became so wound up and confused, he told Franz that the northern lights were in Toronto, people spoke French in Iqaluit, the Mackenzie River flowed southward, and the Pacific Ocean lapped at the sandy foot of Labrador. He deliberately told lies and said that icicles as long as skyscrapers hung in city streets and pack-dogs pulled trains through ice-coated subway tunnels.

One evening, his photos, rocks, and aurora borealis projector disappeared beneath a blizzard of multi-coloured fabrics; the phone was buried and rang incessantly. Because of Sam, Franz had bankrupted himself.

"Do you want my money?" Sam yelled. "Accept it as rent." He would have loved Franz to become financially dependent on him.

Franz finally noticed that the paintings he'd hidden in the closet weren't right side up. Clearly Sam had been leering at them. Weeping, Franz folded and shoved each into the garbage bin.

The next morning, Sam woke to discover all the clothing and Canadiana were gone. The rooms were empty but for the furniture present on his first day there. Franz sat at the kitchen table, polished and intact, every hair in place. His eyes had glazed over. He seemed to have stopped breathing. He was wearing makeup. A mirror glimmered behind him.

"I bought you an outfit," he told Sam. "So you'll look better when we go out."

"You're still ashamed of how I look!"

"No, I like it when you look bad," he confessed. "I wish I could make that matter more. But we're going to an art exhibition and…some people I dated will be there." Sam had been afraid to ask about this. "Don't worry. I wasn't with anyone for long. I always hunt for flaws and end my relationships quickly, but with you," he said bitterly, "everything's—camouflaged. Tonight you need to look decent. You'll never look as good as I do, but, of course, we'll try. Your new clothes are on the sofa." As Sam headed into the living room, Franz said, "*Scheiss*, my hands are rough. I should've bought Swello, that new hand cream everyone's talking about."

Sam felt suffocated in his new attire. The collar was too tight. The glossy leather shoes squeezed his toes into a needle point, and the coarse pants scratched at the inside of his thighs.

On the street, the snow had started to melt. The taxi wheels hissed through puddles. Sam tried to talk of Canada, but Franz made a perfunctory "cut it" gesture with one hand. Sam attempted to catch Franz's eye, glare deeply into his head, his brain, and see the diamond forming, but Franz talked pointlessly on and on to the taxi-driver. "Power," Franz said to Sam before getting out. "I need to be a more powerful person. Power is important."

The men entered an immense ballroom. Horrified, Sam glimpsed his mother and sister in the crowd, both wearing tight-fitting ballgowns. They held cocktails (though his mother didn't drink) and floated among the guests. No one else noticed them.

An enormous chandelier shimmering with tear-shaped glass drops hung from the ceiling like a giant grenade. Rows of men in tuxedoes zigzagged through the crowd like rivers of black ink. Clinging dresses outlined breasts, accentuated pointing nipples, or clutched the pale bottom halves of fleshy bosoms that jiggled like shelled eggs in cups. A small room off to the side contained the artist's lithographs.

Standing before a sketch, Franz said, "'Mosque in Turkey.' Turkey. I always wondered why they named a country after a bird." Sam smirked. Franz's inanities were still hilarious. Then Franz cried, "*Scheiss!* Fuck, mine are as good as these and I didn't get an exhibition." Then he peered at the floor. "Sometimes I wish I were another person. I'm only doing ad work from now on. And I'm moving and getting a condo right in the city *Zentrum*."

They headed back into the ballroom, where an orchestra played. Ladies' laughter sounded like tinkling glass. The chandelier still hung like a plated grenade that Sam knew would drop.

"Looks like I don't know anyone here," Franz said sorrowfully. "No exes anywhere. None of my friends either, but who cares. Sometimes I'm not even sure I even fucking know my friends." He gazed at Sam for a long time.

There was a raucous buzz, and someone stepped to the microphone. "Welcome, everyone, to the *vernissage* of Jean-Paul Gaudet." The roar of applause. "I'm Lukas Warner, Jean-Paul's agent. Jean-Paul's been working on this collection for the past five years, and we're all very proud of him."

Franz hurried over to the dessert table and began speed-talking to a purple-haired woman wearing tiny Statue of Liberty earrings. He thrust his jaw forward. Franz could no longer get excited about other men; might women interest him? "I've often wondered," he said, "what women want. Believe it or not, I hardly know any." He carefully put his hand on the side of her neck and she giggled.

A green-haired man strutted to the mic. "Hello, everybody. I'm Jean-Paul." Ecstatic cheering and whooping. Who says the Swiss are uptight? "So glad you could all come. I want to thank everyone for their support, especially"—he began reading from a long list—"Bettina Schumacher, Joseph Schmidt ..."

Sam's sister drifted by, the train of her dirty dress trailing along the marble tiles.

Sam watched Franz, who now turned toward him and grinned as he put his hand right down the back of the woman's dress. The crowd parted before an enraged Sam, who marched over, enacting the high drama of life that he previously didn't believe existed. This must be what other people feel every moment of their lives, he thought. Sam stepped between Franz and the woman, and this time addressed his lover. "So what exactly are you doing?"

Franz turned away abruptly so he wouldn't have to look in Sam's eyes.

Over the loudspeakers, "and the person I'd like to thank most is—"

All at once Sam's ballgown-clad mother appeared at the podium. She grabbed the microphone and shouted, "The person he certainly wouldn't want to thank is my rotten little son. He's standing over there. He abandoned his sister and me and has only ever thought about himself."

Eyes lowered, Franz said, "You'd do me a favour, Sam, if you'd just leave. This is all too much for me."

Sam just stared at his lover. Behind Franz, they were handing out dishes of syrup-covered ice cream. His mother continued, "And he couldn't give two figs about the rest of us. He'd once been such a sensitive boy, but he changed and we don't know why—"

Suddenly Franz felt a flash of real anger and, thankful for it, reached back, snatched a dish of dessert off the table and, making a swift arc through the air, overturned it on top of Sam's head.

His mother stopped speaking. The room was silent but for the sound of the ice-cream slopping down onto the shoulders of Sam's suit jacket. Everyone turned toward him as chocolate sauce filled his eyebrows, dribbled down his cheek. He tasted sweetness on his lips.

Franz's mouth was wide open. He was amazed at what he'd done. Sam's mother and sister had disappeared. The woman beside him tittered and then someone else laughed and, like fire leaping from tree to tree until the entire forest was ablaze, laughter engulfed the room. Sam pushed past people whose bodies were like tree trunks that wouldn't move, out the main door, and onto the lamp-lit streets. He was crying now.

From behind him, a thundering boom and an ear-splitting shriek. The chandelier had dropped.

Sam began running. What the hell was he doing in Zurich? Why had he ever come here? And where could he go now? What country, what place? Not Canada. This trip had taught him hunger and he'd never feel satisfied in Toronto again. The genie was out of the bottle and Sam couldn't put him back in.

He passed lumbering stone edifices he didn't know the names of, deserted squares, garish over-lit fountains, gleaming windows full of merchandise that appeared and vanished like hallucinations. In an empty intersection he stopped running and shouted, "Why should the Earth be saved? What's so fucking great about it?" To Sam, the only choices were suffocating isolation or pain-fraught involvement in life. "Let the ice-caps melt and flood the coasts! Let jungles turn to deserts! Let hurricane winds strip every bit of foliage from the Earth so our planet becomes a peach pit spinning in space. Who cares? The universe is vast, and there are so many other planets to worry about if we won't worry about ours. And as for that fucking force that moves the world, whatever it is, it's misguided. It should go somewhere else, to a place where it's wanted rather than wasting its time here!" Sam realized these thoughts had long been buried in his mind. He'd worked manically on his research to avoid his true feelings.

At the chalet, he washed himself and threw the soiled clothes into the garbage where, he thought, they belonged. He fell asleep and had a nightmare. He dreamt his mother raised her ballgown to show she had a giant wood pencil for a penis. She shoved it into a hole in the top of Franz's head and began grinding, grinding, filling his head with sawdust. "He never had any brains to begin with," she yelled, "so what difference does it make?" Sam woke in a cold sweat, ran his hand over his body, chest, genitals, kneecaps to make sure everything was still there.

The next morning Sam opened his eyes; his lover was leaning over him. Right away Franz said, "*Es tut mir Leid.* I'm sorry for what I did last night. I don't know what came over me, I just... You don't know how sorry I am. You can stay here as long as you want, just tell me, *sag mir...*" Franz wanted what he hated.

Sam did the best he could. He described wind-swept glaciers and flowers that bloomed once a century in the sun-starved tundra. Snow fell silently in the summer streets of Zurich and a distant fire roared.

Again Sam's genitals became rock, and this astonished him as much as anything. Through Franz, he was becoming the stone Earth; the final border separating him from the planet was disappearing. And this transformation to rock was fuelled by desire, the most ephemeral thing on Earth.

Sam got up and sadly prepared his lunch and backpack. He left a note. "Gone to Zermatt. Be back in two days."

Diamonds are created at a great depth, between 300 and 400 kilometres below the Earth's surface. The deeper a diamond is buried, the greater it grows. Diamonds are brought to the Earth's surface through volcanic eruption. What form would Franz's final eruption take? Sam hoped he'd be present to see the result.

The Matterhorn is a massive crooked finger angling skyward. Sam was conscious of it everywhere in Zermatt and wasn't sure if he was watching it or it was watching him. By a lake at its foot, he studied a sheet of gabbro protruding from the ground. He fingered the angular lumps and pulverized fragments from 300 million years ago, when the continents were united. He ran his fingers over the bulbous rock veins and sniffed the dust on his fingertips. He intoned lines from a speech he could give. "The North American and Eurasian plates were once joined. Present-day Canada touched Switzerland but broke away. Then Spain rotated downward while Italy, protruding like a unicorn's horn from Africa's forehead, rammed upwards into Europe." Staring into the greenish xenoliths, Sam realized that Franz's country and his own contained the same crystalline rock. The gabbro sheet stood before him like a mirror. He could be in Canada now, but he was on the other side of the ocean. Things were the same and different. He'd gone through a looking-glass and out the other side. Feeling spooked, he hurried away from the lake.

He measured distances between outcroppings and wrote numbers in his ledger, but watched himself in the third person. His research, which he once believed necessary for the world's survival, now seemed peripheral. Again he shouted, "Why the hell should the Earth be saved?"

Surrounded by woods, Sam remembered his first days in the forest with Franz. Snow had fallen and pine trees reached for the sky. Franz had shown him hidden caves, cedars struck by lightning, his sculpture garden, the fire at the Earth's centre. He remembered how Franz had been those first weeks—freshly inquisitive, curious, open. That was the true Franz, the best Franz, the Franz forming a diamond; the rest of him—ice cream antics and all those clothes—were the external layers. Could Sam again call forth the rock-eater at his centre? Their relationship was founded in basaltic rock, which takes centuries to erode. He'd never find another merging of compounds with this particular chemical content. Sam remembered things Franz had given him, a triangular photo of a covered bridge, a bouquet of pine needles, artwork, dials with prongs, clay spheres "to use as paperweights," and all those foods Sam had never eaten before. He'd long remember their first weeks and forget the rest. The problem, he concluded, was they should never have left the forest and gone on city tours and to discotheques. Nature had united them. He should bring Franz to the woods here, to the Matterhorn, or better yet, to Canada.

In a valley in the Alps there is a volcanic gash where lava that lies below the Earth's crust periodically bubbles up. The area is off-limits, but Sam called the Canadian embassy and arranged for a research permit. He was now less interested in the Earth's surface and wanted to understand its centre. The rocks ringing the eternal fire survived temperatures of 700 degrees and never melted. It was there that the mystery lay. He stood at the crack in the ground. The lips of the gash were coated with frazzled weeds. A hot breath brushed against his cheek; was that the smell of sulphur?

"Bloody hell!" He hurried from the crack. He would examine the regions below the Earth's surface, but not now, not this month. At this moment, he wasn't ready.

His plane home was due to leave today. He imagined the Swissair Boeing shooting into the sky without him, and felt liberated. On July 31, Sam boarded the train; when he arrived in Zurich, he felt like he'd returned to his first day there. His viewpoint wasn't scientific, but he recognized that at some point in the past month he'd ceased being a scientist.

When Sam opened the door of the chalet, Franz was working at the computer. Looking straight ahead, Franz said, "Ah, you're still here. Thought you'd flown away."

"I missed my plane."

Silence. Both men knew Sam had done that deliberately.

"Going to get another ticket?"

"I'm having trouble accessing my bank account."

Both knew this wasn't true either.

"You allowed to stay on?"

Swiss Immigration. Sam wouldn't mention that fiasco. He hadn't known what it was like to have so many secrets. For a moment all these changes in himself seemed more miraculous than snow in summer, edible rocks, and visitations from the living ghosts of family members.

Franz said, "I thought so." Looking toward the window, he handed Sam a small box wrapped in floral paper. The perfect Swiss host. Before opening it, Sam knew what was inside.

"You didn't have to do this!" The same words he used the first time Franz prepared breakfast.

"This is pay-back time for the ice cream thing. That still sickens me."

Sam removed the paper, opened the box, and eyed the one-way Air Canada ticket to Toronto.

"You have to go, Sam. We could never live together here. Everything is against it. The visa situation. Your employment." The two men looked at each other. Franz confessed, "I am afraid of what will become of me if you stay." Sam searched Franz's eyes for why he loved him. He found it.

"Would you eat a rock for me, Franz? Just this once. Before I go?"

If you love something, put it...

"No, Sam. Let be. Just let be."

Sam did not know what Franz meant when he said this. Let be. He would spend years examining these words. He would study the forms of the letters under a microscope and make clay figures of the words that he then beat into dust and sifted through for some hint of their compositional qualities. He'd play tapes of those two simple, one-syllable words over and over, searching for what connection they had to the sound of plates shifting beneath the Earth's crust and the hiss of steam stealing through underground caves. Diamonds would glimmer, but Sam would not touch them.

The night before leaving Zurich, as Sam lay awake in the dark beside Franz, he could hear the sound of the Earth creaking on its axis. It is an old world we live on. It has spun around so many times that Sam is often amazed its central shaft hasn't rusted and cracked. He and Franz are not the first to touch its surface with their hands. They are not the first to press its glistening rocks against their skin. The snow has fallen many times before and then melted and frozen again. There is so much that we can never know. There are layers of stone from the Precambrian eon concealed beneath rock from the Phanerozoic, and below that, there are stratum, seams, and lamina from epochs we know nothing of, that we do not have names for, that may never be discovered. In our lifetimes, we can only know a small portion of what exists. The world is endless and its treasures are inexhaustible.

Even if Sam could penetrate the Earth's hard skin and journey deep toward its fiery heart, the now-buried diorite and glittering amethyst, the purple-bubbled gabbro and streaked pegmatite would surround him and ignite a sense of wonder that would hold him stationary between the surface and the centre as the Earth spins slowly, so slowly that those who have always lived on its outer rim think the world is motionless and that the sky is moving.

As morning light began to flow around the edges of the window blind, Sam had the desire to clutch his lover's body, but he was afraid to wake him. Franz would be furious. At what? Geography? Let be. The words were an indecipherable tattoo beating in his brain.

After breakfast they headed out into a world where everything had sped up. The Earth spun in reverse as they walked along twisting trails, through moss-rimmed craters, stepped in and out of mud footprints that would, from now on, point in one direction only, passed open-mouthed caves where stalactites had finally stopped dripping. The tram car hurtled through the streets where the last snow was melting. At the airport they got lost in an endless, underground labyrinth where they turned right and then left and then back and around; they followed arrows that pointed up, down, in all directions at once, and finally stood in front of Terminal 3, the wind blowing Sam's hair as his scarf lashed from his neck, and he looked at Franz (a man whose body conquered stone), glanced down at his flapping ticket (to a country no one visits), and when he lifted his head, Franz said, "Sam," and his voice fissured. "We had some good times but please don't write. We must forget. *Danke.*" Then he lurched round and walked stiffly back into the tunnel, and when the glass door closed on his stone-spined back forever, Sam thought: What will become of my country now?

At last Sam stood before the ten iron steps leading into the aircraft. He felt that climbing those stairs would be the hardest thing he'd ever have to do.

When he tore his foot from the earth and let it bang down on the first step, a huge crevice formed in the Northwest Territories and spread south all the way through Manitoba, thus permanently separating east from west. As his left foot struck the second stair, the Continental Divide cracked and British Columbia was thrown into the ocean, never to be seen again. At the third step, the Maritimes were consumed beneath a flash tidal wave. On the fourth, all of Ontario's skyscrapers cracked and every church steeple in Québec shattered. At the fifth, sixth, seventh, eighth, ninth, tenth steps, brush fires lay waste to the wheat fields of the prairies, the Rocky Mountains tumbled into the foothills, the Arctic tundra was submerged beneath a vast inland sea, and in the southern cities, every shopping centre imploded, the subway tunnels caved in, and all the red-bricked walls in subdivisions were jolted into such odd angles, their houses would never resemble each other again.

As the plane rose, Sam looked through the window and saw the remaining snow in Zurich completely dissolve to water that flowed down the streets and into the lake as people ran outside clapping and dancing. With his face in his hands, he wept loudly without restraint as cold winds thrashed his cheeks and snow poured down from a small cloud just below the carry-on luggage rack. Then, above the water, he saw the Atlantic Ocean burst into flame and become one vast, boiling pit.

When he arrived in Toronto, he didn't know where he was. Everything had changed. The CN Tower, which had been in the city centre, was in the north. Streets that ran east-west went north-south or diagonally. The city no longer had seven islands in the lake but two hundred. When he boarded the subway, he realized it had been transformed into an amusement-park train that went in a circle around the business district, while the old subway lines had been moved to the countryside so farmers could more easily transport cattle.

Sam tried to take a taxi home but forgot his street name and his neighbourhood's name. Then he opened a phonebook to search for his address, but the alphabet was in a new order beginning "H R F" and ending "B V E." He ran into his landlady who pointed east (his apartment had been in the west) and said, "One kilometre. Beside the oil refinery." Toronto had an oil refinery? As he walked home, the ground kept fracturing beneath his feet. Lines formed in the pavement as he crossed the street. He had to jump over gullies, steadily widening crevices, and when he reached the edge of a new borough called South York and saw his apartment building in the distance, he had to cross a wind-filled ravine to reach it.

He entered his apartment and stood looking at the empty walls. He thought everything would be fine once he got back into his old routine. He could forget all that'd happened and become his old complacent self again. But the rocks in their plastic cubes had changed from a bright green to pale grey as if they'd died from lack of oxygen. At night, with his head on the pillow, he could hear it: the fire burning at the Earth's centre. Molten lava coagulated into steaming mounds that collapsed into fragments that joined other steaming, shifting masses. He felt tricked, as if a mirror had been pulled from in front of his face to reveal a blank space.

Every morning he saw the bones of Franz's knuckles in stones that littered city construction sites, his kneecaps in the boulders that marked entrances to suburban parks, the ridge of his eyebrows in the curved rocks arching in bungalow flowerbeds, and when Sam tried to shut Franz out and, by staring through a microscope lens, reduce the world to a tiny circle, there in the lit rock were lines like the veins on the backs of his legs and abrupt indentations that resembled the cleft in his chin. Sam could not escape, no matter how hard he tried.

Six months after his return, he threw a stone across a river and started dating other men. He put an ad in the newspaper, followed strangers onto newly built subway platforms, shook hands a second too long with terse-eyed boys at house parties, and discreetly pressed his knee against the seam-strained crotches of slobbering men on barstools who immediately ordered him drinks or put out their cigarettes and left. Men in the dance bars here resembled those in the Zurich disco, and he wondered if this was a franchise. Once he tried to ram a stone through a dancer's lips, but the man dashed off, called the police, and Sam fled.

He hoped sex would sear Franz from his mind and made love in telephone booths, candlelit boudoirs, gas-station washrooms, on top of the CN Tower—but his hand kept forgetting to cover his mouth, which yawned uncontrollably.

Then he threw a stone across another river and started dating women. He mingled at office parties in companies he didn't work for, offered unmatched socks to ladies in laundromats, and his world became filled with the intoxicating odour of rose-petal perfume, the static crackle of fingernails running through red-dyed hair, the humid, nylon-scented heat wafting from pantyhose left drying on radiators. But in bed he kept looking for body parts that he thought had gotten lost in the covers yet weren't there in the first place, and one day, after giving a long, affectionate speech, he realized he was mouthing the lyrics of a pop song he'd heard on the radio.

Then he threw a stone into another river and started dating hermaphrodites, transsexuals, men who were women, and women who were men or both or neither or who didn't know. He dated people dressed as animals and animals dressed as people, and spent an entire evening chatting with a panty-clad blow-up doll that he deflated and inflated for variety.

But amidst the myriad faces of the world's people who sat across the table from him in ten-star restaurants where vichyssoise and shark flambé were just the appetizers, where the table was piled high with long-stemmed roses, where Valentine's Day came twice a week, the violinist never left your side, and champagne bottles popped non-stop, always as Sam finished his drink, he found an ice cube bouncing against his lips, colliding with his teeth, chilling his tongue, skull, and body until, shivering, he had to run to the washroom, where every solid object—the cubicle walls, gleaming chrome taps, tin wastepaper basket—seemed a part of Franz's body.

If only the world would stop spinning and he be released from its centrifugal forces! But no. There was the ground forever beneath his feet, the fire burning at the Earth's centre, winds blowing one way, then another. The problem was the looking-glass: his country and Franz's were the same but opposite. Sam was Franz, and he wasn't. No one else in his home country had the same merging of fire and ice. Sam tried to order *Fairy Tales of Flesh*, but it wasn't distributed on his side of the Atlantic.

Then he drew Franz's jewel-flashing eyes on a piece of paper that he tried to burn, but it wouldn't catch fire. He flushed the sheet down the toilet, but the next day it returned, diamonds flowing through his taps, swirling over the plates he ate from, shooting from the showerhead to saturate his body. He was regularly surprised by mid-summer snowstorms in supermarket parking lots, in dentists' waiting rooms, on lonely beaches where he pulled up rocks from the earth.

Sam was not made for such drama. He was meant to live out his seventy-odd years in quiet obscurity and then be buried a mere two metres below the Earth's surface. He did not expect the world's subterranean plates to shift and collide. He did not expect the oceans to conspire against him. He gazed into horizons. He shouted into windstorms.

Finally one night he raced out into his landlady's garden, hurled himself onto the ground, clawed his fingers into the earth, and dug up limestone, shale pebbles, dolomite, sandstone, gypsum, travertine, and rammed it all down his throat.

The next morning, he woke up in Emergency.

PART TWO

Air

My body was changing. This happens to girls my age, so I wasn't
surprised. In health class I'd learned how our breasts would
swell, our hips billow, and patches of hair appear on our bodies. I
expected everything and, despite Mother's warnings, revelled in
the new flesh covering my bones, the rounding-out of what had
once been level.

One thing that I didn't expect—and couldn't stand—was the
stickiness. A glue-like residue coated my skin, veneered my armpits, the tips of my breasts, and the space between my legs. It was
clammy and viscous, made my thighs cling together and stuck
my arms to my torso. My toes melded into one solid, beak-like
protuberance. I perspired daily, but I did not perspire as other
sixteen-year-old girls did for, you see—*I sweated honey.* This is
not a metaphor but true life. From my pores came liquid, golden
honey such as bees make, such as Father puts on his toast every
morning before he slices it into strips.

"Tests show that your perspiration has the normal levels of
sodium and chloride," said Dr Merton, his voice level, "but its
unusually high levels of sugar make its composition similar to"—
he gulped—"bee-honey."

Mother raised one hand and cried, "God, don't let me lose my daughter just as I lost my son!"

That's you, Sam. She considers you lost.

Although you can not hear my thoughts, Sam, I imagine I'm talking to you. Prayers to the brother who abandoned me. The day after you left Labrador, my honey started flowing. Is my body weeping for your loss?

At home Mother removed my clothes and coated me with sea salt, driftwood shavings, baking soda, coral dust—anything to staunch the flow. She forbade me to eat corn syrup, caramel squares, or Jujubes; she uprooted all the flowers in our garden fearing they'd attract honey-making bees, though bees hadn't been seen in this part of Labrador for decades (the only thing for them here is rock stained with sea salt). One night Mother sneaked into our neighbour's yard and gutted their tiny tulip bed. "I don't know who did it," she said into the phone the next morning. Mother even drove me to Mary's Harbour to get a second opinion, but the doctor there agreed with Dr Merton. "Your perspiration has the standard levels of protein and fatty acids, but there's all that unmetabolized sugar! I've never seen anything like it."

Mother threatened to leave Labrador to get help. Of course, she's afraid to leave. She doesn't want what happened to you, Sam, to happen to me.

Our town, Cartwright, was similar to many other villages along the shore, full of the smell of bonfires and rotting flounder, the cry of seagulls and the thump of wood hitting the earth. Every day fishermen shuffled their feet along the boards of the once-busy port. Gales blew everywhere, wailing up one street and down another. Wind rattled our windows at night, splattered bugs on our walls, and whipped telephone wires. I'd always feared the Cartwright wind but lately would flee our clapboard house to run into it. Some things are greater than fear, and I wanted to know what they were.

Every night, doing my homework I felt honey drops crawling down my neck, beading in the small of my back, collecting in creases around my waist, and dropping in globules from my vagina. Honey seeped through my hair, darkened the fabric of my shirts. Each time Mother threw my clothes in the washer, the agitator got clogged and the machine stopped running. When I took a shower, my sweat flowed down the drain and blocked the pipes in the basement, and Father had to phone the plumber. I was blamed for the pipes cracking beneath the sidewalk, the sewers backing up on our street, and a fire-hydrant that exploded.

School, however, was where things were the worst. When classes started in September, I thought I could hide my affliction, but Mr Schmidt soon noticed syrup beads clinging to my forehead and said, "Sue, are you feeling ill? Do you want to go home?" Whenever I raised my hand to answer a question, my arm made a loud *fffflit* sound and everyone turned toward me. One day when I flung back my hair, a honey-drop flew off and landed on the open textbook of Estelle Beaverbank, Esther's younger sister. Like Esther, she had a mountain of blonde hair lacquered into a complex series of curlicues and a slot-like mouth you wanted to slip a nickel into. She cried out, "Oooh, gross! Sue's a filthy *glue-girl!*"

At that moment, all was lost. "So that's what it is," said Mr

Schmidt. "I wondered why the doorknobs were sticky."

Over the next weeks, my honey flow increased and soon my residue was everywhere—on the edges of chairs I sat on, the side of a doorjamb I'd brushed past, on hall walls I'd leaned against, on the edges of toilet seats, and on the piece of chalk I'd used on the blackboard. Small glue footprints ran up and down the aisles between our desks and along the hallway's square tiles. In Home Ec, the sewing machine needles became jammed and wouldn't budge. In the library, when I put a book on the shelf, students had trouble removing it and when they did, they couldn't open it. A steadily increasing puddle grew beneath my chair in homeroom, and during gym class my honey was splattered everywhere, across the gymnastics bar, along the hobbyhorse, all over the somer-sault mats. The shot-putts became so coated, no one would throw them. The school had to hire an extra janitor to deal with the clean-up.

Mr Schmidt treated me with the condescending tolerance one accords a physically challenged student who, through no fault of her own, is a complete nuisance. "We'll have to delay the geography test until tomorrow," he sighed. "I need to unroll the map of Europe, but it's stuck shut."

After the initial shock, people became fascinated with my physical condition. Groups of girls invited me to walk part-way home with them. Brows creased, they'd glare at the skin on my neck.

"It's all through your hair. Can you comb it?"

I couldn't.

"Is it true you can't wear a pretty formal dress? Estelle says your sweat would wreck anything nice."

"I guess that's true."

I wasn't used to making conversation, but now the pattern of dialogue consisted of a series of simple questions I had only to answer.

"When did you start getting it?"

"It started just a bit seven years ago, the day after my brother left home. But last month on my birthday, it really started flowing."

"Wow," the girls would say in unison. They were my first "friends." When you lived with us, Sam, I didn't see the point in socializing. Now I wanted to meet people.

The boys started inviting me to hang out with them at the end of the school day. Sometimes I'd escape down the alley beside the portables, but one Friday, feeling curious, I shrugged and followed. For a minute I thought I was being led to "the bushes"—a spot at the end of the football field where people hung out or "got friendly"—but they turned the opposite way, toward a large oak tree. We sat in a circle on the shaded grass while the boys eyed me solemnly. No one spoke. Boys up close seemed alarming. Unlike you, Sam, they had dirt-like moustaches and grubby hands, and their clothes smelled like sour milk. The sun hung high in the sky; a dragonfly circled my forehead. Then the boys dared each other to touch me. I studied my legs draped in wrinkled trousers that resembled their own. I felt embarrassed without knowing why.

"Put your finger on the drop on the end of her chin and put it in your mouth. Here's two bucks you won't."

"Touch her ankle and lick it, shitface. If you do, I'm the one who steals cigs from Variety Plus tonight."

"Ten bucks if you put your tongue in her ear; there's a whole poolful in there."

None of them touched me. They leered at a honey drop clinging to the end of my elbow. As they waited for it to fall, their faces stopped twitching, their eyes darkened, and they became stone still. One boy accidentally got some on his hand but didn't put it in his mouth. When he got up to go home—it was dinnertime by then—he just wiped it on the grass and sauntered off, trying to look courageous.

Estelle often chatted with Millie by the north wall. When the boys passed, she'd glance at the stains on their pants. Then her head would turn in my direction so quickly that her neck muscles clicked. Her eyes slitted and her lips formed a perfect horizontal line. "The guys in this school are going mental if they wanna be with Sue."

My downfall was set in motion the day Jimmy Bridock asked me on a date. Jimmy smelled like wood fires, smoked venison, and gunpowder. He had a lick of hair that swung over his forehead like a cow's tail batting flies. His round cheeks were volcanic with acne, and he had moist eyes and cracked lips always twisting one way then another, as if chronically unsure of what expression to make. His father took him to the bush where Jimmy cut the steel-jawed traps that clenched dead foxes. He had a homing pigeon's ability to locate trapped animals. Even when I was a little girl, he'd liked me. When I'd push open the door of the grade-school washroom, he'd be standing in the hall with his head down. I'd walk past him and he'd look away and kick at the floor—but when I turned back, he'd be squinting after me. He'd never spoken to me because he probably sensed that my attention was directed elsewhere, for those were the days when your presence filled me, Sam, and I didn't notice other kids. I think our isolation crippled me. Still, I remember the wonderful contraptions you made for me, pendulums swinging from axles you nailed into my bedroom wall, whirling bike wheels perched on steel prongs, and circular plates that hung from ropes—you'd set everything spinning and turn the radio up full blast, "The Nipper in the Cod and the Codder in the Pail," and it seemed the circles were spinning to the sound and the music was rotating the circles and what we heard and saw were joined to the same relentless, throbbing, rhythmic source.

Now, in grade eleven, with my sweat flowing rapidly, Jimmy became bolder. In shop class one day, I hammered parallel rows of nails into a wooden beam. Unlike the other students, I could whack the silver heads straight on so the iron rods thrust in without bending. Jimmy eyed my forearm moving up and down like the crossbar on a train wheel. *Bang, bang* cried the hammer-head. I stopped to brush away the sawdust. In the silent space between blows, Jimmy spoke to me for the first time ever. His voice started as a rumbling in his throat and emerged as a gasp, then a strange sing-song squeak as his tongue stumbled around the syllables. Did he speak so rarely that when he did, he used tools rusted from lack of use?

"You're stronger than other girls," he rasped. A cloud of sawdust hung in the air between us. A power drill wailed. "If we had an arm wrestle," his voice rose triumphantly over the din, "I bet you'd win."

The room was now full of the repetitive rah-rah sound of saws cutting. I saw that Jimmy had kind eyes. The swath of protruding, unshaven hairs across his jaw was like a fire-razed forest. He smiled a checkerboard grin and walked away. Could he at last replace you in my heart, dear brother?

The next day in the cafeteria, Jimmy walked up to me and knocked on the tabletop. When he spoke, spit flew from his lips and landed on my hamburger macaroni. His cheeks were flushed. Was this because I'd spoken to him yesterday? Was I the first girl who hadn't run from him in terror? He said, "If you don't mind it, we can get together after school. I wants to go to the bushes." Jimmy's smile wavered, disappeared, slanted sideways, collapsed, reformed.

I answered "Yes," like I did when the other boys asked me to the end of the field. The word gave me a feeling of what I thought was power. "Let's meet there."

Jimmy's cowlick quavered like a radar device. His lips parted, spread, lifted, and his smile was so huge I could see the line separating his teeth from his gums. "Great," he said. "Let's meet by the bleachers at four."

When he'd left, I stared after him for a long time. Somewhere in the distance, I sensed winds lashing seaside cliffs. If I found and gave way to a desire for Jimmy, would my honey finally stop flowing?

꽃

Sam, did you know that Estelle and Esther's father owned the new steel foundry? The sisters shared clothes and did their hair the same way. Esther never married. She'd had a series of bad love affairs, but yours was the first, and she believed you'd set the pattern.

Now Esther ran a dressmaking shop overlooking the ocean. She was always furiously whipping doorknobs with strips of fabric and stabbing pins into the eyeballs of mannequins. She only felt satisfied during storms when ships sank at sea and oil rigs collapsed. Few people bought her clothing since it was too fancy, but Estelle often wore her creations, "because I'm a lady," she'd say, "not like you savage bitches." On special days (her birthday, the last day of school), Estelle even wore elegant gowns with ruffles and lace, "because I'm special. Only lady-like girls deserve boyfriends."

In the hallway one day she said to me, "My sister told me your family are goddamned freaks, and I believe it's true. Does your mom love looking at your underwear, too?"

I had the urge to push her to the ground. That'd be easy; Estelle's limbs were pencil-thin, her behind like two eggshells beneath her frilly dress. Sometimes I longed to tear off her clothes and smear wet mud over her ivory-white skin. But

Estelle had a large entourage of admirers, and my status, though higher than before, was tenuous—more than I knew.

❊

Cartwright was playing the visiting Dove Brook team, and we were winning. I met Jimmy in the striped shade behind the crowded football stands where everyone had gathered to cheer. I could see the clump of bushes from a distance, like three ice cream scoops beside a large oak.

"Way to go, Cartwright. Way to go!" *Clap, clap*.

Jimmy leaned against a wood pillar and fidgeted as if his entire body were itchy. He said, "Let's walk by the stands."

The football players ran two abreast across the field. A squad of cheerleaders in yellow blouses and red skirts (I recognized Estelle among them) shook wool pom-poms and screamed, "Cart-wright is all-right! Cart-wright can fight-fight!" *Clap, clap*.

Jimmy beamed as if they were cheering for him. He turned a couple of times toward the crowd. He wanted to be seen going into the bushes with a girl. Was this his way of raising his status? I wouldn't mind. I might have used him for the same purpose. Even before my honey problem, my broad shoulders, thick biceps, and plaid shirts had scared people away. As we approached the wall of bracken, I became frightened. What were we actually going to do in there? Jimmy motioned for me to sit on the shadow-dappled earth, and I reminded myself that I was stronger than him. I worried that Mother would find out, but then I remembered you, Sam, and your advice that I get beyond her power.

Jimmy shyly asked me if he could wipe his finger along my collarbone. I nodded. He wanted a honey drop from the hollow below my ankle, and I said yes. He asked for some sweetness from the space between my breasts, just visible in the V-cut of my shirt. I let him have that too. As he peered at the golden thread hanging from his fingertip, I wondered if I could make myself desire a boy. It was probably interesting to want—*really* want—another person. How fascinating and unusual it'd be to find someone attractive and completely enjoy his or her presence.

A wind blew that rattled the tree branches and brought the scent of faraway forests, pine sap, juniper flowers—a smell part-piquant, part-sour. The wind woke an excitement in my body. It made every pore in my skin open wide and caused my back-bone to straighten so completely that I was sitting more erect than ever before. The mouths of my ears gaped, and my eardrums became as still as the water on a lake so distant and hidden that no wind had ever rippled its surface, a lake that had waited an eternity for something even remotely resembling weather. What was I listening for?

To my surprise, Jimmy brought the honeyed fingers of his hand together and shoved them into his mouth. His large tongue swirled out and round in a long, luxuriant movement, licking the liquid off both sides of his fingers. Drops glimmered on his lips. He stared me straight in the eyes as he loudly and definitively swallowed. His Adam's apple leapt forward once.

A strange expression came over his face. His cheeks slowly

reddened and his eyes grew larger, bulging forward like egg yolks. His chest had stopped moving.

"Jimmy?" I said. "Jimmy? Are you all right?"

Flapping his hands in the air, he raced out of the trembling bushes just in time for the home team to score its final goal. The spiralling football descended through the posts and struck him square in the face. He fell to the earth and, his mouth puckering, thrashed on the ground like a fish pulled from water.

I charged out into the blinding sunshine. The spectators in the stands turned toward me. "Dr Merton!" I cried. "Somebody call Dr Merton!"

When the ambulance arrived, everyone was on the field shaking hands with the winning players. Only Estelle noticed me, her shaggy pom-pom fronds dangling from her hands like tentacles. She eyed me for what seemed an eternity, her head a stuck weathercock, the corners of her mouth upturned. On the front of her cheerleader uniform, below her right breast, a circle of sweat bloomed like a flower.

Jimmy remained in the hospital all night.

The next morning, I learned that my honey had caused the sides of his throat to adhere. Although he recovered, his desk at school remained empty for a month. This wasn't altogether unusual. I assumed he was in the woods helping his father cut open metal traps. It was September and the hunting season was in full swing.

Still, the other students grew wary of me. After Jimmy disappeared, the boys stopped asking me to be part of their schoolyard circle. Girls didn't want me to walk home with them. When students came upon drops of honey on the school steps or the handle of the water fountain, they regarded them at first with annoyance, then outrage, and finally with pure, unmitigated terror. In gym class no one let me join their squads. Exasperated, Mr Schmidt said, "Kids, you can sit beside Sue. She won't bite."

I noticed Estelle everywhere. She talked constantly, her voice no longer high-pitched and metallic, but husky, full of sly hissing s's and cruel, explosive p's and t's. She spoke at an agonizingly low decibel that everyone but me heard. And she listened to people, one hand on her chin, mentally storing this bit of gossip and that piece of information. She'd become a seamstress stitching together rumours and facts; from myriad ingredients, she created a seamless cloth woven together with real needs and deeply rooted desires, all unified by an innate logic. In the end, the story was not hers but everyone's.

Everyone's but mine, that is. In hallways, students gave me a wide berth. I'd futilely search the cafeteria for a table where they'd let me sit. Strangely, boys were more frightened than girls. Some essential balance had been disrupted. The janitor often shook his head as he mopped the hallway.

My new isolation did not trouble me as much as hearing my name whispered everywhere and not knowing what that meant. I peered into the washroom mirror, as behind me, the reflected cubicle doors echoed with a diabolical hiss: "Sssue, Ssssue, Sssssue, Ssssssue." The sound joined to other words or half-words, verbs without objects or objects without verbs or lone, great big juicy adjectives:

"Piggy-girl, Piiiiig!"

"It's 'cause of her condition ..."

"So totally gross ..."

"She dragged him into the bushes ..."

"Stripped him down ..."

"And then the disaster!"

I still couldn't find the through-line to these shattered sentences which, pasted together, now formed the story of my life.

"What disaster!?" I cried. The hissing stopped. Before me a lone, silver tap dripped once into the sink.

In the hallway, clusters of girls huddled by lockers, and everywhere was that infernal susurrating hiss. "SSSSSue ... he had no clue ... her glue ... the stickiness ... got him totally fucked ..." Sometimes I'd overhear a refreshing, "This stuff about Sue Masonty is bullshit," but that was rare. At last, after a month of conjecture, I was able to put the disparate pieces of the tale together. One afternoon, I wandered by the field where the boys were playing flag football. When I stepped onto the bleachers, I heard my name spoken. All the boys had stopped playing; they crowded together, facing me in a tight, protective knot. From hands hung crêpe-paper streamers. Since Jimmy's injury, the boys were forced to play flag football, not the real rough-and-tumble version, as everyone was now more keenly aware of the fragility of the male body. Someone muttered, "Don't let her near us or we'll have to saw ours off too." The wind had ripped one boy's streamer and he knelt sobbing, cradling it in his hands.

It was then that everything fell together in my mind. The story went like this: Jimmy and I had crawled into the space beneath the bushes and proceeded to make love. But when he entered me, he got stuck and couldn't get out. The rumour mill had produced various endings. In one, he had to saw his penis off at the root to get free of me and, full of shame, fled into the forest and was now wandering bloodied and penis-less over the rocks of the Canadian Shield. In another version, he was absorbed by me completely and was now crouched suffocating somewhere amongst the twists and turns of my fallopian tubes. In a different version, the mere sight of my naked honey-streaming body terrified him and his penis shrank into his body.

But hadn't anyone seen him run fully membered from the bushes? I recalled that he'd been lying face down, and most people were fixated on the rotating ball as it descended through the goalposts. No one cared what happened to it once it crossed the line. Only Estelle had watched, so the story was hers.

The boys huddled together, their flimsy flags fluttering. The kneeling boy wept bitterly into his torn streamer. He turned toward me and shouted, "Cunt!" He picked up a stone and threw it. The rock bounced off the bench in front of me.

"I didn't do anything!" I yelled. The other boys crouched and snatched stones from the ground and flung them in my direction. One struck me in the shin; another cut the side of my cheek.

I turned and ran from the field, crying uncontrollably, and when I reached the street, continued running southward. The pounding of my feet on gravel echoed about the silent clapboard houses that seemed to march past in jerky, disjointed steps. Women on porches flapped tea-towels like striped whips as barking dogs thrashed on leashes taut as tightropes. Rows of fence pickets pointed skyward like white knives. The earth was gouged, cratered, and gashed as if hacked with a huge dagger. I passed a man pulling a buggy joined to his waist with a rope; a lady stepped from the white-walled Catholic church, the sides of her hat rim flapping like oars. Down one street I charged and then up another, criss-crossing Cartwright's patchwork of roads. The air smelled of sea salt, tar, rotting scallops, motor oil.

When I reached the open field near my parents' house, I stood panting on the empty plain. The wind struck me square in the face, whipped the bangs off my forehead, fluttered my eyelashes, and dried the spittle on my lips. I looked down at my body, this body I lived in, this body I carted about wherever I went. These calloused fingers, these bulging thighs, this chest rising and falling like the swell of the sea were mine—were me.

It was then that I knew: air will free me. The wind I once feared will lift me high above the earth-bound people of Cartwright. Wind is what happens when air falls in love with itself. I will love the sweetness of my sweat and it will dissolve rocks hurled like missiles at my head. I spread my arms wide to the howling gale that shot into my open pores and roared through my body like Niagara, as a shower of glistening honey drops fell like manna onto the parched, stony earth.

❦

Sam, surely you remember the house we lived in on a hillock a block from the sea? The building's foundation was made of stone, and the walls were of plywood that eternally rattled in the wind. The roof was a silver tin that threw the sun's light back into the blank expanse of the sky.

Before opening the door, I put my ear against it and listened. Inside, Mother was speaking in tongues again. She'd close her eyes and, shivering, raise one hand and feel the Holy Spirit descend, fill her chest, move across her vocal chords; she opened her lips and the Spirit expressed Itself.

When I entered the kitchen, she stopped and said, "Excuse me. I need a way to deal with the stress or I'll end up in the nuthouse."

"I understand," I said.

"Sam still hasn't answered any of my letters," she continued. "The postman has the nerve to ask why I always wait on the porch! This town's full of morons."

Had Mother heard the horrible story about me and Jimmy? It was doubtful; she had little contact with the rest of the town. Sometimes I liked entering the little bubble she inhabited. That day I wanted to embrace her but feared she'd clutch and never let go. She'd wonder why I hugged her, would worry, and Mother had problems enough. When she found my honey-globules on the toilet seat, my bedpost, or the wallpaper, God's syllables burst from her lips. Last week she broke into tongues while waiting at the supermarket checkout; I was so embarrassed I hid behind a stack of canned corn.

Sam, you always told me not to feel threatened by Mother. You said, "When Mother is swallowed by God, say *sayonara* as she slides down His windpipe." But there is more to her than religion, Sam.

Surprisingly, that night, Father showed up for dinner. We

sat before our plates of fries, cod tongues, and salmon rolls. Filling our glasses with milk, Mother said, "I called the hospital in Toronto. Sam was sent home again. Those crackpot doctors believe his stories. They can't see he's trying to hurt himself."

I still don't understand what happened when you went to Europe. After you returned, you began to show up in Emergency wards with rocks stuck in your throat! The last time you could barely breathe. Am I the part of the reason? As kids, we made all those stone castles together, and then you later callously abandoned me. Do you eat rocks to punish yourself? Do you still feel such massive guilt?

"The doctors said if he swallowed and the rock got below his Adam's apple, he'd die. Those knuckleheads think it was an accident. He probably tells them it's part of some experiment. They're scientists so he knows how to deceive them, just like he deceived us. They can't see he's gone bananas," Mother said.

You could simply take a plane back to Labrador and help me, Sam. You could rescue me from Cartwright. There's no need to feel regret forever.

"Don't you both go hiding your opinions," Mother continued. "I know you think I'm the reason he's cracked, but that's nonsense. I see that Sam wanted to hold onto his trophies and collections. I wouldn't have thrown them out if I'd known he was so weak. Remember when he was eight? He loved everything I did. We created those tiny villages made of pebbles on the beach." She still loves the little boy in you, Sam. She'll never accept that you grew up. Do you recall when she tried to un-enrol you from your high-school science courses and you found out? You should never have started dating Esther the week after—that was the worst timing. While you were at school, she'd finger the rocks in your collection, itching to throw them out, but she didn't, at least not right away. Mother can show restraint, Sam.

She stabbed at her salmon roll, pulled off the batter as if peeling the skin off a limb. "He should never have gone to university and taken geology. They taught him to love rocks and now he eats them." Did you know that after you moved to Toronto, she phoned your university and said you'd lied on the application? They checked and found out who the liar was. Poor Mother! Give her points for trying. "In any case," Mother said, "I wrote to apologize for anything I might have done."

We'd all sent letters when you were in the hospital last month—mine was surely the most upsetting—but you never answered us.

Father slurped pop from the bottle, and I wondered what he'd written in his letter. He belched.

"I'm proud of Sam," I said boldly. "He lived eight years on his own and put himself through university to become a PhD doctor!"

Mother replied tersely, "Well, after that, he went on some silly trip to Europe, and now he's ready for the funny farm. If he'd stayed here, he could've gotten a nice job in the steel foundry."

"Yeah," Father said. "Dere's plenty a new posts. He coulda made good money dere."

"Unless they decide to move it somewhere else," Mother stated. "They only built it here because the government subsidized it. Once the managers see the quality of workers in this town, they'll leave without hesitation." She was buttering her bread too quickly; the knife blade slipped and for a brief moment her knuckles shone yellow. "I admit science is good. Because of it, we have electric lights and our cars run." Here she goes again. "But Sam had always taken it too far and now we see the result. I refuse to be blamed for his behaviour." She fears she's the villain in a fairy tale and wants another role.

When dinner was over, Mother put her hand on the table beside Father's. She glanced toward her bedroom. As usual Father shrugged and took down his tin container from the top shelf. Mother stomped into her room and slammed the door shut. After a minute I could hear her quietly weeping and speaking in tongues.

Father placed the container on the table and cranked off the lid to reveal a surface of solidified honey. It was bumpy like pond water that had frozen too quickly. He scooped a large spoonful and, smiling at me, placed it into his mouth. I examined the picture of the bee on the container. It danced a jig in breeches and top hat, one eye winking as his stinger pointed upwards at a perfect forty-five-degree angle.

I stared intensely at the stinger. Then I wrote you another letter.

❧

In the Cartwright harbour, anchored ships spun agitatedly in half-circles; the wharf creaked, ropes became loose, then taut. Men huddled smoking in their canvas jackets or yellow oilskins. Mr Smith and Mr Pool sat glumly, one holding a *For Sale* sign and the other a *For Rent* sign.

Each week ocean ships appeared like hallucinations on the horizon and grew larger until they towered beside our fungus-reeking dock. Tiny lifeboats rocked primly above steel-railed decks. The ships' bottom halves were black and the tops white. Huge whirling posts rose like giant screwdrivers at each end; the smokestacks were parallel flattened tubes, and the backs of the massive cabins were ascending block steps.

Cartwright was the most northerly Atlantic port in the Americas and was a stopover for ships heading to northern Europe; Cartwright is more important than it seems. Some ships travelled with midget boats beside them and others came in pairs mirroring each other. I'd count the storeys (seven), the windows (200). Some had no windows but were flat like huge floating tongue-depressors carrying cranes or levers that see-sawed up and down. I'd mouth the names of the ships in languages I couldn't understand. The blare of their horns was like a cannon shot hurtling through me, and they'd vanish into the distance even faster than they'd arrived.

❦

On Saturday, as usual, Father took me out on his dory. How wonderful to get away from the town, school, and Estelle and her dresses!

Tongues of water slapped the sides of the boat and sent cold saltwater spray over my face and legs. The slat-seat pressed into my buttocks; I smelled wet wood, sea salt, and the Brylcreem in

Father's hair. He sat before me in his yellow oilskin, staring over the raised bow of the boat whose sides joined together like praying hands. A pole bearing a Newfoundland flag stood beside the box-like motor. Along the floor, coils of rope curled like snakes about which small flecks of water scurried. Getting into Father's boat is stepping into a live thing. Near my head, the lone lifesaver rocked and clattered on its pole. Waves smacked at the vibrating hull while the ocean groaned and rumbled beneath us.

"Dere's shoals in dis part," Father said. "Many shoals."

I leaned over the edge of the boat hoping to see glimmering fish, algae, or hidden rocks, but only beheld a grey formless mass. Between our dory and the shore, other boats, skiffs, sloops, and crab-trawlers bobbed in the sunlit water, and I imagined that every man huddled in their hulls was possessed by the same desire for escape as I.

On the shore rose Cartwright in terraced rows of bright white houses with sloping black-tiled roofs and pert, silver chimney spouts scattered across a small peninsula that bulged upwards like an overturned teaspoon. There were few trees in this wind-blown town but tons of bare rock and thrashing leather-leaved shrubbery. Only the T-shaped telephone poles stood motionless, like huge crosses in a cemetery of the living.

Beyond the town, where the land and peninsula met, cliffs towered arrogantly. I had never climbed the precipices that enclose Cartwright, but you, Sam, crossed the line the cliff tops make against the sky and headed east into a valley I'd never seen. On an adjacent hill, the vague outline of the Mother Mary statue stood like a severed finger testing the wind. Farther south, an iron cylinder and a matchbox-shaped building formed the new steel foundry. Nearby, Mother's church crouched like a frog on its haunches and raised its unicorn-steeple into the air. I could not see my school and the football field, since they were hidden by a hillock angling from the earth like an elbow. From here, my town, with the restless waves rolling in the foreground, seemed static and unreal, a still-life painted in a time no one remembered and hung in a place no one looked. For a moment, Cartwright seemed harmless and beautifully inconsequential.

I shifted on my seat and turned starboard to see my favourite sight in the world: the horizon-line on the sea. Beyond lay Europe and Africa. Between this boat and that line was a distance greater than any I'd travelled, a space that made my mind buckle when I tried to imagine it. If we rowed 100 kilometres eastward, my town would shrink and vanish behind a horizon-line of its own, and I'd be suspended gloriously between two lines and not enclosed by either. I'd be alone in a blank space with only the sky stretching overhead and the endless ocean growling below.

A glistening swordfish shot up from the water and made an arc in the air. My father claims swordfish leap to shake off the leeches that cling to their skin.

We eventually came to the spot Father loves. He stopped the motor and lowered the leeboard. He spotted something in the water and patted the hair on his head. His eyes misted over and he muttered into the sea. Embarrassed and feeling I was intruding on something private, I coughed and *ahem'd*; he kept staring and babbling. I wanted to go to the spot where Cartwright vanishes, but clearly Father was imprisoned behind borders of his own.

When his strange reverie ended, he leaned back on his cushion, farted, and scratched himself under the armpits. Father was different from other men, as I am different from other women; we sense this similarity and it binds us.

I decided to speak. "Father, I don't know if you've heard those things kids have been saying about me, but—"

"Hush, hush," he murmured. "No need to prate." Father was the only person not horrified by my honey-flow. He lifted his steel rod, attached a curled hook onto its end, nodded toward me.

I stood and he held the hook between my legs. *Splash–splash.* Two honey globules struck the steel hook, and he threw it into the sea. Years ago you could reach into the water and scoop up shining fish with your hands, but now men rarely come home with even one net full. It's rumoured the government is about to restrict the catch so the stocks replenish themselves. Yet with my honey as bait, everything changed.

Every ten seconds Father pulled in thrashing mackerels, flapping salmon, and frenzied cod gasping their last breath. Over and over my honey splashed onto his metal hook and an hour later the boat nearly sank beneath the weight of a mountain of fish.

As we headed to shore, the men in other boats watched, noses quivering like the ends of horses' snouts suffused with the piquant scent of tuna, the sour smell of mackerel, the acidic fragrance of flounder, cod, and swordfish; as honey flowed in rivulets through all the creases of my body, the men's nostrils, my father's nostrils, the nets, boats, and the whole harbour seemed to explode with the glorious smell of fish, fish, and more fish caught live and glistening on the shallow banks of the North Atlantic. Seagulls cried overhead, and the fish scent entered my hair, clothes, and skin.

The buildings surrounding the port were of the same white-painted wood as the town, but here Cartwright's cube-buildings were elongated into narrow rectangles. On shore near the wharf stood rows of boats nestled between erect wood posts. At the dock was a gate like those at railway crossings, three trucks whose behinds were always turned to face the water, and a huge boulder larger than a house. At its base sprawled a spaghetti-like rope thrown there years ago and never removed. Chained tires hung along the cement wall that plunged into the sea.

We approached the wharf lined with staring men clutching empty nets. Father tossed his rope over a metal mooring. I stood up in the seesawing boat, carefully lifted my right foot, and was about to place it down on the dock's oil-stained boards when—during that one long second that my body was hovering suspended half over land, half over sea, and one metre above the Earth's surface—suddenly in the distance—a sound. All the fishermen dropped their nets, boys by the Dairy-Freeze stopped throwing stones, a mother with a stroller lifted and clutched her baby to her chest, and every head in Cartwright turned northward in the direction of an new, peculiar, unpunctuated buzzing.

I stood with both feet on the wood dock. My honey dripped to the earth. *Splash-splash*, it went. *Splash-splash*.

All the next week, the buzzing continued. At school, students couldn't concentrate. Mr Schmidt closed all the windows, but we could still hear the distant, steady drone.

No one knew its cause. Many said it had something to do with the new steel foundry. My father claimed swarms of killer bees were about to invade. The town mayor said that unionized lumberjacks had gone mad in the woods and were approaching Cartwright armed with buzzing chainsaws. On television, a retired professor said that hordes of ravenous termites were eating their way through forests and would arrive and gobble up our homes. "As our wooden walls disintegrate, we will be exposed naked in our bathtubs or making love on our beds. All secrets will be revealed."

At school, people assumed I was the cause of the buzzing. The sound was strange and I was strange.

"Jimmy's life's a nightmare," Estelle said, weeping before a crowd by the flagpole. "He's alone in the woods and is too afraid to come back. Something awful's happening—all because of her"—she pointed at me—"the glue-pig girl!" In the hallways people jabbed pencils into my shoulder blades and splashed me with soda pop; when I walked home, students hid behind the hillock on Maple Street and threw broken glass and obscenity-covered paper airplanes at me. "Go to hell!" I'd shout back, lunging at people whom I deliberately splattered with honey. During recess, the boys tried to tie me to the schoolyard fence until they were caught by Mr Schmidt and sent to the principal's office.

One day, walking to history class, I noticed that the usual jeers and curses were mixed with laughter. I reached round and touched, on my back, something cylindrical (a drink tin) next to a rectangular object (a French fry container). People had put things on my back that stuck. Estelle's piercing laugh was like a struck tuning-fork pitched an octave too high.

The whole student body participated in this new activity. As I passed, they'd stick chocolate-bar wrappers, empty pop cans, broken pens, crumpled sheets of paper, and cigarette butts on me. I desperately tried to pull things off, but they would just put other stuff back on. I hurled cups, forks, and straws at students, but they dodged my throws. I couldn't believe I'd once wanted to be friends with these people. I'd been right to ignore them all those years.

I tried a new strategy. If I were co-operative, people might pity me and end their game. At lunch hour when the patrolling teacher stepped outside to smoke, I waved and shouted from the table where I sat alone. "Okay! Do it!" People commenced tossing hamburger boxes and sandwich wrappers; they cheered when an object landed on me and stayed there. Boys played a game in which whoever got something stuck on my arms received four points; on the chest, eight points; and on the face, ten. After five minutes, every section of my exposed skin and honey-drenched clothes was coated with plastic cups, straws, paper airplanes, torn-off backs of textbooks, used yogurt containers, empty matchboxes, dandruff-filled combs, Vachon cake wrappers, cracked pieces of soap, and muffin cups.

At night, lying in bed, I screwed my eyes shut and imagined shit falling from the sky into my classmates' open mouths.

Each day the buzzing got louder and my situation grew worse.

First Estelle encouraged people to dispose of their snot-filled Kleenex on my back. Later she said, "What better place to put the tampons that keep overflowing our washroom bins?" One morning I heard hysterical laughter and smelled a horrible stench. I reached around, and my fingers pressed into something soft. My hand darted away; my fingertips were coated in dog poo.

Estelle and her boyfriend created a "turd-brigade." Each morning he found shit—"a different colour every day," sang Estelle—and she directed him to place it in the most aesthetically pleasing spot. I couldn't remove the turds since they were always put where I couldn't reach them. Even if I removed one, it'd be replaced right away or a second batch would be added to my hips or the back of my neck. Mr Schmidt repeatedly ushered me to the washroom for clean-up. The students caught abusing me this way were suspended from school, but returned more hostile than ever.

My hatred of the school increased daily. I hated Estelle more than anyone. I hated her face. I hated her hair. But most of all, I hated her dresses. I went insane on the days she got dolled up and drifted about in a cloud of gauze and lace, the hard angles of her elbows and knees camouflaged by a translucent sheen that softened every movement, making even a raised third finger seem elegant. She didn't walk but floated, fairy-like. From the distance she was a shimmering blur, a faint smudge in the air. Her friends started to emulate her. Her sister Esther got some new customers.

Mother said to me, "Why don't you dress nice, like your friends I saw on the street?"

"They're not my friends."

Walking to the harbour, I discovered a dainty pink belt stuck between two rocks on the ground. I stamped on it, then picked it up and tried to tear it with my hands.

In the cafeteria the next day, Estelle scurried up and attempted to insert a mud-drenched sponge in the small of my back, but I spun around and screamed at her, "You stupid bitch. I may be dirty, but at least I'm not wearing a moronic fairy-dress. I'd rather choke on my own puke than look like you!" I pushed her against the wall, but she was thin, slipped out of my grasp, and ran away weeping.

I had to spend that afternoon at the principal's office. "Everybody's mean to me," I complained. "I didn't ask to be the way I am."

I noticed Estelle waiting in the parking lot. I stopped right before her and we stood face to face on the flat cement plain as if no one existed in the world but us.

"What's with you?" I asked. "What did I ever do to you, anyway?"

Estelle's face was blank. She opened her mouth. I never realized she had such large gaps between her teeth. "My sister talks about people like you. She has nothing else to talk about." She closed her mouth, licked her lips. "When guys admire me, they're admiring her 'cause we're so much alike. She's happy as hell, now that things are going shitty for you. And that's made her dresses even prettier. She's started embroidering flowers into her designs." Her voice became gentle. "When I'm mean, it's to make you change. I'm offering you a kindness. Someone has to be at the bottom and someone at the top, and you've chosen the bottom."

I looked into her large oval eyes that were the same blue as mine. Oddly, for a moment, I felt sorry for Estelle but didn't know why. Her lip quivered. She wanted to embrace me. And I wanted to hold her. Imagine our two bodies pressed together as we wept. She had the same fear as I, because her lips curled abruptly; she spat on the ground, snorted, "Glue piglet," and marched across the parking lot.

On my way home I removed my armour of plastic, Styrofoam, and shit; if Mother saw me she'd start speaking in tongues and never stop. The constant buzzing had already completely unhinged her.

When I opened the door, Mother was sitting with her face in her hands. A fax lay on the kitchen table. I snatched it and read, Sam, that you'd again returned to the hospital with a rock in your throat. This time you swallowed it and almost died. You'd been committed to the York Psychiatric Institute.

"He's in an insane asylum," Mother said. "I spoke with his psychiatrist on the phone. They don't know how long he'll have to stay there. But he's safe now. He can't hurt himself in such a place. The good news is that it's not my or your father's fault. They always blame the parents, but the doctor said a person he met in Switzerland, probably some floozy, inflamed his brain and caused him to eat rocks."

Sam, you astonished me. Somebody you met caused this? You who are solitary were affected by someone else? That woman must be possessed of such force and power like that of the wind that blows or the liquids that churn through my body. Potent forces exist in the universe and you'd been touched by one of them. But there was more to it than this. You'd read my last letter. You want to help me but don't know how. If you smash rock against rock, something has to give, so you went insane.

At that moment, the distant buzzing became louder. I noticed my honey was flowing faster. Two drops fell from my bent elbow and landed on the tablecloth.

When Father entered the kitchen, Mother shoved the note in his face and yelled, "See! I did nothing to Sam. I should've done more to keep him here safe and sound. Now he's in the hospital because someone, some slutty bitch in Europe, has ruined him. And you're the one who always said he should go on dates!"

Father was silent for only an instant. "If me son had a girl, I say good for 'im. Good for 'im."

"He's completely shut down," Mother murmured tearfully. "He won't speak or open his mouth but just looks out the window."

Are you thinking about me, Sam? Are you broken because you see it was wrong to break our bond? You can still find some way to help me, Sam. I believe it!

The buzzing crescendoed.

After dinner Mother took my hand and dragged me up the winding path leading to the highest viewpoint on the tallest cliff, where the Virgin Mary stands with her hands outstretched, her lips shut, her pupil-less eyes staring across the sea. Mother only comes to this spot during crises. Mary thrusts into the sky, and here the heavens were the closest we could get to them.

Yet even here, we could hear the distant buzzing. Mother said, "Just stand here, sweetie," then turned and spoke into the wind. "God, strengthen me! Solidify me! I bring my daughter with me now so she can see the truth and not be as difficult as Sam was." She dropped my hand, totally forgetting me as she spoke alone to her Lord. "God, I know I cling to You to compensate for my faults, the desperation and incompleteness at my centre that has made me shrill and hysterical, but what can I do with this rage that's always within me? So many people in this town are losers. My husband ignores me and loves a stupid mermaid. What can I do about these forces that oppress? Sam is suffering; he eats rocks, and my dear daughter sweats honey. It's all disastrous and now"—she pointed at the distant droning—"Satan's minions are waiting on our doorstep."

I concentrated on a crack in the earth by my feet. Sam, you always told me that to be outside the influence of Mother and her God, I should never raise my head. Whether the atmosphere was blue, black, or grey didn't matter. The Earth was an ever-spinning merry-go-round—and it was there that the true source of life lies. Long ago I decided that this brittle, contradiction-filled woman, who can be so difficult to love, was not my real mother but the stepmother in a fairy tale. I believe my true mother lives in the sky! One day, I will lift my head and see her. She'll be threading long, golden strings of solidified honey, surrounded by open jars and honey pots that are the same colour as her skin; her hair will flow in undulating waves over her neck and shoulders; her whole body will drip—mouth, breast, chin, knees—constantly flowing and being replenished by some hidden spring. As she spins her spinning wheel, the skin on her face will change hue like the shifting shades on a burning candle. She will call me by my name. I will step forward and, when we embrace, our skins will merge. So different she'll be from this harsh woman beating her hands together beside me.

The wind stopped blowing. Mother took me in her arms and held me for a good while. "Everything will be fine." She kissed me on the cheek. Then she stepped away and clenched her fists so tightly that the veins on her forearm bulged. "We'll do something to make things right. God said so. We won't screw up like with Sam. This time, we'll watch."

That evening she made Father install a lock on the outside of my bedroom door. He shrugged, asked, "What's the point?" but obeyed. Mother explained, "It's for you, Sue, if you start having problems. Sam fled at night, and we don't want you to end up in his situation." As she touched the new lock with one hand, she had a rare moment of insight. "Indeed, Sue, my religion didn't make me who I am. I made my religion who I am."

The next day the buzzing was so overpowering, the fish wouldn't come near shore, and the men had to go farther out to sea in their boats. At school the buzzing made the fluorescent lights flicker, rattled the windows, vibrated my chair, and caused chalk dust to rise and fill the room with a pink fog. Estelle's hairdo trembled on her head like a blonde jelly salad. Students glanced toward the windows and shifted in their chairs. Several times Mr Schmidt had to erase what he'd written on the board. "Excuse me," he muttered.

My honey flow was especially heavy, yet no one tried to stick anything on me, distracted as they were by the deafening drone. The sound confused people and sapped their energy. I felt less visible.

As usual the final school bell rang at three-thirty. When I stepped out of the building, the buzzing abruptly ceased. Everyone on the street lifted their heads. The world hung suspended in an eerie silence. Girls clutched books like shields against their chests. A group of boys stood still as a basketball bounced once, twice, struck the curb, and scuttled away.

For the first time in weeks, we heard bushes rustle in the wind. A bird chirped. From a window, a transistor radio. The sky was extremely clear. However, the stillness did not feel like stasis. Nothing was resolved. The air seemed tense and forcibly contained like a breath held in.

I breathed quickly, my chest rising and falling. My honey flow was so rapid that drops hung in rows along my pant hems and the ends of my sleeves; with each step I took, honey splattered onto the sidewalk. I reached the empty field near my parents' house. I stepped into the open space. When I was exactly half-way across, suddenly the deafening buzzing started up like a stereo kicked on at full-blast. I looked up and saw that the sky was filled with a hundred gyrating inkblots. Each blot seemed to contain hordes of buzzing bees. I stood stock-still as the blots came together at the centre of the sky to form a giant axe-like shape. Its edges rippled, as if seen through water. The axe drifted slowly northward, inched slightly to the east. The buzz-roar steadily crescendoed, then quickly stopped. In an uncanny silence, when it seemed the whole world was listening, the shape began to fall down toward the Earth, toward the empty plain, toward me standing in the field's centre like a bull's eye.

I screamed and ran toward the southern part of the field, but the form was falling there; I charged east, but saw the shape was falling there too. The axe was falling everywhere at once.

I searched the open field for a place to hide. There were no ditches, ruts, or gopher holes, just solid crabgrass-covered ground and a few scraggly anthills. Could I burrow underground? I scratched at the stony soil and foolishly pulled up rocks from the earth. The shadow on the earth grew darker. Gasping, I turned round to see the underside of the vast, black shape descending toward me. I cried out every formula I knew to save me. "Help, Mr Schmidt, help! Mother Mary, protect me! Sam, rescue me! Holy Spirit fill me! Ten plus ten equals twenty!" I screamed to every God that existed, but in the end could only fall backwards to the earth.

The back of my skull struck a protruding stone, my vision blurred, my eyelids closed. When I opened my eyes, for one split-second I saw a horrific, black cloud of writhing insects with glistening, armoured torsos, jointed pelvises, legs clawing like flailing multi-jointed fingers, silver wings twisting like twirling blades of cutlery, and jet-black stingers pointed straight down like diviner's rods.

The buzzing blanket of eyes, legs, and pelvises fell upon me and covered my body completely as my heart beat wildly like a fist in a cage and honey flowed in torrents along all the surface of my skin. The bees swarmed along my arms, legs, neck, face; they slid under my T-shirt, flowed beneath the elastic in my training bra, streamed up through the bottom of my pants, along my legs, and crossed under the elasticized line on my panties. They lapped and leapt, snorted, buzzed, and spit.

Thump-thump, went my heartbeat. *Thump-thump* went my heart. I shall listen to my heart and it shall save me. I shall listen to my heart and I'll be free.

Yet as the bees' black-armoured bodies frenetically writhed and shook, as they clambered in and out of my ears, leapt from my upper lip to my lower, crawled in scrabbling masses along my scalp and through the forest of my hair, lapping at the honey tears that flowed in rivulets down my cheeks, I realized I was not harmed. The bees had not touched me with their stingers. I only felt a million tongues licking the pores of my skin and creating a warmth in my navel, a tingling in the crevice behind my ears, a slight tickling on the pale flesh of my inner thigh, and a pleasant scratch-scratching about the follicles on my scalp. My breathing became regular, and though still frightened, I thought, soon they'll be finished; any moment now, they'll leave.

The velvety fur on their backs brushed gently against the inner dome of my armpits, pressed against the sensitive skin on the underside of my jaw. I gazed into the black-bead eye of one bee who peered back into my own from its place by my lower lash. Its body shivered. Its eyes clung to each side of its head like tiny balls of mercury. I wondered, what colour are bees' eyelids? I waited for it to blink but thought, do bees even have eyelids?

All at once several bees shot up into the air. The others followed and formed a roaring, black blanket that hovered and rippled over my body. The shape dissolved as the insects dispersed, flying in all directions at once.

I sat alone in the empty field.

I touched my arm to discover my skin was licked clean and was as smooth as polished porcelain. Still shaken, I walked home sobbing quietly. When I entered our kitchen, Mother asked sharply, "What's the matter? You look flushed."

"It's very windy."

That evening I went back to the spot where I'd met the bees. I noticed that the sky was again very clear. I remembered the softness of the bees' fur, the slight tickling as their twig-like legs stepped hesitantly about the hair in my armpits, and the ululating warmth as their stingers stroked the skin behind my knees. The wind was blowing again. I listened deeply into the distance, heard a cow mooing and an old woman calling, "Come home, Madeleine, come home!"

Having at last admitted I would never belong to a circle of friends at school, I wondered if I could be absorbed by something else, something unknown and so bizarre and beyond logic that it seemed to have sprung from the depths of my own imagination. I snaked my hand up my shirt sleeve and felt the return of that fetid stickiness. For the first time, I felt happy to be who I was.

The next morning we woke to a town bursting with swollen-headed flowers that had bloomed overnight. Pollen-carrying bees buzzed in tremulous haloes about the open mouths of moisture-beaded tulips, lush frilly-skirted chrysanthemums, and rouge-lipped gardenias, which lined sidewalks, filled parks, exploded in riotous displays of colour in once-meagre rock-gardens or crept up the peeling walls of wooden bungalows. From a distance the long-stemmed roses wavered like lipstick smudges in an air now laden with the dizzying odour of floral perfume rather than salt.

Girls ran laughing from house to house picking flowers while boys charged through clouds of bees that, though ubiquitous, were continually out of reach. My mother, terrified by the profusion of blooms in our backyard, closed the blinds and swore she wouldn't go outside even if God ordered her to.

In school, boys fidgeted beside laughing girls who'd placed tulips behind their ears, in their hair, or in the V-cleavage of dresses. Unfortunately, Estelle looked magnificent. I was completely ignored, which pleased me. No one stuck anything on me; the days of Sue the garbage hedgehog seemed over. As I sat writing my essay on the War of 1812, I luxuriated in the glow of my beautiful secret: Cartwright had blossomed because of me.

That afternoon when I left school, the streets were eerily silent. I entered the field and, as before, the roaring swarms of bees gathered in the sky, then descended. I was ready for them this time. My sweat flowed in a honey-torrent over the exposed expanses of my body. I laughed and screamed with delight as they licked and leapt, crawled, nestled, frolicked, snorted or, crouching on the cliff edges of my lower eyelids, stared right into me. Then they disappeared, and I rose feeling cleansed and refreshed.

Back home, Mother was pounding cookie-dough with both fists. She looked at me and narrowed her eyes. Since the bees' arrival, she'd lost the ability to speak in tongues. Their presence in the atmosphere cut off her access to the Holy Spirit, and when she closed her eyes and raised her hands, she caught high-frequency soundwaves that had nothing to do with God. Yesterday she'd opened her mouth and a shriek like microphone feedback emerged. Flustered, she tried again and caught the radio waves of CBNK: "This song's to Donna from George who says you're one hot baby doll." Now Mother put the cookies in the oven, sat down, and braced herself. She'd make another attempt. She shut her eyes and opened her lips, but this time a man's gravel voice emerged. "These walkie-talkies work, Gladys. Lets me know what time your husband leaves and I'll comes out of the bushes."

Mother covered her face. "Oh God, what have I done? Am I not working hard enough? Sue, tell me if you're involved in this!" She rummaged through my closet and dresser drawers for clues, happy to find nothing. She wrote a letter to the newspaper urging that the bees' hives be found and destroyed. "So many insects is unnatural," she argued. She didn't mention God this time, but still the letter wasn't published. "They laugh at what I send," she snapped. "They think I'm a weirdo."

I began to commune with my insects daily. I indulged eagerly, but it was a guilty pleasure. I felt slightly perverse and was terrified of getting caught, so now I waited for the insects in a clearing outside town. We'd meet, then run up and down the bare rock hills, the bees roaring behind me like a furnace; their swarm changed shape—it was like an amoeba, a huge question mark, a whirlpool, or a spinning Ferris wheel. The wind was a giant hand pushing my back as I charged into valleys, up hillsides, over streambeds, along the shores of crystalline lakes, by foaming waterfalls that sprayed and rumbled, in and out of fog-clouds that blew in from the ocean. Brother, you said the pressure in rocks is what moves life forward, but I believe it is the air that drives us, that churns the sea, that brought the bees from their faraway home to be with me.

On the softest spot of earth in the bare field, I'd fall backward, the bees would descend, and I'd be cocooned in the most beautiful darkness imaginable. Although the bees numbered in the thousands, I could distinguish some of them. Each had his or her own habits and I gave names to my favourites. Drooper was the bee whose stinger slanted diagonally to the right. Fuzz-Bucket had an inordinate amount of hair on his forehead. Q-Tip had a long, narrow body with two bulbous ends. Einstein was always pondering the mole on my right cheek. The Dabbler repeatedly touched her stinger over and over to the same eyebrow hair, while Cowardly Kim lingered outside my right nostril wanting to go in, I assumed, but afraid he'd get lost.

I became addicted to the bees, Sam. I just couldn't stop.

At dinner, Mother announced, "Sam has started to speak again. Apparently he actually smiles." Are you thinking about ways to help me, Sam? "He asks the doctors questions. But if anyone mentions Europe, he clams up. He hates that whole continent and finds Switzerland particularly disgusting. I think that's a good sign." You are gathering strength, Sam. I am glad.

Father now spent even more time staring into the ocean depths from his boat. I no longer tried to stop my honey flow. I still visited Dr Merton regularly, but he despaired of finding the reason for my ailment. I suspected its cause was beyond what science understood.

Lying alone on my bed, I'd play honey games. I'd place a fingertip against my leg and lift it to make a luxuriously undulating syrup string. Or I'd clasp then separate my hands to create a gooey cat's cradle. I'd press my lower jaw against my neck and repeatedly raise it, delighting in the wonderful *thwuh-thwuh* sound.

Running with my bees, I'd hold both my arms straight over my head and point my fingers so that my hands and body formed one giant stinger—at such moments I felt I was a bee myself. I'd stop running and the bees would rush ahead, land on whatever was before us—a knotted tree, a wooden fence, or telephone pole—and the ones who got there first would drive their stingers in. Each time twenty or thirty bees expired and lay stingerless below the pocked wood. I didn't play this game often as I didn't want to deplete my swarm, but it was a wonderful sport and I enjoyed it immensely.

The kids at school were too occupied with their new lovers to bother ostracizing me. Everywhere love had blossomed thanks to the thousands of blooming flowers, a side-effect of the bees' arrival. Estelle now had two boyfriends, there were no school virgins left, and Mr Schmidt's wife was pregnant with twins. The old lady on Brown Street was engaged to her gardener, the mayor was having an affair with the baker's wife, and fishermen hesitated before cracking fish's heads with mallets. At town council meetings, representatives winked at each other across boardroom tables and stirred coffee in cups decorated with hearts. In the hospital, nurses asked out doctors who longed to French-kiss patients. Workers at Dairy-Freeze always had ice cream on their faces, and production in the steel foundry slowed because workers took flirt-breaks.

While I enjoyed my new invisibility, I resented that the students who'd tortured me were now happy. Every time I saw a smouldering dog turd, I remembered how they'd felt on my back. When I came upon a rotting lobster claw on the beach, I pictured it stuck to my cheek. One afternoon after playing with my new friends, I glared at the small pile of dead bees below a stinger-filled birch and had a deliciously horrible idea.

I waited outside the change room and, after the girls filed out for soccer practice, I rushed in and slid the plastic clothes-filled crates from their cubicles. It took a while to find one that contained a dress. I snatched a pink one and shoved it up my shirt. God, I hoped it was Estelle's. She'd dressed up today, probably to impress her new boyfriends. This dress could be anyone's, since her friends were now buying clothes from Esther. I scurried into the hall, out the door, and past the crowded football field. On the first street I headed west and didn't stop running until I'd reached the clearing outside town.

When I got there, I noticed something odd: My honey had

stopped flowing. It was only when I removed the dress from under my shirt where it was pressing against my skin that honey again began to seep from my pores.

I shook the dress out and examined it. Pink, made of satin, with a small steel hoop inside the waist. Unfortunately the dress was too big for Estelle but probably belonged to one of her cronies, which was almost as good. I pulled the dress over a bushel of hay and placed a rock on top to resemble a head. I placed my "scarecrow" in the centre of the clearing.

When my bees arrived, I sicced them on it. Oh, how I laughed and clapped my hands as the insects shoved their stingers through the lace on the chest, the ruffles on the short sleeves. When finished, I had them attack three, four, five more times!

⁂

The next day I did something I hadn't done for weeks. I waited for my bees in the park near my parents' house. The insects arrived in their whirling swarm and, as usual, I held my arms out like airplane wings, ran, and they followed me like a giant swinging tail. As we neared a row of clapboard houses, I feared someone would see me so I made a quick detour through the forest. I hid behind the hillock a block from the school where boys had once thrown glass at me, my chin pressed into a dirt groove bordered by ragweed. Before my eyes, a cluster of bull thistles; between them, a sliver of the empty, sunlit street. The black bees spun in a halo above me. I smelled dust and manure.

Soon two boys appeared, talking and throwing a football back and forth. One said, "Wow, check it out!"

"Holy shit."

I ducked.

The silence was very long. When the boys spoke again, their voices sounded closer but shrunken, shorn of bravado. "Fuckin' awesome. I never saw so many together like that."

"Wouldn't wanna piss 'em off."

"Must be a honey pot there."

"Throw the ball at them; see what they do."

"You fucking crazy? Let's go."

Soon I heard only the distant chuff-chuff of the ball being caught. I lifted my head, peeked into the visible sliver of street. Beside my eye, a curling thorn. My bees circled, circled.

In the distance I made out two pink, floating blurs. My heart pounded. My fingers clenched into fists. My entire body stiffened. Estelle. Estelle. Please, let it be Estelle. I heard a cry. They'd seen the bees. I pushed my face down between two rocks. The girls approached.

"So many!" A tinny, nasal voice. I recognized it instantly as Mary-Lou's.

"Oh my God." A lower reedy voice. Millie McAllister. She'd assisted with the turd brigade. Two of Estelle's pals. If I couldn't get the queenpin, I could knock off her henchmen.

"There must be flowers on the other side of the hill."

"Probably."

I was surprised when three bees flew out of the spinning whirlpool and headed straight for the girls in their rayon dresses. Mary-Lou and Millie screamed.

I raised my head. They'd run out of the visible sliver of street.

Now was my chance. I jumped up and leapt off the hillock. My soles landed so hard on the ground, I lost balance and fell. The girls' backs were receding down Bluebird Lane. They'd stopped running and walked hand in hand, their heads down. The bee cloud reeled and roared. I inhaled deeply, joined my hands, locked my elbows, raised my arms above my head, pressed my two index fingers together to form a massive prong at the top of my body. I bent my torso forward and ran straight on.

My feet pounded against the earth like fists, and the whirring bee wings sent breezes down across my body and over the ground; leaves, dust, even pebbles were lifted from the earth. When I glimpsed a faint fog of pink just ahead, I rammed my feet into the ground with such force that my body lurched, then froze with my stinger aimed frontward. The bees hurtled forth like a flaming ball flung from a sling-shot. I spun around and ran back toward the hillock. Behind me, I heard a blood-curdling scream and Mary-Lou's "Oh, Millie! Millie!"

Without looking back, I jumped over the hillock and ran north into the woods where I followed a meandering, rock-strewn trail. I dashed along bare hills topped with sticks in teepee formations. I heard the cry of an ambulance, distant shouts. Into the woods I charged, past boulders draped with moss, through clouds of gnats that entered my mouth and flew up my nostrils. I reached a gravel road full of puddle-filled craters, turned west, and kept running. I stopped only when I came to the one-lane bridge. Its walls of steel criss-crossed upward to its roof, whose intersecting lines split the sky into triangles.

Arriving in my empty field, I threw my arms up, laughed, danced, and sang. Soon my bees appeared in the sky. They descended en masse. I fell to the earth and offered them the nectar that was only mine to give.

The following day, our principal stood before us in the school auditorium. Head bowed, he spoke solemnly. "Yesterday Millie McAllister was attacked by bees and taken to the hospital. She survived but is in great pain."

It took all of my self-control not to burst out laughing. I bit my lower lip, put my face in my hands, and pretended to sob. I thought, next time I'll get Estelle.

After school I returned to the hillock and waited with my swirling bees. This time no one approached. Even the boys kept their distance. Between the thistle stems, I saw a distant cloud of pink. Again I ran with my arms pressed together above my head. I stopped a block away from the girls, afraid they might turn my way. I fled into the trees, but my wonderful bees charged on ahead. Both girls were attacked this time. Unfortunately neither was Estelle, but one was her cousin and the other an Estelle groupie.

The third day I returned to the hillock and saw boys kicking in the dirt and throwing rocks at trees, so I waited until they left.

Over the next week I sicced my bees on anyone wearing one of Esther's dresses. I discovered that I didn't need to use the hillock and could hide behind garbage bins, mailboxes, or wide-trunked trees. Though I rejoiced in my daily successes, I was terrified of getting caught.

The townspeople viewed the first bee attack as a fluke. The second, an unlucky coincidence. The third was part of an emerging pattern. The fourth created panic. After the fifth, Cartwright was consumed by complete hysteria. We even got a headline in the *Labrador Gazette*: "Killer Bees Ravage Seaside Town." In class, students sat quavering with fear. After school, parents drove their children home. I feigned anxiety and reminded myself not to smile.

All the next week there were emergency meetings of the town council, discussions between the mayor and biologists, doctors, and priests. After lengthy debate, the cause of the bee attacks was identified. The enemy was—flowers. The flowers had brought the bees here. Before roses and tulips grew in riotous profusion in Cartwright's gardens, our town was placid and safe. Innocent children were not attacked. If our streets could return to their former state, peace would prevail. The mayor made a public pronouncement: "All flowers shall be cut down and burned in order to starve these bees and make Cartwright undesirable to them. Anyone refusing to destroy their flowerbeds or who is caught with bulbs or seed packets faces fines."

Throughout Cartwright, petunias, gardenias, calla lilies, and roses were placed in stacks and set on fire. The town was full of the smell of perfume and burning ruffage. Bonfires blazed in every yard. The Atlantic easterlies whipped the flames into such high walls of fire that people feared their wooden houses would be engulfed. There was a corresponding rash of couple break-ups.

Estelle lost all her boyfriends. No one talked of love anymore at the town council meetings.

Walking between the fragrant walls of flame, I threw my head back and snorted, delighting in the secret I carried in the very centre of my body.

"I told you something bad would happen when those bees came." Mother was ecstatic. "Nobody believed me. They said I was the freak, but I showed those suckers." Her increased confidence alarmed me. She immediately drilled me on Millie. Did I like her? Were we friends?

I kept my eyes lowered and muttered, "No, I don't know her..."

She delicately kissed my forehead. "Thanks for being so good." Then she abruptly rolled back her head, opened her mouth and sang forth the Lotto-Labrador winners, "1–5–4–7–3. And the daily double goes to 2–4–8..." She'd resisted secular speaking-in-tongues; glossolalia in all forms was a gift from God. Besides, I think Mother realized that she was so full of tensions that if she didn't release them, she'd explode.

The next day she went to the school, as she'd often done when you were here, Sam, and harassed the teachers. "Not enough is being done to protect students from bees. Security guards should be hired. I worry about my own daughter. And there's still too much teaching of science without values," she added. She knew such comments did nothing, but she was feeling powerful and longed to assert herself.

"The people at that school have their heads up their butts," she snarled, scooping lobster chowder into my bowl at supper. Then her mouth twisted; she sighed and said, "Apparently, now Sam is getting aggressive with the doctors. He makes snide, sarcastic jokes at other people's expense. He was never sarcastic with us. The doctors believe he's getting stronger. I'm not so sure."

Something crucial is happening with you, Sam. You are about to commit a major act.

On the radio the announcer said, "The coast guard caught a Spanish boat inside the 370 kilometre limit. The ship was manned with illegal trawl-nets..." Then a woman's voice interrupted: "This just in. There has been another bee attack in Cartwright. Nancy Smitherson was attacked by a horde of bees while crossing the field near the main port."

I dropped my fork. How could this be? I'd not ordered my bees to attack. I'd been at home all evening. But I knew that Nancy Smitherson wore dresses, never jeans. A prong of my fork curled toward me like an accusatory finger.

The next morning while I was skipping stones on the beach, Sandy Higginbott was attacked. Two days later Peter Fitsen, the town transvestite, was swarmed in his rayon jumpsuit when he went to the variety store to buy breath mints.

In my empty field I discovered that the satin scarecrow was more tattered and filled with holes than previously. Clearly I'd succeeded in programming the bees to assail anything in a dress, and now they did so without my prompting. I hadn't wanted the bees to attack indiscriminately. I wanted Estelle to get nailed and, as yet, the bees hadn't poked a single needle into her alabaster skin.

In class while everyone gathered round to admire the new aquarium, I darted to Estelle's desk and snatched three blonde hairs from her chair back and stuffed them in my pocket.

Later I stole two pearl earrings from Mother's dresser drawer because they were identical to Estelle's. Armed with these weapons, I marched past the town limits. I stuck Estelle's hair on top of the scarecrow's stone head and taped an earring on each side. When my bees arrived, I held my arms up and repeatedly practised the long run and stabbing attack on Estelle. "Got her scent, guys? Remember it." The bees spun round the mute body. "She's the one you want."

Shivering, I stripped off my clothes and rewarded the bees for their travails. I shrieked and giggled as they licked the sweat from my skin. "Dropper, you're going too fast," I sang. "Slim-slam, let Kim have some ... Oh, Einstein, you silly boy, try to enjoy yourself for once in your life!"

We played for what seemed like hours. I ran my fingers through the grass as the bees leapt over me. I looked at the tattered "Estelle," its stone face round as a giant eye. Straw fingers stuck through the holes in her dress. A light breeze blew and the three frail hair strands lifted like wings.

"You stupid bitch," I yelled at it. "Pretty soon a hundred bees are going to sting your ugly face!"

Suddenly the scarecrow shook. She jolted to the left, the right;

the stone fell off, and her torso bent forward to reveal two men pushing her to the ground. The taller man pointed the barrel of a rifle at me. The shorter man smiled. He had freckled skin and a cowlick that trembled in the breeze. "Jimmy!" In his right hand, he held the wire-cutters he carried in the woods.

"Don't you move," said Jimmy's father. His lips were stained with tobacco juice and his hair striped red and grey. "We saw everything."

"But I—"

"Shut up! Jimmy, go into town and tell officer Dolsen. I'll keep her right here."

Jimmy watched me, his brow pleated. All the honey on my skin had been lapped off. The bees had vanished.

"I said go!" shouted his father.

Jimmy hesitated, then ran toward town.

❧

An hour later police cars, reporters with cameras, and the mayor arrived. Men in suits examined the satin dummy, poked at the straw with their fingers. One man picked up the Estelle head and shook it. Jimmy's father was speaking with a policeman. "That bitch humiliated my son, so I pulled him out of school for a month." The policeman scribbled on a pad. Jimmy hadn't returned. A uniformed man approached me, touched the skin on my forearm, and walked away sniffing his thumb.

I was handcuffed, pushed into a police car, and driven to the Home for Young Offenders in West Bay. Sitting on a cot shaped like a matchbox covered with a paper-thin blanket, I eyed the bars on the window. They reminded me of the stripes on my beloved bees.

✴

The next morning, Mother stumbled into my cell. Despite everything, I was glad to see her and we embraced. The first thing she said was, "Am I being punished for my pride? And my leniency? Have I not been paying attention?" Being the wicked stepmother takes work. Had she been slacking off? "Maybe I wanted to relax? Forgive me. Or am I too harsh? I know you think me obsessive. Fear is the strongest emotion in me; that's my problem. But people who say disciplinary parenting doesn't work are screwballs. Under no circumstances will you go the way of your brother." She sat down on my bed. "Now Sam has completely lost his hunger for rocks. That means we're doing things right. But he has become very quiet again." You're planning something drastic, Sam. What is it? "Don't worry, Sue. I'm going to take action to make things better for you always."

After she left, I looked out the window, saw the parking lot below, and beyond, the ocean. I put the tip of my finger on the glass where the horizon-line was. I knew that some day I would touch that line with my bare hands. I would lift and hold it between my fingers. I would play jump-rope with it and wrap it, cobra-like, around my neck.

I tried to think back to the days before bees, before honey. Yet I could think only of you, Sam. Was there ever a time when I was not defined by someone else? Could I ever be me, standing separate yet accepted by others? I had only a few scattered memories:

Mrs Bodner, my kindergarten teacher, had three needles protruding from a ball of red hair that crouched behind her head. Once she gave me a gold star to put on my forehead; it complemented my eyes, which she said shone beautifully.

Sandra Morning Star, a tiny Indian girl, agreed to be my friend for five days.

Once I came upon a frog flattened by transport truck wheels. I took it home and hung it like a trophy on my wall.

I was in these memories. Was I anywhere else?

That afternoon, when my honey started to flow, a horde of bees gathered above my cell. I heard Q-Tip's high-pitched whine, Wiggle-Butt's whimper, and Drooper's snorting. The whole room vibrated to the scratching on the metal roof.

"Come, friends, yes, come!" I cried to them.

The sound continued for an hour, then faded. This building was maximum-security. Nothing could come in or go out.

The next afternoon, the bees arrived and again departed. The same thing happened the third, fourth, fifth days. A week later, at three-thirty on a Monday afternoon, I heard the faintest scratching of just one bee on the roof. Was it Drooper? I imagined him pressing his bent snout into the corrugated metal, rubbing it over and over, as tears poured from his eyes. Finally he flew up into the sky and left me. Yes, even Drooper abandoned me to the world of men. I sat in a silence I was sure would never break.

I pictured Estelle sitting before her mirror, surrounded by open jars of gel as Esther moulded her hair into a perfect labyrinth.

Mother was surely praying to God as my father rocked back and forth on his spot on the sea. Sam, were you examining the walls? the ceiling?

I still believed my true mother was in the sky spinning honey scarves, mittens, and underpants on her giant spinning-wheel. When we finally meet, she will sit me down and pat me on the head with her honeycomb hands. Then she will tell me honey stories.

I thought of all the tales my true mother will tell:

First, she will describe the glue-bandit who travelled the world over and, though he left a conspicuous glue-trail behind him, was never caught, for whoever tried to follow the track stepped in it, got stuck, and could never move again.

She will tell me of the honey damsel who let her honey hair flow out a castle window and down to her lover below. When he tried to climb her hair, he got stuck in its folds, and all he could do was watch the sun rise and set or glare at her honey dandruff, which was as large and bulbous as apples.

Then my mother will speak of the glue family. They were stuck together, and only when they accidentally fell into an enormous bucket of paint thinner were they freed from each other. Yet the thinner was so corrosive that two children had polka-dot-stained skin for the rest of their lives, and the youngest child dissolved completely.

My mother will offer me cookies full of caramel and vials of liqueurs that flow so sluggishly that, when drunk, they stop our blood from circulating and congeal our organs as our bodies merge.

My mother was waiting for me in the sky, and only the swarm of bees could take me to her.

The day the bees left Labrador was a day of jubilation in Cartwright. The newspaper headline read, "Labrador Freed from Bees. Teenage Girl's Involvement Still Unclear." Articles described how citizens could walk freely again; fish once frightened away by the buzzing were returning to shore; cod stocks would quadruple, and the town could become a tourist destination.

"Work will continue at the steel foundry," the mayor announced. "We have no reason to fear it will be moved to Mexico."

In court the judge was kind; he sympathized with me. I was simply a poor fisherman's daughter at the mercy of her body's perversity. My family doctor was brought in and chastised for not having alerted the authorities. He said, "I didn't know it was so serious." The judge concluded, "Medical intervention may prevent the appearance of the bees and recommencement of their savage attacks."

On October 30, I was hospitalized in Queen Mary's Institute just outside West Bay. During the following weeks, specialists from every town in the province arrived, each trying to find some way to stop my honey flow. I endured hundreds of tests. Sweat was scooped off my skin with scalpels and deposited in pouty-lipped beakers, and chemical tests were done to me throughout the day. The men, like you, Sam, were scientists, so I trusted them and submitted willingly to their experiments.

They changed my diet, the type of bed I slept on, the hours I slept, how often I bathed. I was put in rooms full of ice, then over-heated saunas, until it was discovered, as I knew, that the honey flow had no connection to my external environment but was a product of my own inner geography. The specialists claimed that my condition was so advanced, there seemed little hope of a cure.

One doctor explained, "We've been studying your sweat glands, Sue. Sweat glands are coiled tubes in the dermis, a layer just below the skin. They are connected by a duct to a pore on the skin's surface. Normally, sweat ducts fill with water that's absorbed from the body. When we eat, our metabolism is activated; our body heats up and we sweat, usually imperceptibly. However, when you eat, the naturally occurring sugar in food isn't broken down but is transferred into the spaces between blood vessels from where it travels into the apocrine sweat glands in your armpits and the eccrine glands found everywhere else—except your lips and clitoris." His mouth twisted. "You are not as abnormal as you think. When people perspire, not all the sweat runs off the skin; most evaporates and leaves a salty residue. On you, it's more sugar than salt. And you sweat at a slightly greater volume. The average person produces between one and two litres per hour, whereas your body produces about four-and-a-half. Your perspiration colour is normal—clear but yellowish under the armpits. You may have noticed," he added authoritatively, "armpit stains on clothes are always yellow."

Mother visited me daily. She had become calmer; a soft light glowed in her eyes. Since the bees had departed, the atmospheric barrier separating her from the Holy Spirit was removed and she was able to speak Godly tongues. While I underwent experiments, I heard Mother in the hall like a constantly rattling air-conditioner. Afterwards, she'd sit holding my hand for hours.

It began to snow as November came and went. My parents celebrated Christmas Day at my bedside. Throughout the winter a tutor came and assigned homework so I didn't lose the school year.

I often asked Mother about you, Sam. She told me you were now allowed to leave your room. The psychiatrists trusted you, and you trusted them. You loved merrily marching up and down the halls. During therapy you related all kinds of personal info without shame. You showed a new curiosity. Oddly, the mention of Europe now excited you. You had a new confidence and appeared giddy and weirdly expectant. "They allow him to read letters now." The psychiatrists had previously asked that we not communicate with you. "I sent him one. He loves reading about what's happening in the outside world."

"Then I'll send something." That evening I wrote my most desperate letter ever, pouring all my weakness into your new-found strength. I recounted everything; the honey, bees, Estelle, and my crimes. "You can save me, Sam! I know it. You can do anything. You were able to escape our home in Cartwright. Do something, please!" I sent the letter, not sure if anything would come of my urgent appeal to you.

The doctors continued to swab sweat from my skin, examine their cotton pads, and shake their heads. They treated me with compassion and saw me as a victim trapped in a body from which she couldn't escape. Yet I didn't want to escape my body. The only emotion I now felt was hatred. I despised Cartwright and didn't care if I sweated honey forever. So many people had been so cruel to me that if I became normal, any kindness from them would be hypocritical. I'd experienced the heartlessness of the Estelles of this world, and in this town they were the majority. I closed my eyes, concentrated on my heartbeat, and thought: honey-pump, honey-pump, honey-pump, let honey flow to all the surfaces of my body; let me be a sleek, glistening eel of sweetness, and make my bees come back.

Imagine my amazement two weeks later when Mother hurried in with her hair all undone and said, "Sam has escaped." She stammered, "He's running wild through the forests north of Toronto. He ran out of the asylum at night when no one was looking. How could this happen? We should sue those blockheads. The airports, train stations, everyone has been notified and Sam seems to know this. The police say he avoids towns and highways and is travelling through fields and forests. The doctors believe he could be dangerous. He is heading east toward Quebec."

A jolt went though my whole body.

"Twenty-four hours passed before they noticed he was gone. Those nincompoops! They should be forced to take a bath in your grandma's outhouse! Sam was becoming arrogant in the asylum, and this is the result."

I couldn't stop shaking. Sam! You were running east, toward Labrador, toward me. It was because of my letter. You know I will help you. We will help each other. The guilt you felt at abandoning me in Cartwright has surely been nibbling at you for years. You will release me from the trap and redeem yourself at last!

I immediately pictured your sparrow chest heaving, your string-thin thigh muscles straining as you climbed over wood fences, ran between walls of wheat, jumped over crabgrass-strewn ditches. Run, brother, run! Run, brother, run! Scrabble across stone-studded fields, through bulrush-bladed marshes Throw your body before skidding, horn-blaring cars as you hurtle across the steel-fenced freeways that slice our country into fragments, but run, brother, run and come to me, come to Labrador and free me! We can escape from Canada forever!

At night I ignored Mother's recommendation to pray but instead recited, "Run brother run, run brother run," non-stop for two hours.

Then the next day, Mother told me troubling news. "They found out that Sam received a letter from someone in Europe—probably the dizzy broad who started all his problems. Whoever it is has changed her mind and wants to see him again. She's invited him back and he's escaped so he can head straight to the lion's den."

Was Mother right? Had you escaped so you could return to Europe? I wouldn't believe this. It was me who had inspired your flight, wasn't it? Aren't I the person on Earth you love most? I still repeated, "Run brother run brother run," obsessively, relentlessly, blindly.

By early spring the doctors were beginning to believe there was a psychological reason for my condition. "When people are anxious, the body's sympathetic nervous activity increases," a specialist said. I was getting tired of these explanations. "Epinephrine secretions from adrenal glands increase and these act on sweat glands. Not all types of emotional experiences cause this process. We need to discover which ones create it in your body."

One morning a woman psychologist wearing butterfly-wing glasses stepped into my room. She had long discussions with me about my family, my experiences at school, my hobbies and friends, or lack thereof. She even interviewed Mother and Father. The next week I was glaring down at the parking lot, where Mother talked excitedly to a blonde woman who looked like a frilly parakeet on stilt-like high-heels. Her full skirt exaggerated the abrupt indentation at her waist, and the exposed skin on her upper back gleamed like marble. One of her thin arms moved like the stick-leg of an insect. I wished I could move my arm like that, so delicately and with such elegance. The woman rotated her head and I saw her spindly nose and pencil-thin lips. It was Estelle! She was dressed up—to impress the doctors. She handed a large bag to Mother, who then marched into the hospital.

That afternoon, three doctors entered my room. One of them said, "Sue, we're going to try a new psychological technique that we're hoping will have a beneficial effect."

The doctors glanced at each other. A fourth man stepped into the room. He carried a frilly pink, low-cut, sleeveless dress, the kind Estelle would wear on her birthday.

"*No!*" I screamed. "No!"

One doctor stepped forward and grabbed my shoulders, the other shoved a needle into my forearm. Immediately my limbs felt heavy, my vision blurred, and I felt myself crumpling downwards onto the shiny tiled floor.

※

I don't know how long I was unconscious. I was not sleeping because I didn't dream. There were no sounds or images, just an impenetrable blackness like the darkness at the bottom of the sea.

Eventually the black faded to grey. Even with my eyes shut, I knew something had changed. I inhaled, but a weight pushed against my chest. My lungs couldn't fully expand. My breasts were pressed together and something hard pushed into the sides of my stomach. I slowly opened my eyes and noticed a white-pink haze below my chin. My shins and thighs felt cold, but my hips and torso were warm. I touched my cheek with one hand and when I lifted it, no glue-string dangled. I lifted one arm, and my armpit made no *thwuh* sound. I sat up abruptly; my head spun and, feeling nauseous, I beheld a ruffling sea of rayon flowing from my neck down the front of my body and all the way to my knees. I gasped—not a full gasp, my tightened corset wouldn't allow that. Below, I saw black, narrow, high-heeled shoes that pointed inanely toward opposite corners of the room. I moved my head from side to side. It felt heavy, and my ears were cold. I carefully raised my hand and with one fingertip discovered that my tangled locks had been twisted into a shellacked labyrinth of solidified loops and curls.

To anyone but me, the dress was astonishingly beautiful, made by Esther during a moment of inspired ecstasy.

The white-walled room seemed to waver. I lay back on the bed and shut my eyes. Wherever they were, the doctors delighted in their discovery.

A week later Mother held my right elbow as I drifted through the parking lot. Car hoods shone like gleaming shells of giant insects. Mother's lips moved, but her voice was muffled. A car door opened like a mouth.

Through the car window I watched as we floated by the hospital entrance. The whole staff stood beneath the portico, their arms waving slowly like seaweed in water. Beside them stood a row of television cameras with leering Cyclops eyes.

At home I stepped into the kitchen. Father got up from his chair, smiled, and embraced me. I heard him say I was prettier than ever. Mother manoeuvred me to my room. She gave me a glass of water and told me to sleep.

I woke up thirteen hours later and discovered that I was still wearing the dress. Murmuring, Mother entered my room. She wet-sponged my neck, knees, thighs, armpits.

The day I returned to school, the streets were silent, but when I passed the bungalows on Maple Street, curtains opened and heads peeked out. My high-heels *pick-pocked* unsteadily along the ground. There was no snow anywhere since we were having another warm spring. I hated the way the dress showed off my small breasts. A breeze blew between my legs. The rocks I stepped over seemed like eyes staring up my dress.

As I neared the school, I heard boys whistle. "Hey, cutie," they yelled. Were they serious or mocking?

A crowd had gathered in the schoolyard. The tri-colour flag flapped limply in the wind. At the front, Estelle was doubled over, her laugh like a high-pitched smoke alarm. She shrieked, "That's too funny! She looks like a piglet dressed up for the circus." A thunder-roar of laughter followed from the crowd behind her.

"Too bad we can't stick nothing gross on her anymore," someone said. "There are some good caribou turds on the football field."

"We're safe from her. That's what counts."

In class I watched from my seat at the back. Two of the bee-mauled girls glared at me and muttered under their breath. None of the boys spoke to me. Though Jimmy had returned and was clearly unharmed, the old story about us lived on. If I hadn't hurt Jimmy, I'd hurt someone they hadn't heard about yet.

Entering the cafeteria for lunch, I tripped on my new heels; my blonde-dyed hair tumbled over my face. Even the janitor tittered. Boys watched intensely, their stares like barnacles on my skin. I ran into the hall to catch my breath.

When the final school bell sounded, I took off my shoes and dashed barefoot down the street. In the middle of the field where I'd first met the bees, I saw the sky was a solid, stubborn blue. No bees would invade it. My pores had closed like a million tearless eyes, and my honey-springs had dried up.

So it had happened. My honey had stopped for good. Some time ago I would've shouted in joy. But now I wanted the bees; they were better than any human being. The poems Mr Schmidt read to us said the touch of another person was the greatest thing of all. I didn't believe this. I silently promised that if the bees returned, I wouldn't sic them on anyone.

Mother greeted me cheerfully when I got home, but I raced up the stairs and slammed my bedroom door. I tried to take the dress off but discovered that metal wires ran beneath the cotton shoulder straps; the chest section was solid brass secured with knobs in the back, and concealed under the thick fabric of the waist was a corrugated iron belt. The dress was girded with metal from Cartwright's new steel foundry.

I rushed down to Mother and shouted, "I want this off now!"

"Really, Sue. We mean for the best. Don't you see that?" and I saw that sadly she believed she was helping me. What Mother next said would become her mantra: "Do you want to end up like Sam?" She added, "He's been spotted north of Ottawa, charging across a highway and into the woods. God knows what he's up to."

News of your journey inspired me. For a moment I felt buoyed into a region of hope. Run, brother, run, brother, run, and rescue me from Mother, Estelle, and the shorn rocky roads of Cartwright. Take me far away!

Mother had spent all afternoon rooting through my dresser, closet, even my bedclothes. As she'd done to you, Sam, she went through my books with a marker, crossing out lines that weren't

Godly or when characters swore or spat. From my *Classic Fairy Tales* she tore out the pages on which mothers were presented negatively. She tried to justify herself: "Sue, I want to clear the bad things from your mind so you don't get depressed like your brother." You fled from Cartwright at midnight right after stealing $200 from our kitchen, so at bedtime, Mother made use of the new lock on my door. When I needed to pee during the night, I had to pound on the wall; Mother would cheerfully escort me to the toilet. She didn't worry about me being out during the day because I couldn't run away without money.

I tried everything to remove that dress, including using my father's chisels, handsaws, and wire cutters. Nothing worked. But when I arrived home from school one afternoon, I noticed a letter poking out like a tongue from the top of our mailbox. The envelope was an unsullied white as if every postal clerk that touched it had been wearing gloves. I slid the letter from the box's metal jaws. The address read: Sue Masonty, 27 Park Rd., Cartwright, Labrador. Our curtains were closed and the house door locked. Had Mother really gone out and missed this opportunity to snoop? Evidently. The envelope wasn't opened. Inside was a fax delivered to the Cartwright post-office. I saw "Sam" beside "Sender" and nearly fainted.

Dear Sue,

The contents of your letter troubled me. I have escaped from the asylum and plan to arrive in Europe before the end of summer. I received a letter from a friend who's had a change of heart and is now waiting for me. I am no longer the boy you knew nor the man I was in

Switzerland. I plan to secretly board one of the outbound ships in Cartwright. I'll wait for you by the octagonal boulder on the beach every night during the week of May 20. Leave with me if you want. I give you that option. Or stay in Labrador. It's your decision.

Stunned, I crept up to my room, lay down, crumpled the letter and stuffed it into my bosom. So I wasn't imagining things. I would see you again, brother. And you would help me. I would follow you out of Cartwright.

Yet the planned escape seemed too easy. Could this be a trick? By whom? No. I refused to believe it was false because there were no other options.

But then I had a horrific thought: I'll still be wearing this dress. I couldn't rip or burn it. Would I have to wear it forever? Time was of the essence. You would arrive in less than a month. I pulled a chisel out from under my bed, sat up straight, and started hacking at my dress.

Mother arrived in the early evening. Her cheeks were flushed and her hair a wind-blown mess. She placed a glass cylinder full of bright, yellow liquid on the mantel.

"What's that?" I asked, alarmed.

She only grinned.

At midnight I swore I could hear a distant pounding and a wheezing in the wind. That was you, Sam. You were heading toward Labrador, leaping over foam-spattered streams, scrabbling up rock-face, your every exhalation an explosion taking you one second closer to that splendid moment when we at last would meet. Run, brother, run, brother, run ...

I began counting the days. I took daily walks by the spot where we'd meet. I studied the anchored ships and wondered what ours would look like. I tried to imagine our new life together, but only saw a blank space before me.

I spent all my free time wandering through Cartwright. I climbed up and down the roads that zigzagged violently right and left, curled voluptuously around wooded knolls, or elbowed toward the sea. I examined the rows of slat-wood houses, the lopsided fences, the sewer water that trickled through pebble-pocked ditches. I lingered by the port, ambled along the creaking wooden boards whose undersides were fringed with strands of seaweed undulating like orange beards. I would leave Cartwright. God, I would actually leave it. I always knew I'd leave at some point but had no idea it'd be so soon.

I watched the boats bobbing like corks on the sea, saw men haul nets of flapping fish onto the dockside, lingered by the women lined up before the foundry pay-office, bought another pack of bubblegum in Variety Plus. With each minute passing, I sensed the town was separating itself from me. A cage door was gradually opening.

I squinted up at the cracks in the General Store sign: "Open Till You Need Us." I breathed onto the moss-covered tombs beside Mother's church. I knew each pothole in every road, each outgrowth of crabgrass in every ditch, which houses had five windows and which had two, which hilltops had grass and which were bald. I knew the best streams to catch frogs in, the seaside boulders offering the greatest views, the ponds with the least flies, and the exact spot where the sun's rays strike the cliff side at dawn. I knew everything in this town as well as I'd known my body before its recent transformations. Yet I recognized that the town's sounds, smells, and sights would soon be replaced by other ones; I just didn't know where they would be or what form they'd take. I removed my shoes when I got to the beach and pressed my toenails into the sand. In the distance, whale backs rose like swelling hills in the sea that gasped out their frail sprays of silver water and disappeared.

Soon I'd be gone.

But how to get out of this dress?

That night in my bedroom, I was about to aim a blowtorch at my waistband when Mother knocked at the door. I slid my tools under the bed. She spoke excitedly. "Jimmy is here. I think he wants to invite you to the prom." Normally she'd never want me to go out with a boy. I went downstairs. Jimmy stood on our porch, holding a handful of freshly picked dandelions.

Without lifting his head, he mumbled, "Will you goes with me to the formal dance?"

Who'd put him up to this? When I was in the hospital, a new story about him competed with Estelle's. In this version, Jimmy and I had made love beneath the bushes, and I became so enamoured that my honey flowed, but Jimmy, an independent man of the world, shunned me. When he later heard the disaster caused by his departure, he returned like a hero to expose me as an insect-witch and save the town from the bees.

Was Jimmy asking me out so he could become a superhero?

Jimmy saves the town and marries the reformed princess? Would dating me kill the myth about his penis vanishing into his body?

Shafts of hair stuck out like windmill blades on top of Jimmy's head. I remembered that he was a trapper and had the best metal-cutting equipment in town.

"Jimmy," I said in a low voice, "are you able to get ahold of your father's tools?"

"Sure. I uses them all the time."

I felt a flash of anger. Why did I have to always be dependant on other people for help? "I'll go to the prom with you on one condition." I whispered in his ear. "Get me out of this dress."

Jimmy grinned lustily. "Sure." He repeated what he'd said before. "We can go back behind the bushes."

"Fine. As you please."

The next day Jimmy took me to his father's shed and showed me the rows of chainsaws, jackhammers, and vise-shaped wire-cutters. I was fondling a jigsaw when the door opened. Jimmy's father loomed in the half-light. He examined me from head to toe, touched my arm with his hand, and rubbed his fingers together. He grunted his approval, snatched his rifle from the wall, stepped out, and abruptly closed the door.

Jimmy picked up a stone chisel. "This here is the safest one. It takes longer but you won't get hurt. I'll tries it now."

"No, not today. On prom night." Sam would be at the beach then.

His eyes glistened. "Right," he replied. "We can do it in the bushes."

"Jimmy," I said carefully, "you know I'll start sweating like last time. You remember what happened?"

"Yeah, I loved it."

"You loved going to the hospital?"

He smirked, embarrassed. "I just ate too much at once. Next time I'll goes slow 'n' sweet. When you was in my mouth," he said, his eyes glowing, "it felt wonderful."

He fingered the blunt edge of a saw, strummed it once like a guitar string. I saw my reflection distorted in the bent steel.

Sam, I knew that at that instant you were racing through canyons, leaping over fallen trees, charging beneath waterfalls. Run, brother, run ...

The night before the prom, I could hardly sleep. My eyes were spring-loaded open and my body flipped as if on a raft at sea.

So much could go wrong. Jimmy might forget the tools or bring the wrong ones. Was the dress that easy to cut through? What if we were discovered while trying to remove it? Would Sam really arrive on time? And what on earth was happening to Mother? The day of my planned departure, she huddled silently on the sofa. She'd stopped ordering me around, and my door was no longer locked. At dinner she studied Father as if from a great distance and her eyes misted over. I worried that she was becoming sick and I wouldn't be there to look after her. She repeatedly went into the living room to touch her yellow liquid-filled cylinder. Many times she crossed herself before it.

I tried not to be alone with Mother because I feared she'd

notice I was distraught and try to wriggle my secret out of me. I ignored Father too—couldn't look him in the eye or a lump would form in my throat, I'd start crying, and all would be lost. I silently promised that once outside Labrador, I'd send a postcard so they'd know I was safe.

I'd just brushed my teeth when Mother entered the bathroom and motioned for me to sit by the mirror. "I'd like to do your hair."

"You don't need to."

"I want to."

I felt the bristles of Mother's brush against my scalp.

"So nice to arrange your hair now that the sweat has gone." She put a hand on each of my shoulders and looked in the mirror. "You were always a pretty girl, Sue, though I know you never thought so. Your face is symmetrical. And look here"—she ran one finger along my cheek—"such a lovely shape. Like the side of a heart. When I was your age and went on my first date with your father, I looked as pretty as you." Why was she telling me this? "I wore a low-cut Flibberty dress that accentuated the hourglass figure I had then." Mother let out an uncharacteristically girlish laugh that sounded like pennies falling on pavement. So rarely did she laugh that I felt concerned for her. She recommended brushing my hair and then swirled it wave-like around my ears. "I know that you've become...distrustful of me over the years because, well, I won't blame anyone." She was going to mention you, Sam. "I just want you to know that"—her voice softened—"you are my daughter. You have always been my daughter. God gave you to me, and I love you, not just because you are His but because you are mine." Swish-swish sang the brush. "I know you find me ridiculous, and I guess I am, but if I'm ridiculous, it's because love is ridiculous and that's what I feel." She sighed and her eyes became moist.

I kept my head down like you told me to, Sam. I wouldn't let her invade me. I tried to think of you and of the swelling ocean waves we'll vanish into. Run, brother, run!

A harsh hiss and a rush of air. I opened my eyes and saw Mother hold a can of hairspray by my head; a million tiny transparent globules gleamed like dewdrops on the waves and crevice-lips of my coif.

Mother waved and her eyes gleamed like steel as I tottered along our street for the last time ever. I tried not to cry. Raising my head, I noticed the big dipper, the small dipper, Orion. I wondered how I'd feel the next time I saw them.

Jimmy stood smoking outside the school. He was wearing his hunting jacket, a white shirt, and a leather necktie tied too short. He glanced at me and threw his cigarette to the ground.

Immediately I asked, "Do you have the tools?"

"They's in the truck."

"Let's do it right away. We'll go to the bushes now."

He clicked his jaw and asked, "Why you hurrying?" He motioned toward the gym. Jimmy wanted to take me inside and show me off first.

"All right," I sighed. This was part of the deal. "But let's not take too long."

From the gym ceiling hung pink and orange streamers undulating in rollercoaster waves. Music thumped as girls in low-cut chiffon wiggled their hips and boys in misshapen suits stepped rigidly back and forth.

"Without *you*, babe,

I can't go on, on, on ..."

Jimmy and I faced each other in the centre of the dance floor. I'd never danced, but didn't care how I appeared now. In the half-darkness, arms thrust and dove, heads bobbed like buoys at sea, and pelvises spun. I was so pumped full of adrenalin, I felt myself exploding into the flood of bodies and sound. I stamped loudly, threw my head forwards, spun my arms like propeller blades. I ceased to notice Jimmy and became a part of the gyrating mass. In my peripheral vision the crowd dissolved into disjointed body parts; shoulders thrust toward walls, red-lit fingers pointed upwards, hair thrashed to and fro. The bodies fragmented, jostled, and disintegrated into each other.

This is how it feels to be happy, I thought. This is what other people feel all the time.

The song ended and a ballad began. The small sea of dancers coagulated into dozens of swaying couples.

"Let's leave," I said.

Jimmy shrugged and nodded. We headed to the bushes. The smokers on the football stands saw us enter the underbrush, which is what Jimmy wanted. We crouched in the light-dappled darkness beneath the overarching tree branches. I peered out onto the lit-up football field. Throngs of students milled around on the distant parking lot.

Behind the gnarled tree trunk we'd stashed our tools and my pack of provisions, including a T-shirt, pants, sandwich, and twenty dollars. Jimmy didn't ask me about my pack, but assembled his instruments: a wire cutter, a razor-edged chisel, a mallet, and a handsaw. We both put on work gloves.

"All right," I said. "Let's get cutting."

I sat down, and Jimmy commenced filing one dress strap with the chisel tip. I attacked the other with the cutters. Beneath the cotton-covered strap ran dozens of intertwined metal filaments that were shiny and taut. I discovered it was most efficient to snap the filaments one at a time. They broke with a loud twang. Every so often I pulled at the cut ends with my gloved fingers to unravel the cord. I came upon nodules where the wires were knotted together. I concentrated so hard that I didn't notice time passing.

Goink! At last one strap broke free of my shoulder. A minute later—*goink!*—Jimmy chiselled through the other strap. He sat down on the ground, exhaled loudly, and wiped a hand across his forehead.

"Jimmy, there's no time for breaks."

He examined the dress's wide iron belt ringing my waist. Jimmy placed a sharp steel rod against the side of my waist and struck it with an iron-headed mallet. The *bang* echoed about the field; all the smokers in the stands turned their heads in our direction.

"Can you be quieter?" I said.

"Do you wants it off or not?"

Bang, bang.

With each hammer blow, I felt a sharp painful jab into the side of my stomach. Was my skin bruising? My organs being shaken apart? I became terrified that Jimmy might accidentally drive the steel rod right into my torso.

"Be careful! The dress is made of steel, but I'm not."

We heard people leave the gym and join the smokers in the parking lot. The music had stopped. Was it eleven o'clock already?

"Hurry up, Jimmy!"

"It's hard to get through; it's really thick."

Bang, went the mallet, *bang, bang, bang.*

The guys in tuxes had noticed the sound. Some drifted onto the field.

Bang, bang.

Five boys climbed down from the bleachers.

"When are you gonna be finished?"

"Do you wants it to stay on or do you wants it to come off?"

Bang!

People stood in groups near the bush where we hid.

I heard voices. "Somebody's hunting gophers."

"It's a knife-fight, steel against steel."

I panicked. Surely you were in the vicinity, Sam. You were waiting at the beach right then.

A larger crowd formed in a choir-like half-circle around our quivering bush. How was I going to make a run for it with everyone there? I wished I'd tried to convince Jimmy to go farther from the school. For the first time I wondered what would happen to him if he were caught helping me.

"Somebody should go in and check things out."

Bang, bang, bang, bang.

The choir parted as Estelle strutted across the field like a queen, her headdress of hair like a multi-tiered wedding cake. On one side was a silver barrette with the word Lovely.

"Finished?!" I hissed.

"Almost done."

Estelle asked, "What *is* that awful noise?"

I counted the final blows.

With a crackling sound, the belt around my waist snapped and the whole dress fell to the ground with a thump. I gazed down at my exposed stomach, hips, the V of my pubic hair. Jimmy's eyes widened in the shadow-shuddering moonlight.

Suddenly, honey gushed from my skin. It shot in waves from the pores in my scalp, filled my eyebrows, and flowed so thickly across my open eyes that the edges of Jimmy's body wavered as if seen through the window of a car in a car wash. The honey had been damned up for so long that it now poured forth in quantities I'd never experienced. It streamed from the crease below my jaw, cascaded in sheets over my breasts, hung in rippling curtains from my forearms, and was like a waterfall tumbling from my vagina. The parched ground below became a foam-dappled honey quicksand that splattered onto my ankles and calves and stuck to the soles and sides of my feet.

Jimmy whispered, "My God." Torch lights burned in his eyes. His mouth hung open. I towered above him gleaming like a goddess in the moonlight. My body was no longer a body but a rushing river. Why had I feared he could conquer me? How could I ever believe that anyone was greater than I? With my untrammelled honey flow, I felt, just for a moment, that the world was mine.

Then—in the sky—a deafening buzzing. The bees had not gone so far away after all.

I looked up through the open space over my head and saw an oozing dark blotch spreading across the sky. It covered half the stars and was slowly filling in the half-moon. The ground trembled. People screamed and began to run back and forth across the field.

As the clouds of buzzing bodies descended, the shrieking crowds swarmed over the parking lot and banged their fists on doors and school walls. "Let us in! Help!" Girls in floral dresses had fainted by the goalposts. Boys grabbed protesting females and tried to use them as shields. Some students piled into the few parked cars and drove off, tires screeching.

I was about to make a run for it when Jimmy lunged forward and threw himself on me; I fell backwards onto the ground. He pressed his open lips over the stream of honey at my waist and sucked loudly, swallowed, belched, sucked.

"Stop it!" I screamed. "Jimmy!"

With all my strength I forced him off me.

He sat dumbly on the earth, his nose, lips, chin, and nostrils shining with honey. His tongue lolled, his gleaming lips formed a perfect O. The O collapsed and Jimmy smiled so wide that every inch of skin on his face wrinkled and his eyes became two crescent moons. His chest had stopped moving. His whole body became as still as a boulder.

"Jimmy!" I cried. "Jimmy!"

He fell sideways like a rock to the earth and lay grinning as the colour drained from his face. His arms and legs twitched and stopped moving completely. His open eyes leered, still lit. I began crying. I ran one hand through his hair, which felt as dry and wispy as a field of wheat.

I repeated, "Jimmy … Jimmy."

Should I cry out for help? Could anyone save him? I looked at his still face, then down at my body, and felt a deeper shame than any I'd ever felt.

In the football field, mayhem reigned. As the bee-cloud neared the earth, people flailed their bodies and shouted, boys wept in each other's arms, others ran insanely along the field's one-kilometre lap, while girls rammed their bodies into the crowded space beneath the bleachers or stood wailing and shaking the goal-posts hoping that would ward the bees off.

When the bottom of the bee-cloud touched the top seat in the bleachers, I knew I had to run. Yet I did not want to be seen as who I was. I did not want the school to know my body bred tragedy. I would not run out naked and exposed with my bee friends, in front of nearly every person in the world that I'd ever known.

So I made a huge mistake. I pulled the severed dress up and over my body and held the broken hinge together at my side with one hand. Honey gushed over the pink rayon.

I closed Jimmy's eyelids with the fingers of my free hand, took a deep breath, pushed through the wall of branches, and ran onto the field. The soles of my feet pounded into the lawn as I charged in the direction of the basketball court. Once there, I'd run down the street to the harbour.

I was half-way across the field when the bees descended on me. I knew they'd alight on my forehead first and lick my flowing honey drops, then slide down my nose, neck, breasts—if I could just make it out of the schoolyard before I was covered—but as the first bee touched the space above my eyebrow, I didn't feel his soft tongue but a sharp, hot needle piercing my skin. The bees landed on me, their torrid stingers shoving into my cheeks, fore-arms, collar-bone, hips, earlobes, thighs, armpits, tongue, and the space behind my knees. I screamed and tumbled writhing onto the ground. Their stingers were poker-hot or ice-cold; some shot straight in or entered diagonally, others grazed the underside of my skin or twisted like knife blades. They sliced the twitch-ing expanse of my stomach, the tender crescents of my lips, the creased cartilage gullies in my ears; they drove into the under-sides of my stunned-open eyelids as my pierced skin reddened and swelled, my heart raced, and my whole body became a fire-lit forest where flames swept northward, southward, over, and across. Needles clung in quivering necklaces, in quilled tufts on my knees, in bull's-eye circles on my forehead, in lassoes around my nipples, and formed lines of artillery in the spaces between toes. My arms flailed, and only when my swollen fingers clutched and pulled the dress down and off my body did the needles stop thrusting. The bees now lapped and whinnied, scooping honey from my seared flesh.

I leapt up, my hands over my breasts and vagina, and ran weeping through crowds who howled with laughter.

"Serves her right!"

"Taste of her own medicine."

"What a bitch on wheels!"

For a moment I was lost in a jungle of wailing gargoyles whose gouged wrinkles framed wound-like mouths. Tongues thrust like rifle tips, fingers pointed like darts. The waves of laughter mounted higher, and above all, I heard a smoke-alarm cry. Would Estelle's scream ring in my ears for the rest of my life?

No one pursued me as I ran down Connor Road. The streets were deserted. Even the bees had vanished. As I ran through the circles of light spilling out beneath street lamps, I heard only myself sobbing and my feet slapping the ground. I feared I'd lose strength and faint by the roadside, but told myself, think east, east, east, think of the ocean, the ocean that will save you, the ship that will transport you to the sky.

At last my soles sank into soft gravel. Frigid water lapped between my toes. My body was covered with an army of protruding needles. With face in hands I collapsed weeping by the shore. Behind me, bushes rustled in the breeze. Before me, the dark sea. No one approached me. No voice called my name.

Sam, would you arrive or had you forsaken me here on the continent's edge?

PART THREE

Ice

Eins, zwei, drei, vier.

Kraut-talk. The manly language. You wanted it, Sam. You wanted my tongue. *Wunderbar! Guten Tag! Raus!*

Swishity-swash, the sound of my paintbrush sweeping across canvas. *Clickity-clack*, my pen drumming a tabletop. These two actions now define my life.

I treated you like crap, Sam. I see that. Do I accept my behaviour? I've had to accept a lot of shitty things. I accept that I'm a second-rate artist. My face will never be on the cover of *Tagesspiegel.*

Scheiss! Verdammung!

Television commentators will never discuss my work's influence on the shape of NASA rocket ships. I live in one of the world's smallest countries, and get diarrhea whenever I near a border-crossing.

Swishity-swash.

What's worse, my hair grows in ripples and won't lie flat on my head even when I use specialized gel. I want my head to be bullet-shaped, Sam, because bullets are associated with power, and I want to express my power through the shape of my head. There should be a connection between a man's hairstyle and what matters to him in life.

You think I'm vain, Sam? *Zum Donnerwetter!*

My hair puffs out like airplane wings, and this grieves me, dude. I've explained this to friends at Wu-Wu Disco; they nod and say they understand, and I believe them. A few years ago in the Zurich gay community, American baseball caps were in vogue because anxiety about hairstyle quality was at an all-time fever pitch.

Clickity-clack.

Yet the most difficult thing to accept, dear Sam, was my heartless treatment of you. Remember the evening I told you about my uncooperative hair? You reacted differently than everyone else. We were wasting our time lined up outside Wu-Wu's, and you were babbling incomprehensibly about geology. "The ground shifts and the shale compounds collide with rhyolite..." I couldn't listen because I was mesmerized by the fantastic shirt I was wearing, a form-fitting Spandex-cotton blend. All at once you cried, "Continents are separate, but the Earth's rotation is the same for all of us!" Your white forehead lit up like a movie screen before the film starts. You'd said something personal, so I told you my hair story. Yet halfway through my speech—"I've tried hot oil treatments, but I'm at a loss..."—you stared at me, and your eyes took on that look that would penetrate, infect, exasperate, and torment me for the rest of my life. How did you fucking do that? Was it something you ate? Did you clench your buttocks so tightly your eyeballs bulged? Your pupils didn't move and your eyes darkened. Then they glazed over with a film—the way the surface of Lake Zurich freezes over and becomes flecked with interlocking bars of silver and white.

Swishity-swash, swishity-swash!

The rest of your time in Zurich, your eyes had that glazed look and it infuriated me. I felt you weren't seeing into me but covering me over—but with what, I couldn't tell.

Du bist ein scheusslicher Mann!

I began to notice you everywhere. Even when you weren't physically present (out lost in some silly library), I felt your eyes on me. I sensed hands reaching into my skull, tinkering with my thought patterns as you seeped into my bloodstream, *clickity!*, travelled through my veins, *flickity!*, crept soft-footed through my pancreas, *strickity!*, nestled in my spleen, sprawled out in my small intestine, then my large, and invaded every bit of sinew, bone, marrow, and tissue—until one day I looked down at my erect penis and thought you were inside holding it up and glaring back at me through the eye-hole of my urethra.

Fick! Christ, you freaked me out!

You made me do things I never do. I touched you gently (I'm not gentle, Sam; I'm a take-charge guy). I confessed I liked you and, *Scheiss*, asked you to move in! I longed to protect you from the bad haircuts of the world. When I fingered you, you'd shiver, then I'd shiver, you'd shiver again, and that damned snow never stopped falling. Winds blew and icicles dripped in every room of my house. I wished the universe would close up like an eye. I wanted to return to a life where the hairbrush before me was everything.

The day I asked about your family, I meant to shrink you into a pint-sized person, but you talked of mermaids and your mother praying to the sky. Sam, scientists are rational, but you made me believe miracles were the root of everything.

Swishity-shit!

In truth, I did not want you, Sam. I wanted the space that surrounded you. You came from a place larger than I could imagine, a country so empty I feared I'd vanish inside it. I longed to vanish. I wanted to run into the space around you and keep running. I wanted to raise my hands to a sky growing more distant by the minute. I wanted to fall in love with distance.

You were possessed of a solidity I envied. So I became nasty. I insulted you, changed the locks on my door, dumped ice cream on you at the gala.

Why were you so skilled at overlooking my meanness?

At the airport when the roaring plane at last took you away, I clenched my eyes shut and thought: he's gone, be glad he's gone, be glad he's gone, be … *Er liebt mich, aber ich liebe ihn nicht.* (The German language is so damned sexy; just hearing it gives me a hard-on; no wonder you wanted me, Sam.)

When I woke the next morning, two eyeballs hovered above my dresser like twin helium balloons. They had that glazed expression that set my blood on fire, made me smash my fist against the bedpost and shout, "*Scheiss!*" Their gaze would follow me and change the way I lived, dear Sam. The eyes watched me during breakfast as I lifted a spoonful of muesli to my lips. They studied a drop of milk dribbling down my chin.

"Get lost," I yelled. "Pick on someone your own size."

The eyes didn't tremble or blink. I decided to ignore them.

Swishity-swash.

I approached my easel, picked up my charcoal pencil. Now that you'd gone, I could open myself up and do art without fearing you'd invade me. But as I shakily sketched a flowerpot outline, I could feel you studying every motion of my hand, judging this line, speculating on that curve, examining my fingers curling when I rubbed my nose, scrutinizing my cuticle as I brushed a hair off my forehead. After fifteen minutes, my canvas was a morass of crooked lines and jagged-edged blotches, as if I'd been drawing during an earthquake.

I flung down my charcoal and scurried into the washroom. I removed all my clothes, stepped into the shower, turned on the water, grabbed my soap-on-a-rope, and started scrubbing my chest. I noticed the parallel dots beaming through the translucent curtain. *Miststück!* I washed my armpits and stomach. While I soaped my genitals, the eyeballs expanded. I leapt from the shower, dried myself, dressed. But your cobalt-blue eyes stayed with me. They hovered above the fire-extinguisher nestled in the wall. I darted away, but they followed me, down the staircase, across the lobby. I hurtled out the front door, slammed it shut, and shouted, "If I can't have privacy at home, I'll have it on the streets of Zurich. Take a long walk on a short dock."

Outside, the air smelled of grass and wet cement. The eyes had vanished. I exhaled loudly and yelled, "*Fantastissimo!*"

Then I tilted my head and saw, up in the sky, your eyes blazing down like two horrible suns. I boarded the tramway, got off downtown, raised my coat collar, and hurried into the fast-moving crowd. The suns remained motionless like satellites frozen in orbit. I stepped into the shade of the huge tower of Urania

Sternwarte. At last you were hidden behind an edifice of steel and concrete.

"Ha-ha!" I shouted out loud.

Right away your eyes glared back at me from the eye sockets of people passing in the street: an old lady hobbling by on a cane, a pink-cockatooed teenager on a skateboard, businessmen swinging briefcases like cleavers, a skipping child blowing bubbles—even a baby in a pram, a pacifier stuck like a sink plug in his mouth, watched me with your still set eyes.

I ducked into Jelmoli where I'd always enjoyed shopping, but as I fingered Dada Damani shirts of speckled cotton or held five-pocketed painter's pants across my waist, I sensed salespeople watching. Every mannequin had his head turned in my direction. Your eyes were everywhere, Sam. They glistened in the plastic heads of dolls I raced past, shone in the flashing sapphire in the jewellery display, and gleamed chakra-like in tie clips on salesmen's chests.

I dashed out onto the street and shrieked at the top of my lungs when a grizzle-furred terrier charged toward me, its mouth barking syllables that sounded like language as its eyes stared the same cobalt glare as yours. I'm going crazy, I thought, staring at the dog who stopped before me and licked his lips.

That evening I walked straight home, drank a full bottle of cognac, and went to bed. I ducked under the covers but sensed you somewhere in my blankets. I took three sleeping pills and fell asleep. When I felt a spongy, wet object slithering up the inside of my leg, I woke screaming.

I went to a psychiatrist, hoping he'd rid me of delusions, but your eyes in his head glared so intensely, my stomach churned. His eyebrows peaked like a chalet roof, and his eyes intensified their regard, blackening like the tips of machine guns. I ran from his office in hysterics.

❦

Der, die, das, dem, den, des. German's six ways of saying "the," like six sexual positions you never knew existed. Hey, I just sprung a boner.

Listen, *Liebhaber*, to hide from you, I knew I had to transform myself. I had to appear to be somebody else. I started dressing in sailor suits, nurse outfits, army uniforms, terrorist balaclavas, and cat costumes, and once went to Wu-Wu Disco in a Little Lord Fauntleroy suit. I became a plaid-suited car salesman, a street vendor with a twirling bowtie, a soot-cheeked waif sucking popsicle sticks beside a garbage can. Yet the day I left my apartment in a baby bonnet and diapers, looked up and saw your eyes still in the sky, I realized that no matter how much I shook my rattle at them, they would never close. You could see me in every form I took. *Mein Freund*, you put the piss in piss off! Still, I continued to search for a disguise that would save me.

I remembered that horrible book you'd loved, *Fairy Tales of Flesh*. The Mr. Potato Head people could detach and exchange body parts. People wore each other's shoulder blades as if they were mink wraps or sported testicles like brooches on collar bones. Everything shifted and nothing was fixed. I should've thrown that book out long before I met you.

In mid-February, I was sitting forlornly in the Odeon café sweating in a Davy Crockett costume as your eyes, as usual, aimed down like rifle barrels between clouds. They forced me back to that time of unexpected snowfalls and breezes blowing powder across iced-over lakes. You were disintegrating me, and soon nothing would remain but trees and rock. Earlier that morning I'd put my house up for sale to move into a cramped city condo far from the forest. Moving wouldn't be enough to stop your eyes from staring. I studied a woman in a cocktail dress and matching pearls sauntering to the café counter. The men in Odeon ignored her, of course; they weren't attracted to women. I remembered the distress you felt when you realized women no longer interested you. "I've crossed a border," you said with pain and elation, "and can never go back."

The thought came to me in a lightning clap: I should become a woman. Then your eyes would shut for good. I removed my fur hat, pondered the raccoon tail swinging against my coffee cup.

The two saleswomen at Lulu's Boutique, Betsy and Reiner, winked in perfect unison when I explained what I wanted. They clapped their hands together and said, "So fantastic. This'll be fun!" But how disoriented I felt when they shaved my legs, plucked my eyebrows, and forced mesh stockings over my legs and high heels onto my feet. How confused I became when they attached foam pads to my hips and a silicone-bubble bra to my chest to give me an hourglass figure. The girls hid my penis by curling it down through my legs and taping it there in a procedure that was disturbingly effective. They dressed me in a shiny silk blouse. The pleated skirt twirled when I walked. Betsy pinned a clamshell brooch below my neck and slipped jangling hoop bracelets on my clean-shaven wrists. Reiner spent a long time on my makeup, which she said I needed to have re-applied daily. The nylons itched against my leg stubble; my new panties felt like an egg cup clasping my pelvis. On my head they placed a heavy wig with feathered, rippling hair. "Its blond highlights," chirped Betsy, "bring out a hidden hue in your cheeks." The girls spent the rest of the afternoon teaching me how to walk and talk. Since I had no female friends or co-workers and only saw women about town, I didn't know how to behave. The girls gave me a new name: Veronika, Franz's voluptuous red-haired cousin.

I stepped onto the street and balanced on my heels, my bracelets jangling, the bra strap digging into my back, Dior perfume making my eyes water. I immediately sensed something had changed. I raised my head and saw, wonder of wonders—no eyes. I cried out in my deep male voice, "Fuckin' A!"

Out of nowhere in the endless blue, two spinning dots appeared that grew into identical spheres. So I lifted my forearms, flapped my hands up and down as if each wrist were an oiled hinge, and remembered the voice Reiner recommended, a descending falsetto, the sound a bird makes falling from a branch. I cried out, "Oh, how nice!"

The globes popped and vanished. *Erstaunlich!*

Navigating Zurich's cobblestone streets in heels was difficult. I remembered not to "walk square" but "flow" as Betsy suggested. Yet new problems arose. One pair of eyes had disappeared, but thousands of new ones opened up. Men leered at me from tram-car windows. Shoeshine boys snapped their rags at my behind. Bandanna-wearing cyclists rang their bells, toothless gypsies asked me to sleep on their sheets of cardboard, and men in suits stuffed business cards down my blouse. As a man I'd been a cool customer. As a woman I was a hot tamale. Every curve, hollow, and mound on my foam-bulging body was scrutinized, but unlike your eyes, which penetrated me, theirs glided along the surface of my skin and slid off.

Not only eyes opened but mouths as well. My life was full of new sounds.

"Nice jugs, Helga."

"You got the curves and I got the angle."

"Let's go to my place and watch your fondue bubble."

Hurensohn! Hands too materialized out of thin air, scampered across my blouse, made beak-like jabs at my breasts, flapped like windshield wipers across my back, or clung to my hips like burrs. Once, when I was waiting for the stoplight, a guy in overalls shoved his fingers up my skirt. I turned, slapped him with my purse, and cried out, "Oh, you cad!"—Greta Garbo's line from *Two-Faced Woman*. I was trying to be authentic.

The constant attention infuriated me. I wished I could walk into a coffee shop without being ogled. I'd always gotten attention from guys in bars but could control the result. I'd snap my fingers and say "Next!" Now, when even some unshaven dork whose breath smelled like horse manure smiled at me, I felt obliged to throw my head back, giggle, and flap both hands in the air like Marlene Dietrich in *Destry Rides Again*. (My mother also flaps her hands.) I was beginning to understand the oppression of women, something I heard about once.

Men ogle, Sam, but women treat women no better. In the Jelmoli washroom, I was sitting on the pot when I overheard a lady at the mirror say, "The problem is that we've lost true femininity."

Another woman answered, "You're right, Elke. We have to choose between independence with no sexuality, or sexuality joined to submission. We lose either way."

I didn't know what they were talking about, but felt I should say something. I knew a lot more about women now. After all, I'd been one for two days.

So I abruptly hiked up my panties and pushed open the cubicle door. How exciting! This would be my first bonding with my sisterhood! "I just want you to know, girls, that I understand exactly what you're talking about." I was disappointed to see that the women were wearing print cotton dresses and wool vests— probably secretaries. "Sometimes my dress clings so tightly to my hips, I fall if I try to run." My voice was as high as a struck tuning fork. "But if I don't run, my hair won't have that windblown look. What should I choose, practicality or glamour? We have such terrible choices."

"Excuse me, but there's a piece of toilet paper stuck to your pantyhose."

Both ladies cackled like witches. It's women against women and men against women in this *verdammt* world! I was learning a shitload of stuff. (Sam, I know you think I'm dim-witted. I've noticed your subtle smirk. Do I mind? Not at all, laugh if it gives you pleasure. I want you to be happy. Please, laugh!)

I decided from now on not to talk but to observe. For the first time in my life.

🦋

Eins, zwei, drei, vier, fünf, sechs, sieben, acht, neun. German is a language of consonants; French, a language of vowels. English can't make up its mind. (Have you made up your mind about me, Sam, you sexy beast you?)

When I beheld myself in the mirror a month later, I no longer felt troubled. I was separate from my former self but now appeared very contained and complete. Huddled over a table at Odeon, I sipped my *Milchkaffee* and flipped through a glossy magazine. I'd been leered at so much lately that I didn't have the heart to glare at others. I remembered judging your bony elbows, Sam, and felt guilty. Darcy and Delial were at the counter, talking hysterically. I wanted to reveal myself to them but feared your eyes would open. My friends gesticulated wildly, sometimes staring into the distance and rarely making eye contact with each other. For a moment, I felt sorry for them.

Out on the sidewalk I frequently heard my name mentioned. I'd stop walking and, ear cocked, lean sideways into my own shadow, balancing carefully on my heels.

"Franz, what an *Arschloch!* I wondered where he went."

"He's a prick if there ever was one."

"He still owes me 500 francs."

I was amazed to hear myself spoken of unkindly. Since I couldn't interject, now I was forced to listen.

"Franz came to my place once, stayed five minutes, got his rocks off, and left right away. Not so much as a thank you."

"The guy's a total sleeping pill."

Unable to defend myself, I felt strangely calm.

"He barely notices you. Before he comes, he'll call you the name of another guy. He doesn't differentiate between men."

Didn't people understand I was the best lay in Zurich? Perhaps the people who'd enjoyed me had been cowed into silence. (I know you want to laugh at me now, Sam. Go ahead! Let 'er rip!)

I touched the corn-cob brooch at my neck and realized it was only you, Sam, who had wanted to make love to me more than once.

Some evenings, cutting bockwurst into bite-sized bits at the Spettle's counter, I heard stories about my unexplained absence. In one tale I'd been kidnapped by an Italian jewellery heiress and was now tied naked to a bedpost in a room on the outskirts of Milan where she and all the town virgins repeatedly milk me like a cow. "He'll never escape," my ex-friend Hugo cried, slapping his kneecap. "Franz's dick's probably so sore he wishes he never had one."

In another story I'd broken a mirror and the shards fell into an open vat of paint. I tried to remove them, but became fascinated by my reflection and accidentally tumbled in. The sides were too slippery to climb and the paint eventually solidified around my body. I was later removed, encased in a congealed beige block, and presently hang in the Kunsthalle Basel. My back is curved, my face pressed against my shins so that my body resembles an O. At first the piece was labelled *The Donut*, then *Pervert's Halo*, then *Franz Niederberger's IQ.* "I'm the one who suggested the last name," Hugo screamed, laughing and slapping his other kneecap, his thigh and stomach. "I'm amazed they used it."

In the third story, I was putting my paintbrushes away but discovered there weren't enough jars. I solved the problem by shoving three brushes into my mouth, one in each ear and nostril, and six up my ass. When I realized I could no longer breathe or shit and was, in fact, dying, I refused to remove the brushes—"He's such a neat-freak," snickered Hugo—instead, I walked quietly into my backyard and lay under a tree. Rain fell and washed the paint from the brushes that protruded from my body like natural appendages. When the sun came out, the grass was stained every colour of the rainbow and I was dead. "Good riddance to bad rubbish," Hugo shouted, whacking his shins, his neighbours' thighs, and my behind.

I preferred this story because of the quiet dignity I displayed entering the garden to die. But when the men continued to laugh uproariously, slapping salt shakers, cinnamon buns, billiard balls, beer glasses, and hot pokers, I wanted to tear off my wig, strip myself naked, and shout, "You stupid assholes, look: I'm Franz. How could I know you never liked me, you dick-shits! *Scheiss*, you think I'm a mind reader?"

But if I did this, your eyes would reappear in the sky, sterner and fiercer than ever, and send down rays that would pulverize me into a pile of ashes. So I snatched my purse from the counter and, remembering to shake my hips, minced out of the bar weeping a high girlie wail. I wiped tears from my cheeks with a silk handkerchief decorated with buttercups, bluebells, and tiny, prancing fairies.

By the time I got home, I was crying. I felt so lonely. I didn't know how to make new friends or get a lover. Should I wait for some *Arschloch* to send me a sheaf of long-stemmed roses? Or hope some loser would throw down his jacket so I could step over a hole in the sidewalk? I was sick of taking steps shorter than twelve centimetres and always aiming my vocal chords at a high D-flat.

Each night, I'd tear off my dress and panties and release my penis from its prison of tape and cotton. From the space between my legs it'd swing forward like an ornery ogre roused from its lair, and I'd breathe a sigh of relief, glad it hadn't dissolved or been absorbed into my body. Some days I'd stop before a shop window and see reflected, in the distance, the glacier-tipped mountains. Why did nature still frighten me, Sam? For the first time I wondered if it mattered if people didn't like me as Franz. Nobody liked or knew Veronika, and, as Veronika, I could deal with that. I recognized how dependent Franz was on others' views. At times Veronika was almost indifferent. Indifference is freedom, Sam.

German has three genders of noun; English has none. German has eight standard plural forms; English only the insipid "s." Do you love my new complexity, Sam, you hot little horndog?

I decided to take a psychological risk and create a painting. Betsy would scold me if I broke a fingernail or got paint on my dress, so I'd protect my nails with oven mitts and cover my clothes with an apron. With Veronika at the helm, my art metamorphosed. Glowing, yellow squares expanded to obliterate the trees. Returning from the art shop one night, I took a detour to see the Canadian flag at International Park snapping rhythmically in the north wind. Feeling elated and delighted by my courage (Franz had been afraid to go to dark places at night), I turned homeward. Little did I know I was about to have a life-altering experience.

I was sashaying down a deserted street, carrying my can of paint and a bag of breakfast groceries (eggs, bacon, and quark). I heard footsteps behind me, an insidious *scuffle-scuffle* punctuated by the *clang*-kick of a trash can. The shuffling sounds blurred, overlapped. There was not one pair of feet but two. Then stifled laughter, muttering, snorts. I walked faster. I passed an *Apotheke* with an iron grid pulled down over its window.

From behind, a raspy male voice. "Hey, foxy lady."

I should've kept walking. I should've kicked off my heels and run screaming up the hill. But I sensed an altercation was inevitable. If I didn't confront these assholes now, I'd have to tomorrow or the day after. They'd keep following until I turned to face them. Also, I thought the man's "foxy" comment referred to the stole I was wearing.

I spun round on my heels and said, "I am not wearing fox! This is mink!" The two men were younger than expected, teenagers with puffy cheeks splattered with pink acne. Both wore ripped blue jeans and running shoes. One guy was cute as hell. He had a square, flat-top haircut, the kind I wished I could grow.

The other had a moustache like a dirt smudge under his nose.

"Whatever it is," said the hot guy, "you look pretty nice."

I tried not to feel flattered. "I don't care what you think. I want you both to leave me alone or I'll call your parents right this minute." I was so nervous that my high-pitched falsetto was starting to break.

"What you got under that coat?" said the cute one. He stepped forward. He lifted one hand and began stroking the fur on my chest. "It's nice and soft. Is it as furry as your pussy?"

I was breathing heavily. Should I say something? Should I shriek? The boy's face was right before mine. His hot breath on my cheeks smelled of beer and onions.

Suddenly the dirt-lipped boy grabbed my forearms and, in one quick movement, yanked my arms behind my back. Cutie grabbed my shoulder and together they dragged me screaming into an alleyway. I was surprised at their strength and my weakness. Since becoming Veronika, I'd stopped going to the gym and my Herculean muscles were becoming pudding-sacs on a stick-body.

In the urine-reeking alley, dirt-lip held my arms behind my back while the other boy tore down the front of my dress.

"Help!" I cried. "Help! Police! Rape! *Rape!*"

He threw my tattered dress to the ground, ripped down my nylons, and with two able hands, slid his fingers under my waistband and yanked my panties to my knees.

All at once, my penis, crouching in its den, came hurtling forward like a massive javelin. The cute boy gasped and jumped back, as my erect penis pointed at him like an accusatory finger.

The other guy released me and leapt to one side. Both boys stared, stunned.

"Stand back!" I said in my man's voice. "Or I'll shoot!"

The head of my penis gleamed in the moonlight. Its arrow-head tip looked sharp as a machete.

The flat-haired boy said, "*Scheiss!* It's a fucking queer!"

He lunged forward and punched me in the stomach. The cruel gleam in his eye—instantly I remembered when I'd dumped ice cream in your hair. These boys and I, were we equally aggressive? What were they afraid of? What was I afraid of?

Dirt-lip tried to hoof me in the balls, but I grabbed his foot in mid-air, lifted it to my mouth, and drove my teeth into his calf. He screeched, fell to the ground, and I spit out his blood. The other boy struck me on the head with my paint can. My vision blurred. I felt dizzy. Nauseous, I collapsed on the ground and gazed into the sea of cobblestones. The boys unscrewed the can lid and poured the whole blue mess over me. Then they opened my grocery bag and broke the eggs, one by one, on my forehead, and shoved a slab of bacon into my mouth before running off.

My breathing slowly returned to normal and the top of my head stopped throbbing. I spit out the bacon and beheld, up in the sky, your two eyes glowing brighter than any stars. In that brightness was not judgement or censure, but acceptance and love.

Egg yolk slid from my forehead and splattered in my lap, and I understood that, totally humiliated here, I was more like you than ever before. Why had I refused to empathize with you?

Du bist ein sympathischer Mann.

I began to shiver uncontrollably. I imagined the worst that could have just happened, and it was more horrible than what I'd feared from you. The terrors I'd clung to had given me nothing, and in reality, I was like these boys. Fear took up so much space, there was room for nothing else.

As I wiped soggy bacon and blue paint off my thighs, I wondered: would losing the accoutrements of my ultra-civilized life be so bad, if you were watching? Your eyes were as miraculous as snowstorms in August. You'd awoken a generosity in me I'd never felt and these boys would never feel. Your staring eyes had turned me toward Veronika, who I now saw was the steadiest part of me. You showed courage by meeting my hostility with affection. With Veronika at my side, could I be courageous?

Sam, it was impossible to escape you—and why would I want to? From now on I'd step boldly before the firing squad of your gaze and get closer to your country. Forests surrounded my city. Trees blanketed your massive home. I'd let nature consume me at last. That was the final step. But I had to give you something back for your gift. What could I offer?

Veronika's hat lay smashed. I felt sorrowful because it had actually been a nice hat with a stuffed bird on top. (Is that ridiculous? Please laugh now, Sam. Just a titter?) On the way home, I ducked into a café washroom to clean up. Then I sat at a curbside table nursing a cappuccino. This was, I decided, my last night as Veronika. I was sad to see her go. I'd stumbled upon her by accident, thinking she was a hiding place when she was, in fact, a transition. You brought out the Veronika in me, Sam. Veronika was self-reliant and independent; she listened and watched.

She'd never be cruel to anyone. In many ways, she contained the best of me.

But she'd taught me all she could and I would now return to being a man because, as a man, Sam, you saw me most clearly. Thinking over the past few months, Veronika began to laugh. (Veronika has a great sense of humour, Sam.) She laughed loudly, her sing-song giggles echoing about the street. Everyone in the café turned to look. Was the woman mad? Had she gone out of her head? Veronika has the most beautiful laugh in the world, Sam, and I hope someday you'll be able to hear it.

The next day I awoke shaking. Hyperventilating, I put on a ripped plaid shirt, dirty jeans, and work boots. I boarded a bus and, still trembling, travelled 180 kilometres south of Zurich to the wildest part of my country—the most like your own.

I stood alone on the shoulder of the road, dust filling my eyes as the bus roared away, and stared up at the Matterhorn, Switzerland's highest peak. I paced there for a full half-hour before daring to step onto the forest trail. Finally, as my boots stamped on the dirt path covered with rocks and bulging roots, I breathed in the pine-scented air. I had become a man again and enjoyed the acrid scent of my sweat and the feel of my cock smacking against the insides of my legs. Your eyes hung in the sky between Mount Alphubel and the Rimpfischhorn.

I approached a wide stream and stopped, suddenly frightened. Veronika came to my rescue and exclaimed, "Oh, goodness." Her hands flitted in the air like birds searching for a resting place as she carried me across the stream. Then she disappeared inside me. I remembered life before Veronika, cocktail parties with Gucci queens on the roof of the Hilton or grope-fests with strangers in bars that smelled like vomit, my endless visits to Excelsior's until I'd arrive home with two-dozen shopping bags, fling open the wardrobe door, and cry, "But what *can* I throw out?" My civilized self would soon be shattered, but what would take its place?

In my pack I carried granola bars, a canister of water, rope, a flashlight, and a hunting knife I'd hurriedly picked up in the toy store next to the bus station; it was plastic but looked authentic. (Sam, you're starting to chuckle! Good!) I spent the morning wandering forest trails, getting nearer the base of the Matterhorn. But my breathing was constricted, my shoulders locked, my hands fists.

I finally came to the edge of a highway along which cars shot fast as bullets. I looked down and saw a brown toad squatting on the shoulder of the road. He was covered with copper-covered warts. I immediately identified with him because when I was seven years old, I had a wart on my knee. I hadn't wanted the wart removed and had begged the doctor not to do so; when he lifted his scissors and snipped off the wart, I felt a second head had been removed. I'd held the decapitated wart between my fingers and looked into its face, certain there were eyes, nose, and a mouth there that would speak if given the chance. The toad leapt once, twice. He wanted to cross the road but could easily get hit by a car. I said to him, "Don't worry, *Freundkein*. I'll help you."

I knelt and scooped him into my hands. He leapt against my

upper palm; the rough, spongy top of his head against my skin felt like hardened oatmeal. His tiny feet and round belly were sticky as glue on my lower palm. He was no heavier than a prune. "All right, hold your breath, dear friend."

I ran into the traffic. Horns blared. I dodged flying cars; halfway across I crouched on a white line while a northbound, eight-wheel tractor-trailer hurtled past in a whirlwind of dust and stones.

Safely on the other side, I deposited the toad on the gravel bed. Immediately he jumped back onto the road, a BMW heading straight toward him. I leapt forward and grabbed the toad in one hand. A horn blasted, brakes shrieked, and the car veered. A man yelled, "*Arschloch!*"

Back on the shoulder I held the toad in front of my face and scolded him. "Idiot! You just came from across the road and now you want to go back? You make no fucking sense! Look before you leap or you'll end up a blood-and-bone pancake." His black eyes peered unblinking like two ball bearings. I put him down and again he leapt onto the road.

"*Jesus Christus.*" I jumped out, snatched him up, and again ran to the opposite side of the highway. "You don't know your ass from a hole in the ground, you know that?"

I put him down on the spot where I'd first met him. Again he jumped onto the road. Swearing uncontrollably, I snatched him up—"Don't you understand a *verdammt* thing?"—and carried him across. However, this time I continued straight into the woods. I walked twenty minutes and at last lowered the toad onto a rock in a stream. Just before leaping from my hand, he left a toad turd in my palm. It was a symbol for something, but I didn't know what.

I returned to the highway and spent the morning helping other animals cross the road. A coffee-coloured June bug was ambling clumsily through the crabgrass on the roadside. I cupped her in my hands, ran across, and placed her on the lawn. I scooped a dozen crawling ants into my hand and later helped a fidgety grasshopper. Each time I placed the animals into the opposite ditch, I exclaimed, "Animals, be free!" Unlike the toad, none of these tried to jump back onto the road. "Animals, you are blessed," I cried.

By noon I was famished. I ate my granola bars, but that wasn't enough. I started walking along the side of the highway. Soon, Sam, I came upon something from your country. I stood speechless, my mouth gaping. Before me stood a white building with ceiling-high rectangular windows. On the top of a post was a sign shaped like a horizontal teardrop coloured white and red: "Dairy Queen." I'd once thought it was an American franchise, but they put it in a forest so that meant it came from your country. Plus, the sign was white and red, like your flag. This place was authentically you, Sam. I had never been inside a Dairy Queen. They were new in Switzerland, but surely they were everywhere in your country. A map of Canada would probably show one in every town.

I braced myself and pushed through the steel-rimmed door. Entering the Dairy Queen was like stepping into the cavern of your skull. I was closer to the centre of you than ever before. My stomach churned. The walls were frosted white, and paper snowflakes dangled on strings attached to hanging fluorescent lights. Somewhere violins were playing a finger-snapping melody against a catchy cha-cha-cha rhythm. Mysterious messages hung on the walls—"Pecan Surprise. We're as Nutty as they come" and "Choco-Avalanche—Drown in a Landslide of Cocoa"—accompanied by photos of multi-coloured ice creams towering like skyscrapers from transparent cups or blooming like orchids in lava-coloured cones.

I stepped to the counter, stuck my chin forward, and spoke, the force of nature making my voice gravelly and hoarse. "I want a Brownie Delight."

Almost immediately, a gigantic mound of whiteness dripping with tar-coloured sauce and haloed by ruffled skirts of whipped cream was handed to me. Tiny nuts winked like eyes. I sat down on a plastic seat that couldn't move forward or backward but pivoted from side to side. I put a spoonful of ice cream into my mouth, tasted the sweetness of vanilla, and instantly thought of other ice creams: the cone we'd shared at the Zurich fairground; the cherry sundae that, laughing, we tried to eat with chopsticks; and the ice cream I dumped in your hair at the *vernissage* gala. *Ich schäme mich!*

Here in the Dairy Queen, I'd make amends. I'd do what was necessary to make me understand what I'd put you through. I must destroy my self to become part of something larger. In one swift movement, I lifted the plastic cup directly over my head and turned it upside down. I felt a numbing coolness as chocolate sauce streamed down my forehead and filled my eyebrows; vanilla rivers flowed into my ears carrying nuts like little rafts;

icy liquid cascaded down my cheeks, over my half-open lips, and chunks dappled with whipped cream did suicide leaps past my earlobes and onto my shoulders. One blob rushed along the ski jump of my nose and splattered in my lap. An unfamiliar coldness crowned my skull and seeped into my groin.

Across the aisle an elderly lady holding a snowcone stared motionless. I heard a child laugh and a woman hiss, "Be quiet!"

Damned philistines!

Finally I rose to my feet and stood statue-still there in the centre of Dairy Queen, my whole body dripping with desire for you, Sam. The music had changed to a snappy waltz; a merry clarinet sang against a crisply stuck snare drum. I became riveted by my reflection in the mirror, my head engulfed in a swirling river of striped darkness and light while ovals of whipped cream drifted like ambulatory clouds down across my torso, pelvis, and legs. Like a demigod, I marched toward the exit and pushed through the glass door that for one second held my image.

In the parking lot, I raised my dripping head and beheld your two eyes blazing in the sky. They melted the ice cream that now flowed fast and fiercely over all the surfaces of my body. (Oh, laugh, Sam! I know you find me ridiculous. Veronika finds it hilarious too! Laugh with her!)

I re-entered the forest and reclaimed my natural essence. Birds fluttered overhead. Snakes slithered between my feet. I cried, "Fly high, birds. Enjoy your freedom. Slide fast, snakes. Hope your stomachs are slippery. Run fast, squirrels. Don't fall into any holes." Three chipmunks bobbed on a quivering tree branch. A raccoon's head popped out from a bush like a jack-in-the-box.

Encircling my face, a halo of darting flies delighted in the taste of melting ice cream. *Freheit, mein Sam. Ich habe Freiheit gefunden*. I have found freedom.

❧

Darkness fell and I slept on a soft bed of grass beneath a sky of precisely etched stars.

Early the next morning when I woke, the ground felt like a block of ice against my back. I got up, brushed dirt from my clothes, and started walking south. The sun was rising when I reached the small lake at the foot of the Matterhorn; its stone wall of pink wrinkled rock shot skyward. Clusters of scraggly pines clung perilously to its stone cliffs.

Lifting my head and straining my eyes, I scrutinized the dazzling summit, a snow-frosted, pyramid-tipped rock finger curling into an endless blue and haloed by frail wisps of cloud. My whole personality would soon be pulverized. Who would be the "I" about which I constructed my new self? I yearned to find out.

Down the mountain's face, a glacier rippled in grey and white like the foam-crested waves of a raging river that had frozen there. At the mountain's base the glacier thrust forward like an outstretched tongue whose tip touched the edge of a slate-grey lake. Twigs cracked and earth crunched beneath my feet. A stone tumbled into a rock-rimmed cavern and the *pop* sound struck my eardrums violently. I passed squat currant bushes with dense, impenetrable foliage and climbed onto a flat-topped boulder standing by the water's edge. Just above the eastern mountain summit, the sun huddled like a sniper; it bathed the opposite peaks in a hallucinatory glow, yet the valley below was in complete shadow. No breeze ruffled my hair or shook tree branches. I felt I was the first man in the world's history to come and stand at this spot. The surface of the turquoise lake was as flat and still as my washroom mirror. I held my breath for fear that my exhalation would ripple the water surface and bring to life a world suspended in an unearthly yet intoxicating slumber.

But I finally exhaled, and mountaintops didn't tumble into the lake, trees didn't fall against each other like bowling pins. Rock remained solid. Ice was ice. I breathed in the frigid air, imagined my lungs becoming bright pink as they expanded and shrank. Somewhere water dripped. In the forest, I heard the ascending call of the snowfinch. Below, in the lake, were swirling clouds of dirt specks. I couldn't see the bottom; the lake was guarding its secrets. It was a perfect oval, the oval of an eye or, as you would say, Sam, the oval of the Earth's orbit around the sun.

I felt terrified and cried out, *"Erlöse mich!,"* my voice echoing through the valley. Forcing myself into direct contact with nature's potent force, I removed all my clothes—my shirt, boots, trousers, and underpants—complete exposure. I was now defenceless. Let the Matterhorn have its way with me. Oh, *Mein Gott, Ich habe Angst!* With your eyes blazing down, I stood naked on the boulder beside the Matterhorn lake and stared straight into the water.

Then the miracle happened.

The obscuring clouds of grey vanished and, on the flat water surface was reflected—stone-hard, stolid, and unconquerable— my own body. The reflection was astoundingly clear, stretching across the entire lake, and my raised arms touched two shore-lines. Yes, my body had at last seamlessly merged with nature. I observed my forehead, rectangular as a movie screen; my smooth skin, coloured a lustrous honey hue. My eyes gleamed with a steely brightness; my symmetrical nose jutted straight as a knife blade. My capacious, glistening lips throbbed with an iridescent sensuality; my jaw was crude-cornered, fierce in its unbreakable angularity. My shoulder muscles swelled outwards and dove-tailed into my protruding, bulging biceps, solid as concrete while myriad forearm muscles twisted like the knotted cords of sail-or's ropes. My pectorals flickered in an ivory chest studded with auburn hair in patterns once seen on Viking shields; below, the lower edge of my stone-solid ribs protruded, and the indenta-tions between each fat-shorn abdominal muscle were like brutal-cut trenches in enemy battlefields.

Dummkopf that I am! Why had I been afraid of the truth?

Directly below, my burgeoning penis loomed, monstrous in girth, leviathan in length, and with such an intensity of presence that, yes, Sam, it seemed not of this world but a fierce, feral extra-terrestrial flown in from another planet, attached to my body and, though one-eyed and mute, able to command the universe. (The Veronika in me awoke and looked out through my eyes; she was especially impressed.) Its ample head ballooned toward the sides of the valley; the tree trunk stalk was covered with a network of clutching, claw-like, throbbing veins, behind which two testicles bulged like ears listening with a savage, annihilating intensity amidst a riotous profusion of pubic hair, twisting and interlock-ing like multiple passages of an endless labyrinth, all set against the backdrop of two stone-pillar legs holding the whole massive structure in a high, rarefied air, out of the reach of mortal men and certain to endure for all time.

Language blossomed in my mind. Three simple words burst forth like the first words Man ever uttered, three words that fit together like the long-lost pieces of a Divine puzzle, three words containing the beginning and end of everything. A stone skipped down the side of the Matterhorn, leapt into the centre of the lake and at last exploded my reflection into a thousand pieces as three words, like rifle shots, blasted through my brain: *Ich—Bin—Fantastic!*

(Oh, laugh now, Sam! I'm a crackpot! You can't hold back any longer. Yes, I can hear you—*ha-ha-ha-ha-ha-ha-ha-ha-ha-ha!*)

Bodies like this give sexual desire its meaning! It's for this that penises rise like drawbridges and vaginas become engorged with blood! It's for this that people throw snot-nosed kids into ravines, cross raging rivers, or ice-pick up the wrong side of frozen waterfalls! It's for this that politicians undo their flies in election season, porn magazines with their pages stuck together are found stacked in church basements, people chop off body parts and mail them to ex-lovers, risk hair on palms, stolen wallets, planes flying into buildings, and lice that hop like chess figurines on a board whose players are ever changing. It was for this that people do everything they have ever done, and my body was at the centre. And it was this I would offer you as my final act of generosity.

Why had I feared that I'd disintegrate? Some days I spoke English, other days German; I was an artist, then an ad designer,

Sam's lover, Veronika, a wandering vagabond. Though I changed, my body was constant; it was the stone monument that remains after an earthquake. And I realized it was this I deprived you of when I turned my back on you at the Zurich airport. It was this I took from your life with those three other words, "Please don't write."

Of the six billion people in the world, you were the one who could most profoundly appreciate the masterpiece of my body. Your sallow face and hell-on-wheels fashion sense put you farther from me than anyone I'd ever met, and that distance awoke in you a desire for me greater than that possessed by any other being on this whole planet. (*Jawohl!* Of course Prince Charming is gorgeous!) Yet I had cast you aside.

My shoulders started shaking, my lungs heaved, and I collapsed sobbing on the boulder. I wept because I'd treated you badly. I wept because I'd refused to see life through your eyes. I wept because I'd forced you to leave Switzerland. That morning beneath the summit of the blessed Matterhorn, I realized that it was my destiny to give pleasure to the world through my body and that the person most capable of receiving all I have was you, Sam. (Sounds loony? Of course it is, Sam, but that's the guy I am!)

I looked up at the mountain peak and saw your eyes radiating like suns from which liquid gold poured. I stared unflinching into those searing eyes and said, as I say in this letter I'm writing now: Sam, *mein Liebling*, come back to Zurich. Put my body under a microscope and find the uncharted connections in the constellations of my pores, hairs, beauty spots, and pimples. Remove my limbs and preserve them in your labelled jars. Cover my skin with angles and lines. I'll never be afraid again. Make graphs on my Adam's apple, tables over my cheekbones, and pie charts on my buttocks. Describe every atom of my body in sentences so long they'll reach right around the world, and their commas, periods, and exclamation marks will be like lights that flash on meteorites passing through outer space.

You never thought I could talk pretty, eh, Sam? You inspire me, *Liebhaber*. You make me greater than I've ever been.

Come meet me at my chalet. I'll expect you any day. And this time you won't leave, for my country's borders will become walls you can't cross. You'll be as trapped as I am, but you'll love it. A part of my bed is reserved for you. There is a plastic bowl with your name on it, and if we buy ice cream, this time it goes in my hair, not yours. I've got a wonderful Veronika inside me, but know that you like me best as a man. *Du bist fantastisch, Sam! Ich liebe dich! Swishity-swash! Klickity-klack! Ha-ha-ha-ha-ha!*

We will stand and laugh together, and once we start, we'll never stop.

I am back in Zurich and am waiting. I've renewed my gym membership and bought a new wardrobe of skin-hugging spandex you'll love. You are on my mind every second. Lifting barbells, I observe my vein-pulsing biceps and think of you licking your lips. I finger the curves of my calf muscles and feel your delight. Your eyes are on me always and, for you, my northern

Romeo, I do cartwheels in city parks, pop ping-pong balls from my right thigh to my left, pull coins out from behind an ear and pretend it's magic, or clench and unclench my abdominal muscles to the rhythm of Bolero. Your eyes make my hair shine with more lustre and my spray-on tan look authentic. Your eyes make me hand tips to street cleaners, compliment women on scarf-belt sets, give my credit card number to the homeless, or walk into elevators and for no reason press every button. Your eyes make cash registers ring and customers place francs into hands that are like mouths opening and closing. Your eyes make news vendors cry out headlines in voices that—when the breeze is blowing from the north—sound like music.

Your eyes make the wind blow down the stone streets of Zurich, the sun move from one corner of the sky to the other, the moon go crimson and once every twenty-five days angrily turn its back on us; your eyes make cold fronts move while snow collects in my eyebrows as I stare up into a uniform sky that stretches away from me on all sides forever.

At night I hear, from every corner of the Earth, the voices of people gazing skyward and humming melodies they'd long forgotten. Sam, I feel your eyes on me this instant.

Please. Never stop looking.

PART FOUR
 Rock

In the psychiatric hospital, the tests performed on Sam are endless. Never has he endured examinations so exhausting. Never has he been analyzed so obsessively. Every thought in his head is dragged out and chopped into chunks that are then diced into miniscule slivers. Hands lunge down his throat to yank up strings of sausage intestine, only to stuff them back down again and then drag them back up. He throws himself screaming onto the asylum floor or weeps into the cotton smocks of doctors who, shuddering, push him away.

He was sent to the hospital after arriving four times at Emergency with a rock in his throat. The first time, everyone believed his story. Walking in his garden, he'd felt hungry because the full moon reminded him of his life's emptiness. He saw a rock, thought it was a candied apple—what the hell, Halloween was two months off—and stuffed it into his mouth.

The second time, he claimed he was on the beach. It was still the high tourist season and he was surrounded by Americans nasally accentuating the diphthongs of their every word. He observed a row of rocks caked with dirt. If cleaned they'd be beautiful spheres reflecting the face of anyone looking into them. He had no handkerchief so he knelt and polished the rocks with his shimmying tongue. In the process, he accidentally swallowed one, two, three—damn—four rocks. "But I did it for the Americans," he explained on the stretcher, "and for the health of our city's tourist industry."

The third time the interns were sceptical. He said his body needed extra zinc. "Dieticians claim it's important. They should explain that the zinc in fossils isn't the same as in broccoli."

The fourth time in Emergency, no one believed anything he said. "I thought the scoops of a very hard ice cream cone had fallen to the ground and preferred they melt in my mouth rather than into the earth, which is already saturated with acid-rain."…"I always wondered how I'd look chubby-cheeked and once they were in my mouth, my Adam's apple called, 'Come on down!'"

We are allowed a limited number of fictitious stories on this Earth, and after they're told, nothing else we say is believed. Sam's rocks were too heavy to be held up by the gossamer threads of language, and he was transported to this cell where everything, the mattress, padded floor and walls, even the apples he gets for dessert, are soft as pudding.

He spends his time looking out the asylum window. The white lawn below is a perfect rectangle. Sometimes a dog walks out, urinates, moves on; its signature in the snow is an inane dot or squiggle, as meaningless as a punctuation mark without a sentence, a body without a head. An old man often chases scraps of paper across the blinding white. One day a boy and girl step into the blank space. They both wear green coats and are holding hands. Sam watches carefully as they lie down on their backs and flutter their arms and legs. When they stand and see the angels they made, they leap onto them, stamp and kick with their rubber boots, then run off the field. Sam peers into the bumpy, crater-filled blurs that were once torsos with skirts and wings and feels satisfied. The dog trots out and pees on the spot where a head had been.

The Earth is still in danger. There isn't enough snow on the lawn, and though it is January, rain drops crawl down his windowpane. Yet Sam rarely thinks anymore about that enigmatic force that moves the world. How can he solve large problems when his own life is a catastrophe? He collapsed merely because he met a man in Europe. He understands now that his fascination with Franz was partly a fascination with himself being fascinated by Franz. Yet the man contained a diamond. Or so Sam thought. Or the man would become one. There was a crack in logic, and now Sam is imprisoned in this palace of psychology where Reason dominates everything.

A knock at the door. The gangly, pimple-cheeked orderly shuffles in with his pail of soapy water. The uneventfulness of institution life magnifies trivialities, which grow like ivy to take up all the space in Sam's mind. The orderly splashes water across the floor, and Sam becomes angered by the irregular rhythm of the mop slapping tiles.

"You're not getting at the dust in the corners," complains Sam. "Use a little elbow grease, for God's sake." Two coffee stains darken the orderly's shirt. "You're dirtier than the floor you're cleaning...And that soapy water should be pink, not burgundy." The intern is quiet today, lost, Sam thinks, in his adolescent dream-world. Whenever he does speak, his words are startlingly pointed. His shoulders are square like Franz's, whose body remains superimposed over every aspect of Sam's life. "Get a haircut or a hairnet." He hears, in his own words, his judging of his Swiss lover. Sam had harshly assessed the frivolity of Franz's life, and Franz had crudely appraised Sam in return. Another reason, Sam thinks, why things ended as they did.

Before leaving, the intern says, "See ya, dude." The door slams. Sam wonders: In what way is he a dude?

He glances at the people on the television he received yesterday. Initially the doctors wouldn't let him have one, fearing that, as he'd eaten rocks, he might try to swallow the copper filaments or the IC chips. They conducted *laissez-aller* experiments in which unplugged televisions were placed beside his bed for two hours. In the end not even the channel converter had teeth marks on it, so they ordered a Toshiba 20A22. Sam didn't want a television, but the doctors believed the glare of the screen would rouse him out of his torpor. They succeeded only in enraging him.

On the round-cornered screen a woman simpers, "How old do you think I am?"

Sam shouts, "Ninety-five, you old battleaxe!"

"I tried hot wax treatments and anti-bacterial shampoos, but still got a case of the greasies."

"Try salting your hair with carbolic acid!"

"My teeth were yellow before I discovered Crest tooth-whitener."

Everyone relentlessly obsesses over the trivia of their bodies. Sam understands such people now.

He touches the slit in his pillowcase and remembers a zippered pencil case and Esther's labyrinth of hair. He unplugs the television and peeks down through the window at the battered snow angel. He silently thanks the boy and girl and wishes they'd return.

The world is quiet. He no longer notices the chafing of underground plates and booming thuds as chunks of lava collapse into each other. The fire at the Earth's centre has stopped roaring. The same sky hangs relentless above, becoming dark, then light, dark, light, as if a cheap plastic switch were being regularly snapped on and off. The Earth is so silent at night, Sam swears he can hear the hydrogen crackling on the surface of the sun. He wonders where unsatiated desire goes. Does it evaporate? Or cannibalize itself? Energy deprived of an outlet continues to exist somewhere.

He sees his own face in the windowpane. He remembers studying himself before his first date with Franz. He tilts his head backward and his cheeks narrow, raises his face and the edges waver. Just by angling his head he can have the face of someone else, the orderly, Esther, the Swiss immigration officer. Could be he become anyone he wants? Perhaps that had been his problem. He'd thought we were singular when each of us is plural. As usual, his reveries are broken by the visit of the doctors.

"Here they are," he says. "Carrying clipboards with edges sharp as knives and pens they'll poke into my eyes if I keep them open long enough." Sam's words were once soft-centred like plump grapes. Now he spits out hard-edged words whose consonants clatter together like tacks in a jar. Sarcasm is the language of people whose emotions are dying.

The doctors see the unplugged television, stare as if at a freshly killed animal. The two men don't sigh but, as usual, smile faintly. Why are they never angry? When Sam was a geologist, he had many days of frustration, and rocks are more co-operative than people.

He notices that today is another "special" day. The doctors have brought a rock into the room. They do this only when he's chained to his bed while two security guards stand by the door with arms crossed. The rock is placed on his desk. The doctors' pens are poised like aimed darts above their clipboards.

The doctor with a moustache (Sam's given him the warmly personal name Doctor #1) says, "So, Sam, what do you think of when you see this rock?"

Sam sighs. Here we go again. "I think of teeth," he says without thinking. "Molars or bicuspids."

The furtive scratching on pen on paper.

"No, not bicuspids. Incisors."

The whip-like slash of pens crossing out words.

"No, not incisors or bicuspids. Not even the teeth of humans."

Scratch. Whip. Scratch.

Lately his thoughts have started to ricochet, surge, and explode into fragments. In the past, they were tight and cramped, proceeding step-by-step up narrow staircases. "I think of dog's teeth. The teeth of dogs ... that have been swimming in the ocean so long that their teeth look like fins."

The two doctors glare. They don't like this answer. The guards uncross, then re-cross their arms. Sam is not deliberately being difficult. He wants to be honest. Psychology is not his field, but he figures if he's as frank as possible, the doctors might leave him alone. At times he admits they could even help him. "The rocks remind me of bosoms."

Both doctors start as if shot.

"Yes. Great, big lactating tits." The image intrigues Sam because he remembers the stories in *Fairy Tales of Flesh* and still longs for interchangeable body parts. If elbows could become knees or the ends of toes, necks turn into thighs while vaginas transform into armpit cavities or great gaping mouths, then he'd be freed—but from what he doesn't know. "Boobs. Great big ones. The best ever seen. With beautiful curves and nipples that bulge forward like eyeballs. Each has a nice drop of moisture on the tip."

The doctors are sitting up straight, their cheeks flushed as they write. The pens screech and cry. Sam is giving the right answers for a change.

"Boobs," he repeats.

One guard reaches into his pants pocket, makes an adjustment.

"Or no," he says, troubled. "Actually, the boobs have no nipples... because they're afraid of looking like bull's eyes." *Scritch, yowl, shriek*, go the pens. "Or maybe they're not boobs. In fact, those rocks are—*testicles*," he shouts, excited. "Great big, swinging knackers. Cleansed of hair and freed from the dictatorial penis. And round, round as globes or women's bosoms. In fact, those testicles *are* bosoms. They are testicles that women have instead of boobs. There they are, always flapping against training bras, or swinging like grandfather-clock pendulums, or dangling forward when she's doing the laundry, or leaping off a diving board, or they drop low-low-low and become narrow, looking hollowed out as they lengthen like a reflection in a funhouse mirror when, after swim practice, she takes off her bathing suit and steps into the crowded sauna where everyone is looking."

Both guards are sweating and have loosened their ties. A maelstrom of scratching until one doctor's pen explodes and his clipboard falls to the floor drenched in ink.

After the session, the doctors step into the hallway. Their voices go so fast they sound like bees buzzing. Doctor #1 steps into the doorway and proudly announces that Sam had a break-through. "You're making tremendous progress." They always say this, but today, for the first time, Sam believes them.

"Sure, if you like," he answers.

Doctor #2 says, "Pay attention to your dreams tonight."

Sam eyes the thread dangling from the psychologist's collar and knows it'd be easy to deceive these men. The surface never matches what's beneath. Sam had once ignored the distance between the Earth's surface and its centre. He recalls the gap between Franz's frivolous life and the fact that his penis made snow fall in summer and his intestines broke down stone. Franz had taken a great personal risk approaching him at the confer-ence. Only now does Sam understand his generosity.

But that night, Sam can't sleep. At three a.m. he gets down on the floor and puts his ear to the cold tile, but only hears pipes clinking.

At seven he is woken by the orderly who places orange juice and a bowl of apple crumble on the table. Sam requested a sugar-filled breakfast and the authorities complied. Sam sticks a spoon into the dessert and asks, "Why is there so much crumble and so little apple?"

"I didn't make it."

"You're serving it. That makes you responsible."

"Quit being hard on me. I'm only doing my job."

"Only doing your job? What kind of job is that? And I'm not being hard on you."

But Sam knows he is. He's spent his life assessing people—when he deigned to notice them at all. No wonder he had no friends; he didn't judge Franz in the early weeks, but as he got to know him, he quietly mocked him.

He says sadly, "All right. I'll see if I can choke it down."

❧

That afternoon Doctors #1 and #2 bring in a cardboard-backed map of the world.

"Today we'd like to talk about sexuality."

That again? Sam feels sorry for these doctors because they remind him of how he once was, fixated on details and over-defining everything. Franz had done that too. He'd said, "The first time I saw you, I knew you were homo." Sam had disliked the label's fated quality. "You weren't more Liberace than Rock Hudson, but you fit on the scale somewhere. If you were with a woman, you wouldn't know which way was up. At first glance I thought you were asexual. I couldn't imagine you'd be lying here naked with me." That comment still bothers Sam. He lives in a body. When he dreams of his lover, blood floods his loins and he wakes, the sheets wet.

Doctor #1 points at the map and asks Sam which country's colour appeals to him most.

"Christ," Sam mutters. They want him to talk of Switzerland. His fourth time in Emergency, a nurse overheard him mumbling about the Alps, deliriously repeating Franz's name and describing his chest, the lock of hair that fell like a comma over his forehead, the shape of his penis "pointed like a tomahawk," and the diamond growing inside him. She told everything to the hospital psychiatrist who passed the information on. People in the sciences forget nothing, Sam knows. He was once like them. Even today the structural formula of boron-bearing cyclosilicate is engraved on the insides of his eyelids. Sam sympathizes with these men yet scorns them, consumed as they are with fact-fetishizing inquisitiveness.

All our old methods! Sam regards them as rusted machines in a historical museum. How afraid we are of the gaps between words, the space separating the dot of the "i" from the stem, multiplication tables complete but for one missing number. Sam is the fraction whose top half won't dance with its lower. He's the digit whose square root is reducible to nothing. He is two lines that never intersect, the fulcrum two degrees short of north and one degree east of west. He is the phrase with no subjects, two objects, and five verbs that don't accord but is a sentence nonetheless. Doctors murmur, "Such a shame, a brilliant, educated man." The doctors fear he rode the rails of logic and fell off, and if he can't be saved, they can't either.

Sam pities these men for they'll never hear the fire roaring at the Earth's centre, see snow in summer, touch icicles hanging from shower curtains, or discover that a man's sweat tastes like liquorice one moment and molasses the next. Deep within Sam, he feels a rising wave of sorrow; he's going to burst into tears. The walls of the room are horrifyingly white. He chokes down a sob, trapped as he is here in the palace of Reason. Yet he will not give Franz to these doctors as easily as the Earth once offered him her secrets.

He studies the map of the world, sees the continents as multi-coloured Rorschach blotches on a turquoise sea.

"Pink is a nice colour," he says. "The British Commonwealth is pink, except for Lesotho, which is as red as a stubbed toe. Or a flattened tsetse fly." *Scratch-scratch.* They love his metaphors. He feeds them more. "Or a mashed tomato. Or a ketchup stain on a tablecloth." The worse the image is, the more honest it seems.

Yellow. Switzerland is yellow. Half-conscious in the emergency ward, he looked through the window and thought the sky was yellow.

The doctors shift in their chairs, cough. Finally Doctor #2 speaks. "We were thinking about what you said yesterday about testicles." Ah, Sam knew they'd come back to this. "Have you had any other thoughts on that? Especially as pertains to your relationship with your father."

"I've never seen my father's testicles."

"Never?"

"Never."

"Is it possible you've seen them but forgot?" asks Doctor #1.

Doctor #2 says, "Maybe you repressed the memory."

Sam reflects. His father wore chequered boxer shorts. They were wide-legged and he had trouble stuffing them into his pants. He wore hip-waders overtop. "No, I never saw them. He was a fisherman."

"Well!" Doctor #1 sniffs. "Fishermen do have testicles."

"I know that."

"And?" says Doctor #1.

The pens are still.

"Yes, and?" repeats Doctor #2.

Sam says, "And what?"

Both doctors stare.

Sam explodes. "Look, if I'd known my father's balls were so important, I would've asked to see them before leaving Labrador, but I never did, and do I regret that? Maybe I do, maybe I don't. When you're living on the ocean, you don't think about looking at your father's nuts. All that salt-water exposure would have made them wrinkled anyway."

"Your father's testicles anger you," observes Doctor #2. "The mention of them strikes a sensitive spot."

"Are you disgusted by the body in general?" asks Doctor #1.

"Or perhaps," chirps Doctor #2—he grins and his teeth shine like blanched almonds—"you're afraid to realize your father's testicles look like rocks!" He lets out a little crow and sits up, beating his hands together.

The other doctor frowns. Sam was supposed to come to this conclusion himself.

Doctor #2's shoulders sink, and he *ahems*.

Sam wonders if he is afraid of the human body. He remembers

the curve of Franz's lower ribs visible where his stomach sloped into its magnificent washboard. "No," he says. "I am in love with the human body. Never again will I number, diagram, or measure it. It is enough as is."

The two doctors glare tight-lipped. Their pens hang like skydivers caught in mid-fall. Today Sam hasn't given the right answers. When they leave, Sam leaps down, puts his ear to the floor. Still, only silence.

❧

Sam hates when the psychiatrists dredge up his past. He feels they're building an invisible house around him, locking him in patterns he should flee. The ghosts of his mother and sister appeared in Zurich because they knew they were being abandoned. The past pulls hardest when it's in danger of losing you to the present. Any woman he slept with was always in danger of transmogrifying into his mother, who'd sneak in slyly and he'd wake up in her arms.

At eight in the morning, the intern says, "Breakfast time, big boy."

Immediately Sam sees that the bowl contains peach cobbler, not apple crumble. A peeled peach half gleams like a severed buttock. Sam goes berserk. "You call yourself a hospital orderly and you can't tell the difference between two kinds of fruit!" Again he hears the judgment in his voice and pities the man, but can't stop himself. "I am a person who eats apple crumble. Hear that? Apple crumble for breakfast and from time to time melba toast when the mood hits."

"Don't you think it's time for a change, dude? It's why you're here." The intern has a silver cap on his front tooth that catches the light and sparkles like the mineral zircon. Sam never noticed it before. "Things change, don't they? I'm not wearing the same underwear I had on last night, and if I were, you wouldn't like the stench."

The realization is like a pole rammed into his ribcage: things change. Every organism continually transmogrifies, and if it stops doing so, it dies. He recalls how Franz's penis altered; some days it seemed a weapon, then a writing implement, a comfy armrest, a feisty Aunt Mabel, a stern schoolmaster, a lance raised in battle, then a droopy sad-sack friend who never goes to the movies no matter how often you ask. Perhaps Franz is still changing now, the hidden gemstone taking nutrients from all parts of his body. Sam himself had changed so much in Zurich that it'd terrified him. Why can't he move forward now? Why cling to an iron-rimmed identity he's been carting along the Earth's surface for a quarter of a century?

He snatches the bowl in his trembling hands. With a spoon he tentatively scoops and slides the syrup peach-buttock between his lips. The sweetness is revolting, the syrup thick like slime, but he chews the firm flesh and swallows. All of a sudden there are tears in his eyes. The orderly winks and heads out the door. Sam is learning more from him than from the doctors.

Sam decides to set in motion a process of change to align himself with this formative principle. He moves his bed to the north side of the room, puts his pyjamas on inside out, practises standing on his head until his face is borscht-red, and instead of muttering about Franz and the fire at the Earth's centre, he conjugates French verbs out loud. He knows he appears outlandish but is beginning to see that the ridiculous is closer to life's source than the sensible.

The doctors enter the room and gasp. Doctor #2 writes a whole paragraph. They sit on their chairs and clear their throats.

Then Sam says, "Can I ask a question? Why are there always two of you treating me? You're like Bobsy and Dobsy. Or Jekyll and Hyde. Or Sonny and Cher."

The men's eyes brighten. Doctor #1 puts his hand on his chin and asks, "If that were true, which one of us do you think would be Sonny and which would be Cher?"

"That's a stupid question," Sam answers, disgusted. "I thought you considered me intelligent. You, sir, have a bat-like hair growth below your nostrils—and would obviously be Sonny. Whereas you, sir," he glances at Doctor #2, "are a voluptuous, leggy brunette and could only be Cher. I'm amazed you'd ask such a silly question. I think the role assignment is clear."

The moustached doctor frowns. Evidently he wanted to be Cher. "You have two doctors," he says, "because your high IQ makes you a challenge to health-care professionals. Your recovery is very important to the scientific community. If you recover, we all recover."

"So I've got two."

"Yes," he answers. "Two mints are better than one." And to emphasize his point, he pops a mint into his mouth and bites it.

Sam doesn't want to talk about his life today, so he describes the cracks in the ceiling, their resemblance to seismograph lines or to the frenzied scribblings of a junkie trying to write his own name.

The men sit still as totem poles. Sam sighs again. He sighs so much that eighty percent of the air in the hospital must be made up of his carbon dioxide. Clearly, the doctors want him to talk about his family and childhood, so as usual he nestles down into his chair, as if in preparation for a bedtime story someone else will tell. He closes his eyes, concentrates, and begins to recount the tales of his life. He refuses to see patterns, but describes things randomly with no beginnings, middles, or ends. Yet sometimes the events arrange themselves into forms Sam wasn't looking for. The stories connect to the ones told the previous day or are as self-contained and alone as a single star in the sky. As he speaks, the men's pens stroke lovingly at their sheets, moving back and forth, up and down, rhythmically like waves. He expects to see their pages covered with curlicues and fluid, elegant spirals when, in fact, they are printing sentences that march compliantly between narrow lines that shoot straight across the page.

"My father was a fisherman," Sam says. "He was a fisherman living on the edge of the ocean. He spent all his youth hauling in nets of fish that gleamed like jewels and fluttered like fingers wagging until one day, there were no fish left. Now he floats staring dumbly into dark water. He curses and fidgets, and gets so tangled up in his nets that he cannot move but sits baking in the sun like a fish caught in a net. I have had to paddle out in a rowboat to rescue him. As I cut through the net to free him, he continues to gaze into the watery depths. Looking for what?

Fins flickering? Hands waving? The flash of an eye that opens and closes?"

"Do *you* look for eyes in water?" asks the Sonny-like doctor.

"What do you mean?"

"Do you look for eyes in kitchen-sink dishwater, toilet bowls, or the wonderful minestrone soup they serve here on Fridays?"

"You mean Mondays," corrects Cher.

"One of the two days," continues Sonny.

Sam says, "I don't think I look for eyes anywhere."

"Do you look for naked bodies in water? Is that what you look for?"

He recalls grey water rippling against white porcelain. "Thursday night was bath night for our family. My sister always took hers before mine. Sitting in the tepid water, I could still smell her body."

"Your sister. Yes. Tell us about her."

Sam speaks honestly. "My sister has spent her life winking at people who won't wink back. She's fluttered her eyelashes, and my lashes have tried to match their velocity but failed. We played together, painted purple dots on neighbours' doorsteps, draped our bodies over clotheslines and pretended we were shirts drying, ran up and down the valleys, our arms outstretched. But my sister is attached to my mother who is, in turn, attached to my father, and the same electricity flows through all of them. When I became aware of the rocks in the ground beneath my feet, I abandoned my sister and hiked to the steel city where I live. Still, my sister wanders up one street and down another and the footprints she leaves are larger than the shoes that made them. She lives trapped where the edges of buildings are blurred by sheaths of fog, sunlight makes flat windowpanes appear concave, and at night the ocean futilely bangs its head against the shore. Sue has heard the distant pounding, but will she ever wake?

"I hear her voice call me in the early morning and the sound becomes a rope that coils around my neck and pulls. I want to free my sister but don't know how. She trusts wind more than stone, but air brings you nothing and that's what she has. My father has fish, I have rocks, but my sister has zero."

"And your mother," Sonny asks. "What about her?"

Sam speaks honestly. "My mother does not have zero. Every number added up is hers. She looks up into the sky and it is an extension of her cerebral cortex. She looks down at the earth and those are her feet growing lichen and grass shrubs. When the wind blows, she falls to her knees, the world enters her, and she opens her mouth and gives the world back to itself in long, unbroken syllables. Bonfires glow in every corner of her skull, and her skin conceals muscles of such strength that she can fell trees with one blow of the hatchet and crumble shale rocks in her hands. She has braided the hair of my sister into such iron-solid scrollwork, a smithy's poker can't undo it. My mother gives and takes as does the universe, but there are things beyond her fingertips, and she can not accept this. When I was a child, Mother towered so high, I could not believe there could be a sky above her. She is an ocean that bubbles and pitches, but is so all-encompassing and formless that only the solid, defined edges of rocks could save me, and so I smashed stone against stone until I built a world she couldn't touch and would fear if she knew it existed.

For she is merciless. She pours bleach onto the bright, upturned faces of sunflowers so the birds that eat the seeds die. She hacks at the roots of raspberry bushes that are more fruitful than the womb that bore us. One day I discovered my second rock collection covered with blood; she'd tried to smash the stones with her bare hands. The next day she mail-ordered a Charles Atlas wrist-strengthener, and a week later I could hear her in the basement groaning as she squeezed the latex balls. After dinner she challenged my father to an arm-wrestle and won. That night my rocks in their trays looked like sugar cookies that would dissolve when touched. At midnight I put my rocks in a box under my arm and left Labrador for good. As I passed my sister's door, I pressed my lips against the polished wood. She'd be in hysterics in the morning. I was creeping through the living room when my father walked in, still wearing his oilskins. I held one finger before my lips and we stared at each other for a long time. Then I passed through the doorway and, for the first time in my life, climbed up and over the lip of the valley and headed east toward the city."

Sonny's voice becomes very quiet. "And this," he says, "Franz person. Tell us about him."

Sam jerks up his head. Four eyes and two ballpoint pen nibs glare back.

No. He will not speak honestly. He will not offer Franz's body on a platter so that they can separate pelvis from torso. He will not let them peel Franz from his brain and shape him into whatever form suits them. There's a type of cave lichen that's killed by the light that makes it visible. Let them shine their flashlights elsewhere. The world's centre remains stone-circled for a reason.

Sam has thrown story after story at the doctors—"Here, catch this"—and they race to catch a ball arcing high in the air, but one ball is never enough, and Sam has to juggle, volley, and lob in all directions to keep their over-washed, antiseptic-reeking hands off Franz. He peers at a stain on the wall and tells them Franz was a rosy-cheeked milkmaid living in the high Alps and that his skin was white as cream and his hair soft as lamb's wool; together they'd stand in alpine meadows and blow long, curling horns, then prance about fields with bells on their necks until they fell naked beside piles of sheep dung and proceeded to make love. At the moment of climax, Franz would yodel; his voice echoing about the mountains caused avalanches and made goats fall off cliffs.

"Can you impersonate this yodelling for us?" asks Sonny.

Sam can't, so he explains that Franz was a seventy-year-old blacksmith who beat metal beside the lake below the Matterhorn; the sound of pounding metal was so infectious, Sam would perform avant-garde interpretive dances on glaciers, jutting his hips to and fro and clawing his fingers before his face as if scraping hardened frost from the air.

"Can you perform this dance now?"

That's impossible, so Sam tells them Franz was a Zurich housewife who incessantly polished delicate china figurines on mahogany shelves; the last time Sam visited, he'd swung his coat over his shoulder and a statuette of a shepherd playing a hornpipe fell and smashed on the hardwood. Franz picked up each glass shard and dropped them into a bin with no injury to himself, but when Sam touched just one piece, scratches appeared on the palms of his hands and every finger bled.

"Could you show us the scars?"

On and on it goes. "Tell us about Franz! Franz! Franz!" repeating that name over and over; it is so disorienting to Sam that his own words stick like mud to the roof of his mouth, and he is no longer his new derisive, sarcastic self. Blood slows to become sludge in his veins, his brain spins like a weathercock in empty space; he feels he is sinking and can only see the terrible distance between his body and Franz's. As he huddles finally brain-naked before them, the doctors lick their lips and go for the kill. They hurl questions like stones at his exposed flesh.

"How could six weeks with one person have changed you so utterly?"

"Was it because he was your first real lover and the betrayal so sudden?"

"What is this diamond that has become so important?"

"And why Switzerland, why not Austria, Sweden, or Italy? For God's sake, why not Italy?"

"Surely there were signs you'd collapse before you met him. What glue held you together?"

"Why did this glue stop working when you entered Switzerland?"

They attempt to uproot desire from its hiding place, give it dimensions, weight, a back and a front. But once you describe something, you destroy it. Sam writhes beneath the onslaught of language until he collapses weeping on the floor before them. "I don't know why anything's happened! I don't know who Franz truly is, why the ocean exists, why rocks don't fly, and why we can't walk on water! I don't know anything anymore! Please let me be!"

The two doctors look at each other. Have they peeled off a layer of resistance?

"I don't understand why you're so harsh with me, Sonny." Sam wipes tears from his cheeks. "And you, Cher, I really had high hopes for you." He looks up at the two doctors and says, "Sonny and Cher, I'm disappointed in the both of you." At the mention of their linked names, the men beam.

Sam confesses a secret. "I feel embarrassed because I've had this relationship that you, as scientists, know is meaningless. It can't produce offspring and is an evolutionary mistake. I don't know why I'm a biological non-sequitur."

Sonny looks directly at Cher. Then he reaches over and takes her hand in his.

❦

The next day the security guard unlocks Sam's door and grunts, "You have walking privileges. You can go through the hallways and the hospital grounds if you want." Sam is shocked. He immediately has the desire to race from his room, then recalls that he has nowhere to go. Sam will leave his room but not right now. He spends the day by the window gathering energy. He knows all organisms require a vitalization stage when a change of form is imminent. Again he watches the blank rectangle of lawn. Snow is starting to melt. Small islands of green rise like bruises in the endless white. From the hall, he hears a water cooler gurgling, announcements on the P.A. "Dr Finstein wanted in Sexology clinic."

In the late afternoon, Sonny and Cher arrive, and when Sam hears their voices, even without looking at them, he knows something is different. He turns to see that the two men are no longer clothed in lab coats. Instead, Sonny wears white bell-bottoms and a vest that flashes with bits of tinfoil, while Cher wears a strapless, low-cut dress decorated with teardrop sequins. His curly hair has been straightened and hangs down his back. Sonny is blushing. Sam pretends not to notice their new clothes so as not to embarrass them. He likes the change because during today's session, the doctors spend more time looking at each other than at Sam. They keep losing their train of thought; often, for no reason, Cher abruptly wiggles her shoulders, and sometimes when Sam is speaking, they look at each other and hum.

However, their attention turns to him completely when Sonny offers Sam an envelope with his name on it. Sam carefully takes the paper rectangle. The postmark is Labrador.

"Now that we can trust that you won't eat any stones," explains Sonny, "we can safely give you your letters without fearing you'll choke on the sealing glue."

Sam glances at the Queen, whose face is crossed by four parallel ripples. He is amazed that someone in the world knows he is here. He is not as sequestered as he thought.

Something at the centre of him shifts. He lifts his head and strains to hear into an empty distance where he searches for the slightest sound. Somewhere in this building is a passageway between his life and the rest of the world. Somewhere a bridge exists. At that moment, he thinks: why do I forget that life never repeats, that minutes don't return, that life transforms itself each second? Why clutch at phantoms? My time with Franz had little to do with happiness and much to do with something greater. He slowly rips open the envelope and finds a long letter. He reads:

My dear son,

You are imprisoned in a psychiatric institution and pain is all around you. You must know I love you as God loves you. You are in my heart and my hopes follow you everywhere...

He folds the page. "It's from my mother," he says. "Doing her usual *schtick*."

Sam wonders what is happening to his name floating about the outside world; how many other people know he's here? What stories are being told about him? Sam knows that on this dynamic planet everything goes in circles. There are the cycles of day and night as the ground alternately heats and cools, and cycles of seasons as the Earth orbits the sun. There are cycles of the wobble of the Earth on its axis. Even the movement of lava below the Earth's crust is cyclical; it rises up, melts, descends, melts, then rises up again. Everything rotates—planets around space, the moon around the Earth, the Earth around itself.

At that moment something—the way the knife-blade of sunlight lights the top knob on the bedpost, or how Cher's lipstick covers only her lips and never crosses the line onto her skin, or how when he looks out the window, a bird the colour of hazelnuts is flying in a rising arc through the sky—makes Sam feel that miracles are possible. He senses he will see Franz again. Despite the iron bars of logic that imprison him, he is sure he will meet him one last time.

The force that fuels the world still exists somewhere.

"This mail arrived directly," explained Sonny. "Other letters are forwarded here." Ah, they read his letters to find the final piece of the puzzle. "If you're co-operative, we'll share them with you."

His door will be open this afternoon. He'll search for the mailroom, that wonderful conduit between this hospital and the world outside. Trying to act blasé, he gives the letter to Cher. "I don't need this," Sam explains. "Crumple it up and put it in your bra. Your left breast is bigger than your right."

"Thank you, Sam," she says, her voice a husky vibrato.

The next day Sam crosses the line separating his room from the hallway.

His slippered feet scuffle along the white-tiled floor and he hears new sounds: moans, cries, rattling trolley-carts, laughter, humming razors, static-y intercoms, and bedpans clanging like cymbals.

He glances into the common room furnished with rocking chairs, a painting of a sunset, round-cornered coffee tables, and an ankle-deep shag carpet the colour of clay. Farther down the hall is the gym, where armies of people move their limbs like pistons; torsos on mats fold themselves up and down like giant wallets opening and closing. Old women and young men hobble along a running track that takes them back to where they came from and then sends them off again. How interesting the world is, even this little community within the walls of the asylum. So much variety, motion, activity, and colour. Why had he once scorned human beings? Why had he liked to feel separate? What the eye sees is so different from what actually is. He remembers Delial's horror when Sam tried on a yellow shirt in Excelsior's. "It doesn't match your skin colour; you look like a cadaver," he'd said. Why did people's gazes stop at the surface? He recalls how he'd disdained Franz's stacks of clothing and realizes that he assessed his lover unfairly. He should've appreciated Franz's creativity, the way he viewed his own body as a canvas to be covered with an endless cavalcade of textures, colours, and forms, transforming himself into a different person every day.

Sam now wants to enter people's minds and hear their thoughts. How are they different from his? What a burden it is to be just one person limited by a single psychology. Why had his curiosity extended only as far as inanimate geology? He tried to save the world but was blind to the people in it.

Down in the basement Sam discovers the hospital kitchen. He peers through the round window in the door and observes rows of bran muffins nestled like chicks in tin cubby-holes. A baker with a white cylinder on his head is swinging a rolling pin in the air. Farther along, the boiler room; next, the humid laundry room, the security office, and finally, in the hall's dead end, the mailroom. He stands at the open doorway. Inside is a silent counter with a button-bell on top. If he goes in and rings it, will what is rightfully his be given him?

Back in his room, Sam lies on the bed, not in foetal position, but for the first time in months, flat on his back.

Sam finally asks Sonny and Cher if he can have access to his own mail. They now wear very elaborate costumes. Sonny sports flashy ties and macraméd vests, has a gold ring in one ear, and is growing sideburns. Cher has jiggling bracelets on her wrists and carries a feather boa. Her long glitter-sparkling nails curve elegantly and her breasts seem to be getting bigger. Perhaps it's the effect created by her dress, which pushes her chest flesh forward, or maybe she got implants when no one was looking. The sessions are repeatedly punctuated by her neigh-like laugh. Sonny and Cher's trust of Sam increases with the strength of their new identities and love for each other. Sonny says they can allow him mail access as long as he agrees to discuss his letters with them.

"I will," Sam says. "Believe me." And he means it.

Each day he munches his peach melba and enjoys it. One morning he spontaneously embraces the startled orderly.

Franz's growing diamond begins to obsess Sam. Unstable transition metals like nitrogen and carbon would be required for this gem. Franz surely contains such substances, for he changed constantly. Gemstones need highly fluctuating temperatures, evident in Franz's manias and paranoia. Diamonds do not form near the surface but must be deeply buried, at times as far as 400 kilometres below the lithospheric plates. They are often brought to the surface through volcanic eruption. The suspense of not knowing what form this eruption will take in Franz is agony to Sam. Although his belief in Franz's diamond seems like faith, he knows it is based on geological phenomena and grounded in fact.

❧

The first time Sam requests his mail, the postal clerk asks his name, then runs one hand along her right breast and says, "Nothing today."

The second time, she runs her other hand over her other breast and says, "Nothing today."

The third time he asks, there is mail.

The letter has no return address. He runs up to his room, tears it open, and recognizes his father's handwriting. He reads:

"Gishy-fish. The fins flash and the waves splash. Mishy-mish. The boat croaks and the tokes smote. Where is she with the flaxen hair and the scales that shine and flippers that flime? Gishy-fish. And the curves seen through brine as her hair undulates like seaweed at the seaside? My son, I have loved you more than the—lishy-kish—more than the—kishy-wish—take the sun and put it in your pocket for my heart goes out to—gishy-fish, mishy-mish …"

Sam doesn't need to read any more. He folds the page and puts it back into its envelope.

That afternoon he explains Father to Sonny and Cher. "He's lost at sea always searching for a glimpse of the mermaid that only exists in myth." He fears Sonny will start asking about his father's testicles, but he only says, "That's a beautiful story."

⚘

The next time Sam visits the postal clerk, she drums her hands on the counter.

The following day she pokes one finger into her cup of yogurt.

The third time there is mail. Sam runs up to his room and tears it open to see his sister's handwriting. He reads:

"Everyone in town hates me. My honey flows but the bees no longer come to see me. Is it my fault that my body is this way? If only you could help me ... "

He reads more of this letter than the others. He feels exhausted for the rest of the day.

Sam tells the doctors, "I have no idea what's happening to my sister now. She wears me down like water over rock. She has the same clutching fingers as my mother, but she doesn't try to penetrate my inner organs in the same way. The ocean stretches east from Labrador; to the west, a wall of stone barricades Cartwright from the rest of North America. I long to free Sue, but too many years have passed. I hate being powerless and think I could help her if she'd help herself. I don't know the solution. If you have an idea, tell me."

Rivers of tears run down Cher's cheeks and blotch her makeup. "That poor girl," she blubbers. "That poor sweet thing."

Sonny reaches over, pats her hand. "There, there," he says. "There, there."

That night Sam dreams of fog creeping over wind-scarred cliffs and leaping swordfish shaking their tails at the pinnacle of arcs so high the fish appear to be flying.

✻

One day Sam tells Sonny and Cher, "The day before I left Labrador, my mother was at her most difficult. The Bhopal disaster in India was still recent news, and when my father said that could happen here, she replied, 'No, it couldn't. We're a Christian nation. They're suffering because they're not with God.' When she went to buy groceries, I snatched her silver crucifix from the living room mantel and buried it in the back yard, beside the tree where the neighbourhood dogs piss. That evening, in tears, she phoned the police and said that the two town hippies had stolen her treasure. She glanced at me nervously but refused to believe I could do this. I still picture that silver Christ bathed in dog piss and feel guilty. I should've left her a note explaining why I was leaving."

"You shouldn't feel guilt," Sonny explains. "Urine, in fact, prevents precious metals from oxidizing. I have a silver copy of Rodin's *The Thinker* and polish it daily with my urine and want to use Cher's, but she won't give me any."

"We don't know each other that well, Sonny," says Cher. "These things take time."

The next day when Sam asks for mail, the clerk brushes her teeth.

The following day, she puts anti-wax drops in her ears and runs an electric razor over her armpits.

The third time, she does nothing. "There is no mail," she blurts. "That's all there is to it."

The next weeks are long and agonizing. Sonny and Cher become so taken with each other that they stop visiting Sam. He looks out at the lawn that's now half-green, half-white like the flag of a newly created country.

He wanders the hallways, watches janitors slosh grey water over tiles, sees cooks throw Oxo cubes into steaming sauces, and studies the laundry woman beating her hairbrush against a mustard stain on a duvet.

Finally the mail clerk gets sick and has to take time off. When she's in, she spends her time in the washroom spitting phlegm or coughing up hairballs. Sam eyes the curtains that lead to the forbidden bowels of the post office. There, secret documents are stored. Somewhere beneath that wall of velour is the mailroom loading dock, the conduit to the outside world. He longs to run through the curtain, but if he's caught, Sonny and Cher will lose faith in him, and he'll be locked in his room forever. Everyone but Franz has sent Sam a letter. Outside his window, birds keep flying in rising arcs. The suspense becomes too great.

On March 2, the clerk is in the washroom having one of her hairball days. When she hacks, it sounds like two sticks being struck together; to Sam, each cough has a veiled message: "Go." "Run." "See."

He takes a deep breath, dashes into the fur-soft slit in the curtains, and suddenly is in a lit-up room crowded with rows of slotted boxes. Pillars sport alphabet letters. One aisle is ABCDEFGHIJKL; the other, ZYXWVUTSRQPONM. He rushes into the labyrinth, stops before M, shoves his hand into a box, and pulls out some envelopes. He shuffles through Manning, Mappens, then finally reaches Masonty.

He sees the Swiss postmark. He nearly faints. Then, as he clutches the envelope, his penis tents his trousers. Through the curtain slit, he glimpses the back of the mail clerk. She's furiously stamping squares of paper. Sam crouches hiding behind a box and tears open the envelope. As he reads the twenty-page-long manuscript, a thousand disconnected thoughts roar though his mind at once.

He sees that Franz is a flawed vessel, yet opposites are interwoven in all organisms. The carbon necessary for diamonds comes from both organic and inorganic sources and Franz contains both. Sam is perplexed by Franz becoming Veronika, loves him deeply when rescuing the toad, feels vengeance when the ice cream splatters in his hair, and experiences a sense of synchronicity when Franz has his revelation by the lake. Amazingly the entire cycle of Franz's present life, all his transformations, agonies, and massive adaptations, were set in motion by Sam! Yes, Sam and his staring, glowering, hypnotic eyes! He'd reoriented Franz's life. Or so it seemed. And he wasn't even trying. He'd been in his Toronto apartment, then in this hospital, the whole time. While astonished, he recognizes that he expected this all along. What would happen if he were there with Franz now? How much more good he could do! Sam's power seems, to him, astronomical. He can smell Franz's cinnamon skin-scent on the letter. He remembers Franz's diamond and realizes that the final geological force that will push it to the surface is himself. From the start, he'd been that Earth-balancing energy.

Franz's diamond hasn't quite formed; falling in love with his own body before the Matterhorn lake is ridiculous (and Sam's so glad Franz asked him to laugh). The Matterhorn is merely a way station, and Franz still hasn't found the key to himself. Clearly he has experienced the eruption of kimberlite or lamproite, an inferior volcanic rock that presages the surfacing of diamonds. The gushing forth of garish lamproite indicates that diamonds are on their way soon, but first Franz must abandon everything about himself, his body included. Who can help him on his path? How will he reach a transformation point? And why can't one person be interchangeable with another? Why must Franz's penis be so exciting? Why not his elbow or chin? Shouldn't body parts mix and match? The fairy tale about the people who freely detach and re-attach appendages still inspires Sam. He remembers the character who interchanged his earlobes and testicles so he could acutely hear his ejaculations and enjoy a tightening at the side of his head whenever the weather got cold.

Finally Sam reads: "Sam, *mein Liebling*, come to Zurich. Put my body under a microscope …" Then he hears it—the fire roaring at the Earth's centre. The ground begins to shake; plaster flecks fall from the post office walls. All of Franz's resistances to

Sam have evaporated. Now he wants him without reservation.

Sam longs to knock over every wooden box in that room and dance about the scattered envelopes, waving Franz's letter like a flag of victory. But if the clerk sees him, she'll telephone Sonny and that will be the end of everything. He's gotten past the troll at the gate. Now he must find the exit to the outside world. Sam will return to Switzerland. But this time, not only for himself. He will be the geological force that makes continental plates collide and drives the Earth's inner riches up through its crust. Sam shoves the sheet into his underpants, scrambles along an aisle and, at the end of a row of boxes, charges into a dark hallway. His feet clang on the steel floor and he stops running. Did the troll hear? He listens to a distant *clat-clat-clat* as she stamps letters on her wooden desk.

He sees, at the end of the long tunnel, the loading dock that opens onto the parking lot. He dashes through the passageway, arrives at the end, and stands wobbling in the square opening that divides the hospital from the outside world. A wind smelling of rust, oil, and wet hay pushes the hair off his forehead and flutters the edges of his hospital gown. Below stretches a cement plain covered in criss-crossing yellow lines dotted with cars, their windows blackened. The parking lot is bordered by fences with raised floodlights pointing down like rifles. Beyond is the wonderfully disorganized world he's long feared and never truly been part of. Why were there no security guards here? One large window on the ground floor is lit and he hears a thudding bass beat and someone singing, "We won't find out until we grow…" He clenches his fists so tightly that, in the half-light, they look like rocks stuck to the ends of his forearms. If anyone tries to prevent his escape, they'll get a stone blow to the temples or balls or both.

Sam leaps from the loading dock, and his feet strike the pavement with such force he's surprised the hospital doesn't collapse behind him like a house of cards. Head lowered, he runs along the outer fence, the music growing louder in his ears. "Babe, I got you, babe." Opposite the lit window, he sees Sonny and Cher singing on a stage before a swaying crowd holding hands above heads. So that's it! Everyone, including the security guards, has been drawn to the concert. What a lucky break. Thank God for Sonny and Cher!

He runs onto the muddy lawn he's studied for so long and looks back at the wall of square windows. His curtains are closed but the lights are on; he sees the shadow of a slim figure waving—the orderly wishing him good luck.

"Thank you," Sam whispers. "From now on I'll know friends always come disguised as strangers."

The last sound he hears from the hospital is a thudding bass beat and Cher's voice singing, "I—got—yo-u-u—b-a-a-b-e!" Sam charges across a deserted road and plunges into the darkness of a barley field.

※

He knows he's heading east because the moon is in the sky's fourth quadrant. Although shock waves whiplash through his body as his slippered feet strike the earth, he runs. Although plants strike his shins and tree branches slash his cheeks, he runs.

Although mosquitoes fly into his hair, eyes, and up his nose, his hands blister as he climbs wood fences, and his calves, thighs, and face become splattered with mud and manure, he runs.

He cartwheels over stone walls, hurtles through crabgrass-devoured ditches and wanders, panting across light-drenched, sign-flashing highways where cars charge trailing flames of light; horn blares are like sudden explosions.

A strange second sound fills the air and becomes louder as he heads east. At first Sam thinks it's a train whistle, then a tuning fork struck so hard its prongs will oscillate forever. The pulsating ringing is coming from the northeast. The sound enters his ears, seeps into his lower cranium, and journeys down through his torso until all his bones and interior organs, hard and soft, vibrate to the same rhythm.

In the morning, the sun puts one blunt fingertip above the horizon-line and lights up the apartment blocks of Peterborough. His hospital shirt and pants are in shreds and his feet bloodied and swollen. He attempts to comb his hair with mud-caked fingers. Sam heads north toward the airport and arrives an hour later. His feet slap the pavement as he races across the parking lot. He pushes through a plate-glass door, steps inside. Directly in front is the Air Canada counter and a smiling woman in a navy blazer. When he approaches the desk, the woman stops smiling.

"I want a ticket to Zurich," Sam says. "For the next plane."

A deep crease forms in her forehead. "We don't have direct flights to Europe, sir. You have to fly to Toronto and get a connecting flight there."

"I have no time for that." When Sonny and Cher discover he's escaped, a warrant for his capture will be published immediately. "I want Zurich now!" A queue of people giddily flapping yellow cards shuffles through a doorway below a flashing light. "I'll give you all I have." He realizes he has neither money nor I.D.

The woman politely says, "Just one minute, sir." She speaks into a microphone. "Security. Desk number five."

Sam curses, runs to the front of the queue, throws down a man in dreadlocks, knocks over a lady in purdah, hurls a pen-clicking businessman against the wall, and charges through the door. Inside is a tunnel crowded with more people. "Get out of my way!" he shouts, pushing through. Shrieking passengers fall like bowling pins; crutches and canes clatter on tiles, but he races ahead without mercy. At the end of the tunnel is a red line on the floor and beyond, the stairs into the plane. If he crosses that line, he can storm the plane. The pilot will take him wherever Sam demands, and if he refuses, Sam will clobber him senseless and fly the plane himself.

Hands suddenly clutch Sam's shoulders, pull his arms behind his back. Two men in grey uniforms. Security pigs.

"Let go of me!"

Their grip on his forearms tightens.

Then an amazing thing happens. As he thinks of Franz standing with arms outstretched on the other side of the world, the words from the letter in his underpants cross the divide separating paper and skin, seep into his pores, enter his bloodstream, and shoot to all the extremities of his body. His pituitaries go into hysterics and erupt every last bit of adrenalin in their reservoir, and Sam becomes possessed of a strength he's never known.

His biceps swell, ripping his sleeve seams, his pectorals flicker, thigh muscles bulge, and deep crevices etch themselves into his once soft stomach.

In one quick movement, Sam spirals his arms like propellers and the guards are hurled to the ground. He charges forward down the tunnel only to be stopped—*bap!*—by a wall of sheet metal that strikes his forehead, nose, and kneecaps, and clangs a high C. He pounds at the plane door with his fists, he scrapes and paws, puts his fingers into the crack and pulls.

The guards on the ground are radioing for help. "Terrorist at Gate Five."

Swearing, Sam hurtles back out through the tunnel, inadvertently steps on the hands and faces of people he'd already trampled once. "Not again!" they scream. "No!" Outside, the woman in the blazer is bellowing, "Reinforcements at Gate Five!"

Sam sprints through the glass door and finally stands alone in the wind-swept parking lot. He does not run far. A half-kilometre from the airport, he climbs down into a rainwater culvert and lies there panting. Rings of corrugated metal circle his body. He stays there until nightfall. Then, after dark, when a plane arrives, he'll storm the runway.

All day as he listens to the screech of planes taking off, the circular ridges of metal around him hum and vibrate, pressing so deeply into his flesh, he fears he'll have zebra patterns on his skin for the rest of his life. He rolls onto his stomach, and an iron ridge rises up to his eyeball. His bangs feel sticky on his forehead; his lips pucker into a steel ridge. Sam clicks his jaw, stretches his feet, and his toes fan outwards. He notices his heart pounding as perspiration trickles along his scalp, tickles the hair in his armpits, and pools in the small of his back. As his lungs expand, the two halves of his ribcage separate; his flattened testicles sprawl outward like elephant ears. This is his body. This is him. He feels his mind at last sliding down into the heat of his torso, stretching out tentacles into his four limbs. He takes possession of his body as never before. He is it and it is him. He refuses to separate himself from it ever again.

Sam smells something sour, hears rasping, and feels a tickle on the top of his head. He raises his chin, and peers into the bloodshot eyes of a snorting rat, its tongue flickering. Sam bangs his hands against the metal and the animal scurries away but reappears at the other end of the tunnel where it grunts and shuffles.

Sam instinctively puts his hand in his torn pants to feel the edges of Franz's letter. It is still there. No one will take it from him.

The sun sets and the drain darkens. Sam crawls out of the hole. He stares down at his feet; the moonlight makes them appear thicker and wider. He lifts each foot and notices his swollen soles have hardened into inch-thick calluses and his toenails are now hooked talons. Opening his mouth, he places his fingertip against the incisors that are now surprisingly long and sharp. A stab of pain. He examines his finger, marvelling at the pearl of blood on its tip. He uses his teeth to gnaw a hole in the airport fence. Crouching, he watches a staircase on wheels drift onto the runway, float about indecisively, then veer toward a small parked plane. When the stair lip touches the plane's shell, a jolt goes through Sam's body. He races out onto the lit-up tarmac, but just before he reaches the stairs, a herd of pot-bellied security guards stampede out of a wooden hut and surround him. Some men have batons in their hands, others carry lemon donuts and a few, crullers. All are chewing. Sam kicks one man in the stomach, hoofs another in the balls, then joins his raised arms like a hatchet and hacks a third man on the head. He turns and charges up the staircase. At the top—that same damned high-pitched ringing! It's not an alarm but a shrill throbbing coming from the eastern forests, from the direction of—Labrador. The plane's steel door closes against his face.

He dashes back down and races through the sea of writhing security guards wiping jelly off their faces and babbling into walkie-talkies. Sam knows he can't come to this airport again. Next time surely the entire police force will be here, and as strong as his body was becoming, there are limits to what it can do.

※

So he runs all night and all the next day. Outside Belleville's small airport, he encounters and challenges the same floating staircase, the same guards, the same flight and escape. And again in Kingston, Gananonque, and Smith Falls. When Sam reaches the Perth airport, he peers through the wire-mesh fence to see the armed guard assembled on the runway. He resigns himself: he'll have to travel to Zurich by sea.

The closest Atlantic port is Ogunquit, Maine, but Sam could get caught crossing the US border. Percé, Québec has too few ships. Halifax, too many people. The best bet seems to be Sydney, Nova Scotia. Beneath the cover of night, he'll sneak into the cargo hold of a Europe-bound ship.

Suddenly the constant ringing sound pops, sputters once, twice, and forms syllables. "Run, brother, run! Run, brother, run!" His sister's words extort him to approach the future by returning to the past. Cartwright has a port, and he knows the schedule of departing ships by heart. But he does not want to return to Labrador. It's too far out of the way. The detour will take too much time. He's spent his life extricating himself from the fires of Cartwright. Why return to a place he so desperately wanted to leave? He's not responsible for his sister's welfare. Let Sue save herself. But strands of guilt thread themselves through his whole body.

"Run, brother, run! Run, brother, run! Run, brother, run..."

The next week he sleeps by day and runs by night. His sister's voice continues to call across a great distance. There it is beneath the sound of his feet thumping the earth, leaves *shushing*, tree branches creaking, and the roar of cars passing on the nearby highway. Should he really go to Cartwright?

He passes dried-up streams, brittle forests about to burst into flame. Global warming has wreaked its havoc here. Is Sam strong enough to return to the town of his birth?

He finds soiled newspapers and, curious, reads them. One morning he discovers a piece of newspaper with a photo of his own face glowering below the words, "Escaped Mental Patient Attacks Airport Staff. Sam Masonty, a schizophrenic psychotic has escaped from the York Mental Institution. Doctors Browning and Silversen say he is a threat to public safety…"

Sonny and Cher. Those assholes. After all he'd done for them. Sam knows he has difficulty trusting people, and now Sonny and Cher made his worst fear come true. He reads on: "Joe Baxter, an orderly, was fired because he witnessed the patient's escape but waited hours before reporting it." Sam can't bear to read more. He crumples up the paper and buries it. He will have to steer clear of all human habitation.

He travels northward through the deep wilderness, and his body continues to change each day. By the time he reaches Hyndford, his torso is a tree trunk of pulsating muscle. The last patch of clothing falls from him, and hair now sprouts from every pore in his skin, claws protrude from his fingertips, and the centre of his face expands outward to form a very definite, cone-shaped snout. The wilderness affects him in ways he hadn't anticipated. Sam doesn't mind his new body—the fur keeps him warm at night, and his claws are particularly good for digging up acorns and peeling off tree bark. He subsists on a diet of swamp grasses, berries, birch branches, and squirrels that he catches, places between his lips, and decapitates with a quick, downward thrust of his upper jaw.

His penis has grown particularly long. He has to lift it up when he walks over logs or sharp-tipped rocks. Sam grows tired of it slapping against his shins and calves. While he climbs hills, it drags along the ground; when he crouches to drink from streams, his penis becomes coated with mud. If he rotates his body too quickly, it swings out at a ninety-degree angle and thwacks an adjacent tree trunk, causing a storm of leaves, acorns, and irate chipmunks to land on his head. Still, his penis reassures him. He realizes he can clutch and pull at it violently, but it will never come off; it is attached to his body for good. His erect penis can crack open nutshells or overturn rocks. Walking through close-set rows of trees with a hard-on is awkward, and he's glad his penis's default setting is flaccid. He once had a dream that through the strength of his will he could make his penis rise and fall, just as he can raise and lower a leg. Now he understands that would kill the most meaningful part of him because things that happen outside our volition are truly mysterious and important.

Everywhere in the forest, sunlit rocks leer brazenly, and he thinks about sex more than ever. Some days he feels he's nothing but a giant whirling mass of testosterone. Franz's body, Esther's labyrinth of hair, and the giant legs of the wooden kicking man ricochet about his brain and he ejaculates every half-hour. His semen glitters on rocks, fills gopher holes, sticks tree branches together, and rushes downstream to clog the sanitary systems of riverside villages.

But each night lying on the forest floor, he sees Sue's hovering, grief-creviced face. Igneous, metamorphic, and basalt rock towers around him on all sides, each containing layers of sediment accumulated over centuries. He recalls how the phantoms of his family sabotaged his relationship with Franz. "Run, brother, run..."

As he watches fish leaping through rapids, bears galloping down mountains, deer circling him nervously, or hoards of flies attacking his moist snout, he begins to think about the force that fuels the world. Perhaps it's not only in inanimate geology, but here in wild animals and in him. Is that power present in his outstretched arm, in his fur bristling in the cold, in his jaws crunching berries, in his vocal cords when they make unconscious exclamations out of fear or delight, or in his penis filling with blood that then drains upwards like nutrients flowing from the roots of a plant?

One night when the moon is full, Sam falls asleep in the mouth of a gigantic stone cavern. He dreams that he meets Franz at last by the Alfred Escher statue. The two men fall to the ground and have constant sex for seven days and seven nights. The dream images become so vivid and passion-infused that he sleepwalks out of the cave and across meadows, in and out of babbling brooks, his eyes shut, lips murmuring, penis pointing like a wand, as he ejaculates non-stop.

In the morning when Sam wakes, every inch of the forest is covered with foot-high piles of semen that twinkle in the sun like manna descended from heaven or some primeval pus oozing up from the deepest pores of the skin of the Earth. The gleaming whiteness rises in glorious, undulating mounds about the feet of trees, hangs in dripping cobwebs from drooping branches, clings in a sheen on the smooth surfaces of rocks, engulfs low-lying bushes, foams on the banks of clogged rivers where cum-toupéed frogs belch spunk-bubbles. A torrid crushed-apple scent suffuses his nostrils. Leaping fish leave ivory arcs that slowly collapse, folding into themselves with balletic grace. Everywhere Sam senses transformation and fecund life while a billion invisible sperm-tadpoles snap their tails as they whip up and down the shining roller-coaster hills that have changed a dull, muddy forest into this alive, frenetic, gleaming paradise.

"Run, brother, run! Run, brother, run!"

Then Sam realizes his body created all of this. This glittering paradise came from him. He studies his own body, this powerful, hulking, heaving, massive, sperm-exploding body, and wonders how he could ever fear anything.

"I will go to Cartwright," he says confidently. Surely he can confront the town and all it represents. He shudders and a warm liquid floods his veins. He has never felt such relief. He will heal the world. Things are not so difficult in the end.

"Run, brother, run, my wonderful brother, my wonderful brother..."

He stumbles across the soft-sticky mounds and, standing completely still, opens his mouth to let out a laugh so loud, it echoes among the distant cliffs. What is he laughing at? He is laughing at Sonny and Cher, Veronika, Franz's obsession with hairstyle, his mother's glossolalia, Sue's honey-sweat—he laughs at everything that is life, his laughter celebrating all the illogical things that don't fit into a system and never will.

He changes the trajectory of his journey; instead of southeast, he heads northeast, toward Labrador. Over the following weeks, Sam races through the forests laughing at the top of his lungs. The sound fills the still air above empty meadows, vibrates the outstretched branches of pines, drowns out the roar of waterfalls, wakes grizzly bears from slumber, and makes coyotes cock their ears to the wind. The cry of "Run, brother, run" grows louder until Sue's voice and Sam's laughter intermingle, become one and the same sound.

In the evenings, Sam performs exercises to prepare his body for love-making with Franz. He practises kissing (something he'd once hated) by smooching deer lips, antelope ears, frog anuses, and the great, whiskered muzzles of sleeping bison. He improves his petting skills by necking with juniper bushes and pine tree trunks with such passion that the bark snaps and sap runs, or with such tenderness that the whole forest goes silent and swallows nest in his hair. In Zurich, with Franz beside him in bed, Sam slept poorly, so now he builds sleep tolerance by spending nights on rocky ground where chipmunks repeatedly scamper over him and acorns fall on his forehead. To improve oral sex skills, he shoves arm-thick tree branches down his throat to destroy his gag reflex. Then he grabs and twists his own genitals into a myriad of fascinating forms: sailor's knot, mandrake root, ballerina tutu, ticking metronome; and he ejaculates in lassoes, rainbow arcs, or machine-gun fire. Franz will be amazed by Sam's new prowess.

Sam is troubled that Franz's letter is becoming soiled and frayed. These sheets of paper are the scientific proof he lacked in Zurich, the incontrovertible facts written in Franz's own hand, without which he'd again be unanchored and drifting in conjecture. By the time he reaches Labrador, the writing will be illegible. He decides to briefly re-enter civilization.

Fent's Landing is a hamlet accessible only by floatplane. Sam arrives at dawn and creeps down an empty gravel road flowing between prim, wooden houses. In front of the general store, a cat stretches, yawns, and claws the air once with a paw. Sam glances into the window of the Blue Star restaurant; a waitress in a yellow jumpsuit has her back to him. He's startled by how attractive she looks, with her hourglass figure. He begins running, his wide feet slapping the ground; his breathing is loud and hoarse; he makes occasional grunts. What will he sound like if he speaks? He thinks of the lectures he once gave, those insipid balloons full of air.

He notices a hand-written sign taped to the inside of a storefront window: "Photocopies ten cents a sheet." The door is cheap plywood and easy to break down. Sam finds the copier at the back of the store. He nimbly presses the on button with his right claw. The machine hums to life. Sam unwrinkles the sheet and presses it against the glass. He reads a sign: "E-mail stations coming in June." So the world wide web, which he'd used for research at the university, would now be utilized by the general public; it will kill the romance of letter writing.

Sam snatches a plastic bag from the garbage can and puts his eight backup copies in it. He turns and sees, in a cracked mirror, his grinning wolf's head. His black eyes glitter like polished marbles, his triangular ears are raised, and steam streams through his snout's nostrils. Not a bad face, though unusual. He spreads his cracked lips and a tongue creeps out that dangles a foot long.

He's enjoying himself here. The stacks of paper remind him of his old life. As he picks at lice crawling in his stomach hair, he remembers his Bunsen burners, microscopes, plastic cubes, and books—walls of books within which every dimension of the world's surface was recorded. All that is beyond him now. He is running into a world without numbers and the obsessive analysis of details. The world is spinning, but he can put one foot forward and walk without falling. Gravity is his friend. It keeps us from touching the sky, yet without it, we would drift helplessly in a sea of air. Such seems his sister's fate. Reminded of her, he finds a fax machine in the shop and sends the Cartwright post office a fax for Sue.

Sam eyes the staff photo. How attractive everyone is in their green polyester uniforms. If they were here, he wouldn't ignore them, as he'd once snubbed people like Heidi, but, surrounded by the hum and click of the photocopiers, would have an orgy with everyone. The more Sam hears the fire roar, the more insignificant people's appearances become. Lips, toes, dicks, foreheads, anuses, and ear lobes are equally desirable to him now.

On the street, a boy aims a slingshot at a telephone pole. He turns, sees Sam, drops his weapon, and runs away, wailing. Sam hurries along the road, the plastic bag flapping. If captured now, he'd be taken to a zoo. He finally feels safe hidden behind a protective wall of foliage.

The day Sam crosses the border into Québec, everything changes. The air becomes full of the scent of baked ham and pea soup, the sound of laughter and fiddle music. People in toques sing around campfires; they hail his welcome and offer him drinks of *Le caribou*. They assume he's costumed himself as *Le Bonhomme Carnaval*'s mythological cousin, *Le Chien Fou Carnaval*. When they realize it's not a costume but his own flesh and hair, they're impressed.

"You really go to the end, *hein*?"

"You take a party-time seriously." His harsh voice so distorts his French that they think he's from a faraway country.

When he says he was in Ontario, they reply, "How sad. The people there are terrible. Here we may be poor but we're friendly." They offer him venison pie and maple syrup fudge and then hold hands with each other and dance in large circles. Afterwards, everyone takes off their clothes and has sex in the snow, all the while saying, "See, we're not Puritan like in Ontario. We're sensual 'cause we're Latin. It's so much better here."

The Québec countryside is dotted with gleaming crucifixes (his mother would like those), but people throw snowballs at them and say, "We hate the crucifixes but keep them for historical purposes. We express our hatred with snowballs because we're not hypocritical and we're sensual because we're Latin."

In forest clearings, people scream and push each other about in the snow, outraged over the pronunciation of words.

"It's not 'ee', it's 'oo.'"

"It's not 'oo', it's 'ee.'"

"But we're not afraid to fight openly," they tell him, "because we're sensual and we're Latin."

Then they look at each other, take off all their clothes again, and have sex in the melting snow beside the roaring campfire. People are always having sex in this place, and Sam thinks that when he's reunited with Franz, they can return and live here. Québec's forests have more rock than he has ever seen.

❧

Finally he enters Labrador and comes upon a narrow cement road. On each side a person stands facing him. My God. Sonny and Cher. They are holding a large net between them. But the doctors are no longer singers. They've shed their sequined outfits and are wearing the same grey tunics they had on the first day Sam met them. In silence, they look him square in the eye.

Sam studies Doctors #1 and #2 and sadly shakes his head. "No," he says. "You want me to return so I can rechristen you Sonny and Cher and give you the identities you desire. But if you can't imagine who you truly are, then no one else can do it for you."

The doctor who was once Cher has tears in his eyes. If he were wearing eye-liner, it would be running. Sam steps forward, swipes one clawed finger in the air, and slices their net in two. The strands fall and lay at their feet like piles of intestines. Sonny and Cher vanish into the air. Then Sam looks up and sees the ocean. The sea level is higher than it should be. Clouds are forming on the distant horizon. This coast is the spot where 200 million years ago the North American plate joined the Eurasian landmass. Sam falls to his knees and begins crying.

The Earth does have value. He sees now that he should fight for its survival.

Sam heads northward and one week later ascends a steep purple cliff and looks down at the town of his childhood. Cartwright's white wooden cubes lie scattered across the rounded peninsula. To the north, the placid cove speckled with boats, and beyond is the curve of the beach where he'll meet Sue.

He notices the statue of Mary whose clothes and skin are the same white stone, making it impossible to tell if her clothes are part of her body or her body part of her clothes. At his feet, broken steel animal traps lie like severed jawbones.

He climbs down the hill and hurries across a wooded lot. Through the foliage he glimpses the rows of clapboard houses on sloping streets, his mother's white-washed church with its delicate needle-like steeple, the red-bricked library. Somehow he expected to be horrified, furious, or mournful, but Cartwright stands silent and unreal, as if behind glass.

He discovers a boulder covered with dead bees. At the end of Maple Road, he scurries into his parent's backyard. Right away he knows no one's home. At this hour, his father is usually listening to fiddle music on the radio and his mother clanging pots and pans. He warily approaches the house, glances through a window. His room hasn't changed; there is his poster of a windmill on one wall, his stack of *Scientific Americans* in the corner. His bed's been left unmade, as if time stopped when he left home. His family refused to believe he'd grow up. That was always the problem. Through the living room window, he sees a cylindrical glass containing a yellow liquid. Its presence bothers him, so he leaps over to the tree and begins digging. He still feels guilty for burying his mother's damned crucifix. He lifts up Christ, brushes dirt from his eyes, and drops him in the mailbox. Sam patters back into the bush, glad he didn't have to confront his mother.

Nearby, he hears a man's voice: "Caesar ran barking in here and I never seen him since."

Sam races into the woods, runs in the direction of the beach. He pauses by his old school, observes the track, the football fields. He hears music, sees men in blue jackets milling in the parking lot. One of their silly dances. Sunlight catches the golden hair rising on top of a woman's head and Sam feels a tug at his heart. In his mind, wooden-legged men do can-cans.

He finally arrives at the cold windy beach, but no one is there.

❧

He has been waiting behind the hardwood shrub for hours. Fuzz-dappled leaves tickle his cheeks. Waves crash rhythmically, hypnotically. Before Sam are the bare components of the universe: water, sky, and earth. Yet whatever the universe contains, it does not include his sister. He decides to sneak back into town and find her. Then he hears a distant roar, rumblings, the sound of an avalanche, screams. A percussive pounding like fingers on a tabletop—and like a bullet, an object shoots into his line of vision.

Not having seen Sue for eight years, he has no idea what she'll look like, but he quickly concludes that this tall naked woman covered with red dots and black needles isn't her. The woman crouches at the ocean's edge, pulls at her hair, and pounds the earth so savagely, Sam is terrified. Best to head back into the woods, but then he hears a voice. "Sam, you forsook me … you forsook me." My God—Sue's voice? It's Sue?

His whole body convulses. Steadying himself he calls out, "Sue, is that you?"

The woman stops moving.

"It's me. Sam." His voice is clearer than he expected. "I'm here."

She darts around but sees only a quivering bush.

"Please don't be afraid. I look different, but I feel great." He takes a deep breath and steps forward.

Sue shrieks once, covers her mouth with both hands.

"I've had an eventful trip. I see you've had your own adventures. You'll have to tell me about them when we get on the ship."

She bats her eyelids twice. The wrinkles on her forehead smooth out. Sue takes one step and embraces the monster. The side of her head presses against his furry ears. Sam feels her fingertips nestling in the small of his back. The high-pitched ringing in his ears has stopped and a syrup-scented silence descends to drown out all but the sound of their breathing.

PART FIVE

❧ *Water*

When Sam and Sue boarded the ship, they didn't know that their Mother was waiting inside. They thought they could sever their links to the past and remake themselves completely. They thought they could simply look in the mirror and say, "I want a thinner face, a more aquiline nose, eyebrows that don't join like Boris Karloff's but are lightly sketched curves." They didn't realize that their Mother was crouching in the darkness at the bottom of the ship and would unexpectedly spring up like the monster in an amusement-park funhouse and, with razor-tipped fingers, shred the tender buds of their freedom. How do I know? Hearken, Reader! Their Mother is narrating this section!

There it is! Ha! I spit in your eye! You think that everyone shall have a story but me? You think I want to be the sourpuss everyone laughs at? "I may not be perfect," you say, turning to the next chapter, "but at least I'm not like *her*."

A pox on thee! I am not a bitter old hag and refuse to play the villain. My desires are as real as anyone's, my needs as legitimate, and if you think I'm but a stuck-up Jesus-freak, then it's you who wear horse-blinders to bed. Remove them and behold! Realize there's more than meets the eye! Read between the lines for a change, you stupid little ass wipe!

I am not the wicked stepmother in this fairy's tale. Sam and Sue were once in mine body and of mine body, for mine body created them. I gave birth to all the major characters in this book (except Franz, that perverted cockatoo; if he ever poked his hairsprayed head out of my vagina, I'd ram him back in again crying, "He's not mine! Wait a few minutes and somebody else will come out.")

Everything on Earth cometh of me. I am the salt of our springs and the rock of this Earth. My blood floweth in my children's veins and the arc of my bone is the contour of their skulls. I am their Mother, and God is our Father, our *real* Father, not that silly man tangled up in nets on the ocean.

How horrid to be marooned, as we all are, in this atheistic century!

May Mary shower us with sweet milk from her tender swollen breasts!

When thou standest on the ground, thou art standing upon mine body. Put thy head into the sky and thou brushest against mine cerebral cortex. Each breath thou takest is of oxygen from mine nostrils; the food thou eatest was plucked from dirt wet with mine sweat, and the water thou drinkest is but mine urine that evaporated to the sky to return like God's rain into our open mouths.

You laugh at me, reader? Yea, I know you do. Yet I say hallelu. I cry, praise ye the Lord. "No one speaks like you," you whine. "You're not real; you're a stereotype, like someone on *Saturday Night Live*." Lo, each subculture hath its own language, and verily I am not a parody. You don't believe me? Get with the program, crackpot! Take thine head out of thine arse.

Oh, I have tried to restrain my desires to mould my children. Yes, my own hands have maimed them. But I cannot help it. A Monster rises within me and I give in.

Twenty-eight years ago, I spread my legs and Sam fell from my vagina like a rock. He had a hard head and left a dent in our linoleum that endures to this day, but I picked him up (Lord, he was heavy), washed him off, and as his lips closed over my breast, he sucked so loudly that everyone, my husband, the midwife, and Pastor Benson, gasped. Praise God and Jesus whose golden hair gleams in the sunlight and contains no dandruff whatsoever! I didn't know the Lord back then. My husband—what a wiener he is—still gave me flowers for my hair and sat on bended knees to sing me "The Sailor's Hornpipe." He said I was beautiful and I beheld him, a warm fluid flooding my limbs. The angle of his hat set off his butcher's-knife jawbone; his eyes flashed like sunlight on fishing tackle.

Yet as my husband examined the baby swaddled in my arms, I noticed he had a crevice in his forehead, which I resented, for it divided a space that should be unbroken. Also, his head was spherical—I prefer cube-heads—and his hairline had receded, so his face resembled a swollen cabbage. What had happened to my husband?

I feared he would claw this new life from my hands and hurl it into the sea or place it amongst forest rocks so similar in shape to it that Sam would be lost to me forever. Perhaps I should have offered love, not complaints. Regrets follow regrets, but I had to feed the Monster within. I turned my back to him.

The next day he went out in his rowboat and, though he'd return for meals, he never leered at me again. Pastor Benson said that he'd found a mermaid—could that happen? Outside, the sky was so vast, I felt tinier than a freckle on my dear boy's face. God descended to comfort me. He filled me; my bone marrow stirred like a sludge-filled river flowing, blood pooled in tight knots beneath my skin, and my vocal chords, long clenched tight as fists, unknotted, and I sang. How glorious to hear one's own voice for the first time! Yea, the mind of Jesus is a gleaming jewel and the mind of Satan is a mushy turd!

One night in a stupor of drunkenness and rage, my husband came to my bed. He touched my shoulder, and I said, "All right," for now I saw God's will in everything. Thus, Sue was begat. Again my husband dragged his nets to the sea. When my daughter was born, the stillness in our kitchen was broken, and a wind knocked the sugar dish from the shelf and sprayed sink water on the floorboards. She had a full head of hair that riffled like seaweed underwater. The first time she saw her brother, she cried out an explosion of sound—what word did she say? Sam smiled at her and punched his thigh. When I wrapped my arms around my children, their backs became shields, as mine was to my husband, as the house walls were to the steep valley slopes, and as those slopes were to the outside world. Shields against shields against shields. At church Sue never listened to sermons but huddled in the pew, ears cocked toward the wind-shook windows. "Rattle, rattle," she'd hiss, "rattle-rattle."

At twelve years old, Sam said to me, "I hate your church. Going inside is like entering the honeycomb of your brain." I burst into tears. His sister cackled, and the two of them joined hands and ran shrieking out the door. I knew then I'd failed and had turned my children against me. Lord protect me from Satan whose skin is scaly and his breath foul no matter how many Certs he chews!

I have repeating nightmares, and when I wake, the bed sheets are so wet with sweat that, wrung out, they fill buckets. In one dream Sam is swimming and cuts his feet on knives hidden like coral reefs in a ketchup sea. He doesn't know he's bleeding for his blood is the sea's colour and he continues to swim, bleed, and shed his skin until he dissolves into the ocean red.

In another dream, my daughter lies in a tub of mayonnaise that soothes the blackfly bites she got running in the hills. I chide her, "Get up for church; today is the Easter Cantata." She ignores me. The mayonnaise hardens and she stops breathing, still grinning. Workmen try to chisel her out but can't tell where she and the mayonnaise begins and ends, and they hack her to bits. The tub is full of white-beige rubble; each piece resembles the meringues sold by the Ladies' Auxiliary, except some are crunchy with bits of bone and others have eyes staring out.

I have dreamt of my children turning blind, having mustard fights. I have seen their skin on fire beneath storm clouds that rain salsa. God hath no place in the liquids of this world. He baptized with water, not honey or drinkable yogurt. My children shall be saved by the lithe resourcefulness of the body. But whose body? Satan huddles behind my sewing kit and, in an unexpected moment, I'll shove a needle into his eyeball!

The day I intercepted Sam's fax to Sue, I knew that God was on my side. I read Sam's letter in one breath, put it back into the envelope, resealed it with melted candle wax and re-deposited it in the mailbox for Sue. If we were all going on a trip, she needed to know the details.

I emptied my bank account and purchased a ticket, sensing that I was embarking on a doomed voyage. What could be achieved by following my children? I imagined their surprise upon meeting me on board, their cries of horror and outrage. I could scream, shout, thrash about on the floor, and pull my hair out by the roots, but I'd already tried these strategies and they hadn't worked. When Satan is picking his nose, may his finger get stuck and remain up one nostril for eternity!

I know I over-control my children. I choke them to compensate for my life's emptiness. A week before our departure, I carried a jugful of water up the winding path that led to the highest peak on the steepest hill. The humid air was a hot hand pressing my face; water beads sprouted like diamonds on my forehead. In an air full of sea salt, the cry of gulls, and the sound of waves pummelling rocks, I knelt before the Virgin. Her body is solid stone, her legs concealed inside a rippling rock dress. A stained hood swirls around her alabaster face, and her pupil-less eyes are beacons that gaze east toward Africa and Christ's birthplace. Her nostrils flare. Mary's unblemished face shows calm, but her hands clutch each other so tightly that the veins bulge like snakes.

I poured clear water over her massive boots and placed the empty jug beneath her. "Mary, I don't know what to do. I bully and scold my children. Why can't I let them grow up and trust you'll look after them? I long to bring them to Your Grace, return them to Our Fold, but Satan has coated Sue's body with the sticky mire of Earth and shoved rocks into Sam's saliva-dripping mouth. The world's ingredients are greater than I. When I polish the bathroom taps, the cleanser corrodes my nail polish; I hold clip-on earrings near my lobes and they snap like leeches into my skin. If I let my children go their merry way, they'll turn into a couple of sickos and will reject you and my love forever. What should I do?"

I stared at the bare stone surface of her shins for hours. The winds died down. Mary's white lips didn't part, but amazingly, I heard her words! Her voice was as clear as a dewdrop on an erect blade of grass.

"You have been a faithful servant," she intoned. "You have prayed, you have sung to the Lord. You have cooked, cleaned, and washed windows for the Lord. You have baked brownies for the church bazaar, good brownies with almonds in them, a highly original recipe. But remember: God is stronger than the world. God releases the enslaved from enslavement. Baptize your children with my wetness, and God will fill them. You shall then bid them farewell, and they will enter adulthood, the mark of your love imprinted on them forever. Remember that one day all our bodies shall be One, and the Kingdom of Heaven shall reign on Earth just as it did that split-second long ago when seed touched egg in your womb."

"What do you mean 'wetness'?" I asked.

Some people might accuse me of having delusions, but what happened next was so concrete that I shall register it in the *Eucharistic Book of Miracles*. From between Mary's legs squirted one, two, three times, a yellow liquid that filled the jug on the ground. I lifted the bottle toward Mary's impassive face and gazed at the fluid swirling in sunlight. A nectar of God more sacred than the waters of Lourdes.

A horn wailed and I beheld, far below, a flag-decked ship that tapped against the harbour dock. The boat's sides sloped gracefully from the water like two outstretched hands. On its deck stood three squat, symmetrical stacks. Sea water flickered like a million winking eyes. At that moment, the ship, the dock, and the water were the most beautiful sight I'd ever seen. I knew then I would succeed. My children would remain in my life, for God knew I couldn't be without them.

All hail the Lord of Lords whose throne is a real throne and not the toilet some people mean when they say "throne"!

✿

The day of my departure I combed Sue's hair, then watched her stumble up the street. I wanted to cry. I hurried down the hill. If I ran into a neighbour, I'd say I was visiting my sister on Goose Island. Of course, my husband was out on his boat. I left no note to explain my absence. I'd spent a lifetime worrying about him. Now let him fret about me. Still, the guilt of those who abandon filled me. I told myself that I respected my children's wishes and was simply embarking on this trip because the Virgin Mary had commanded it. Yet as I approached the harbour, my cheeks felt hot with shame.

At three a.m., alone in the dark, I watched the ship arrive; it would leave again in two hours. Luckily Sam and Sue weren't here yet and didn't catch me boarding. The white-uniformed guard glanced at my passport and third-class ticket. He nodded. "Level Two. Corridor One."

Then I crossed the arched bridge between dock and boat and descended into the bowels of the ship, far deeper than I wanted to go. (I'd asked for the cheapest room.) I headed down the dimly lit halls and entered a small cabin containing a cot covered with a foam mattress and a wafer-thin blanket. I sat nervously on the bed knowing that, at this hour, the passengers who'd boarded in St. John's or New York were asleep. Now was the time to explore the ship.

Beside my room I discovered a square archway above a rectangular counter. Behind hung rows of jackets, dresses, and pants wrapped in cellophane. A hand-painted sign read "Weldon's Complementary Dry-Cleaning."

My flat-soled shoes padded softly as I continued down the hall, one hand flitting over the handrail. My other hand half-covered my face. Sam might be already on board and could catch me here. I also worried he and Sue would miss the ship; the whistle would blow and I'd be dragged from my old life and thrust into something new I never wanted. I made quiet, careful steps, almost afraid that if I stamped my feet forcefully or opened a door too suddenly, the vessel would split apart.

I discovered a mailroom, cook's quarters, a water purification centre, and several storage rooms. I liked the spareness of the corridor but not the rows of harsh and flickering fluorescent lights. There were only two directions to go, forward or back; no turns, detours, or cubbyholes. I felt as exposed as if on a fashion-show runway.

At the end of the hall was a door marked "Warning: Boiler Room. Do Not Enter." Of course I went in. There, a steel cylinder trembled, gurgled, and spat on frog-leg haunches. I enjoyed the clatter and noise of this room. If somebody opened the door, he'd be distracted by this shuddering metal monstrosity and not notice me. In Cartwright, I felt as though I towered into the sky like a colossus, casting such shadows that those below didn't know if my body or the Earth's rotation caused the arrival of night that stained the sky black. Yet I was not just any old colossus, but one with hips that swung and fingers that snapped, with Yvresse-scented, bouncy-curled hair, and thrusting, jelly-jiggle boobs that poked you in the eye. You silly reader, I am not a hung-up prude, and if my husband had known what was good for him, he could've had this throbbing, more-luscious-than-Lovelace body to have and hold.

However, on this ship, I needed invisibility. Behind the boiler, a metal ladder ascended into a narrow cleft in the ceiling. I put one hand on a metal slat, the steel beautifully cold against my palm. As I climbed the ladder, the boiler made *hubba-hubba* sounds. Entering the opening, I felt like mist ascending. I reached a landing that connected to two catwalks that went in opposite directions. I followed a second ladder to discover other catwalks, another landing, and more ladders. Hallelu! The entire inner framework of the ship was accessible to me.

At the top was a squat metal door. I pushed its lever forward and walked out onto an empty, windy deck; I saw railings and, beyond them, the lights of Cartwright. Pipes rose on each side of me, and a swinging rowboat teetered over my head.

I re-entered the ship and returned to my cabin. Alone in the dark, I reassured myself that Sam would be on board and he'd succeed in getting Sue on too. He was a genius; he hadn't won the Labrador science prize for nothing. But this could be a trick. What if he and Sue had no intention of leaving and the fax was sent to get rid of me? I remembered combing Sue's hair; her hands shook, her eyes watered. Such excitement was hard to feign, especially for Sue, who was a terrible actress and only good at playing herself.

My children would be here and they'd be miserable together. They'd often directed their chronic resentment at me, but now they'd aim it at each other. I especially pitied my daughter, who had fewer gifts than her brother. How I longed to take both my dear children in my arms and kiss them—but they'd pull away disgusted. May Mary shine upon my offspring with her beautiful uncapped teeth!

Wood creaked and the ship rocked. I reached into my purse, touched the bottle of Mary with my fingertips, and discovered it was warm. I lay down and tried to sleep. I would discover things I hadn't known about my children. Perhaps terrible things. For a moment I wished I weren't here but safely at home.

A horn-blare shook my eardrums, and I sat bolt upright in bed. The porthole, round as the dot on an "i," was filled with sunlight.

I looked out and beheld leaping waves as we pulled away from shore. I was leaving Labrador. For the first time in my life. May God bless Cartwright while I'm away. May God smite the evil-doers of Labrador—especially rock-music groups with names like Donny and the Dicky-Demons or Lucy and the Lucifettes. Despite everything, I was amazed at my own courage. Had we crossed the line separating Canadian waters from the open sea?

Suddenly in the centre of the porthole appeared a bright white dingy. My husband stood in it, his torso covered in the vein-like cords of his nets. Arms outstretched, he spoke to the water. Did he talk with his mermaid? Then he leapt into the sea. Was he trying to catch fish with his bare hands? He and his boat passed out of view.

Feeling shaken, I pressed my face to the glass, closed my eyes, and prayed long and hard. My husband was decent but a fool. Should I have concentrated more on his decency than his fool-hardiness? I had much to be thankful for today. I had the privacy of this isolated room and its unvisited corridor. I had the dry cleaner's with the army of hanging clothes. I had the skeleton of passages I'd discovered.

I opened the small box of Halloween prosthetic devices that I'd bought at Cartwright's One and Only Joke Shop. I spent the next hour before the mirror, carefully attaching a plastic hooked nose and a square chin to my face. I used flesh-coloured putty to seal the creases. I was still recognizable, so I covered my cheeks with lumps of more putty, completely distorting my face shape. I coated the creases with beige-hued skin makeup, then inserted the contact lenses that changed my eyes from blue to brown.

God was clearly helping me. My transformation amazed me, but would my children be fooled? My height, body size, and voice could give me away, but I reasoned that they'd never expect to meet me here. The underhandedness of the disguise troubled me. I was obeying the Monster within, but God had offered no other choices.

I put an ear to the door, then slowly opened it. The hall was still empty. I scurried along the rug, ducked into the dry cleaner's, and rang the bell. No one appeared. I waited thirty seconds. Perfect. I rushed to the rack of clothes and flipped through as if it were a giant deck of cards. My fingers skipped over business suits, lingered on skirt pleats, skimmed through silk blouses, cleaner's aprons, and cocktail dresses whose tiny sequins shone like shark's teeth. I touched nurse uniforms, security-guard jackets, psychedelic satin shirts, and a wedding gown so bright a white it hurt my eyes. Which identity would provide access to my children's lives?

I snatched a gold-trimmed, brass-buttoned military uniform hanging in the first row. I undid my cotton dress, which slid from my body and lay in a puddle on the floor. I found a white shirt and black tie. The long jacket covered the extra fabric of the trousers (they were too big on me). I wrapped a belt around the outside of the jacket and fastened it, then grabbed the matching hat from a ledge. The front brim jutted like a bird's beak and sported a coin-like circle with the inscription "Canadian Navy." I stuffed my hair under the tight-fitting rim, clicked my heels together, brought three fingers to my temple, and barked, "Ten-hut." The rows of clothes hung mute. My Monster was satiated.

Suddenly I heard steps in the corridor. I ducked behind a mink stole. Someone clattered into the shop. A girl's voice said, "There has to be a blanket or something." Her voice was high-pitched and tinny. Sue's voice! God be praised! I nearly wept. She was answered with an indecipherable voice that sounded like bricks being dragged across concrete. Bits of mink dust travelled up my nostrils, tickling at my sinuses. I was going to sneeze.

"Help me find something," said Sue. "I can't do everything myself!" Right away I could see her profile; her nose curled outward like a lick of whipped cream, her auburn hair rippling to her shoulders. Yet what had happened to her? She was naked and her skin prickled with tiny black needles. She turned and I saw that a constellation of protuberances travelled all the way down her back and buttocks. It came to me in a thunderclap: bee stingers. The bees had turned on her. It took all of my self-control not to burst into laughter. So this is what her "freedom" added up to! Oh, but I was ashamed of my glee. Her skin didn't shine. Her honey had stopped flowing (I'd find out why later). Then I pitied my daughter. Yea, I would have plucked the pricks from her skin with my teeth.

Sue hurried away, and into the space where she'd been stepped a monster, a gorilla-donkey-ogre with eyes bulging like egg whites full of red spider-webs and beads of coal. Fangs protruded from its cracked lips, and his entire body was covered with frizzled hair, half-concealing skin the texture and colour of corrugated cardboard. Worst of all, a gigantic penis hung between his legs like a viper. His hand clasped a plastic bag overflowing with papers. He took the bell from the counter, sniffed it, then bit off the top button. He stepped away, and I scrutinized the mutilated bell. What was Sue doing with this demon? And how did they manage to get on the ship looking like this? I remembered Mary's bottle locked in my room and understood how necessary it'd be.

"How's this look?" Sue walked into my view. "It's so comfortable." She had put on my polka-dot dress. I rammed my upper teeth into my lips to stifle laughter. "Look. It twirls when I walk." Tears filled my eyes, my stomach cramped. Dust danced up into my sinuses, and I let out a loud laugh-sneeze-cry, "*Agaroo-ee!*"

Sue darted from view. In the tense silence, I realized I couldn't hide any longer. I nervously adjusted my hat and straightened my spine, then stepped forward. The clothes parted and closed behind me like doors sliding shut. But where was my dear child?

I observed four lower legs like tree-stumps below a row of clowns' costumes. I reminded myself to speak at as low a pitch as possible. "I see you, my friends," I spoke with a Mainland accent. "Come out. Don't worry. I won't tell anyone. I, like you, am a stowaway here."

Neither the hairy nor the red, swollen feet moved. Did Sue sense who I was? Please God, help me, I silently cried.

"I am a soldier who has fled the army," I said. "I fled because"—because what?—"the fighting was very violent, and I wanted none of it. If you are castaways, let us be castaways together." How difficult it was to speak so low. My throat hurt. I began to cough. "I have a cold." The four feet remained motionless as goalposts. "Come now. If you stay here any longer, the workers will arrive and all shall be lost."

At last they shuffled out, both looking at the floor. The monster lifted his head and glanced at my belt buckle, which I defensively covered with one hand. Sue didn't recognize me! Was I under a spell? Perhaps the prosthetics and makeup I'd bought in Cartwright's joke shop were magic; God had directed my hand to the supernatural packet!

"I've been here two days," I continued. "I boarded in Maine and have suffered alone. I wanted to make friends with people who'll help me and whom I can help." Sue raised her head and stared at me. She accepted that I was who I said! Oh, how I rejoiced. I felt the urge to speak in tongues but commanded the Holy Spirit: Not now. Later.

"Why would you wear a uniform if you've deserted and don't want people to know you're a soldier?" Sue asked. I hate to say it but my daughter's intelligence always takes me by surprise.

"That's a good question." The pitch of my voice rose. "I decided to wear my uniform so that people like you would not believe I was a deserter." God, forgive my lies, for I told them because I felt so alone.

Sue whispered to the beast, then said to me, "Help us, then. We need something to cover him so people won't freak when they see him."

She lifted a folded sheet from underneath the counter and turned to the monster. "Stay still." He didn't move as she draped it around his body. She fastened the edges together with pins.

"Hold this end," she said to me, gesturing toward the fabric draped over his shoulder.

I glimpsed the tangled hair on the monster's neck. He stank of tar and manure. Did he have lice? I studied my own hand, which seemed astonishingly clean. Lord protect me, I muttered, pressing my fingertips into the cloth. I could feel the warmth of his body through the fabric, his pulse throbbing into my hand. He kept his head lowered as Sue pinned together the ends of the sheet dangling beneath his groin. The hair on the nape of his neck was extremely thick. It must be itchy there. For a moment I felt sorry for the beast. He was like an unloved puppy returned to the pound. His breathing was a harsh, sandpapering sound. Sue abruptly flicked the sheet out from beneath my pressing finger and for a second my fingertip lay directly on the sticky skin laced with steel-wool hair. "Ahhh!" I cried and snatched back my hand.

Sue eyed me sharply.

"Excuse me." I lowered my voice. "Excuse me. I was afraid you'd rip the sheet. We wouldn't want your friend walking around in ripped sheets, would we?"

Sue scrutinized the monster. "It looks great. No one'll notice you now." White fabric flowed over his head and body. His darting eyes were visible through a slit. Sue put gloves on his hands and socks on his paws. She said, "We'll tell people he's sun-sensitive."

When they were about to leave, I asked, "Where are you staying?"

"Down below."

"What are you eating?"

"We're not."

"Then, my new friends, you'll have to accompany me to the dining hall."

"What?!"

"Yes. You are officially a passenger now with your charming dress and your ... well-covered friend. Are you not going to eat?" Oh, I was clever! I applauded myself for my quick-wittedness. "All shall be well," I continued. "People will assume you're a paying guest. Why else would you be here? Stowaways are something from a fantasy story, and this is not fantasy but real life. I don't know where the dining hall is, but together we can find it." I reminded myself to stand straight. I offered her the crook of my elbow. "Shall we go? If you are seen with me, people will be less suspicious. You will seem more respectable."

Sue looked at me, then at the monster staring at the wall. She lowered her head, blurted, "Okay," and put her hand tentatively upon my arm. I felt like we were man and wife with our strange pet padding behind. Sue used her free hand to pluck out the stingers in her face as we walked. I tried to smile but was worried. Why wasn't Sam with Sue? Was he hiding somewhere or had he missed the ship? And what or who was this creature?

"How did you two get on board?" I asked lightly.

Sue said, "A guy was wheeling a box of canned chowder onto the ship. We sneaked from the bushes, and dumped the tins out of another box, threw them into the harbour, then climbed inside the box. Later the man wheeled us on board."

Did Sam get on at the same time?

We climbed several levels until we were in a beige-carpeted lobby. Gold-framed mirrors reflected light from a huge chandelier of shimmering glass tears. Sue's grip on my arm tightened. We passed a cluster of men staring into their day-planners. I remembered to take long strides. I kept my hips as level as a tray carrying glasses that could slide off and shatter.

At the end of the lobby was an arched entranceway and a sign: "Welcome, Remston Batteries Inc. Complimentary brunch served six a.m. to nine a.m." Good. At least one meal each day was free. I didn't have enough money to buy us three meals a day.

Sue stopped picking at her face. She squinted through the doorway at the expanse of tables encircled by people in business suits. I patted her hand and mumbled, "All shall be well." I was speaking to myself more than to her. Sue's mouth was a horizontal line.

We entered the dining room. The sound of clinking knives and forks competed with the voices of men shouting. "Tokyo stocks won't go down!" "The target audience for transistors responds to print ads ..." I scanned the crowd for Sam but didn't see him. Few people glanced at the white-clad being lumbering behind us; most seemed too interested in themselves to notice. We found a small empty table in a quiet corner.

It wouldn't make sense that Sam's plan had failed. Putting on a brave face, I said, "We'll have a jolly good breakie this morning. Some good, old-fashioned flapcakes and sausage will put grease on our lips and hair on our chests. Or at least on my chest. I would never imply that you'd have a hairy chest, Miss."

Sue hissed at the monster, "Sit down!"

He dropped onto a chair.

"Yes, the brekkie-eckkie is going to be splendi-endi," I said, with great gusto.

The beast had removed one glove and a talon rested on the edge of a plate.

Sue said, "If you do that, people will notice!"

Then he spoke in a hideous, hoarse voice. "I've spent years fixating on the surface of life and not seeing what's below. Don't be as I've been, Sue." The sheet accidentally fell from his face, revealing his blunt snout and dripping fangs.

"Be careful, Sam!"

His name was like a rock smashed into my forehead. It took a whole minute before I could speak. "What did you say his name was?"

The beast's thick, green tongue flicked like a windshield wiper across his blood-spittled fangs.

"He's Sam, my brother. Please, tell him he has to cover his face!"

I was going to start crying. I would go into hysterics. My body automatically stood up. "I have to"—down, voice, down!—"go to the washroom." With a will of its own, my body hurled itself across the carpet whose fronds now seemed to be a thousand ululating tongues. I told myself to walk with long strides and stiff legs, but my torso twisted, writhed, and tossed above buckling legs. I was so upset I almost went into the women's washroom, but swerved and charged straight through the door sporting a Gumby stick-figure. Three men adjusted their ties before the mirror. I bent over the sink, splashed water on my face, retreated to a cubicle, and shut and locked the door. I pulled my pants to my ankles so no one would get suspicious and hid my crotch behind one hand.

So my beloved son had become a monster. My brilliant son with his astounding intelligence, who'd partially redeemed our family. What had they done to Sam at that hospital? What did he do to himself? I imagined every possible scenario: they grafted ape genes into his skin; he acquired an infectious disease, one of the African ones, and became possessed; or, while fleeing through the forest, he'd met a clan of sasquatch, foolishly slept in their beds, ate their food, and shared their toothbrushes. Whatever had happened, Satan had embraced him. He was farther from me than I had imagined. Maybe I had already lost him for good.

I closed my eyes, opened my mouth, and the Holy Spirit descended and entered me. The imprisoned words burst forth from my windpipe and filled the air. My voice rose and I revelled in the sound—I didn't care who heard me; luckily the toilet kept running and Muzak played loudly.

When finished, I wiped tears from my cheeks and thanked God for bringing me peace. The solution to the problem was simple. In soldier's guise, I'd find out all the information required and then invite Sam and Sue to my room where I'd baptize them with Mary's urine. Before leaving the men's, I stuffed a wad of toilet paper into the crotch of my panties; it bulged impressively. I pushed open the door and stood before the rows of chattering men in dark suits. With deliberate indiscretion I reached into my pants and moved the Kleenex from my right side to my left, removed my hand, and gave my hips an abrupt little shake. I straightened my hat and strutted into the room, completely secure in the world of men.

The waiter walked away from our table just before I arrived. Sam had put the sheet back over his face.

"We ordered you the English breakfast," Sue said.

"Very good. I love that. You've got me down pat."

Sam was scraping the paint off a teacup with a talon. I couldn't bear to look at him.

From the loudspeakers came a *rappa-rappa-rappa*. A fresh-faced man stepped up to a microphone. "Good morning, ladies and gentlemen." Diners applauded. "Organizing this conference was a challenge, and we hope you enjoy it. A conference at sea is an incredibly original idea! We needed a full week of discussion before meeting our conglomerate counterparts in London, so we decided to do it en route! Now we've officially started our North Atlantic tour!" People cheered. "Such innovative thinking is at the root of the success of Remston Batteries. Just last week, CEO Benson said to me, 'Youngster, when I was your age, the world was an oyster. I can't eat oysters now because the juice stains my dentures, but I hope that when you're my age, you'll eat oysters all day, even if your teeth turn green permanently because'"—the man's voice wavered; he was becoming emotional—"'you deserve them.'" He was going to start crying.

A woman shouted, "You're a real trooper, Hank."

Reviving, Hank yelled back, "Yes I *am* a trooper, and when we arrive in Bristol, those Brits are gonna love our fine products!"

The crowd hurrahed and clattered their cutlery.

Our food arrived. Taking a utensil in each hand, I asked Sue, "So, why are you here?"

She looked at me warily. "Because I want to be here."

"Want to be here? What do you mean by that?" I put a salty piece of bacon in my mouth and munched loudly.

Sue lifted a piece of toast, held it level before her face as if balancing a marble on top. "I had to leave where I was. That's all."

"Where are you going?" I countered cheerfully. I sliced my ham-circle in half.

Sam burst out, "Switzerland." He clutched a greasy sausage in each trembling hand; froth splattered from his mouth onto the tablecloth as he spoke. "When I left Zurich, I thought I had been forced to leave, but it turns out I left of my own corrupted volition."

My poor son. I was going to start weeping. Luckily Sue distracted me. "My town in Labrador was awful. I hated everything there. The kids, the school, my mother." Surely she didn't realize the weight of the word "hate." She was speaking with adolescent bravado, but still I felt wounded. Her eyes reddened. She swallowed round a lump in her throat. She was not honest about me.

A man at the mic said, "How great to see so many company-men and women in one room."

I continued, "This mother of yours," was it my imagination or was the ship rocking? "she can't have been that bad." I spoke each word as notes in a descending scale, "Because, she, gave, birth, to, you."

"Gave birth?" Sue's eyebrows raised. "No. She's not my real mother at all."

Restraint. I had to learn restraint, for at that moment I wanted to scream. I know her idiotic story about a honeycomb mother in the sky. I stared at my daughter's bulbous head. The stories she tells are clouds of mist, not rooted in flesh and blood. I'd heard Sue blubbering at her open window. "Come Mother, come!

I want to touch your drops of sweetness." Hiding in our alder bushes, I flung a rock that bounced off the house. She gasped, shut the window, and turned off the light. That's her sky mother for you. Faced with the slightest opposition she disappears like a vanishing ring of smoke.

"So why is your brother going to Switzerland?" I asked.

Sam gnawed on the tip of his fork. When he removed it from his mouth, two prongs were missing.

"Who knows?" Sue said. "I thought he'd come along to help me, but he has other things on his mind." She studied a patch of skin on her forearm now cleared of stingers.

"But why must he leave Canada?"

Sue's eyes narrowed.

I was asking too many questions. "I ask this question because," I spoke in an off-hand, relaxed tone, "because I have fled many things myself. I fled the army and before that, I fled an office job. Before that, I fled my high school, grade school, I fled my kindergarten teacher, and I fled my nursery. I fled the hands of the doctor who pulled me out with forceps. The thing I regret most is fleeing my mother's womb. I should've stayed inside. The placenta walls fitted my body perfectly, her cervix was as comfy as an ottoman, and fallopian tubes hung like party streamers. I have fled many things in life but long to turn flight into its opposite, rest."

Sam blurted, "The opposite of flight is chase." He grabbed the salt shaker and began nibbling on it. Sue glared at him.

My children's disjointed lives lay in pieces before me and I could not find the thread to join them together. Lord, help me unravel these mysteries and return my children unto me. I remembered Mary's gold liquid and the miracles it promised.

As we headed out, I glanced at people talking together at the tables. It occurred to me that I'd never really had friends of my own. Religion is supposed to expand your life, but without my God I'm nothing. In Cartwright I could have developed other parts of myself.

Returning to the lower corridor, I said, "It has been wonderful meeting you both. I'd like to invite you to my cabin for a—" A what? For once my imagination failed me. "To look out my porthole. I have a fantastic view."

"We're very tired," Sue answered carefully. "We didn't sleep much last night."

"Let's meet later then. For a ... martini. Before dinner. It's on me."

Sue's forehead wrinkled. She needed me for my money and the appearance of normality I provided. She was terrified of arousing suspicion and probably feared that if she offended me, I'd report her. "All right. We'll meet. Later." My children scurried down the hall and ducked into a curtained space beside the boiler room.

I entered my room, locked the door, took off my hat, and let my hair fall down my back. Here no one could see me except— through the porthole—flying seagulls and those horrible, leaping swordfish. I cradled Mary's vial in my hands as if shielding a flame from the wind. Praise God for His succour and may those with dirty minds not snigger at the word "succour"!

I could hear the boiler room door opening and closing. The elevator bell rang incessantly as workers transported things out of storage rooms. From the dry cleaner's came a steady hum followed by a loud hiss. At noon a man began to shout and curse. He was the soldier who'd come to get the uniform I was wearing.

In the late afternoon things quieted down. I tucked my hair under my hat and crept into the hall. I lingered by the wall near where my children were hiding. From behind the curtain I heard a scraping sound like a stick rubbed across a washboard—Sam snoring—punctuated by occasional sighs. Sue was awake.

Soon Sam woke and he and his sister started giggling together. Through a crack in the curtain I observed Sam lying with his head in Sue's lap. She stroked his hair. They were happy together! For an instant, I felt superfluous. Something was growing inside them that I wasn't privy to. A waiter carrying a box appeared in the hall. Afraid he'd speak to me, I darted into my room. An hour later I returned to the curtain. My children were arguing, which reassured me.

Sue said, "This isn't what I expected. Everything's so difficult—and dangerous. And what's with that creepy soldier who keeps asking questions?"

Sam began to wheeze, a mountain of phlegm in his throat. "We don't have one identity but several, Sue. We change from one personality to others every second of our lives. Only submitting to passion keeps us safe."

My body curled like a comma over their hiding place, my ear as wide open as a trumpet-mouth.

"What do I have now?" continued Sue. "I no longer have Father and his dingy. And when we get where we're going, what'll I do there? Sam, quit picking your crotch, I'm talking to you! You're no help at all. You've been creating all these problems, and *I'm* the one who has to look after *you*. I'm afraid of you, Sam. Surely if you shaved off all that hair, things would be fine. Oh, quit reading those stupid letters! Why won't you even tell me anything? Why are you going to Europe? I told you all about what happened to me. You have to learn to trust somebody, Sam."

"Maybe you're right," he said. "Maybe I'm not on track."

A loud thump. She'd leapt to the floor. "I'm going to find out where the washroom is."

I flew like an arrow to the end of the hall and ducked into a closet; its shadowy shelves were lined with plastic goats with silver eyes and spring-necked puppies whose heads nodded as the ship rocked. In the corner, a bunch of naked Barbies lay like a pile of flesh-coloured kindling. I heard Sue's feet *pick-pock* past the closet. She was wearing my shoes. Then—*bam-bam-bam*— Sam's heavy feet followed her. When I saw him in the doorway, I noticed his hands were empty. Where was his bag?

I counted to ten, raced out into the hall, arrived at their empty hiding-place, knelt, and drove my head through the curtain. Piles of rope, pails, steel poles and, in the corner, a small rock beside a shopping bag. I snatched the bag, stuffed it into my pants, marched purposely down the hall, entered my room, and slammed the door with such a loud bang that I imagined the ship swayed from side to side and waiters fell onto trays as plates and cutlery slid off tables. The ship's horn gave a disgruntled blast.

I plucked one piece of paper from the bag: "*Eins, zwei, drei, vier*. Kraut-talk. The manly language. You wanted it, Sam. You wanted my tongue …"

I read further and the words entered my eye sockets, seeped into my bloodstream, and flowed to my brain, my heart. Colour drained from my cheeks. My lips quivered. I briefly experienced life without faith.

Now I understood the reason for this trip. That this Franz Niederberger—a pervert, a debauchee, a degenerate spawn of Satan, a pantywaist homo-boy—had breathed his rank, polluted air into the nostrils of my boy, poured poison-peppered saliva onto his tongue and with a touch of one suave, manicured fingernail laid waste to Sam's entire body.

Listen, reader. My son was never a skirt-twirling ball-sniffer, a flitting, pulp-sucking guava-girl, a purse-flapping fruitfly, a pirouetting, zipper-kissing Pansy McBride until Franz hurled his body against him like a comet that collided with the Earth.

My fingers began to flail. The Monster in me was let loose. I could crush Franz's testes like grapes, tear out his penis by the roots, and chop up the rest of his body into bite-sized chunks, each no bigger than a Shreddie that I'd scatter over all the oceans of this world. A storm of weeping descended upon me and I tumbled to the floor. No wonder Sam's pores sprouted hairs that curled like tarantula legs.

Suddenly in my mind's eye came a horrible vision: two ruler-hard penises crashing together like swords. They smashed against each other, one slanting upwards and the other down, or the tips struck—bam!—directly against each other. Then they clumsily whacked at the other's sides, poked a swinging ball, or rebounded from flabby stomach skin, shuddering but not vanquished. On and on they continued thrusting, thrashing, clobbering, jabbing.

It was a nightmare vision! Each penis desired that the other submit, but the skin surfaces were too solid, unyielding, and self-enclosed, so the dicks lunged, pummelled, and pounded at each other relentlessly. The sight was dizzying, repulsive, gut-wrenching, and exhausting.

I skimmed the other sheets, and they all told the same story. Then I thought: Lo, I shall defy ye, beast from Zurich. Lord protect us from Satan whose Hell-heated head is so hot, it melts any toupée you place on it!

I knew my actions had only pushed away those I love, but the Monster was too strong. I crammed every last page down the front of my pants, fled my room, and dashed up the metal stairs. In a daze I wandered the main deck. Where should I cast Franz's words? A woman with a beehive hairdo eyed the bulge in my pants and licked her lips. I couldn't cross my legs, for Franz's sentences were too long.

The ringing of the lunch bell was like a slap awakening me. The deck cleared. I limped toward the stern and stood alone at the back of the ship. I observed the strip of bubbling foam the vessel left in its wake. It swung back and forth like a tail. I undid my pants, and a gust lifted Franz's words from my drawers. The pages flew up and over the water. They hovered for a moment in mid-air, then fluttered down to be absorbed by the rolling waves. I zipped up my pants and sighed profoundly.

I kept the first sheet of the letter as criminal evidence of Sam's deeds, quickly folded and stuffed it into my jacket.

When I returned to our corridor, Sam was running in circles, squealing and rocking his head from side to side. Sue chased him, yelling, "I didn't take your papers. How could I have? I was with you! Could you at least tell me what was written on them?"

"What on Earth has happened?" I exclaimed.

Sue told me the story. Sam twisted his hands and moaned. I glanced at my groin freshly emptied of Franz's words. She implored, "Did you see anyone down here, sir?"

I shook my head. "How terrible indeed. To lose letters that mean so much. Absolutely dreadful."

Sue asked me where they stowed the garbage.

"On the third level at the bow."

"We can get them before they're dumped overboard."

"I wish you the best of luck," I called after them. When I re-entered my room, I laughed so loud, the people in the dining room above probably heard me. I stuffed the remaining page of Franz's letter into a hole in my mattress.

At dinner my children joined me at our table in the corner. Sam kept muttering and Sue tried to console him. "I'm glad you finally told me about Franz, Sam. And I'm really happy that you'll see him again. You shouldn't be afraid to tell me other stuff about you either." Sam gnawed on his dessert spoon. "Don't be so upset. Losing the letters is nothing. You still got that rock you can give him instead."

Sam put the spoon on the table. "Maybe you're right. Letters are less important than he is." He spoke more clearly now. Perhaps he was learning to control his bizarre vocal cords. "I will not get trapped in illusions. I must remember a diamond is being formed."

"That book you told me about is so neat, Sam. Mr. Potato

Head people who can remove and share each other's body parts! Just thinking of that gives me a weird happy feeling, and I don't even know why."

Soon Sue's arms were grazed clean of stingers. She bent her foot and picked at her dotted shins. Her tongue flicked lizard-like; her fingers leapt and darted so quickly, they appeared to be fluttering. By the time I finished my fruit cup, she'd cleared her whole kneecap.

"Ah," I said cheerfully. "I see that your skin is nearly free of its … ailment." I spoke lightly. "What is that all about anyway?"

"A little mistake I made." She stabbed a pineapple chunk with a toothpick. "At least *you've* noticed. Sam doesn't notice me any-more. I don't think he ever did. He's useless to me, really."

She's starting to understand the truth. She's alone in the world. My son is intelligent, but he isn't her saviour. "If you're feeling upset, come to my room this evening for a cognac."

Then I heard my husband's name. "Ted Masonty." A business-man sitting behind us said: "A fisherman from Cartwright. He was found floating dead in the wake of our ship. The town wants to blame us, but the captain swears he saw him jump into the water deliberately. They say it was suicide, but the corpse had a grin on its face that the undertaker couldn't remove."

"He must have purchased one of our products."

Sue asked, "Excuse me, did you say Ted Masonty?"

The man nodded; she turned abruptly and, trembling, clutched Sam's arm. My hand flew to my face. Then I saw a man running toward me. He was wearing a white T-shirt, track pants, and had a military haircut. "Gimme my clothes!"

I leapt from the chair and raced to the exit. I charged down to the lower level, dashed into the .boiler room, climbed the ship's inner skeleton, shot out on the deck, and was again at the V-shaped stern of the ship. I stripped to my underwear and threw the jacket, shirt, tie, pants, and boots overboard, then hid behind a rowboat.

A minute later the man ran on to the deck. When he saw his hat floating on the water, he cried, "Jesus Christ!" He didn't go back inside but stared at the water for over an hour. He left, and other people arrived, drinking from shot glasses.

Huddled in a ball, I shivered in the shadows. I watched the moon rise and cast a strip of light on the sea. The line's edges wavered and were crossed by abrupt slashes of darkness. At last alone and unobserved, I wept for my husband and me. His death was the end of a long process, and I felt half-responsible for the failure of our marriage. Yesterday I had at last left him alone in an empty house, but did that free him? He threw himself into the ocean to be with his ridiculous mermaid. That desire was always in him. I asked God to be gentle and forgive his faults, which were many. As were mine.

"We could bottle this seawater," a man said, "and sell it in the Sahara. The people there wouldn't know the difference."

A breeze fingered the hair on my forehead. Now was the proposed hour of my children's baptism, but I was trapped here. Tomorrow I'd have to strike up an acquaintance with them as a whole new person. It was all so exasperating! When Satan is clipping his toenails, may he get confused and chop off his whole foot!

Finally the deck cleared. The midnight gong sounded, and I scurried naked to the galley door, made my way to the lower deck, hurried to the dry cleaners, and stole some new clothes.

My children were still awake. Sue stopped sobbing and said, "If I'd known I'd never see him again, I would've said goodbye. I'm trying not to blame myself because I always do that."

"I could've stopped him," blubbered Sam, "or talked sense into him."

"I'm worried about Mom. How'll she feel now?" I silently thanked my dear daughter for saying that I mattered.

My children wept together. I hoped my husband's death would kill their new spirit of adventurousness. Dread had always sharply defined my own character, and I'd hoped to pass on that fear in my breast milk.

Sue said, "Let's do the flowers."

An hour later I watched from a shadowy cubbyhole on deck as my children tossed plastic roses pilfered from the dining room into the wake of the ship. They quietly sang, "The Nipper in the Cod and the Codder in the Pail." I hummed along. My husband was gone: it was now more imperative that my offspring not abandon me. Still, staring at my children holding hands, I felt sad for them, targeted as they were by the ferocious need within me.

That night in my haze of grief, I still had the sense to know I could douse them while they slept. I carefully carried Mary's magic bottle into the hall. Sam was snoring but Sue was awake, sighing and weeping. The situation was infuriating!

The next morning I dressed as a gypsy-girl in clog-soled sandals that slid on the floor when I walked. My torso and hips were concealed beneath a silk dress printed with garish parrots, macaws, and cockatoos in bright grasses. When I moved my hips, the fabric flashed like myriad winking eyes. To conceal my hair I knotted a topaz-streaked kerchief around my head. I attached a longer plastic nose to my face and added more putty. Perhaps it'd be easier to become acquainted with my daughter as a female. Still, I worried this disguise would be less convincing than the first. God, are all the disguises you offer magical?

I picked up Mary's bottle, left my room, and approached the closed curtain. All was silent. Now was the time. I unsealed the bottle, crouched, and thrust myself through the curtain to see— coiled rope, pails, and Sam's rock in the corner. Where had they gone? Today was the day for the miracle. I could wait no longer. If necessary I'd splash my children in public. I worried that Sue would recognize the container and flee before I could baptize her. I'd displayed the bottle on our mantel in Cartwright in a moment of foolish pride.

Back in my room I tried hiding the container in my under-pants, but it was too big, seemed wrong anatomically, and could easily slip through my panty elastic and shatter on the floor. I headed into the storage room. At the back stood shelves lined with broomstick ends, soap cakes, and coils of wire. I opened a wooden box and found Geronimo dolls, a Snakes and Ladders set, and several dice. At the bottom, I saw a plastic water pistol. God be praised! I returned to my room, filled the gun with some of Mary's urine, and stuffed it into my bra. I pointed it upwards so no liquid dribbled out.

I waited all morning at our table in the dining room, but my children didn't arrive. I ate a croissant and glanced forlornly at the crumbs lying on the tablecloth like tiny eyeless heads. All day I searched for them; I climbed about the ship's inner skeleton, wandered through rooms where people played billiards or watched videos. I discovered a small chapel that, not surprisingly, was empty. My children were hiding and mourning.

The ship's main deck was thronged with bodies stretched out on identical plastic lawn-chairs. In a world of so many people, why did I feel I had so little in my life? The air was scented with coconut; transistor radios buzzed like boxes of bees. Frying hamburgers sizzled; a man shouted, "Get your red-hots. Get 'em while you're red and hot." The sea of exposed flesh broiled and sautéed, becoming as dry and desiccated as horse leather. Plaid bikinis-cups rose like prim little hills. Wrinkled boxer shorts ruffled in the breeze and nylon Speedos gleamed as smooth as jade or bulged with concealed anteater snouts. Coloured sun creams shone in diagonal lines on cheeks. Over eyes lay plastic glasses like overturned spoons joined at the tips. Hills on eyes matched hills on breasts, and for a second everyone seemed to have breasts for eyes. I glanced at my own bosoms, glad they were down on my chest and not on my face.

Men muttered "We must increase the flow of goods" and "Governments must be weakened." They talked about eradicating borders again. I walked past teenagers playing volleyball, a clown juggling sticks, an ice cream vendor pushing a coffin-like box on wheels. He slid open the lid and, amidst clouds of steam, pulled out cones the colour of bone. People stripped off the tin foil and licked.

"Mmmm," they said.

All we are doing is eating death.

Leaning on the railing, I yawned ferociously. I'd been up all night obsessing over the gaps in my marriage. I returned to my room, removed the plastic pistol, and lay on the cot. I fell into a deep sleep and again had nightmares: Two penises clashed in a lance battle that never ended.

I woke in darkness, my hands clutching the bedspread. In the porthole, moonlight bled onto the waves. Footsteps outside my door. I turned the doorknob, stuck out my head. Sue's back was receding down the hall. I was about to cry out her name but realized I wasn't supposed to know her. In a high-pitched soprano, I yelled, "Hey, you there, girl!" Sue spun round. "How you do," I said. "I guess I your neighbour. We didn't meet before. I Cheryl."

Sue observed me. Would she accept this woman pasted over the soldier pasted over her mother?

"What you doing down here?"

"I'm looking for someone," she said, "who's always running away." Again she believed my costume was me! How wondrous! Thank you, God!

As she headed down the hall, I called out, "Maybe I can help." I shoved the pistol into my bra and followed. Lord, she moved fast! I headed up the metal-clanging steps and was panting when I reached the top. Out onto the wet, slippery deck a storm raged and water splashed across the rows of lawn chairs. I clutched my kerchief with both hands, fearing the wind would rip it from my head.

Sue disappeared through another doorway. I heard a distant

thumping, as regular as a heartbeat. I scurried down a steep stair-case and entered a low-ceilinged room full of crowds, smoke, tables with waxed tops, flashing lights, and blaring loudspeakers:

Sexy mama, shake your tush
I wanna hold you, oh so much…

A rectangle of gyrating bodies drowned in sheaths of flickering, multi-coloured light. The bass beat throbbed so loudly my kerchief, collar, and dress hem vibrated, and Mary's gun twitched spasmodically against my nipple. The place smelled of stale beer, cigarette smoke, and nachos. Why was Sue here? My children weren't grieving. They were in a disco! The soldier, in his T-shirt, stood talking to a woman in a leopard-skin dress. I feared that the woman whose clothes I was wearing was here and would attack me. I hurried past hands holding glasses of a red liquid that swayed as the ship rocked. The pounding music stopped and a voice over the loudspeakers yelled, "Everybody! We've just passed over the ocean-canyon and are entering the mid-Atlantic!"

The crowd cheered, but the floor immediately dropped like a freefalling elevator, then pitched violently upwards. Drinks spilled, a man on crutches collapsed; the bass beat began pulsing again, lights flashed, and everyone laughed. A loud hiss and a raised funnel spewed white smoke that concealed the dancers. In the darkness on one side of the room, a white-sheeted figure wriggled like larvae in a cocoon. Sam. The power I felt at that moment was incredible.

I pushed through the crowd that parted as the Red Sea once did for Moses. Sam kept bending over, then standing up. He was examining the tops and undersides of tables. Behind him,

Sue gesticulated and yelled, but her words were drowned beneath *"Sexy mama, shake your tush..."*

The speakers buzzed; the song changed. Against a clashing of symbols, a rhythmic yodelling. Sam stood statue-still. A horn sounded followed by a cooing soprano.

'Cause I want you, mountain babe,
I give you edelweiss, edelweiss, edelweiss...

With arms raised, Sam leapt onto the dance floor. Sue lunged, grabbed his hands, and tried to pull him from beneath the lights. Sam broke from her and pogoed amidst the gyrating bodies.

Come here I need some Swiss loving,
I give you edelweiss, edelweiss, edelweiss...

Pretending to dance, Sue spread her arms wide so no one could see him. Her body jerked back and forth like a metronome. Sam and Sue, side by side. Just where I wanted them.

I hurried onto the dance floor and weaved my way through the crowd. When the strobe started flashing, everyone's bodies were chopped into a million pieces. The strobe stopped, and legs, torsos, and arms reassembled themselves. Pelvises thrust and receded, heads rolled in circles over shoulders, arms spun like windmill blades or jerked like rotating turnstile prongs. At last I came to my children: Sue's face was lit blue, red, and orange, then was obscured in darkness; Sam's whole body glowed in a yellow spotlight.

Delighted, I wiggled my hips, watched my dress swirl voluptuously. I had been a great dancer in my youth. I raised my free arm, bent it sensually at the elbow, and stepped so one of my hips touched Sam and the other Sue. The bass beat pulsed through every cell of my body. Even my bones were humming. I shook my behind like a hula dancer. Any moment now, I'd start singing. Was this life as it was meant to be lived, my children and I locked in a sensual embrace? The singing stopped and trumpets blared. I snaked my hand into my bra, clutched the pistol, placed one finger on the trigger. I'd baptize Sue first.

A leather-clad man with slicked-back hair shook his groin toward Sue and grinned. She stepped away, glanced out over the crowd.

Oh mountain babe, I give you edelweiss…

I took a deep breath and pointed the gun at Sue. I whispered, "Be gone, Satan!" and squeezed the trigger—but either the ship lurched or the man attempted to throw himself on Sue, for she fell and he landed in the crossfire. Mary's urine splashed off the side of his face, drenched his hair, and filled one ear. He tumbled down onto the floor and, thrashing his legs and raising both arms, cried out in tongues. For God so loved the world that even screwballs like this loser shall receive God's grace!

Amazed and horrified, I accidentally dropped the pistol, which shattered on the floor. People stopped dancing, stepped back. The music ended and lights came up.

"Epilepsy," a woman muttered.

But Sue and Sam knew what was happening. They had lived with me. Sue grabbed her brother's hand and the two ran from the room. I fled lest someone would point me out as the pee-shooter. Stepping into our corridor I heard murmuring behind the curtain.

Sue said, "Someone like Mother is on this ship. That guy kept leering at me and then he started speaking in tongues. I don't know which was worse."

"I'm worried," Sam rasped. "I hiked across all of eastern Canada but have more challenges here."

"Stay away from that guy who spoke in tongues, Sam. And quit running from me! You've got to let me help you. Turns out I'm the one who can protect us, not you. I'm not a little girl any-more … You know, when I think about it, I probably could've looked after myself in Cartwright. I didn't need you to come rescue me, Sam. I think I only trusted you because I didn't realize I could do stuff on my own. Now it's my turn help you."

Sam moaned the "Mmmm" he makes when pondering a new idea.

"I feel kind of sad," continued Sue, "'cause there's no one for me to depend on now. But there's something solid in me, though I don't know what, exactly." Where had my daughter learned such wisdom? I felt inspired yet saddened. "When I figure it all out, I'll tell you, Sam. Now go on with your story. What happened after you moved out of the hotel and into Franz's chalet?"

I couldn't bear hearing about this disgusting Franz, so I returned to my room. I shook the bottle of Mary and watched the yellow waves claw the inside of the glass. That night I again attempted to ambush my children in their hiding place, but this time Sue slept and Sam lay awake sighing and muttering, "Franz, I'll surrender myself as never before."

I nearly vomited. Yes, at times I'm horrible. The Monster triumphs. Looking through the porthole up at the dark sky, I addressed God: Would I have been better without You? Or You without me? Would I still have ended up so desolate? Are things not working because I bully You too? I received no answer. Oh, that my children could return to our house by the sea and live with me forever.

The next morning I'd thrown the gypsy clothes overboard and became a pinstriped businessman with a black fedora and shiny, lacquered shoes so new they crackled when I walked. I no longer worried about my disguises; my children would accept everyone I chose to be. From the storage room I snatched a large plastic vial from the cardboard box. I poured the remainder of Mary into it, screwed on the lid, and put it inside my breast pocket.

My children were chatting behind the curtain. "That's wild, Sam. Snowstorms in summer and icicles on curtain rods. I want to meet Franz some day. Here, let me remove that flea behind your ear." Sam playfully groaned. "Now listen: I notice that there are times of the day when the hall is empty and times when it's full of workers. I prepared a schedule so you can walk without getting caught. I wrote it on this napkin. And don't go to that disco again." Sam grunted. "I want you to hold my hand this morning. It's going to be scary, and you need my help."

"Okay, sis. Thanks." He'd never been so openly affectionate before. My children were becoming unrecognizable.

I waited outside my cabin door, and at last Sam and Sue crawled from their hiding place. They headed toward the iron stairwell. With one hand on my hat, I sprinted toward them, the tie flapping in my face. I approached Sue's back and held my breath—a light bulb was right above her head, so I cast no shadow. I reached into my pocket and removed the vial. I stopped to remove the lid. When I looked up, she was already in the stair-well. I ascended the stairs, vial in hand. As I rounded the last landing, the lid slipped off and clattered down the metal steps. My children passed through a door, entered a hall, and ducked into a room. Hallelu, they were cornered! I raced into the corridor, turned right, and was suddenly in a beige-walled office where Sue stood talking to a nurse in white.

The nurse turned to me and said, "Ah, Mr Jones. Good of you to bring your own sample." She snatched the vial from my hand.

"No ... wait!" I cried in an undeniably woman's voice.

Sue's head jerked toward me.

"Relax, Mr Jones. Many people are nervous at check-ups, but I'll put a safe lid on this and we'll label it for testing." She vanished behind a curtain.

I tried to hide my panic. I cleared my throat and tightened the tie.

Returning, the nurse addressed Sue. "You were saying, dear?"

She spoke quickly. "Something's happened to my brother. Please don't get upset when you see how he looks."

The nurse joked, "Don't you worry. We've seen everything here."

A door opened and a lady in an afghan shawl hobbled out on a walker. The nurse smiled and led Sue and Sam into the room.

As soon as the door closed, I raced behind the curtain. To my horror, there was a tray with a hundred identical vials of urine! Had everyone on the ship been here to give samples? I began frenziedly taking each tube from its slot and reading the labels. They were numbered but had no names. Where was Mr Jones's vial? There must be a corresponding list somewhere. I skimmed through the papers attached to the wall—Jameson, Jennings, Jorgens—no Jones? I overturned the wastepaper basket, fished through Coke cans, and unravelled bandages. I opened a cupboard to discover only an unplugged coffeemaker.

From the next room came a bloodcurdling scream and Sue pleading, "He's not like he looks! He won't hurt you!"

I stared hard at the hundred vials nestled like eggs in their slots; one of them was Mary's. I took a deep breath, lifted the huge tray, carried it into the waiting room and, balancing it on my thigh, opened the main door with my elbow. In the hall, the half-naked soldier passed me. I walked quickly, the vials rattling violently in their slots. Finally safe in my room, I examined each vial and tried to guess which urine was secular and which was Holy. I sniffed each container. I touched the liquid surface with my fingertips. All had a similar colour, consistency, temperature and, when I tasted them, were equally salty. I couldn't splash my children with vial after vial until I found the right one. After just one baptism, they'd get suspicious. Sue already thought something was up.

There was only one solution. It would be time-consuming, frustrating, and exhausting. I prayed to God for the strength to do what was necessary. I retrieved a box of empty vials from the storage room, poured half of each urine sample into two vials, and labelled them with the same number and an A or B. A was the test vial. I would douse a random stranger with A; if it turned out Holy, I'd use the corresponding B on my children. I gazed at the 200 vials of urine. Mary's power was being divided, diluted, and becoming invisible as it entered the world of Man.

I waited until evening, trashed the business suit, darted into the dry cleaner's, and emerged as a voluptuous eccentric with a breast-thrusting cocktail dress, mesh gloves, hiking boots, and baseball cap. I slunk sensuously up the staircase and onto the deck where knots of people clustered at the railings. The full moon was a hole punched in the sky. A portly, middle-aged man leaned on the rail near the bow. He was clearly a conference man in a pin-striped suit like the one I'd sported this morning. I sauntered over and cooed, "How are you, sir?"

His head rotated and one eye twinkled. "I'm quite fine, young lady." His hairline forked violently at his temples, making the rectangle of hair on his head look like a giant thrusting tongue. "And how are you, sweetie?"

I spoke musically, each word half-sound, half-breath. "I'm feeling fine, with the moonlight, the waves, the water." My voice trailed off, faded like a dying breeze.

The man's eyes were bright as polished eggs. If he'd had antennae on his head, they'd be standing straight up. "Well, dearie," he chortled and stepped closer. My index finger snaked into my other glove, removed Vial 1A. "I'm glad you're having a good time." My finger pried off the lid. I heard it clatter somewhere in the dark. "I'm here with Remston Battery." His hot hand rested on my hip. I could smell his cinnamon cologne and a mix of onions and mint on his breath.

All at once I hissed, "Be gone, Satan!" My hand flew upwards and the urine struck him—*splat!*—in the face. His collar was drenched. But he didn't fall to the ground or speak in tongues.

He stood blinking with beads of liquid on his eyelashes. One of his hands wiped at what was clearly secular pee. He sniffed it. "What the hell!"

I raced into the ship and practically threw my body down the staircase. Late that night, I dumped Vial 1B into the ocean. One down. Ninety-nine to go. Over the next four days I baptized thirty men and twenty-five women, but they all cried out the words of Man as laic pee soaked tie-knots or darkened ball-gowns. Each night, moonlight made a vertical slash on the ocean that now contained vials one through fifty-five and the dissolving remnants of Franz's words.

I had many close calls. Once I aimed incorrectly and the urine landed in a man's soup. Not noticing me, he took one, two sips and grimaced, nothing more. Another time I missed a woman and struck the dog she was walking, who barked and began chasing its tail. Once I flung urine into a man's open mouth. He immediately turned and spat it at his wife. I thought I'd have two tonguers for the price of one, but they threw themselves on me. I pulled myself out from under their beating fists and ran beneath the hanging rowboat upon which, following me, they both struck their foreheads and collapsed with cracked, bloody skulls. I decided to approach only those who were alone on the deck or in the stairwell.

Word got out that a pee-thrower was on board, and I became terrified of getting caught. I made more use of the ship's inner skeleton and changed clothes three times a day. I'd hide Mary's vials in my socks, amongst the curls in my hair. Sometimes she protruded against my bandannas like a tumour or bulged like strange growths on my hips or buttocks. As I spilled each vial without finding Mary, my frustration was balanced by the knowledge that I was getting closer. The odds were one in a hundred, then one in ninety-nine, ninety-eight, and eventually I'd strike gold and have the power of pure Mary in my hands.

I dumped so many clothes overboard that travellers now showed up for dinner half-dressed. Pot bellies bulged against undershirts as men tightened imaginary ties; women adjusted bra straps before stepping to the podium to speak. By the fifth day, nearly all the conference attendees were half-naked or wore clothes with pee stains on them. I'd eye the dark sphere on the crotch of a man's pants or the exclamation-mark-shaped shadow on a woman's dress and know these clothes would be in the dry cleaner's tonight and on my body tomorrow.

As wrath at both the pee-thrower and the clothes-stealer mounted, accusations flew and paranoia took hold of the ship. I watched as a young girl with daisies pinned in her braids was cornered by a mob of fist-waving men in boxer shorts.

"Those aren't bobby pins in your hair," they cried. "You stole our tie clips."

One night I shivered in terror as feet stamped in the hall and Sue shrieked.

"She's the one," men yelled. "Why else would she be hiding down here!"

When she didn't return, I correctly guessed she'd been locked up and was being interrogated. I performed a record thirty pee-throws in two hours. My strategy worked. No one can be in two places at once, and at three in the morning, Sue was released.

Back in her hiding place, she wept until daybreak. How wonderful it was to have her near me again. I wanted to enter her cubbyhole and embrace her.

Most passengers blamed the first man I'd baptized, the greasy-haired loser who now wandered the ship shouting, "Hallelujah," or "Praise God. Let us bless His Holy Name." He sat alone at the breakfast table twisting croissants into the shapes of crosses. He'd say to the waiter, "You saved the toast from burning just as Christ keeps our souls from sinning." He had been interrogated several times, yet the thefts and pee-throwing continued. Many believed that he was using spiritual powers to ruin the conference.

"I betcha he's an anti-free-trader. I can tell by the shirt he's wearing. If you flutter your eyelids, it looks tie-dyed."

"If I find out he stole my Armani, I'll crack his head open with the No Blood for Oil placard he's probably got hidden in his closet."

Luckily Sam was never accused of stealing because he always wore the same now-filthy sheet and was assumed to be a clothing victim himself. Ever since we'd crossed the ocean midpoint, he'd stationed himself at the ship's bow where he lay outstretched on the bowsprit that pointed toward Europe. He wrapped his arms around it, his eyes focussed on the horizon as the wind whipped and billowed his sheet. In the evenings he'd relax on deck with Sue. One evening I heard her say, "My honey started flowing the day you left Cartwright, Sam. And it increased when I turned sixteen, but it stopped when I met you on the beach. I guess that means I'm still dependent on you somehow—which I think isn't good. I'm really attached to you, Sam, deep down, in a way that is bad, probably. I've got to start finding something important in myself, whatever that is, and I'll never find it if I'm always hanging around you. So I'm going to move out and sleep in that closet at the end of the hall."

"You're not going to leave me alone? What happens if someone finds me there at night?"

"Then scream. I'll hear you and run from my room and boot them out."

"I don't know," he said. "I keep thinking of those stories you told me. I wish I'd never heard them."

"You mean Estelle's tale about how Jimmy couldn't pull his penis from my body and had to chop it off? Or how his penis disappeared into his body? All because of little old me." She chuckled. "I used to be upset by these stories, but now I see they're a joke. The most important things in life are the most hilarious."

"I think having one's penis recede into one's body would be horrible. I sure hope it never happens to me. When I'm sleeping, could you check on me from time to time to make sure my penis is still there?"

"You're a riot, Sam."

"I'm serious. I'm going to get rid of this rock, though. You're right about that; it's just another thing I use to avoid having contact with real life. I fixate and put these things between me and what I love, and then I can't be open to what's around me. I've just got to find the best way to get rid of it."

Security guards were finally stationed at the dry cleaner's. I lost access to the clothes and began wearing a sheet like Sam's. This costume was actually better than any disguise. So many people now wore sheets that I blended in beautifully. After tossing a vial of urine, I could run into a crowded room and be indistinguishable from everyone else.

Sue spent less time with her brother and would only wave at him lying at the bow. She preferred standing at the stern and looking westward, toward home. I took this as a positive sign. She wanted to return to her old life, to Cartwright, to me. Oh, I felt such a rush of love for her then.

One morning I spied Sue doing can-can kicks to the rising sun. Then she leaned on the railing and peered, transfixed. Her eyes, face, her whole body was glowing. At lunchtime I asked, "Mind if I sit with you?"

"Yes, of course. I love having company." Her habitual paranoia had vanished.

A man in red underpants was speaking at the microphone. "We must strive for the free flow of goods. Imagine a world with Chinese broccoli and Guatemalan cheese on every table. Produce has its own mysteries and we should let it flow where it must. Money is the motor of the world. Let's respect that!"

What foolish men. Money doesn't move the world, even in this atheistic century. It's hard to believe that so many people that live on the Earth's surface today are such complete and utter morons.

Sue crunched a burnt bacon slice between her teeth and giggled.

"You're in a very good mood today," I commented.

"Oh yes, yes, yes!" Watching her pop grapes into her mouth, I believed I could ask her any question at all and she'd answer honestly.

"Are you happy because you're no longer living with your friend?"

"Leaving him changed everything in me."

"Changed everything? What do you mean?"

Sue tittered, jumped up, began dancing, then sat down again. Was she on drugs?

"Well, you see," she said. "I had some friends. Once upon a time." She yelled, "Once upon a time," then sing-songed, "very special friends who visited me regularly. They gave me great pleasure. But I didn't appreciate them." She looked straight into my eyes. "Everybody said it was wrong, and I sort of believed them." She became very quiet. "But I loved them dearly. Really, I did. I couldn't understand it all then because everything was—strange, so wonderful, beautiful, and strange." Her hand absent-mindedly caressed the table top. "There was nothing wrong with me at all. I never needed to leave the place I was born because the best thing I had I carried with me wherever I went. I mean, I *am* my body. That's what I've been looking for. My body has been with me since birth and will be with me for the rest of my life. I'll never be able to get rid of it—even if I wanted to. And it'll never abandon me, the way, for example, Sam did. So I don't need to worry. My own skin supplies me with more pleasure than I've ever known." She let out a tinkling peel of laughter. "It's like a fairy tale I heard about, where Mr. Potato Head people could shift around their body parts. I define my own body and make it do what I want." What was she talking about? Her speech was becoming as cryptic as her brother's. Was I the only person here aware of more than herself? "In the end, my friends turned against me, but that was because I was afraid to show the world how much I really loved who I was. That won't happen a second time. I refuse to feel shame ever again."

What a blabbering, mindless freak! Still, her vulnerability touched me. Nervously, I said, "What you say isn't true. Only your soul is important. The body is not a means to salvation but a distraction, unless, as a mother, it creates something." But Sue wasn't listening. A minute later she said, "Ta-ta!," lifted both arms like airplane wings, and glided out of the room. She spent the afternoon at the stern, standing in the cusp of the V, one elbow on top of each railing. The wind ruffled her hair, flicked at her dress. Her head didn't turn but remained straight like a stuck weather-cock.

Mine two children are stone gargoyles at the head and foot of a ship crossing the ocean. I am the energy moving between them. I imagined Sue's body hardening to stone as she gazed westward toward a long-vanished continent. When the dinner bell sounded, she stepped back. Passing me, she smiled dreamily. I marched to where she'd been standing and, like her, put each elbow on the railings. Looking ahead, I tried to see what she saw. But the sky was clear, the horizon bare.

Then I felt on my elbows a mucus-like viscidity pressing into my skin. I lifted my arms, saw thin dangling threads. I gasped: it was there, honey-drops in a row on the railing, honey on the metal post she'd pressed her pelvis against and, on the floor, honey footprints glistening in the sunlight! In horror, I looked up and stared hard at the western horizon. Was it my imagination or did

I hear, from the direction of North America, a subtle, distant buzzing?

Clutching my sheet I hurtled down to the cabin, burst through my door, slammed it shut, and exploded into a torrent of weeping. I banged my fists on the floor, screamed at the porthole, kicked the walls of the room. Had it all come to this? In racing ahead was my course but a circle, and we were back where we started? The vials stood like soldiers in a depleted army.

The twenty-first century is the problem, so detached from the Christian past. My children must not live in an era where science is all that's left or they will be cut off from their roots. Without God the world becomes a mechanistic whirligig, and you can be as exposed as those businessmen's bodies, but there's nothing to see but rows of pimples and birth-marks. Without God, ye deny the mystery of life and mine womb. There are huge parts of myself that even I don't understand. The womb is all and I accept no other truth. The ability to desire cometh from me. Sam thinks he loves Franz, but that's simply my love that's flowed into him and which he's twisted. Sue believes that the bees are an extension of herself, but her pleasure is but the energy that at her birth flowed from my body to hers.

I admit it now: I am a selfish, bitter shrew. I am our civilization's suffocating past whose presence still lingers and is despised. I know my domineering ways have damaged those I love. I recognize my personality's limits but can't escape them. It's the way God made me and I am too weak to change. Applaud me for my insight. This is my epiphany. It's not much but it's all I shall get. Not everyone has the chance to see the Matterhorn in one's lifetime. We know about Biblical floods. The Earth was born in catastrophe and shall end in catastrophe. I surrender to the Monster. What pleasure at last to give way to the strongest force in oneself!

Tomorrow I shall throw all of the remaining vials, find the magic talisman, and bring my children back to me before this foul century swallows them for good. That they had been born before Newton imagined his first light bulb!

I could not sleep all night. The infernal buzzing filled the air, the boat was rocked by strange winds, and dark waves lashed the porthole. I got up on my bed and besought the Holy Sprit to descend, but the accursed droning kept Him locked in the sky. When I finally slept—nightmares. I dreamt that I threw Mary's urine, but the wind shifted and it was I who was splattered. My body grew before my astonished children's eyes and I became as tall as the statue of Mary. But I was not happy because this made me more separate from my offspring than before. Then I dreamt I doused my children, but it was they who grew large. Next I dreamt that, after a perfect baptism, Sam and Sue's faces transformed to resemble mine. At first I was delighted, but in public no one could tell us apart. People called our names and Sam turned or I turned or we all turned at once until we were moving frenziedly like doors flapping in a windstorm.

By morning the buzzing was so loud that the cabin walls were vibrating and the sea covered with trembling goose bumps. I snatched the page of Franz's letter from under the mattress and stuffed it into the cleft under my breast. Sheet-swathed and armed with every remaining vial, I, for the last time, marched down the hallway and up the stairs.

Everyone on the ship stood on deck half-dressed or blanketed, staring at a sky half-covered with a steadily oozing inky blotch.

"Mother of God," I whispered. "Help me in my hour of need."

The bees were sliding like a car sun-roof over the world, slicing in half that wonderful space between Heaven and Earth. People cried and wailed. "What is it?" "What's happening?" The man who'd praised CEO Benson crouched in his stained undies, pounded his fists on the floor, and screamed, "Eight months of preparation for what?!" In the ocean, swordfish leapt in bright silver arcs. My grip closed tighter around the ten vials concealed beneath my sheet. I pushed through the crowds. Women thrashed against walls, shrieking men pulled at the hair on their heads.

My daughter stood at the stern, her back erect, arms outstretched, and face shining as she laughed into the darkening sky. Shaking with fear and fury, I ran to her, quickly unscrewed one lid, and cried, "Be gone, Satan," as I flung the pee onto her back. The wet coolness made her turn slightly toward me. She smiled and said, "Hi, friend."

I unscrewed and threw a second batch and got her right in the face. She wiped off her cheeks, giggled, and looked back at the sky.

"It's him! The pee-thrower!" someone yelled.

"Yeah! I saw it too!"

I spun around. A dozen men in boxer shorts faced me. I was still clutching eight vials in my hand. Visible criminal evidence. I pulled my arms inside the sheet.

"We've gotcha, you asshole," one man said. He stepped forward and yanked down a corner of my sheet. "He's the pee-thrower, guys. There's his stock inside."

The crowd lunged. They pinned down my shoulders, tore the sheet from my body. One man kicked me in the face, and my prosthetic nose flew off and bounced on the deck. "Holy shit!" he said. Fingers scrabbled at my putty-coated cheeks. Plastic and gels were wiped from my face, and as the magic fled, I cried, "Help me, God!" and clutched the vials to my chest. When the men discovered I was a woman, they hesitated only a moment. A man stuffed my panties between his teeth, another snapped off my bra and flung it into the sea.

Suddenly, above us, a loud *boom* as the bee clouds joined and began descending.

The men froze, gazing upwards, no longer noticing me. I leapt to my feet and, completely naked, turned to Sue.

But now she saw me. She knew. She stared motionless. Her arms stuck straight down at her sides, her fingers rigid as popsicle sticks. Her mouth opened a hair's breadth and a wisp of a voice emerged: "Mother."

I drenched her with a third vial. Sue seemed to come to; terrified, she jumped down and began running toward the other end of the ship. I followed, flung a vial full into the small of her back, another onto her shoulders. A week of practice had made my aim exemplary. My feet pummelled along the floorboards that steadily darkened as the bee cloud descended. The roaring increased. Businessmen screamed and moaned, threw themselves onto the deck.

I still insist that my daughter is two grams short a kilo. She could've darted into the crowd and lost me, or run into the ship and vanished in its interior. But in her hour of need, she went to the worst place for her—yet the best for me. She galloped to the bow to alert Sam.

I followed until I stood panting before my cornered children. I proudly lifted my two remaining vials in the air, the final Holy duo that had taken me so long to find. All the waters of Man had to be spilled before the power of God could reveal Itself. And now that power was in my hands, and my children were at my mercy. Restraint, sensitivity, diplomacy, and all these foreign stratagems had never fit me and were in the past. At last I was the colossus I was meant to be.

Sue huddled, weeping. "Please, Mother, please!"

Sam turned and recognized me. "What the hell!" he gasped. "What are you doing here?!" His eyeballs shrunk to pinpricks. His mouth was open so wide, I could see his tonsils.

I let out a shout that echoed from one side of the world to the other. "Ha! I've been everybody on this ship! I changed from one person to another, and now it's *your* turn to be changed! I converted that freak in the leather jacket, and now I'll convert you. I control it all! It was me, Sam, that found those horrid letters from Switzerland and threw them overboard, just as I now do with the last disgusting sheet." I pulled out the letter, unfolded it before my quivering son, and mockingly read its final sentences. "'Your eyes are on me this instant. Please. Never stop looking.' What horse manure!" I flung the sheet into a cresting wave and Franz's words dissolved beneath the ocean surface. Sam screeched and began thumping his feet and pounding his fists against his stomach.

"Do you think you can defy me, who gave you love and life? Thou hast wandered far from thy home in Cartwright, and thy bodies have become infected with poisons. Yet I shall heal thy flesh, re-sanctify thy souls, and take thee back to the place where thou belongest. From now on, thou shalt be on the side of God, yea God, the true force that moveth the world. He is in thee, as I am in thee, for He is me, and I am Him, and so we are, forever more! Satan," I bellowed, "be gone!"

Yet it was here that I made a fatal mistake. Just as Sue, out of shame, had once pulled a dress up and over her streaming body, just as my husband leapt into an ocean yearning to grasp a vision he hoped would save him, just as Sam boarded a plane in Zurich before realizing that Franz truly loved him, just as Franz raised his arms beside a lake and called, "You inspire me, *Liebhaber*," though Sam was too far away to hear him, just as all these things shouldn't have happened but did, so did I, caught up in the moment and yearning for a liberation from the relentless calcu-lations of measurements and numbered vials, so did I risk all on one moment and throw care to the wind—I greedily tossed not one vial, then the other, but my two vials *at exactly the same time*, one from my right hand and the other from my left. The twin streams joined to form a golden river that hung in the air like a wraith between me and my children for one perilous second.

Yet just when my elbows leapt forward from the sides of my body, so did a swordfish with silver scales bright as flashing eyes and a bill pointing not east or west but north, shoot up from the watery depths and travel in a perfect arc between me and my offspring. At the highest point of its trajectory, it shielded Sue and Sam long enough for the rushing stream of urine to splash across its body, saturate its skin, seep into its gills, and spurt off its bill, before completing its half-circle and re-entering the sea. The gash made in the water closed like a healed wound.

Immediately all around us, the ocean burst forth with the Glory of God. Leaping salmon sang the Hallelujah chorus. Schools of dolphins passed wearing choir gowns. A whale rose spurting the water of Lourdes, as on its forehead a preaching mackerel clung. Starfish changed into crosses. Shark fins were adorned with scripture verses, "For God so loved the world" and "Seek ye first the Kingdom of God." The sea was of God, but this boat and my children were still of Man.

"No!" I screamed. "*Nooooooo!*"

The empty vials fell, rolled and knocked together on the floorboard of the atheist ship. Sue's laughter was so high-pitched and cruel, I felt wires were being driven into my eardrums. She leapt down onto the deck and clapped her hands together. Darkness fell as the black swath of scrabbling legs and multi-sectioned torsos closed over the ship like a massive hand. If I could not save my children through the power of God, then my body would suffice. I grabbed Sue by the hair and pulled her toward the cabin entrance that gaped like the maw of a huge mouth.

"Let me go!" she screeched.

How small and frail she seemed then, with her sparrow bones and spaghetti-noodle muscles. She thinks she's so fantastic, but she's a stick-girl, not a real person at all. As I dragged her, honey splattered across my face, neck, lips; I tasted the horrid sweetness on my tongue. I pushed her down the staircase, wrapped both arms round her chest, and hauled her, while she pleaded to be let go. Her legs thrashed on the carpet. She tried to hook her feet around the guardrail. In vain she struck her head against my chest. Her honey flowed in waves over both of us, melding our bodies together. I was horrified yet excited. "You want to stick to everything," I gasped—I shoved her into my room—"but that everything includes *me*." I locked the door behind us. "We're going to wait until the bees pass and then, holding hands, we'll pray for the Holy Spirit to descend and fill us. Then we and your brother shall return to Cartwright."

Honey flowed from her bent knees and splattered loudly on the floor.

"I want to be … like a friend to you from now on," I said. The floor lurched and we heard the deafening roaring of power drills all around us; another jolt and a furious whining. The floor, walls, ceiling began to shake. A light bulb popped from the ceiling and hung swinging on its wire. Amidst the deafening roar was a ghastly creaking sound.

Sue's eyes were lit as with a thousand torches. She cried, "Yes, Drooper, Snagglepuss, Einstein, come, come, *come!*"

"Who's Drooper?" I yelled, shaking her. "What's happening?" I abruptly slapped her across the face as hard as I could. She collapsed onto the floor, a red crescent-moon glowing on her cheek.

She moaned, "Come, come!"

Before I could stop myself, I grabbed her head, struck it once, twice against the wall. "Make this stop," I shouted. "Whatever's happening, make it stop!"

Weeping, she murmured, "Drooper…"

On the wall, beside her cut cheek, appeared a rotating spiral that bulged into a spinning anthill, another whirling sawdust circle grew beside it, then one in the ceiling and another on the wall; two, four, five, seven, ten above my head, rows on every wall. We were trapped in a horrid room of spinning eyes shedding sawdust tears.

What happened next was so sudden, unexpected, and of such magnitude, I would not have believed it possible and had neither the time nor ability to assess its significance. The pulverizing realization that what one most wishes for in life has been irretrievably lost, mixed with the horror of death and transformed the sad body I lived in into a writhing avatar of blind terror and panic; the ship, now hole-ridden as cheesecloth, exploded into a thousand fragments.

I was plunged down into the frigid sea; my body thrashed and flailed in the icy water; blank greyness pushed into my eye sockets and down my throat. My arms and leg muscles cramped. My lungs shrieked for oxygen. Flapping my hands like featherless wings, I slowly rose until eventually my head burst up through the sea's surface. I coughed as I inhaled air and my lungs ballooned. Above, in the insanely blue sky, the sun bounced up and down like a yo-yo. A flap of drenched hair hung over one of my eyes.

Debris danced on the ocean waves. Dismembered sofas bobbed like gigantic buoys and enormous wood beams rocked back and forth. Plastic lawn chairs spun in whirlpools, crepe-paper streamers flowed amidst the debris like strings of multi-coloured blood. Shrieking businesspeople clung to seesawing boards, floating wood rails, and severed tabletops. Some men wore life jackets upside-down or inside-out; they paddled around shouting and angrily pushing people off boards.

Small waves smacked my face like hands; I tasted blood on my tongue, and salt burned in my eyes and on my cheeks. "Sam!" I cried. "Sue!" The horrific buzzing still filled the air.

A man shouted, "Give me your life-jacket, asshole."

Off to the side, a swarm of flickering bees hovered in a perfect oval above the water. A growth swelled on its top; the whole vibrating form looked like a giant, wavering hat. A section of the upper growth separated itself and stuck out like a tree branch. It was an arm. A person sat upon it and had turned toward me.

It was Sue, her long honey-hair dripping down her back, her wide open lips melting as they formed first an O, then a crescent-moon smile. Her arm moved, waving lugubriously like seaweed under water and she let out a laugh, but even it, normally bright-pitched and metallic, faded the moment it sounded. The bee canopy rose and shot up into the sky, carrying my daughter farther from the Earth than she'd ever been. I watched the oval shrink, become half its size, then a third, a quarter, an eighth. Before it disappeared completely, a giant, gold-threaded spinning wheel flashed for a split second, revolving in the endless blue like a Ferris wheel. The mother in the sky. The mother in the sky existeth!

A wave swelled, and I was submerged. Wood specks and salt water flowed up my nostrils. I re-emerged into the sunlight, coughing and weeping. I cried out, "Sam!" He was all I had left. "Sam, where are you?!"

I paddled through a mass of cellophane-wrapped dry cleaner's clothes flapping on the water. My thighs and shoulder muscles were stiffening; my jaw had taken on a will of its own, and my teeth clattered together like dice in a jar. "Sam!" I screamed. I passed two men grappling on a floating door and realized it'd been my door. Sam clung to a piece of wood and sobbed. His sheet had fallen off, and his wolfish body was completely exposed. Wet fur clung to his skin.

Swimming towards him, I shouted, "Sam!" I took a breath. "Sue's gone." I was still weeping. "She's gone…for good. And now it's just us together. I so want to be with…my intelligent son. Oh, Sam, let's find a way back to Labrador. Let's try to make things work this time."

For the first time in years, Sam looked straight at me. His eyes were a network of red veins tipped with soot-black pupils. Frizzed hair framed his face and sprouted from the creases in his cheeks. He was not the beautiful boy I'd known.

Still, I could get used to it.

I spun my arms like propeller blades, and my body rose out of the water and up to him. Sam opened his mouth wide and his green tongue swept over jagged teeth. He closed his lips. Was he going to kiss me? For a second I wished he would. Instead he said, "For fuck sakes, Mother. Do you always have to bloody well wreck everything?" He lifted a closed fist above my face, opened his hand, and let drop a stone into my open mouth.

Without thinking, I swallowed it. The rock lodged in the space between my Adam's apple and windpipe. Sam didn't smile or frown. No light shone in his eyes. The rock lingered for a moment between my head and my torso, then sunk down like a comet falling to the earth. The weight of the rock pulled me into the ocean; I raised both arms to my son and the vanishing sky and cried silent words to the boy, sky, and world, which I saw were all, at long last, leaving me. "Everything cometh of me! I am the root of thy entire civilization. Mine body conceived this world and gave birth to it. I am the rock surface thou walkest on, the salt springs thou drinkest from. I am the foam in thy mouth and the spittle on thy lips. I am the solidity of thy bones, the wetness of thy kidneys, and the dog-ear aorta-flaps of thy heart. In my absence, no wind whips ember into flame, water leaves no pattern on rock; ice hardens not, and clouds are pinned like prisoners to a sky they cannot cross. I am the electricity that floweth through nuclei. I am the eye that never closeth, the finger that forever points, the wheel that spinneth relentlessly, and the axle that runneth from the North Pole to the South. Trying to escape me is trying to climb from the skin that encaseth thee. The walls of mine womb are the furnace that forged the world, are of the world and are the world. Abandon me and thee abandonest thyself, for I am the Alpha and the Omega. I am the Beginning and I am the End!" Descending into the sea, I shut my mouth and accepted everything.

Light faded.

The waters closed above my head, and I was gone forever.

PART SIX

Rock

Sam clutches the slippery edge of a bobbing wooden plank as waves swell like lungs inflating. Flicking fingers of water slap the plank's edge and dissolve into sunlit spray that showers his cheeks with bullet-bright drops. The pungent seaweed scent shoots up his nostrils, and fur shines slick against his body. His legs dangle in the water, the hard plank edge thrusting into the soft folds of his stomach.

Amidst bobbing chunks of splintered wallboard, sofas spinning in circles, wood pillars chugging like pistons, thousands of dancing Styrofoam balls, the wreckage is dotted with the swaying bodies of people wailing.

"Somebody save us!"

"Help me! *He-elp!*"

Their exclamations are punctuated by the creak and groan of wood and what sounds like giant billiard balls clacking together.

Sam glares into the whirlpool where his mother vanished and wonders how she could have so successfully concealed herself from him and Sue. He'd thought her incapable of functioning outside Cartwright, yet she'd lived incognito in the clothes of more than a hundred people. He imagines the terrific stress of her non-stop camouflage, the constant threat of being discovered.

Her God must have given her something. The energy that moves the world can't only be in rocks. Whatever the Earth's vital power is, his mother had possessed it.

Feeling exhausted, Sam mutters to the sea, "Mother, it's not your fault you were the way you were. You were limited; I'm limited; we all are. But I refuse to feel guilt. Sorry, but you deserve what you got. Of course you raised us, and I will never forget that." There is sadness in his voice. He slowly paddles past a drifting chest of clothes and gets momentarily stuck in a mound of gluey foam.

Sam beholds the blue sky where his sister vanished and feels such a rush of love that he chokes on salt water. He's touched by her kindness. She offered him a strength that she'd once expected from him but which he couldn't provide. Sam didn't save Sue; Sue saved Sam. Reversal is a cornerstone of life. How wonderful it was to depend on someone. He wishes Sue were here to help him now. Amazing that he could be deeply affected by someone other than Franz. He never suspected such strength in his sister or mother. Why does he continue to look only at life's surface? From now on, he won't trust a fraction of what he sees. His sister's flight to the sky fills him with wonder. Wherever she is now, Sue has found happiness; Sam's sure of it, and is delighted for her.

Below him, sharks circle, flashing scissor-sharp teeth; manta rays' magic-carpet bodies undulate like severed wings filmed in slow motion. As Sam contemplates his sister's generosity, he feels the range of his concern for the world expanding outward. When a sobbing woman tries to clamber onto a nearby banquet table,

Sam paddles over and says, "I'll hold the table steady while you climb on." But all around him there are gasps, screams, shrieks— he's forgotten about his appearance. Flying bars of wood strike his forehead, a camera smacks him on the mouth, and two teeth fall out. "It's him!" people shout. "He caused all this!" In a torrent of whizzing plastic balls and wood chips, he swims away. Sam is not angry at the business people; they look only at the world's exterior, and need to learn what his mother and Sue have taught him about what lies beneath.

He fingers his cut lip, paddles past seesawing wooden panels and somersaulting barrels. Soon he can no longer hear the frenzied moaning as the ship vanishes behind waves. Gurgling sounds rise from the depths below; the wind sighs. Sam tries not to panic. The edge of the plank repeatedly jabs like a blunt sabre blade beneath his ribs. He pulls himself up onto it, but the plank sinks slightly, and the strands of his fur splay outward like the hairs on a Venus flytrap. He listens to the wheezing of his lungs as he pants. Before his eyes, foam-tipped waves gather, curl, and crash forward, over and over, steadily, rhythmically, like a million sentences beginning and ending.

The sky into which his sister vanished is as clear as a pupil-less eye.

What the hell is he supposed to do now? The ship voyage had already lasted six days, and they'd travelled past the midpoint of the Atlantic. How far is the European coast from here? He could linger near the wreckage until help arrives. A helicopter will surely be sent. But if he's taken to Europe, he'll be put in a zoo. If he's returned to North America, Sonny and Cher will get him, and he'll never see Franz again. By studying the angle of the sun to the sea, Sam determines which way is east. He scrutinizes the horizon, which looks like the line across a 1950s television screen about to explode into moving images.

Again he feels a flash of anger at his mother for wrecking everything. But he bravely intones, "On your mark! Get set! Go!" He starts paddling, the bald sun beating onto his skull. It occurs to Sam how ridiculous his situation is. Logic clearly has no place in life. He, a scientist who loved logic, has ended up a monster paddling a board in the middle of the ocean. The truest things in life, he sees, are the most ludicrous. He and Franz were ludicrous; two men—a fact Sam still finds peculiar—from the two most unromantic countries in the world, and they weren't opposite (opposites attract, don't they?) but similar; they ate rocks amidst summer snowstorms; one of them was a nerd, the other a narcissist, and their social worlds didn't overlap. Logic is a house that's burning, and nothing remains solid for long. Nature's frayed edges keep evolution happening. Sam believes now that people repeatedly collide with each other swiftly, brutally—not to produce children but to shatter their sense of self, and be thrust into a creative space beyond reason, where anything can happen. Only through the destruction of psychological borders is freedom possible. That must be, Sam concludes at last, why other people exist on Earth.

He glances into the sea. If only there was the flash of a fin or a bubble ascending to the surface, but the relentless grey water is as blank as the blue sky overhead. Sam says out loud, "What if I don't make it? What if I never get to Europe? Or, if I arrive, will things be as I expect?" How many days has it been since Franz sent his letter from the base of the Matterhorn? He'd changed so quickly from wanting Sam to turning against him and then wanting him again. He could turn against Sam if he thought he'd never show up. Maybe he's forgotten him already. Perhaps the diamond stopped forming.

Sam kicks his legs in the water and is soon puttering up and down the roller-coaster waves. He will not stop paddling until he sees the European cliffs rise like herds of blue dinosaurs lifting their heads into the sky. His skin could turn green, his muscles dissolve to skipping ropes of tendon, and his dehydrated torso become a solid lump of salt, but his thighs will pummel like fists into the face of the grey, unrelenting sea. Somewhere on the ocean floor, he knows, runs the seam marking the meeting point of the North American and Eurasian plates.

Kicking, Sam murmurs, mutters, babbles, his voice crescendos into a high-pitched falsetto of terror. "What if Franz doesn't want me anymore? Will he be there when I arrive? What if my desire doesn't last the journey and I'm indifferent when I meet him?" No, Sam will fight the forces within himself that could destroy his desire. Each phase of his journey is not a chapter but a book. It seems years since he was trapped in that asylum, decades since he writhed in a garden, his stomach full of stones, centuries since that pterodactyl-winged airplane snatched him from Zurich's runway and dumped him onto Toronto's cruel streets, and though he ran non-stop from his country's centre to its circumference, the journey, when viewed from this rocking stick of wood on the North Atlantic, seems to have lasted since the dawn of time. Every wave that slaps the plank is a passing second in the interminable epoch before he meets Franz again. The time-line of life, though elastic, only stretches so far before it snaps.

Why is returning so much more difficult than leaving? His body points like a rifle at his lover's homeland. But the water against his skin is too warm (Sam estimates it's thirteen degrees Celsius), an effect of global warming.

Though the ocean depths are opaque, Sam knows he's paddling over underwater mountains, buried volcanic islands, and vast landslides. The sea floor holds particles from distant deserts as well as volcanic ash and dissolved fragments of fish skeletons, whale ear-bones, and sediments from icebergs that melted. Along the sea bottom scuttle blind shrimp, eyeless crabs, and mute clams that live off white smokers. Is Mother enjoying her new neighbours?

The waves ascend and descend with a hypnotising monotony. Sam swears he won't stop kicking until he smells baked bread and sees cobblestone streets. At mid-day, the sun's rays blaze into his skull, and images of Franz fill his mind: Franz throwing a snowball, Franz wearing a bowler hat, Franz smiling on a merry-go-round horse—wait a minute! Franz was never on a merry-go-round horse! At some point the Franz in Sam's mind separated from the real Franz and spins in a self-enclosed circle. What happens if Sam arrives in Europe and the imaginary and real Franz don't match? Will the two Franzes have a fight? Which one would win? Sam worries that if Franz doesn't believe he's returning, he'll find someone else. Sam should've sent him a postcard the day he left Sonny and Cher, but he had no idea his journey back would last an eternity.

Sam tells himself to remember his sister. She was strong and conquered insurmountable obstacles. Recalling the profundity of her pain, the arduous road she travelled, he promises that he'll never feel sorry for himself again. He tries not to think about her or he'll start weeping, and the ocean is wet enough. He marvels at how much power people can have inside themselves. As he mounts the crest of a wave, he feels he's being pulled by the hidden strength of all the people he's ever known.

In the late afternoon, hunger claws at the inside of his stomach. When a school of blue fish flow beneath the plank like spilled paint, he shoves his claws into the sea, squeezes his fingers shut, and drags up two salmon that flap in the air like severed hands. Their eyes, round as globes, can't blink; the lips throb, gills flutter like featherless wings. He stuffs their bodies between his lips, bites once, then rams their torsos into his mouth and munches. He gulps loudly as the trembling bone-crunchy mass slides down his gullet. He belches and all the horizons hear him.

Later shark fins break the water's surface and circle Sam. Their lead-black eyes glimmer; their teeth, rows of jagged pyramids, gleam in lipless mouths. He leaps up and lands—*baff!*—on a slippery shark back and claws his fingers into its spongy surface. The fish buckles and thrashes but he holds tight as if to a rodeo horse, working one claw through the outer skin. Finally he shoves his whole hand into the hot mucus-like flesh. With one thrust, he rams his arm in right up to the shoulder; his fingers, trapped in a sticky pudding, graze the beating heart. He clutches and yanks it up through the opening and stuffs the bloody, dripping mess between his lips. The other shark flees.

The wooden plank floats in a lily pad of shark blood, drifting sticks of cartilage, and masses of porridge-like flesh. The shark gristle gets stuck between Sam's teeth; the cartilage is wiry and must be bent into curlicues before swallowing; the outer skin has a sticky membrane that's tricky to peel off. The shark's organs, especially the pancreas and gall bladder, taste spicier than the outer extremities. The fins take a lot of chewing, and the eyes explode like grapes between Sam's teeth.

All night Sam lies flat on his back, listens to his breathing, the creaking of wood, and the endless start and finish of sentences that will never be spoken. Above, the stars are spread across the sky like a million unblinking eyes. The moon is a half-crescent. Sam can make out the beige dot of Venus, the ghost-planet.

He's come to love his own planet deeply. He loves its colours, its multitude of landforms, the way mountains are hidden under the ocean but visible and garishly ice-capped on land. He loves the Earth's sensuality, its dripping stalactites, river-rumbling gorges, hot and cold regions, wet and dry spots. There are many people like Sue on Earth. He will not just sit back passively and watch the world turn into a monochrome cinder devoid of the opposites that keep energy circulating. If he reaches Europe, he'll fight to preserve the ice and fire that maintain life. He'll find that source that fuels the world and discover a way to reinforce it. Then the Sues on Earth will be saved.

The next morning, the sun rises shyly above the eastern horizon. The sky is the grey-green colour of a gall bladder. He sits up, and the plank descends and then bounces up as if on springs. He scratches his salt-crusty armpits, rotates onto his stomach, shoves his legs into the mouth of the sea, and begins egg-beatering.

Occasionally flying fish fly over him. Pods of dolphins pass, their bodies arching like horses' necks. A seagull swoops and scoops a fish from the water. Sam gasps—birds mean land. Or did this one follow the ship and is now lost? He stares hard into the blank horizon, tries to will into existence a blue cliffside curving like an elbow. Waves lift and drop, his plank lifts and drops, his body lifts and drops. The sky is an azure expanse stretching from one horizon line to the other. He sprawls face-down on his plank, pummelling his callused feet into the dark skin of the sea. But he remembers the bird, its sudden drop and quick ascent.

Later that day, he sees a second seagull. "Tell Franz I'm coming," Sam shouts. The sun warms his cheeks and the wind ruffles his hair; he hears his sister encouraging him, "Kick, brother, kick…" He remembers the wonderful movement of body parts in *Fairy Tales of Flesh*, and how penises could be interchanged with the tips of toes, how Velcro-backed nipples could be stuck onto kneecaps. Now he knows that tale is true, as nothing is stable in this world.

More fish swim in the water beneath him now. Eels flap like trailing bits of streamers amongst the rows of plankton reaching up like fingers. Sudden splashing as out of nowhere, sturgeons leap in parallel arches. Schools of silver fish race through the striped shadows, their scales winking, as overhead, pelicans fly with fish dancing in their beaks, the beat of their wings like laundry flapping on a line. He paddles over glimmering mazes of boulders, through swamps of seaweed. In the late afternoon, a whale surfaces beside him, and a rainbow-coloured geyser spurts from the top of its head. Sam quenches his thirst by grabbing and sucking blood from a tuna.

The next night, he endures a storm at sea. He desperately grasps the plank, terrified it will slip out from beneath him. Waves spin him like a poker wheel, fling him skyward like a Frisbee. Whirlpools rage in his ears and eyeballs; enswathed in flying streams of brine, breaking whitecaps, somersaulting salmon, boomeranging driftwood shards, and air bubbles that pop like fire crackers, he feels he's never been so close to the core of nature and senses that chaos is the root of everything. Chaos is the transition point as forms change into each other. Where there's chaos, there's movement and energy, and what has energy is most alive. Chaos is creating Franz's diamond. Sam kicks his feet, and a kinetic jolt shoots from his soles to his cranium. If he survives, he won't return to his civilized, over-planned life. How he loves the disorganized present in which he's a free radical ricocheting with an energy all his own. Waves breaking sound like whips cracking the air, and Sam is ecstatic. He longs for mayhem, confusion, extremity of all forms, a destruction of limits, and the explosive energy released when systems break down. For a moment, he wants to become the sea.

In the morning, the ocean is as still as a pane of glass. The surface of his board is coated with seaweed slime and barnacles. Sam kicks, and his body crawls slug-like across the glimmering expanse. On his fifth day alone at sea, Sam notices his body is changing. His matted coat of fur sheds to reveal his old pink skin; his claws have started to recede into fingers, his snout shrivels into the blunt bump of his nose. The rippling muscles of his shoulders, thighs, chest, and biceps dissolve to taut violin strings, and his ribcage and skull shrink.

At first he thinks this is due to non-stop physical activity, lack of rest, and an unbalanced diet. He is losing his hunger and some days eats very little. *If you love something, you put it in your mouth.* If he feeds on anything, he feeds on himself. Yet as he moves farther away from his time in the woods and closer to Franz, his sparrow-like body is returning. He remembers Franz's buff fashion-obsessed friends who took steroids and spent hours in gyms. He scrutinizes the gentle curve on his sparse thighs, his button-like kneecaps, the sensitive gully of his stomach, his delicate fingers. He puts a hand on the skin on the inside of his thigh and it seems the softest thing he's ever touched. So this is what it means be to be human. This is what everyone has been afraid of all along.

Only Sam's penis doesn't change but retains the serpentine form it developed in the forest. When it's erect, Sam uses it as a rudder so he can travel straight east and not on a diagonal. He drapes the flaccid penis across his shoulders or over his tender nipples to prevent sunburn.

If you don't truly live in your body, he knows now, you're not truly on the Earth and can't feel the fire at its centre. The people who believe that we're souls without bodies are the ones who damage the world. Has Franz learned to possess the skin he lives in or is he still observing himself from the outside?

Days pass and no land appears. Any seagulls Sam meets are as lost as he is. The horizons are purple with the pollutants that now roam across the globe. In his third week at sea, he loses the power to count days and panics. He sees his famished, shrinking body, and in his head a thousand bells chime. The sun ascending is like a rotating clock-hand. His legs thrash at the mercilessly flat sea face, and his arms flail like feather-shorn wings. The moon chases the sun across the sky, and then the sun chases the moon; by studying their angles, he estimates he's at forty degrees north, the same latitude as Portugal.

Staring east, he prays for a bulge, a hillside, a slight dribble of land, but there is only that agonizingly straight line with the sun peeking over it. Knowing he's closer to Europe than North America torments him—he can almost smell Franz's spicy cologne, is sure he hears Zurich's tram-cars clattering; squinting, he can see the Matterhorn peak. Whatever Franz has become is within reach: the *splish-splash* of waves sounds like Franz's laughter; the moaning wind is Franz's sigh after he ejaculates; the darkening horizon is the shadow he makes when he steps in front of the bedroom window.

One morning Sam wakes, his head dangling over the plank like that of a doll with a broken neck. The sea grazes the tip of his nose, a sliver of air separates him from the depths. In the clear water, a pencil-thin fish darts once, twice, as if jerked along a wire. It is then that he lifts his head and sees the Portuguese coast. Mountains of umber rock undulate between ragged peaks above a beach across which groves of shaggy palm trees shake their heads in the wind.

A wave swells, lifts him skyward, and it seems everything that ever happened in his life has been for this moment. The sky is an azure dome and the burning sun blazes in its eastern corner. The seawater somersaults around itself, its farthest reaches bathing edges of prone continents. Far below, the ocean floor is unfissured and deeper still, the Earth's core is safely encased in its protective stone ring. Switzerland rests snug inside its borders, its mountains as hard as steel thrones, and Canada sprawls across its paralyzing mantle of ice. For the first time in Sam's life, the world's principal substances, those main building-blocks of life—Rock, Ice, Air, and Water—are locked in a perfectly balanced tension. Then he hears that distant roar, the fire burning at the Earth's centre.

Nearing the shore, he sings out Franz's name at the top of his lungs when immediately he is caught in a fast-flowing coastal rivulet; waves foam, lash and whip, and his board seesaws wildly like a bucking stallion. Sam clamps his hands around the seaweed-slippery edges and presses his cheek against the wood when, to his horror, the plank slides forward and leaps skyward as if shot from a cannon. He is pulled down into a raging torrent; bubble-flecked water pummels his eye sockets, roars in his ears, and arms of water ram their fists into his mouth, down his throat, and into his lungs. The undertow catches his ankles, and as he hurtles head-first toward boulders looming on the sea floor, he is gripped by a fear of death, all the more ridiculous because he's just about to see Franz and fulfill his most profound desire, a desire that is itself ridiculous because Franz is ridiculous, and their relationship is ridiculous. All at once the ridiculousness of everything—his impending death, Franz, ships exploding, girls sweating honey, supernatural urine, the Dairy Queen, men loving mermaids, summertime snowstorms, skies full of bees, Pentecostals at sea bottoms, giant spinning wheels, steel dresses, earthquakes on the far side of the world, and this Earth spinning so blindly on an axis without oil—assaults him, and the wonderful illogicalness of Life stares him in the face like God. The Earth was formed by driving forces, fire, wind, granite melting—yes, for one golden moment *rocks and fire were exactly the same thing*; Sam realizes his obsession with Franz is as strong as these thrashing currents and central to life's beautiful implausibility. Desire fuels the world, dissolves the edges of our selves so that we're freed into formlessness and releases a potent energy that makes plants grow, rain fall, planets go off-course, stars explode, the sun harden, lava drip, and volcanoes open their mouths to the sky.

As his arms and legs flail in the fast-moving currents, he is confident that his body will save him, for it is matter, part of a universe that endures. One of his feet strikes a boulder; his head is above water, he wheezes, coughs, and vomits. The waves have stopped buckling. He sees a beach where people are running back and forth. Sam begins to cry. Kerchiefed men race into the water yelling words that are lost in the wind. The men approach, shouting, "*Vindo! Vindo!*" Their hands reach under Sam's armpits and lift his body, which now seems as light as driftwood. He shivers uncontrollably and his teeth clatter like stones in a cup. The men lay him carefully on the wind-bitten earth. He rotates onto one side and instinctively curls into fetal position.

People holding nets mutter. "*É surpreendente!*" They are troubled by his protruding ribs, yet amazed by the length of his penis whose end trembles on the sand like a sniffling elephant snout.

Someone throws a blanket over him.

Before his eyes, sand spins in miniature whirlpools. He smells damp earth, oil, barbecued chicken. A seagull cries overhead. The lost bird?

✻

The day Sam leaves the Portuguese hospital, all the nurses, doctors, and nuns give him gifts for his voyage—sweet bread, *caldeirada*, *chourico* sausage, clean clothes, and some money. The employees had taken a liking to him and treated this mysterious man without a passport. Touched by their kindness, Sam wipes a tear from his cheek. How different they are from Sonny and Cher. He takes one last look at the crowd-thronged building. Dressed in the freshly pressed clothes of an orderly, he steps forward onto the cobbled streets of Europe.

But it is not the Europe he visited before. Everywhere, the sky is full of bees. They hover on top of mailboxes, shoot across open fields, circle the heads of monuments, and spin in kaleidoscopes before the camera lenses of stunned tourists. The bees arrived on a wind from the West. Sam comes across hordes of bees lying dead in ditches or mounded in empty fields; their armoured bodies gleam, stingers like rusted rifles pointed skyward.

When Sam reaches the Portuguese-Spanish border, a strange frisson goes through him; it's one of the last borders he'll cross. He thinks of how he was once a science geek, then an awkward Romeo, a lunatic, a criminal, a beast, a sheik on a ship, a disaster survivor. Sue taught him to grow beyond the borders of himself.

He recalls his mother's transmogrifications on the ship as well as Franz's letter describing his multiple identities. We were so many people at once. What will Franz be like when Sam arrives? This man of his, yes, this *man*. Now Sam accepts his own desire. "I'm a gayrod," he shouts marching through crowded plazas. "I'm in love with a man, and I want men. That's what I want. I want man, man, man!"

Spain fascinates Sam. Boys with betel-stained lips run chased by bulls down long, winding streets. Because he's dressed as a hospital orderly, Sam's often called upon to aid men lying gored in back alleyways. Women with riotously coloured flowers in their hair flamenco dance in sunlit squares, their torsos gliding as if on greased wheels. Pork flanks sizzle over crackling fires, girls throw tulips from balconies, matadors strut adjusting codpieces or flicking their Mickey Mouse ears. City centres are full of the *clackity-clack* of castanets; people wear them on their shoes, hands, armpits, and beneath their chins so that every syllable pronounced is accompanied by *clackity-clack*. It's a nervous sound, like heels trembling against marble floors or rocks skipping down mountainsides. Sam shouts to the same rhythm, "Man-man, I want my man-man." For the first time in his journey Sam doesn't sense clocks ticking, time passing, and the world spinning. Walking through sun-baked tomato fields, he comes upon rivers that he has no urgent desire to cross. He rejoices in detours that increase the suspense leading up to the final meeting that hovers like a beautiful water drop about to fall. He lingers before windows displaying hazelnut candies like tiny chicks with ribbons on their heads. He is uncharacteristically complacent. Franz is in Switzerland, his body as solid as a glacier wedged into the Matterhorn's stone flesh.

At night he listens to that distant fire roaring. During his time with Sonny and Cher, he believed it had been extinguished. How ridiculous—the fire is stone-ringed and eternal, and there are many ways to hear it. He scrutinizes the townspeople. That man buying a plum, can he hear it? That lady with parsley stuck in her teeth? Who else has felt the heat of fire on their feet and the coldness of snow on their foreheads? Sam is in love with everyone now.

He follows roads that head east, hitches car rides, jumps onto the roofs of fast-moving trains, rides abandoned bicycles, pogo-sticks, does cartwheels, crawls on all fours, or swims, his clothes tied in a knot on his head. Halfway across France he notices the countryside starting to buckle. He is nearing the Alps. He is nearing Switzerland. When Sam reaches the sign, "Geneva 50 km," he kneels and bows his head reverently.

Suddenly one of the new freak heat waves hits Europe and the temperature tops forty-one degrees Celsius. Sam staggers along the road. At night the temperature finally drops and Sam has a wet dream that lasts until morning. He wakes exhausted in a ditch and has to eat a huge breakfast that includes plenty of almonds.

At the Swiss border, Sam sees a wooden hut beside the road. He creeps toward the building, which is empty but for a dog that barks once whenever a truck passes. Since the erosion of trade barriers celebrated by those businessmen on the ship that sank, no one mans the booths that once teetered on all borders. Sam examines the road, the painted line separating Switzerland from the European Union. Stepping across this border is the mirror-image of jumping from the loading dock in the Toronto asylum. The yellow line is cracked in two places. A ladybug crawls along its centre.

※

Sam arrives in Zurich late in the evening. He'd almost expected cheering crowds waving signs, "Go, Sam go," announcers screaming through bullhorns, cheerleaders shaking American-style pom-poms in bright bony hands. But the streets are empty. A sheet of newspaper blows by like a phantom; it smacks and is pinned against a telephone pole, its edges fluttering. From a back alley, a cat meows. Sam steps through crescent moons thrown by lamps, passes windows full of hanging plants. A woman in high heels clatters over to a Volvo, ducks her head and jumps in; the car whizzes off, leaving a cloud of blue smoke.

This city, long stewing in the broth of Sam's imagination and coloured the shades of ecstasy and nightmare, now seems strangely banal. Unbelievably, people lived here without know-ing who he was. He approaches the *Haltestelle* of the tram that had taken him to the airport the very last time. He remembers sobbing, clutching the tram ticket in one hand and Franz's shirt-sleeve in the other, and he pities his younger self. If only he'd known he would return one day. That day is now. He gazes long-ingly down streets remembered only in dreams.

A jeweller's sign pulsates with turquoise light. The splash

of water in the Escher fountain sounds like applause. As the steel and stone monuments of civilization rise around him, Sam thinks of his appearance. Should he have gotten a haircut? Do his clothes need cleaning? Maybe he should rest up in a hotel overnight so he's at his best when he meets Franz. It's been over a year since they last saw each other, so what's one more day? No, he thinks, boarding the tram, the world does not stop spinning; he hasn't hesitated once on this journey and won't now.

He makes a wrong turn at Seestrasse and misses the trail to Franz's chalet. He's troubled that the map in his mind doesn't match the real Zurich. At the trailhead he dashes up the twisting path. The clearing is lit by the full moon, but Sam does not see chalet walls, windows, or a porch. Where the building once stood are four squat stone pillars and stacks of burnt wood, smashed glass, and piles of ash.

Sam cries out, puts his hands to his face, and sinks to his knees. Franz's disks and poles, which had filled his grounds, are also gone. Sam can't bear to behold this scene, clutches his own arms and, choking, hurries back down the trails and into town.

He sprints over to a policeman handing out parking violations, asks, "*Herr Wachtmeister*, what happened to that house on the hill?

"The Niederberg chalet? It burned down."

"Was anyone hurt?"

The police officer shrugs. "Don't know." He writes another ticket.

Sam rushes into a telephone booth and frantically searches the phonebook for F. Niederberger. Sam phones all five Franz

Niederberger's in Zurich, but none are the one he wants.

He checks into the hotel where he stayed before, buries himself under the covers and prays for sleep.

Only certain diamonds are durable enough to survive fire.

❧

Sunlight on his pillow wakens Sam, and through the curtains he sees the city he remembers. Quaint trolleys full of smiling tourists clatter past, their bells ringing; men with flour-coated forearms carry trays of butter-scented pastry; women with shopping bags run in and out of boutiques as if playing hide-and-seek. Sam notices, in the distance, a white glacier twinkling on a mountainside. "Franz exists in this city," he states confidently. "I only have to find him."

Glancing down at himself he notices his giant penis has shrunk to its former size. Unconcerned, he studies the rows of people in identical trench coats on the street below. One of them has to be his lover. Yet the charred chalet is a scar in his mind.

Sam dresses and marches purposefully to the Odeon café where Franz used to drink a *Milchkaffee* every morning. Sam orders one and surveys the crowded room; if Franz isn't here, maybe one of his cronies is. He smiles at two men in tank tops. Did they know Franz Niederberger? "Never heard of him." He asks a man in an Afro wig and then a tuxedoed guy carrying a guitar case. No one knows Franz. Sam is surprised. Perhaps Franz's circle of friends was tinier than he let on.

By noon he has drunk thirteen coffees, his limbs are jittering, and he stutters when he speaks. The manager threatens to throw him out. "What are you asking everyone? For money? You don't look like a tramp."

"I need information about Franz Niederberger. Do you know him?"

The manager shakes his head. Perhaps Franz was here but Sam doesn't recognize him. Does he have a new look or a startling hairstyle? Has he stopped going to the tanning salon?

He sees a man at the counter with a rooster's tuft of blond hair on the top of his head. "Darcy!" he shouts rushing at him. "Darcy! Wait!"

The man's nose is painted with stripes like a parrot's beak. "I'm not Darcy," he blurts.

"Oh, sorry. Do you know Franz Niederberger?"

By one o'clock Sam has spoken to eighty-five people. The manager yells, "If you don't leave right now, I'll call the police and have you arrested for harassing customers."

Sam struts defiantly out the door. He'll come back tomorrow in a disguise. His experience has shown him it's often easier to be someone other than yourself.

He goes to Franz's gym. "I'd like a membership," he says to the desk clerk.

"No problem, sir. You get a complimentary trainer for the first week."

What if his trainer were Franz?! Sam is disappointed when a slender blond man approaches him. Sam yanks at levers as metal lozenges clatter along poles. The trainer yells, "Concentrate on what you're doing and quit watching everybody. You're cruising

∞ 351 ∞

desperately, and it's pathetic. Most of the guys here are straight or in couples."

"I'm looking for Franz Niederberger. Do you know him?"

They check the member registry. No Niederberger.

Sam eats dinner at the café where he'd encountered Heidi. He scans the waitresses and doesn't see her. If she were here, he could pour out his soul, and she'd tell him exactly what to do. Two Americans are chatting at the table behind.

"I think we can do the lake cruise after breakfast."

Sam remembers how he'd expected something major to happen in his life when he first got to Zurich and it had. If this, the end of his journey, doesn't turn out the way he wants, does that mean that everything leading up to it has no value?

At midnight Sam chokes on cigarette smoke in Wu-Wu Disco. There is the same dry ice, pounding music, muscle shirts, and sailor's caps as last time. He snakes back and forth through the crowd, asking, "Do you know Franz Niederberger? Do you know Franz?"

At last the barman, a bare-chested peroxide-blond, nods. "Yes. But I haven't seen him in at least a year."

"You know him? The man whose chalet burned down?"

"Oh right, that old place. Filled the suburbs with smoke for days."

"Was anyone hurt?"

"Hadn't heard that."

So Franz must be alive and well. Every muscle in Sam's body unclenches; he nearly tumbles to the floor. The lone woman behind the bar says, "The owner cleared out all the contents and set it on fire. The police fined him big-time."

If he was in trouble with the law, might Franz have left Switzerland? Where would he go? The world is enormous. How many countries are there? Sam becomes exhausted thinking about it. What if Franz had gone the opposite way, toward North America, searching for Sam? Did his letter suggest that he no longer feared crossing borders?

The next day, on Bahnhofstrasse, Sam glimpses the man who once took him shopping for clothes. Sam can't recollect his name but shouts, "Franz's friend!" He lunges and clutches the man's shirt sleeve. "Remember me? We went shopping when I was with Franz Niederberger."

The man's eyes widen. "Oh, yeah." Sam recalls that he's called Delial. "That's right. You're the one who changed Frankie."

"Changed him? What do you mean?"

Delial bites his lip, plucks a petal from the flower in his lapel, drops it to the sidewalk, and crushes it beneath his feet. "Is Franz all right? That's a matter of opinion."

"But where he is? Is he in Zurich?"

"Yes, he's here."

"He is! Thank God! Where?"

"I can't tell you." His lips close firmly then open to say, "I can't tell you anything. I'm forbidden to."

Sam clenches a fist. "Listen! I've come all the way from Canada. I'm not interested in playing games. You wouldn't believe what I suffered through to get here." He'd willingly tell Delial about his adventures but knows he won't be believed. Little does Sam know that Franz's story strains credibility more than his own.

"Let's talk about it in Odeon tonight then. At ten o'clock. At a private table, where no one can hear us." Delial twists his lips and steps into the flowing stream of pedestrians.

❧

As promised, Delial arrives at the café. His fuschia top is covered with sequins that clatter together when he folds his arms.

After a double martini he says, "Sam, I thought that I have no right to tell you the story of Franz. But I will, because I hope you can change things for him. We all miss our old Frankie so much." Delial lowers his head; a tear streams down his cheek. Sam lets him have his moment. Delial wipes his face with a napkin, clears his throat, and says, "The sun shines after even the darkest storm. And now I'll tell the tale of Franz Niederberger. It goes like this: After you left, Franz started behaving oddly. He was often frightened, paranoid and, for a while, disappeared from view."

"I know all about that. He described it to me in a letter he sent."

"Yes, he did send you a letter. We know about that. He invited you back, but you took such a long time, such a long, long time to return. You're here now, but it's too little, too late. He stopped believing you would ever come, Sam. Time passed and you sent no news. Why couldn't you have sent a letter? A postcard? A dove with a olive branch in its mouth? He thought you'd forgotten him, or that you'd never forgive his treatment of you, you snarky bitch. Why did you abandon him like that?"

"I didn't!" Sam says. "There was no way I could contact him. I was locked in an insane asylum, then lost in a forest, and then stuck on a boat crossing the ocean, which exploded because of my stupid, fucking mother. I did worry but assumed that as long as he was in my mind, I was in his. But what's happened to Franz? Tell me!"

"Some say a tragedy has happened. Some say it's wonderful. To me it's such a massive change—and all change, except how hemlines change when the fall line is introduced, terrifies me. First he burned down his chalet to destroy all evidence of his past life. Presently he lives in a tiny apartment just off Viederplatz. He's practically a hermit; he rarely goes out but has food delivered. As you may know, after he disappeared from view, his early artwork, the spinning wheels, etcetera, have been discovered and *Tagesspiegel* claims he's a genius. But he refuses all exposure, no interviews, photo gigs, or television appearances. But worst of all—" Delial chokes, can't speak.

"Most of all what? *What?*"

"I can't describe what's happened." Delial grabs his handbag from the counter and storms toward the exit. "And it's all your fault!" he shouts, racing out. Sam scribbles Viederplatz on the back of a matchbox.

The next morning, he stands in the centre of the square. Franz is in one of these four buildings. Sam imagines Franz sleeping behind one of the walls, his butt rising in the air while an erection dents the mattress. He looks at every list of entry buttons beside every door. None has Franz's name.

At seven a.m., two Asian men wearing toques cross the square;

at seven-fifteen, an old lady drags an empty grocery cart along the cobblestones, then returns at nine-thirty, her buggy full of apples. At one, two, and three minutes after ten o'clock, three men in business suits march past, their lower legs flicking like jack-knife blades. At eleven o'clock, a stray dog runs over and pees against the square's lone tree, and Sam remembers the dog he saw from the asylum window. Two policemen stroll through at eleven-thirty; at noon, a woman rushes out, her hair tied in scraps of newspaper. Sam doesn't leave the bench to have a snack or use a toilet fearing he'll miss something. In the late afternoon, he walks over to a man sweeping leaves to ask, "Do you know in which of these *Gëbaude* Franz Niederberger lives?"

"Sorry, I don't."

He asks tenants exiting or entering buildings. Always the same answer. He wonders if Delial lied to him about the address.

The next morning, he posts himself on the same bench and studies people's faces more closely. Perhaps Franz made an appearance yesterday but was unrecognizable. He scrutinizes a man's cleft chin, the nostril of a teenager, the cheek of an old man who scuffles by in broken shoes.

The third day, Sam despairs. Franz is nowhere. At dusk he watches a young boy carrying groceries to the apartment tower. The boy puts a key in the lock; the door opens, and he enters. He reappears a minute later without the bag. He tosses a coin in the air. A delivery boy. Franz's delivery boy? Sam charges across the square. "You," he cries. "Were you just at the Niederberger residence?"

The boy cracks gum between his teeth. "What's it to you?"

"I need to go there. I need to get inside. Please tell me the address. Give me your key."

The boy crosses his arms on his chest, sensing that, for once, he has some power. Sam has to give him the 200 francs in his pocket, and agree to deliver groceries for the kid all next week. He must wait an agonizing six days before the boy gives him the passkey. The Niederberger delivery is only once a week. Finally Sam has the key in his pocket. The apartment number is 1000. He carries a bag full of eggs, muesli, and orange juice. Franz must be on a health kick.

"You're not supposed to knock at the door," the boy says. "Just put the bag down and leave."

Sam struts confidently across Viederplatz. The key fits the lock perfectly. After stepping inside Sam makes an effort to control himself. He climbs the stone steps. Each *clop-clop* of his shoes is like the *tick-tock* of a clock that's been counting the minutes since his birth, has been ticking throughout this book, and will tick until the world's end. He climbs to the second landing, then the third, fourth, fifth, sixth, seventh, eighth, ninth, tenth.

Sam trembles before the door of apartment 1000. It has one eye-hole. he becomes self-conscious. He combs his hair with his fingertips, tucks in his shirt, cups his hands, and smells his breath—so silly, he who was once a beast in the woods. In his mind he repeats the sentence he'd practised over and over while floating on the wooden plank, "Franz, at long last we meet again. I have crossed the Earth for you."

He clears his throat. He knocks once, twice.

From inside, silence, then a cough and the creak of a chair.

Percussive footsteps approach the door. The spy-hole snaps open and an eye—an emerald-green eye, yes, Franz's eye!—fills the hole. Sam hears a gasp. The rattling of chains, the door swings open violently, bangs once against the wall.

Franz Niederberger is standing facing Sam Masonty.

But Sam cannot give his speech because Franz is not what he once was. He is what he has become. He has become Veronika.

The story goes like this: one year ago at the foot of the Matterhorn, Franz sent Sam a letter. He returned to Zurich and waited. The sun crossed the sky a hundred times. Each morning Franz put on a new shirt, gelled his hair, sprinkled his neck with lavender, gargled with a lemon-lime spritzer, and sprawled across the divan, his arms spread, an inviting smile on his lips, and his erect penis pointing like a wand toward the closed door. The door never opened. Weeks passed. Months passed. Franz started wearing shirts that weren't so new or were un-ironed or stained with ketchup. He clutched the VCR remote and watched snippets of soap operas and infomercials all day. The door remained shut.

Huddled on the floor, he glared morosely into the carpet. Little did he know that by this point, Sam had received his letter, escaped from the asylum, and was futilely trying to board planes in Ontario airports. Franz assumed Sam had already arrived in Zurich but was having second thoughts, or didn't know if he wanted to again involve himself with such a pompous prick. Crippled with indecision, perhaps, Sam was hiding somewhere in the city. One day Franz charged from his chalet, slamming the door so hard the living room window cracked. He hunted every street, searched bars, laundromats, telephone booths, and the city council chambers. He spent a whole month searching for Sam in the Earth Sciences department of the University of Zurich before their security guards threw him out.

On the summit of Mount Käferburg, Franz spread his arms above the city of his birth, and bellowed, "I'm here, Sam. Take me!" He repeatedly pounced on bespectacled pedestrians he thought were Sam. Franz took to getting drunk in village bars. He blubbered non-stop to anyone who would listen. "I've done the math; he should've arrived six months ago." He was ashamed of the letter he'd sent, sure it had disgusted Sam. He concluded the Matterhorn experience was simply his ego wrapping round itself.

In the chalet, everything reminded him of Sam: the jar of Nutella Sam had poked his finger into, the Lake Louise towel he deliberately forgot, the shirt he borrowed from Franz for the gala. The day Sam crossed the border into Québec, Franz, in a tormented fit, poured gasoline over the floorboards of his chalet and, with matches from Sam's hotel, burned it down. He moved to the city where he rented a flat on this quiet square. He sold his remaining artwork for pennies. He resolved to support himself by creating placemats and Christmas cards for the rest of his life.

Franz never left his apartment. He was sometimes seen at a window shaking a broom or staring mournfully at the moon. He hoped solitude would purge Sam from his brain, but it intensified his ex-lover's presence. He listened to mind-control tapes, performed self-hypnosis, even purchased a device that shot electrical currents through his penis whenever he got a hard-on when thinking of Sam.

One night he drank fifteen bottles of Swiss beer and three bottles of Canadian whiskey. In a blind furor, he stumbled out onto the street. Hours later he woke up in the alleyway where the two boys had tried to rape him when he was Veronika. This time he was completely alone; Sam's eyes no longer watched from the sky. As he lay face-first in a puddle of his own vomit, he recognized that the thing he'd feared most had happened. He had disintegrated. His personality had dissolved. All those forces he'd opened himself up to when he risked going to that geology conference, then approaching a Canadian, taking him to have sex in a forest, and afterwards eating rocks day after day, all those gigantic forces had come hurtling into his life with hurricane strength and finally obliterated everything. Franz hadn't been wrong to fear nature. He should've respected his own phobias and lived protected inside his small, trivial life. He once dreaded that the Matterhorn would pulverize him, but in the end it was Sam who accomplished that.

Franz rolled over and peered at the full moon bathing the grey stone street in a soft white light. He scraped his dinner off his eyebrows and continued to lay there for hours. Then he heard a voice, a woman's voice. "Franz, you must put everything back together. You have broken into fragments, but you must assemble them differently this time, in a better way, into a superior form." He knew the voice was coming from himself. It was the voice of Veronika, the woman born beneath the warm rays of Sam's gaze so long ago. He seldom acknowledged her. But he remembered her fondly now. As Veronika, he was never pompous or self-obsessed. She'd listened when he was criticized.

How courageously she'd acted when those two boys assaulted her. She'd strutted about Zurich self-contained in her nifty outfits, needing nothing from anyone. She didn't seem capable of viciousness. Veronika was strong and indifferent yet open-minded—everything Franz wasn't. Veronika never needed her ego stroked. She was non-judgmental and, as an artist, much freer than Franz. Light exploded on her canvases to create the most beautiful paintings Franz had ever seen. Maybe she wasn't an accident. Franz recognized that Veronika was more significant than his own superb body. If he'd gone to the Matterhorn as Veronika, the outcome would have been very different.

Most importantly, Sam's eyes had closed when she existed. As Veronika, he'd be free of Sam. Franz could start anew. Was his epiphany at the Matterhorn a zigzag in his path and Veronika the ultimate goal? Should he reassemble his shredded self into a fabulously new form with jewel-decked fingers that snap, dagger-sharp eyebrows, and a torrent of flame-red hair that, when shaken, crackled like fireworks? If he wasn't completely satisfied the first time, why accept her now? The only options he knew of were old Franz or Veronika. No other choices existed. The decision was easy to make.

He ordered a dress from Cartwright, Labrador, his lover's birthplace, because he assumed it would best neutralize his desires for Sam. He asked for a used dress suffused with the scent of Canadian life. When he opened the box, he discovered a pink rayon dress with thin shoulder straps and layers of ruffled gauze. One side had been torn but repaired. The fabric smelled strangely sweet. The label read Fashions of Esther Beaverbank.

He put on the dress and, when he looked in the mirror, he saw a Veronika that was absolutely ravishing. Here was the outfit she was meant to wear.

The dress had a steel-ringed belt that, once snapped shut, couldn't be reopened. Would he accept living the rest of his life as Veronika? He nodded into the mirror and said, "Yes." He clicked the clasp and felt the deepest satisfaction he'd ever known. At this point, Sam's ship was halfway across the Atlantic and about to explode.

So Franz lived as the new Veronika. He worked hard designing "We love you, Santa" cards by day and doing serious art at night. He'd never been so productive. But if people loved his work (and they did; his pieces sold for thousands), he didn't care. Veronika didn't need admiration. When Delial showed up asking Franz to come to Odeon to bitch about the snotty new bartender, Veronika calmly said, "No." The old Franz wouldn't have been able to resist.

The dress exerted its power. His hair grew longer, curlier, and developed bright highlights; his skin appeared smoother, softer, and his voice got higher in pitch. His chin rounded out and hair fell from his jaw. He could stop shaving his face. He barely noticed the changes because as Veronika he didn't obsess over his body. The knobs of his knees receded and his thigh and calf muscles curved sinuously. In bed he sensed his pelvis widening. His hips swayed as he sauntered about his new apartment. He no longer copied gestures from Marlene Dietrich. Once he'd decided Veronika was here for good, everything fell into place intuitively. He'd been transformed into a natural woman and completely inhabited his body. By the time Sam lay panting on the beach in Portugal, Franz had settled into his new life.

Franz felt better yet wasn't entirely happy. Ghosts from the past hovered at the edges of his grey life and he dreamt about Sam every night. Moonlight shone on his pillow and he'd wake sobbing. His hours were a steady movement back and forth from muted pain to numbness. His days passed unpunctuated and flowed together so seamlessly that by the time Sam arrived in Zurich, Franz felt he'd been living at Viederplatz for a thousand years. He assumed that nothing further would happen to him. This was to be the end of his tale.

When Sam knocks at the door, it's as if someone had slapped Franz across the face. Was it the delivery boy? Did Franz give him the wrong change? Or is it someone else? He remembers the boys who'd attacked him in the alley. As Veronika, he'd conquered aggressiveness in himself, but it still existed in the outside world. Veronika grabs a butcher's knife from the kitchen counter.

She looks through the keyhole to see a man she doesn't know. Veronika clutches her knife and pushes open the door.

The man does not grab at her dress or try to rob her, but simply stares. His eyes expand; his thin lips open and a tongue, like the tip of a billiard cue, emerges. At that moment Veronika realizes, my God, it is Sam. She screeches and drops the knife; its tip pierces the wooden floor and the handle wobbles back and forth. Immediately she becomes aware of her body. She feels embarrassed yet proud. She knows she is beautiful.

Sam finally forces out the words, "Franz, is that you?"

Veronika's voice is velvety smooth. "Yes, it is. And I see it is true: you have come back to me."

Although the pitch of her voice is as high as a train-whistle, Sam recognizes the percussive t's and c's as his lover's. She *is* Franz. Sam throws himself into Veronika's arms, and she crushes his head against her breasts.

"I've waited so long for you," gasps Veronika. "And you're here, finally here." She begins to cry. "Why the hell did you take so long?"

"I couldn't help it," Sam sobs into her neckline. "I had to escape a mental institute and hike a 2,000-kilometre forest, rescue my sister, kill my mother, and swim half the Atlantic. But none of that matters now. I'm here, Franz. I've arrived." Sam sniffles. "But before we go any further, let's get you out of this dress. Why are you wearing it?"

Sam's fingers slide along the gauze; they graze the metal belt and leap as if touching a live wire. "My God! You're wearing Sue's dress?" Sue had told her brother every detail of her story.

"I was afraid to go to your country, so instead a piece of your country came to me."

"You ordered this from Esther's? Oh my God! Do you have a chisel or wire-cutters?"

Then Sam remembers the climax of Sue's story. The one man who'd broken through her dress—Jimmy Bridock—had died. This time, things would be different. Jimmy had been greedy and wanted to possess a body without the owner's permission. He'd tried to steal Sue from herself. He didn't realize that all bodies— men's and women's—are fragile and must be handled gently so as not to hurt the people living inside them.

For the first time in history, desire transfused by the tender glow of love would cut through the magic belt.

"Hold on!" Sam runs from the apartment and returns carrying a rock snatched from the grounds of Franz's chalet. He plucks Veronika's knife from the floor and aims its tip at the gown's belt-lock. Sam strikes the rock against the end of the knife handle— *bang, bang*, sings the stone—*bang, bang*—filling the long-silent kitchen with a sound that once roused cruel, boutonnière-wearing teenage boys gloating on a football field.

Veronika exclaims, "Stop. You're hurting me." Sue had used the very same words.

"Sorry, cupcake. I'll be more careful."

Eventually the dress cracks opens like an egg, and Veronika and Sam sigh at exactly the same time.

"Free at last," says Veronika. Franz's naked body towers over Sam, and he leaps back astonished. For what had seemed an eternity, the dress had bound Franz's unresisting body, and its power was absolute. Sam scrutinizes the perfectly formed D-cup breasts, the hairless expanse of the stomach, the sides of the torso curving inward. Sam's hand flies to his face as he sees that Franz's penis— the once-indomitable, colossal sceptre with its mighty tomahawk head has, as prophesied in a story told long ago, receded into his body, to be replaced by a swath of elegantly crimped pubic hair and a perfectly formed vagina that glowers from between his legs like a sullen eye that never blinks.

Franz has long known about his own loss and gain. Over the past months, he has noticed changes in his genitalia whenever he urinated or whacked off. By the time Sam reached the Portuguese-Spanish border, Franz's transformation into a woman was complete.

Franz shrugs and says, "You win a few, you lose a few."

Mystified, Sam, who's learned to cherish man-to-man desire, looks helplessly up and down the body of the naked female before him. Where is the masculine cleft in Franz's chin, the steel thigh muscles that, when contracted, bulge upwards, his clock-pendulum testicles, his foreskin, one moment as loose as an elephant's snout, the next as tight as the skin on a broccoli stem—the list of Franz's desirable male body parts was endless. Sam senses that the whole universe is laughing at him. The truest things in life are the most ridiculous.

Veronika examines this man born on the outer edge of the universe who'd claimed he'd travelled half the world for her. Was this true? "Have you crossed the Earth for me, darling? Did you really do that for me?"

Sam feels he's being observed by someone else. Is it God or one of his henchmen wanting to get in on the action before the book ends?

Sam knows he's being tested. He can make the right decision and save his life and the Earth he lives on or make the wrong one and destroy everything. An unseen power he neither knows nor understands is pushing him toward Veronika, who now lies on the sofa beckoning with open arms and puckering lips. Something is pressuring him into the banal life he hoped to flee. Will he become as boring as everyone else? From now on, will he simply be another unremarkable, suburban heterosexual man?

If he rejects Veronika, would that mean getting trapped again on the surface of life? The Franz he loves is in Veronika and will always be there, even as her body ages, withers, stiffens, and dies. Sam knows there is a fire at the centre of everyone, and a fire has at last created a jewel on Earth. He remembers that story in *Fairy Tales of Flesh* about the Mr. Potato Head people who exchange body parts. The story didn't have a climax or dénouement because no real tragedy had taken place; it didn't matter what body parts people had because the *you* uniting them was always the same; you could have ten, twenty, even a hundred penises or your every pore could be a vagina smiling its toothless grin, but you were the same person underneath. The surface is but a dazzling show of interchangeable patterns—mesmerizing, hypnotising, and wonderful—that blind us to the fire inside. Yes, Sam decides at last, he will stay with Veronika. He will share his life with her.

"I love you, Veronika," he says. "You are the most beautiful person I've even seen. You are the diamond found at the end of my quest."

All at once the fire at the Earth's centre roars so loudly, everyone in the world hears it. Police shout "Halt!" in 6,000 different languages, traffic stops, people fall down staircases, waiters drop plates, lovers have orgasms, elderly people wake up and decide to die, government leaders resign, and babies cease fidgeting and spread open palms to the world. The Earth's core detonates, and lava shoots up through the planet's vents and longitudinal fissures, blasting the tephra stoppers from volcano mouths as, on every continent, streams of torrid molten rock hurtle into the atmosphere. Earthquakes shatter mountain ranges, mile-high waves pummel cliffs, steaming lava engulfs valleys and riverbeds, and Arctic winds thrash at the Earth's two poles, freezing its crowns into impenetrable scabs of ice. A crack opens up in the main street of Cartwright, and the town is blown off the face of the Earth.

Sam rips off his clothes, throws himself onto Veronika, and the two claw at each other's skin, this frustrating outer layer as if they could tear it away and slide effortlessly between the ribbons of veins, could penetrate flesh and enter tissues to search for the very centre of the person they love. Where is the centre located? In the heart? Pancreas? Small intestine? They'd soon discover that the self continually flees from one body part to the next and is so hard to catch that when you've explored every organ and arrive at the very last one—perhaps the pituitary gland—the person you seek has gone to the organ you visited last week. But which one? *Which one?* That was the agonizing question that could never be answered.

✾

The next day, Sam and Veronika move in together. A week later, they are engaged to be married.

When Sam visits the University of Zurich, the director of the geology department remembers him from the conference and offers him a job. Armed with an offer of employment and the name of a Swiss citizen soon to be his wife, he marches over to the immigration office. The officer who once rejected him is ecstatic. "Glad to see your life's turned around. I'm giving you an *Arbeitserlaubnis* that can be renewed each year. Congratulations, and welcome to Switzerland."

Six months later, Sam and Veronika move into a wonderful chalet in the country. Veronika furnishes it with tables and chairs from IKEA. Sam spends his days researching environmental problems. He writes articles for scientific journals and once a week gives a lecture at the university. Veronika hasn't given up her job but works out of the chalet. Sam is hoping to attend the Kyoto Conference on climate change; if not invited, he and Veronika will join the demonstrators. Veronika bought Sam a bullhorn and he's been practising shouting through it. Veronika's gift-card business becomes a roaring success. Her "Happy Easter" cards are translated into several different languages, and she's planning on developing a "Happy Summer Holiday" series.

Every evening, Sam returns from the library famished. He has rediscovered his hunger. Veronika makes him wonderful cakes, which he thoroughly enjoys, though sometimes she cheats and buys him the frozen Sara Lee kind.

They have sex twice a week. Loving a woman has been an adjustment for Sam, and he's learning to appreciate a whole new type of beauty. Each day he wants her more. Veronika often sets her hair in a labyrinthine structure that she's discovered drives him wild with desire.

On weekends, Sam likes to take Veronika to the lava pit in the Alps. They stand holding hands near the crevice from which lava steams, bubbles, and hisses. Sam fears nothing now and will step past the markers placed by the Swiss authorities and kneel at the edge of the crack in the earth. Veronika calls, "Be careful, sweetie."

Feeling no trepidation, he rams his arm in, right up to the elbow. Rising steam singes his fingertips, hot vapours burn his cheeks and make his eyes water, and the pungent sulphur scent fills his sinuses; he feels at one with the planet as he touches this live current of electricity connecting him to the centre of the Earth.

Sam and Veronika also like to play sex games on the weekends. "Pow, pow," he yells, chasing her with his erect penis. He remembers Franz's story about his own penis becoming a weapon. "And now I've got the loaded gun," he states proudly, "or a flying missile, whichever you prefer." Veronika laughs at the ludicrousness of the game. The most ludicrous things are the truest.

"Your penis isn't a weapon," she asserts. "No offence, but it reminds me of a toy from my childhood, a hairless puppy-dog head I called Snoopy-Doopy." She chuckles. "Want to call your cock that?" She pats Snoopy-Doopy's stiff little head, which bobs up and down, as if nodding and answering, "Yes, please do!" Then she throttles Snoopy-Doopy until he ejaculates and, for a moment, flying sperm arcs in a white rainbow above the bedspread. Sam remembers the forest dripping with his semen in northern Ontario, his sister's honey splashed on rocks, and his mother's stream of urine flying through the air and understands that bodily fluids are the most wonderful thing in the world; they are the oil that lubricates the Earth's engine.

❧

Not everything is rosy. One afternoon in the town of Singen, Sam and Veronika are in the Walmart parking lot loading patio furniture into the trunk of their car. Sam is having trouble with the striped table umbrella. He throws it to the ground. "I'm upset, Veronika. I'm sorry, but I've been depressed all day."

Veronika puts down her potted bamboo plant. "Why, honey?"

"When we were choosing briquettes for our barbecue, I just …" He sighs. "I wondered why we've ended up like this. Think of all the adventures that you and I have had over the past years, all the ecstasy, torment, moments of terror and beauty, our spectacular reunion—and we end up here, a suburban couple like the rest of the boring people on this boring continent."

Veronika ponders. "Perhaps being boring is your destiny. You always say we shouldn't cling to our identities, and now life has given you the role of being a boring and tedious little man. Maybe you should accept that."

"But I don't want that. It doesn't match with … everything!"

"Or does it?" Veronika turns toward the parking lot. Suddenly light flashes from a chrome fender, piercing her eye, and she has a shattering revelation. She opens her mouth and says the most insightful thing Sam ever heard or will hear. "Everybody is us, Sam. We are not boring; everyone is fascinating. Look at them all." Her face glows as she gazes at couples pushing strollers, blinking cars turning into parking spots. "Everyone has had the same experiences. They've gone from being one person to another, had their moments of exaltation and terror, their journeys across oceans, flights through forests, rapture before mountain lakes, but they didn't have to leave the country, and it all happened when they weren't paying attention; they were asleep or look-ing at dry cleaning bills or wondering why the television remote stopped working or if little Natalie should take tap or ballet. No one is dull *inside*, and it's never the end, Sam. There's no final stage! Other adventures will follow, and we'll keep changing. I'm so excited about what our unknown future together holds, just as I'm thrilled we bought these barbecue briquettes and can't wait to see how delicious our steaks will be."

Sunlight reflects off every single hood of the parked cars placed in perfectly parallel rows all the way to the horizon. "Thank God," Sam says with tears in his eyes, "I've got such an intelligent wife. I'd love to make love to you right now. Let's go inside and do it on the bedding display." They both laugh out loud and will not stop laughing for a long time because they know laughter is the root of everything.

When they get home, they hurl themselves onto each other's naked bodies and recommence pawing, groping, and scratching at this barrier of skin that keeps them from reaching one another's core, which beckons so tantalizingly, that you swear you could touch it with your fingertips, but can't. Not quite.

Sam purchases a new car—a Subaru electric model. He buys grey flannel suits. Veronika hires an assistant to do her file management, leaving her free for more creative work. The lovers rekindle their friendships with Holder, Darcy, and Delial. Sam and Veronika enjoy having them over for dinner, for they're nostalgic reminders of the past; also, having gay friends is a testimony to their open-mindedness.

"Even though we're suburbanites," Sam chirps happily, "that doesn't mean we're Nazis."

One Saturday morning there is a knock at the door. Sam

assumes it's Darcy, who forgot his braces and knit cardigan at their house. (Although only twenty-eight, Darcy has taken to dressing like an elderly man. "Senior chic is the latest trend in the gay community," he says. "All the guys at Wu-Wu's wear slippers and have pretend walkers.") Yet when Sam opens the door, to his amazement, Sue is standing there in her old pigtails and jumper.

"I've been travelling a lot," she says in a confident adult voice. "I've seen the world and decided to stop by and say hi." Sam bursts into tears, and the siblings embrace.

When he introduces her to Sue, Veronika is overjoyed. "Oh, sweetheart," she says, "I've heard all about you!"

Over croissants, Sue says, "Switzerland—it reminds me of home, almost, but not quite." Yes, Sam thinks, she's become a victim of the looking glass.

The next day, Sue's bees arrive. They perch on the backyard tree, which shimmers like a giant lollipop. Veronika has heard the story and knows not to be afraid. She and Sue get along fabulously. They play catch in the backyard, stroll arm and arm along the Lake Zurich boardwalk, and shop for clothes on Bahnhofstrasse.

On the day Sam and Veronika get married, Sue gives them the best wedding gift of all, a pencil case with a picture of a mountain on it. On their wedding night, they unzip the shiny case to find inside, a joint-limbed man made of rocks. Sam tears him into two pieces. He devours the head and torso, and Veronika nibbles the pelvis and legs. The lovers swallow at exactly the same time. Outside, it starts to snow, and it won't stop for a very long time. Before going to bed, they open *Fairy Tales of Flesh* and re-read their favourite story about the Mr. Potato Head people.

"If you were in this tale, which character would you be?" Veronika asks. "The man who keeps trying on penises hoping to find one whose size corresponds to his body weight, or the woman with two assholes who exchanges them for a foreskin she can wear as a sunhat?"

"Neither. I'd be the man with breasts for testicles and a penis where his chin should be. What about you?"

"I think I'd be the foreskin lady. I've always wanted a good sunhat."

Three years later, they all gather beside a glacier at the base of the Matterhorn. Veronika claps her hands, and Sam shouts, "Go, buster, go," as a spry toddler with twigs stuck behind his ears scampers into the arms of Aunt Sue. Overhead, a cloud of bees swarms, their stingers glinting in the sun.

Sam, Veronika, Sue, and Little Sam.

Did they live happily ever after?

It's anyone's guess.

The Earth kept spinning, and many other things happened to its inhabitants.

Epilogue

And so the wind blows.

Breezes circle the southern tip of our Earth, speed across frozen, sunlit plains, suicide-leap over ice cliffs, grate at the ragged edges where glacier meets sea. As the Earth spins, the centrifugal force whips wind into fast-moving, ever-widening arcs, and the streams of air spiral northward, pick up moisture, and join other gales to become one vast, buckling, rioting river that ascends, flattens, bifurcates, and whips ocean waves into walls that crash into other water walls and against cliffs, as far below, lava gurgles, spits, and crackles, and seismic plates lurch and buckle, eternally tortured and tension-taut; overhead, dizzying wind-blasts lasso mountain peaks, volcano mouths disgorge pulsating black balloons into the atmosphere, the Earth whirls like a ball too slippery to grasp and, as cold fronts clash with warm fronts and with fronts that are hotter still, CFCs gobble the ozone that replenishes itself and is devoured again, continents tremble like toys shaken in plastic packages, the moon hurtles in its orbit like an out-of-control whirligig, and as air, waves, clouds, and winds collide like cymbals crashing, clashing, clanging in this endless orchestra of the Earth, we all stand up, sweat rising to the surface of our skins, our nostril hairs quivering like radar devices detecting approaching storms, and then we feel it, the lava burning in our bones.

Acknowledgments

I would like to thank Brian Lam for all of his hard work and Susan Safyan for her insightful guidance. Thanks to James C. Johnstone for his support and hospitality and to Robert Jennings for his encouragement and unfailing sense of humour. I also thank Terrie Hamazaki for her feedback and for answering all my inane questions.

I am grateful to all those who read the manuscript in its various incarnations, including Patricia Anderson, Dayle Berke, Mary Frances Coady, Kelly Dignan, Peter Dubé, Matthew Fox, Amelia Gilliland, Claude Lalumière and, in particular, Zsuzsi Gartner.

Thanks to the participants at the Sage Hill Novel Colloquium 2005, especially Marilyn Bowering.

I also acknowledge the assistance of Julie and Rachelle Horne, John Mingolla, Jean-François Roulier, and the staff and my colleagues at Marianopolis College. Thanks to Derek Webster of *Maisonneuve* magazine and Zsolt Alapi of *Writing in the Cegeps* (Siren Song Publishing) for publishing the excerpt "Sweat."

I am indebted to the following texts: *Theory and Problems of Introductory Geology* by Richard W. Ojakangas and *The Earth* by Martin Redfern.

I am grateful for the generous support of the Canada Council for the Arts and the Quebec Arts Council.